3

li

THE
GRAY
WOLF
THRONE

BY CINDA WILLIAMS CHIMA

The Heir Series

The Wizard Heir
The Warrior Heir
The Dragon Heir

The Seven Realms Series

The Demon King
The Exiled Queen
The Gray Wolf Throne

THE
GRAY
WOLF
THRONE

A SEVEN REALMS NOVEL

BOOK THREE

CINDA WILLIAMS CHIMA

HARPER
Voyager

HarperCollins*Publishers*
77–85 Fulham Palace Road,
Hammersmith, London W6 8JB

www.harpercollins.co.uk

Published by Harper*Voyager*
An imprint of HarperCollins*Publishers* 2012

1

First published in the USA by Hyperion 2011

A catalogue record for this book
is available from the British Library

ISBN: 978 0 00 745914 8

Printed and bound in Great Britain by
Clays Ltd, St Ives plc

MIX
Paper from
responsible sources

FSC
www.fsc.org
FSC® C007454

For my maternal grandmother,
Dorothy Downey Bryan, a gifted musician and
indifferent housekeeper who had the second sight. Grandma
had a lap that would accommodate several small children,
but she always kept a shotgun in the closet.

And in memory of Ralph M. Vicinanza,
who left us too soon.

THE
GRAY
WOLF
THRONE

CHAPTER ONE
IN THE
BORDERLANDS

Raisa *ana*'Marianna huddled in her usual dark corner at the Purple Heron, picking at her meat pie. She'd learned to stretch a meal and a mug of cider over an entire evening.

It was risky to sit out in the common room of a tavern every night. Lord Bayar's assassins would be searching for her. They'd failed to kill her at Oden's Ford, thanks to Micah Bayar, Lord Bayar's son. But the High Wizard's spies could be anywhere, even here in the border town of Fetters Ford.

Especially here. Bayar would prefer to intercept Raisa before she crossed the border into the Fells. It would be tidier that way, her murder easier to conceal from her mother the queen and her father's people, the Spirit clans.

Still, she couldn't hide out in her room all the time. She needed to be visible to the people she *wanted* to find her. Somehow she had to get home, reconcile with Queen Marianna, and confront those who meant to take the Gray Wolf throne away from her.

The name Rebecca Morley was no longer safe. Too many of her enemies knew it. These days she called herself Brianna Trailwalker, a nod to her clan ancestry. Her story was that she was a young trader returning from her first journey south, held up by the turmoil along the border.

After a month in the limbo of Fetters Ford, she knew the regulars at the Heron—mostly pilots from the ferry service on the river, and the blacksmiths, farriers, and stablers who serviced travelers along the road. Locals were in the minority, though. The town churned with the comings and goings of wartime.

Raisa scanned the room, picking out the strangers. Two Tamric ladies occupied a corner table for the second night in a row. One was young and pretty, the other sturdy and middle-aged, both too well dressed for the Heron. Likely a noble lady and her chaperone fleeing the fighting to the south.

Three lean young men in Ardenine civilian garb played cards at a table by the door. Four had come in, but one of them had left a while ago. Several times, Raisa looked up and caught one or another of them staring at her. Apprehension slithered down her spine. Thieves or assassins? Or just young men showing interest in a girl on her own?

There were no easy answers anymore.

Most of the rest of the patrons were soldiers. Fetters Ford swarmed with them. Some bore the Red Hawk of Arden, some the Heron of Tamron, others carried no signia at all—either sell-swords or deserters from King Markus's army.

Any of them could be hunting Raisa. It had been a month since she'd escaped Gerard Montaigne, the ambitious young prince of Arden. Gerard hoped to claim at least three of the

Seven Realms by overthrowing his brother Geoff, the current Ardenine king, invading his former ally Tamron, and marrying Raisa *ana'*Marianna, the heir to the Gray Wolf throne of the Fells.

Any day, they expected to receive word that the capital of Tamron Court had fallen to Gerard. The prince of Arden had laid siege to it weeks ago.

When Raisa arrived in Fetters Ford, she'd planned to ask the local Tamric authorities to send a courier to the garrison house at the West Wall in the Fells. They in turn could send her message on to her father, Averill Lord Demonai, or to Edon Byrne, Captain of the Queen's Guard—perhaps the only two people in the Fells she could trust.

But when she arrived in the border town, there *was* no authority. The garrison house was empty, the soldiers fled. Some might have gone south to the aid of the beleaguered capital city. Likely, most had melted into the general populace to await the outcome of the war.

Raisa was left with the hope that her best friend, Corporal Amon Byrne, and his Gray Wolves might follow her north and find her here in Fetters Ford. She could travel on, hidden in their midst, as she had in the fall, on her way to the academy at Oden's Ford.

As the future captain of her guard, Amon was magically linked to Raisa, so he should have a rough sense of where she was. But the weeks had dragged on and Amon had not appeared. Surely if he were coming, he'd be here by now.

Her other plan was that she might fall in with a clan trader heading back north. She was a mixed-blood; with her burnt-sugar skin and thick black hair, she could pass for clan. But that hope had also faded as weeks passed with no traders passing through. With Tamron in turmoil, most travelers preferred to avoid the marshy Fens and sinister Waterwalkers and use the more direct path through Marisa Pines Pass and Delphi.

A shadow fell over Raisa's table. Simon, the innkeeper's son, was hovering again, summoning the courage to ask if he could clear away her plate. Most days, it was an hour of hovering to three words of conversation.

Raisa guessed Simon was her age, or even a little older, but these days Raisa felt older than her nearly seventeen years— cynical and jaded, wounded in love.

You don't want to get involved with me, she thought glumly. My advice is to run the other way.

Han Alister still haunted her dreams. She would awaken with the taste of his kisses on her lips, the memory of his scorching touch on her skin. But in the daylight it was difficult to believe their brief romance had ever happened. Or that he still thought of her at all.

The last time Raisa had seen Han, Amon Byrne had driven him off with a sword. And then she'd disappeared from the academy without a word—abducted by Micah Bayar. Han wouldn't have fond memories of the girl he knew as Rebecca. Anyway, it was unlikely she'd ever see him again.

By now it was near closing time, another day squandered while events at home rushed ahead without her. Perhaps she'd been disinherited already. Perhaps Micah had escaped Gerard Montaigne and even now was proceeding with plans to marry her sister Mellony.

Someone cleared his throat right next to her. She flinched and looked up. It was Simon.

"My Lady Brianna," he said for the second time.

Bones, she thought. I have to get better at answering to Brianna.

"The ladies over yonder invite you to join them at their table," Simon continued. "They say as it can be awkward for a lady, dining alone. I told them you'd already eaten, but . . ." He shrugged, his hands hanging like twin hams at his sides.

Raisa looked over at the two Tamric women. They leaned forward, watching this exchange with eager expressions. Women in Tamron had the reputation of being pampered hothouse flowers, socially ruthless, but physically delicate beings who rode sidesaddle and carried parasols against the southern sun.

Still, it was tempting. It would be a pleasure to converse with someone other than Simon—someone who could carry one half of a conversation. And perhaps they had more up-to-date news about events at Tamron Court.

But, no. It was one thing to fool Simon with a story of being a trader stranded in a border town. Simon wanted to be fooled. It would be another thing entirely to sit down with highborn ladies with a talent for ferreting out secrets.

Raisa smiled at them and shook her head, gesturing at the remains of her dinner. "Tell them thank you, but I'll be retiring to my room before long," she said.

"I told 'em you'd say that," Simon said. "They said to tell you they have a prop—a job for you. They want to hire you as an escort across the border."

"Me?" Raisa blurted. She wasn't exactly the bodyguard type, being slight and small-boned.

She gazed at the ladies, her lower lip caught behind her teeth, considering. There might be safety in numbers, but *they* wouldn't be much protection to Raisa. While their social weapons would be finely honed, they would be no good in a physical fight, and they would slow her down.

On the other hand, no one would expect her to be traveling with two Tamric ladies.

"I'll talk to them," Raisa said. Simon went to turn away, but froze when Raisa put her hand on his arm. "Simon. Do you know who those men are?" she asked, nodding toward the card players without looking at them.

Simon shook his head. He was used to such questions from her, and understood what she wanted to know. "Came in first time tonight, but they're not staying here," he said, scooping up her plate. "They speak Ardenine, but they're spending Fellsian coin." He leaned closer. "They asked some questions about you and the Tamric ladies," he said. "I didn't tell them nothing."

Simon's head jerked up as the tavern door opened and closed. It admitted a rush of damp, chilly night air, a splatter of rain, and a half dozen or so new customers—all strangers. They wore nondescript boiled-wool cloaks, but they had a military edge. Raisa shrank back into the shadows, heart flopping like a stranded fish. She strained to catch any stray bit of conversation, hoping to make out what language they spoke.

How long can you keep doing this? she thought. How long could she wait for an escort that might never come? If Gerard gained control of Tamron, how long before he closed the borders completely, bottling Raisa in? Maybe it would be safer to cross the border now, rather than wait for an escort.

But the borderlands swarmed with renegades, thieves, and deserters, and she risked ending up robbed, ravished, and dead at the side of the road.

Stay or go? The question reverberated in her brain like the rain pounding on the tin roof of the tavern.

On impulse, she stood and threaded her way to the Tamric ladies' table.

"I'm Brianna Trailwalker," she said in a gruff, businesslike voice. "I hear you're looking for escort across the border."

The stocky woman nodded. "This is Lady Esmerell," she said, nodding at the younger woman. "And I am Tatina, her governess. Our home has been overrun by the Ardenine Army."

"Why choose me?" Raisa said.

"Traders are known to be skilled with weapons, even the females," Esmerell said. "And we would feel more comfortable with another woman." She shivered delicately. "There are many men on the road who would take advantage of two gently raised ladies."

I don't know, Raisa thought. Tatina looks like she could knock some heads together.

"Did you mean to cross via the Fens or the Fells?" Raisa asked.

"We'll go whatever way you choose," Esmerell said, her lip trembling. "We just want to get away and take refuge in the temple at Fellsmarch until the Ardenine brigands are driven from our lands."

Don't hold your breath, Raisa thought.

Esmerell groped in her skirts, pulled out a fat purse, and clunked it onto the table. "We can pay you," she said. "We have money."

"Put that away before somebody sees it," Raisa hissed. The purse disappeared.

Raisa gazed down at them, debating. She couldn't wait for-ever for someone to come fetch her. Maybe it was time to take a chance.

"Please," Tatina said, putting her hand on Raisa's arm. "Sit down. Maybe, if you get to know us, you will—"

"No." Raisa shook her head. She didn't want to be remem-bered sitting with the ladies in the tavern if anyone came asking questions. "We had better be early to bed if we're going to make an early start tomorrow."

"Then you'll do it?" Esmerell said, clapping her hands with delight.

"Hush," Raisa said, glancing around, but nobody seemed to be paying attention. "Be at the stables at daybreak, packed and ready to ride all day."

Raisa left the two ladies and returned to her table, hoping she'd made the right decision. Hoping this would get her home sooner rather than later. Her mind churned with plans. She would ask Simon to pack up bread, cheese, and sausage to carry with them. Once in the Fens, she could make contact with the Waterwalkers, and they might . . .

"You look like you could use cheering up, young miss," a rough male voice said in Ardenine. A bulky stranger dropped heavily into the chair opposite Raisa. It was one of the newly arrived patrons, his face shadowed within his hood. He hadn't even bothered to remove his cloak, though it dripped puddles on the floor.

"You, there!" he called to Simon. "Bring the lady another of whatever she's having and a jacket of ale for me. And step lively, now! It's almost closing time."

Raisa's temper flared. One of the hazards of dining alone in a tavern was being seen as fair game by any male who wandered in. Well, she would disabuse him of that notion right away.

"Perhaps you were under the mistaken impression that I wanted company," Raisa said icily. "I prefer to dine alone. I'll thank you not to intrude on me again."

"Don't be like that," the stranger complained, loudly enough to be heard across the taproom. "It's not fitting for a girl like you to be sitting all by herself."

The soldier leaned forward, and his voice changed, became low and soft, though he still spoke Ardenine like a native. "Are you sure you can't spare a moment for a soldier long on the road?"

He tugged back his hood, and Raisa looked into the weathered gray eyes of Edon Byrne, Captain of the Queen's Guard of the Fells. Eyes uncannily similar to his son Amon's.

It was all Raisa could do to keep her jaw from dropping open. Questions crowded into her mind, threatening to pour out. How had he found her? What was he doing here? Who knew he could speak Ardenine so fluently? Was Amon with him?

"Well," she managed. "Well, then." She cleared her throat to speak, but just then Simon brought their drinks, slamming Byrne's ale onto the table so hard that it sloshed. Byrne waited until Simon slumped away before he spoke again.

"Fetters Ford is no longer safe," he murmured, still in Ardenine. "We've come to take you home." Byrne looked beyond her, scanning the room. He smelled of sweat and leather, and his face was stubbled from days on the road. Though he slouched back in his chair, Raisa noticed that he'd raked his cloak back to expose the hilt of his sword.

"Let's talk," Raisa said, hope blossoming in her heart. "Meet me in the stables behind the inn in ten minutes."

She rose abruptly. "If you won't leave, I will. Go and bother someone else." She turned toward the stairs. The Ardenine ladies fluttered and clucked sympathetically, likely thinking Raisa should have accepted their offer to join them.

"Miss! You forgot your cider," Byrne called after her, drawing some catcalls and snickering.

Raisa strode past the stairs and through the kitchen, where Simon was kneading bread for the overnight rising. "My lady?" he said, looking up at her.

"I need some fresh air," Raisa said. Simon stared after her as she walked out the back door and into the rain. Shivering, she drew Fiona Bayar's wrap more closely around her shoulders. It had come with the horse she'd stolen from the High Wizard's daughter—one of the few things of Fiona's that fit.

The stable was warm and dry and smelled of sweet hay and horses. Ghost poked his head out of his stall, snorting and blowing bits of oats at her. She stroked his nose. Two stalls down, she recognized Ransom, Byrne's large bay gelding, a mountain pony cross.

The stable doors creaked open and Byrne entered, followed by a handful of bluejackets. Though they could hardly be called bluejackets, since they wore a mixture of nondescript cold weather clothing in browns and greens.

Raisa scanned them quickly, but to her disappointment,

Amon wasn't there, nor were any of the other Gray Wolves. These soldiers looked more seasoned than Amon's cadets, their still-young faces inscribed by sun and wind.

Byrne carefully latched the stable doors and set one of his company to keep watch. The others went immediately to work, leading out their horses and saddling them up.

"You mean to leave tonight?" Raisa asked, nodding toward the others.

"The sooner the better," Byrne said. He stood gazing down at her, chewing his lower lip, examining her for damage. "It is a relief to find you still alive."

As if he wouldn't have known if she'd been killed. As if he wouldn't have sensed the blow to the all-important Gray Wolf line.

"What's happened?" Raisa said. "How did you know I was here? Where is Amon? Why is Fetters Ford no longer safe?"

Byrne took a step back, retreating from the onslaught of questions. He nodded toward the tack room. "Let's talk in there."

Raisa remembered the Ardenine ladies. "Oh—there's one thing. Those two ladies I was talking to in the taproom—I agreed to travel on with them tomorrow. Could you send someone to let them know my plans have changed?" It was cowardly, she knew, but she was too weary to deal with Lady Esmerell's disappointment.

"Corliss." Byrne motioned to one of his men and sent him back to the inn to give Esmerell and Tatina the bad news.

Unlatching Ghost's stall door, Raisa led the stallion into the tack room and cross tied him, then fetched his saddle and bridle from the rack against the wall.

Byrne followed her in and closed the door. He watched Raisa work for a moment. "Isn't that the flatland stallion Fiona Bayar was riding last time she was home?"

Raisa nodded. Fiona went through horses like her brother Micah went through lovers. "I borrowed him." Dragging over a step stool, she climbed up so she could fling her horse blanket across Ghost's broad back.

"I'd like to hear that story," Byrne said.

"You were about to tell *me* the story of how you came to be here, Captain Byrne."

"Yes, Your Highness." Byrne inclined his head, giving in. "Your father intercepted a message that suggests Lord Bayar knows where you are and has dispatched assassins to murder you."

"Oh," Raisa said, looking up from her work. "Right. I know about that. He sent four of them to Oden's Ford."

Byrne raised an eyebrow, which so reminded Raisa of Amon that her heart stuttered. "And?" he said dryly.

"I killed one, and Micah Bayar killed the other three," Raisa said.

"Micah?" Byrne said sharply. "Why would he—"

"He'd rather marry me than bury me, apparently," Raisa said. "He kidnapped me from school and was hauling me back home for a wedding when we were overrun by Gerard Montaigne's army on its way into Tamron. That was just north of Oden's Ford. If Micah survived, I think he'd assume I'd go back to school rather than on to the Fells. So it's unlikely Lord Bayar knows where I am now."

"This was a recent message," Byrne said, frowning. "I'm not sure it refers to the earlier attempt."

It's unfortunate, Raisa thought, shivering, when so many people are trying to kill you that you can't sort them out.

Byrne lifted Ghost's saddle and positioned it atop the tall horse. "If you would like to go fetch your belongings, I'll finish him up."

Raisa was familiar enough with Byrne avoidance tactics to know when she was being played. "*Corporal* Byrne taught me to take care of my own horse," she said, ducking underneath to buckle the cinch strap. "Who else knows that you were coming after me?"

Byrne thought a moment. "Your father," he said. "And Amon." He bit down on the last word as if he regretted saying it.

Raisa stood on tiptoes so she could look over Ghost's back. "Did Amon contact you? Is that how you knew to come here?"

Byrne cleared his throat. "When you disappeared from Oden's Ford, Corporal Byrne thought perhaps you had gone home, willingly or not. He guessed you might take the western route, since you'd come that way last fall. He sent a bird, suggesting I try to intercept you here in order to avoid a possible ambush at West Gate." Raisa could tell he had been shining up this story for some time.

"Really?" she said. "How did he know I survived? We left a bloody mess behind at Oden's Ford." She buckled Ghost's bridle while the stallion lipped at the bit, trying to spit it out.

"He . . . ah . . . had a feeling," Byrne said. Raisa snorted. He was no better a liar than Amon.

"If he thought I was here, then why didn't he come here himself?" Raisa tugged at the cinch strap, unconvinced that it was as tight as it could be.

"He thought I could get here sooner," Byrne said, shifting his weight.

"Why? Where is he now?" Raisa demanded.

Byrne looked away. "I don't know where he is right now," he said.

"Well, where was he when he messaged you?" she persisted. "We had no birds at Oden's Ford that would carry a message to Fellsmarch."

"He was in Tamron Court, Your Highness," Byrne said, like an oyster finally yielding up the meat within.

"Tamron Court!" Raisa straightened, swiveling around. "What was he doing there?"

"Looking for you," Byrne said. "He'd received word that you'd been entangled in a skirmish between Montaigne's army and a scouting party from Tamron. He thought you might've taken sanctuary in the capital. So he and his triple went there to find you."

Raisa stared at Byrne, her stomach clenching as certainty set in. "He's still there, isn't he?" she whispered. "And Gerard Montaigne has the city surrounded."

"That's why it's important that we move quickly, while the Prince of Arden believes that you are in Tamron Court," Byrne said.

"What?" Raisa whispered. "Why would he think . . . ?"

"It's a long story." Byrne rubbed his chin as if debating whether he could avoid telling it. "Montaigne has threatened to level the capital if they don't surrender. Whether he can really do that or not is anyone's guess, but King Markus seems convinced that he can, so he leaked word that you were inside the city, hoping the prince of Arden won't destroy the city with you inside. Now Montaigne is demanding that King Markus hand you over or he will put everyone in the city to the sword. So Markus sent a message to Queen Marianna, asking her to send an army to rescue you."

"Isn't he afraid I'll surface somewhere and prove him a liar?" Raisa asked.

"Corporal Byrne told him you were killed during the skirmish with Montaigne's forces." Byrne grimaced. "In fact, Corporal Byrne was the one who suggested this scheme to Markus after Montaigne laid siege to the city."

"But why would he do that?" Raisa asked, lost.

"Corporal Byrne guessed you hadn't yet crossed the border. He'd rather that those hunting you believe you're in Tamron Court, and not here in the borderlands. So he and his triple have made themselves visible in the city so that any spies working for Montaigne or Lord Bayar see that members of the Queen's Guard are still there and assume that you are also."

"No," Raisa whispered, pacing back and forth. "Oh, no. When Montaigne finds out he's been tricked, he'll be furious. There's no telling what he'll do." She stopped and looked up at Byrne. "What about the queen? Will she send help?"

"Given the situation at home right now, we cannot send an army into Tamron," Byrne said flatly. "It would destabilize a fragile situation. War may break out at home at any moment, depending on what happens with the succession."

"But . . . if my mother believes that I'm trapped in Tamron Court," Raisa whispered, "wouldn't she send an army anyway?" In truth, Raisa wasn't sure of the answer to that question.

"I told her not to risk it, that you were not there," Byrne said, his gray eyes steady on hers.

"But—but—but—that means that Amon—and all the Gray Wolves—will *die* there," Raisa cried. "In horrible ways."

"There is that possibility," Byrne said quietly.

"Possibility? *Possibility*?" She stood in front of Byrne, hands fisted. "Amon is your son! How could you do that? How *could* you?"

"Amon made this decision for the good of the line, as is his duty," Byrne said. "I won't second-guess him."

Raisa went up on her toes, leaning toward Byrne, her fury ringing in her ears and freeing her tongue. "Did he even have a *choice*?" she demanded. "He told me what you did to him—that magical linkage you forced on him."

Byrne frowned, rubbing the corner of his eye with his thumb. "Really? He said that?"

Raisa didn't slow down. "Does he even *have* free will anymore, or is he compelled to sacrifice himself to save the bloody line?"

"Hmmm," Byrne said, still damnably calm. "Well, I would say he has some free will or he'd not have told you about the bond between queens and captains," he said.

"What about the Gray Wolves?" Raisa said. "Did *they* have a choice?" She thought of her friends among Amon's cadets: Hallie, whose two-year-old daughter waited for her in Fellsmarch. Talia, who would have left her beloved Pearlie behind in Oden's Ford. And poor Mick, who had offered Raisa his clan-made saddlebag as consolation for losing Amon Byrne.

Tamron Court is standing in for me, she thought. It was arrogant, she knew—the notion that the invasion of Tamron was all about her. Gerard Montaigne wanted Tamron's wealth, a bigger army, and a throne to sit upon. She was just the filling in the nougat—a chance to claim the Fells as well.

"We have to go after them," Raisa said. "There has to be a way to get them out of there. What if—if I showed myself and drew Montaigne off. Or if I offered to negotiate. Or maybe there's a way to slip between their lines, and . . ."

Raisa didn't really believe any of these things would work as she spoke them. And Byrne knew it, because he just looked at her impassively until she trailed off.

"We don't even know if he's still in the city, or if he's still alive, Your Highness," Byrne said softly.

"He's still alive," Raisa said. "The linkage goes both ways. I would know if he were dead."

"The city may have fallen by now," Byrne continued. "How do you think he would feel if you went to the capital and were captured by Montaigne, and all of his efforts were wasted?"

Unable to contain herself, Raisa kicked the door of the tack room, hard enough to splinter it. Ghost tossed his head, yanking at his tether. Furious tears burned in Raisa's eyes, then spilled down her cheeks as she turned back to Byrne.

"Amon Byrne is better than you, better than me; too valuable to throw away, and you know it," she said, her voice trembling. "He is—and always has been—my very best friend."

"Then trust him," Byrne said. "If anyone can get out of the city, he will."

Raisa rubbed away her tears with the heels of her hands. "Captain Byrne, if anything happens to Amon, I will never, ever forgive you."

Byrne took hold of her shoulders, gripping them hard, the light from the lanterns gilding his face. "What you can do for Amon now is survive," he said, his voice husky and strange. "Don't let them win, Your Highness."

Raisa strode back across the stable yard toward the inn, her mind churning with worry about Amon and the Gray Wolves, still trying to devise some kind of rescue plan.

It was after closing time, and with any luck, the taproom would have cleared. She'd pack her few belongings and they'd be on their way.

When she looked ahead, she saw Esmerell and Tatina hustling toward her through the rain, lifting their skirts above the mucky ground.

Great, she thought, rolling her eyes. Just what I need.

Then two of the card players Raisa had noticed earlier burst out the back door, charging after the ladies at a dead run.

Raisa's mind grappled with what she was seeing, and came to a quick conclusion. The men *were* thieves after all, and likely had seen the purse the wealthy Ardenine ladies had been waving around.

"Look out behind you!" Raisa yelled, sprinting forward.

The women didn't look back, but increased their speed, running faster than Raisa would have expected. The card players were yelling something as they ran. Something Raisa couldn't make out. She heard the stable door bang open, then shouts and pounding feet behind her.

"Get behind me!" she shouted as the ladies closed the distance between them. But then something slammed into her, throwing her sideways to the ground. She rolled to her feet in time to see the Ardenine ladies go down under the card players.

Edon Byrne seized Raisa's shoulders in a viselike grip and held her fast.

It took a moment for Raisa to gather breath enough to speak.

"What are you doing?" she spluttered, struggling to free herself. She was soaked through, muddy and shivering, her teeth chattering.

Slowly, the guards disentangled themselves and stood. The ladies lay flat on their backs, unmoving, blood and rain soaking their fancy dresses.

Run through by the card players.

"Good work," Edon Byrne said gruffly, nodding at them. "But next time don't let them get so close to the princess heir."

The card players yanked their blades free, wiping them on the ladies' voluminous skirts. One of them knelt and efficiently searched the women. He came up with three knives and a small framed picture. He scanned the picture, then mutely extended it toward Raisa.

It was a portrait of Raisa, done for her name day.

Byrne kicked something away from the two bodies, stooped and picked it up with two fingers.

It was a dagger, delicate and feminine and deadly sharp.

CHAPTER TWO

PICKING OVER OLD BONES

Han Alister encountered more traffic than he had anticipated on the road to Fetters Ford. Hollow-eyed refugees streamed north as Gerard Montaigne's army scorched the countryside to the south. They looked witch-fixed, some of them, stunned by calamity, still dressed in the ruined finery that said they were bluebloods.

It seemed to Han that all of Tamron was on the move—country folk seeking refuge in the cities, and city dwellers fleeing to the countryside. How likely was it that he could find one girlie amid this chaos—traveling alone or with two wizards?

The road traced the Tamron River north from Oden's Ford. To the east lay Arden and the dense broadleaf trees of Tamron Forest. To the west lay the fertile fields of Tamron, now overrun by fighting. Smoke spiraled up from charred farm buildings and manor houses.

Sword-danglers seemed to like to burn things up.

Tamron might be the breadbasket of the Seven Realms, but

these days food was hard to come by even for those with money to spend. Small villages lined the road, a day's ride apart, like knots on a frayed string. Each was guarded by a motley local militia armed with pitchforks, staffs, and longbows, ready to drive off the ravenous hordes—soldiers or citizens—that threatened to overrun them.

Fortunately, Han was used to going hungry.

In every village there was at least one inn. And in every inn, Han would ask the same questions. "Have you seen a girlie, a mixed-blood with green eyes and dark hair? She's small, she'd be this tall." Here he'd hold out his hand below shoulder height. "Her name is Rebecca Morley, and she might be traveling with two charmcasters, a brother and sister. You'd remember them— both tall, and the sister has white-blond hair and blue eyes, the brother has dark hair and eyes."

Some of those he asked tried to make a joke of it. "What's the matter, your girlie run off?" But most seemed to take a cue from Han's expression, or the amulet that hung around his neck, or his travel-weary appearance in these desperate times.

Missing girlies in wartime were no laughing matter.

The dead were everywhere. Bodies hung from trees like grisly fruit, spinning slowly in the southern breezes. Here were battlegrounds littered with the bodies of dead soldiers, lorded over by carrion birds. Clouds of flies rose from the carcasses of animals along the roadside, and bodies fouled many of the waterways.

Han traveled most days with the stench of decay in his nose. It reminded him of Arden, when he and Dancer had traveled through on their way to Oden's Ford. Had it really been nearly a year ago?

This was the poison that had spread into Tamron and threatened to sicken the Fells.

Stay out of it, Alister, Han said to himself. You have enough battles to fight as it is.

One innkeeper thought he remembered a girlie matching Rebecca's description traveling alone, riding a gray flatland stallion far too big for her. It seemed a thin lead at best.

Han could hope that Rebecca's party had passed through unmolested; that the reports that put Rebecca in the way of Gerard's invading army were wrong.

It was possible she'd turned aside and taken refuge in the capital of Tamron Court, now under siege by Gerard Montaigne's army. Han considered detouring west, toward the capital, but there was no way to tell if she was there or not. And nothing to be done if she were.

Han took a deep breath, released it, forcing himself to relax his neck and shoulders, to unclench his fists.

Anyway, Corporal Byrne and his Gray Wolves were headed that way. Han had his own path to follow.

If not for his worries about Rebecca, Han would have been in no hurry to reach the Fells. Why should he be eager to take his place as the magical sell-sword of the upland clans who'd misled and betrayed him? Why should he rush to confront the Wizard Council? Did he really want to play champion to Marianna— the queen responsible for so many of his losses? The queen who likely still had a price on his head.

Even when he reached the Fells, Han couldn't trust the clans to have his back. The Demonai warriors despised him because he was gifted. He was their throwaway piece, intended to buy them a little time.

If not for Rebecca, he could have run the other way. As long as he stayed out of the mountains, he might avoid those he'd pledged to for months or years. He could always find a flatland hidey-hole and lose himself.

He snorted. As if that would ever happen. Han had loved Oden's Ford, but he didn't like the flatlands. Though a city boy, he'd been raised in a mountain town, and it made him uneasy to have vacancy all around him. He wanted to wrap himself in the mountains again.

Anyway, he'd never had much luck lying low. Sooner or later, he'd have a crew, a gang to support, and people depending on him. People who'd pay the price for his failures.

So he hadn't seriously considered breaking his agreement with the clans. Not by running, anyway. It wasn't enough to be on the winning side. He would do whatever was necessary to make sure he, Han Alister, came out on top.

Han and the clans had a common enemy. Lord Gavan Bayar, the High Wizard of the Fells, had engineered the deaths of Han's mother and sister. He'd tortured and killed Han's friends in an effort to find Han and retrieve the amulet he'd taken from the Bayars. The serpent flashpiece had once belonged to Han's ancestor, Alger Waterlow, the notorious Demon King. Han now wore it against his skin.

Then Rebecca Morley had disappeared from Oden's Ford, and Lord Bayar's son Micah with her. If Han found no trace of Rebecca along the way, he would hunt down Micah Bayar and wring the truth from him. If Rebecca were still alive, it was an urgent mission. If she were dead, he would make the Bayars pay.

Han had been overconfident at Oden's Ford. His own words mocked him.

You Bayars need to learn that you can't have everything you want. I'm going to teach you.

He'd spoken truer words to Rebecca, the last time he'd seen her.

When I put things aside for the future, they disappear on me.

He was returning home, like a Ragger streetlord walking into Southbridge, with enemies on every side. Only, this time, if blood spilled, it would be on the other side.

Which meant he needed better weapons. He'd have to risk a return to Aediion and make up with his former tutor, Crow.

Crow had lied to Han, too—had played him for a fool, had ruthlessly used him to try to kill their mutual enemies, the Bayars. But Crow had taught Han more about magic during their late-night tutoring sessions than he'd learned from all of the faculty at Oden's Ford put together.

Han wanted to get a commitment from Crow before he crossed the border into the Fells. He needed to enter Aediion from a secure place, since his abandoned body would be vulnerable during the time he was absent. About a day's ride south of Fetters Ford, Han found a camping place in a small canyon where a creek ran into the larger river.

He spread his blankets on the slope above the stream. Scraping a rude pit in the rocky earth, he built a small, smokeless fire at the bottom, which wouldn't be visible except from directly above.

Han ate his standard supper of waybread, cheese, smoked fish, and dried fruit, washing it down with tea made from water from the stream. Then he paged through his book of charms, leaning close to the fire so he could see.

Crow could create illusion but did not seem to be able to do magic on his own. He lacked flash, the wizard-generated energy that interacted with amulets to make things happen. So if magic was the only tool that could do damage in Aediion, Han should be safe in returning. *If.*

Han still wore the rowan talisman Fire Dancer had made for him, the one that had prevented Crow from possessing him during his last visit to Aediion. He had to trust that it would protect him again. It was a calculated risk, but Crow shared his hatred for the Bayars, and Han needed an ally. Crow was likely the only one able and possibly willing to teach Han what he needed to win.

Taking a deep breath, Han focused on the Mystwerk Tower room, their meeting place over his months at Oden's Ford. He guessed it didn't matter where he chose, but it was as good a place as any. He visualized the battered floorboards, the huge bells hanging overhead, the pattern of moonlight on the wall. Closing his hand on his amulet, he spoke the traveling charm.

Han opened his eyes to find himself standing in the belfry in Mystwerk Tower, dressed in finely tailored blueblood clothes. Quickly, he scanned his surroundings, keeping his hand on his amulet. He was alone.

He breathed in warm, moist air—southern air. Outside, a cart rattled over cobblestone streets. If he ran to the window, would he see it? If he walked outside and made his way to Hampton Hall, would he find Dancer there? He couldn't quite get his mind around that.

Han waited. A minute passed. Another minute. Maybe he'd been wrong, and Crow wouldn't come. Disappointment swelled within him. Patience, Alister, he thought. It's been a month, and likely Crow doesn't expect you back.

Finally, the air quivered in front of his eyes, brightened, then seemed to compress.

It was Crow, but different from the Crow Han remembered. The image was frail, insubstantial, his clothes rippling around him like angel wings. Han's former tutor stood at a little distance, feet spread, arms raised as if for defense. And his hair, which had been soot black, was now a pale blond, nearly translucent, though his eyes remained the brilliant blue Han remembered.

"Hello, Crow," Han said.

Crow tilted his head, watching Han like he might be jumped at any moment. "Why are you here?" he asked. "I did not think I would see you again."

"This may be the last time," Han said, as if he didn't care either way. "But I thought I'd give you a chance to explain."

"Why should I explain anything to you?" Crow said, eyes narrowed. "You've gained considerably more from our relationship than I have. I handed you the chance to be rid of two of the Bayars and you fumbled it."

"Fine," Han said. "Guess this is a waste of time. Good-bye, then." He took hold of his amulet and opened his mouth as if to say the closing charm.

"Wait." Crow put up his hands, then slowly dropped them to his sides. For once, he'd left off the baubles and the fancy rigging. "Please stay."

Han stood, his hand on his amulet, waiting.

"Was there something specific you wanted me to explain?" Crow said, with a sigh. "In the interest of efficiency?"

"I want to know who you are, why you don't want me to know who you are, why you have a grudge against the Bayars, and why you wanted to partner up with me," Han said. "That's for starters."

Crow rubbed his forehead with his thumb and forefinger, looking done in. "Wouldn't it be sufficient if I promise not to treat you like a fool in the future?"

Han shook his head. "That's not enough."

"Even if I tell you the truth, you won't believe me," Crow said. "That's always the way. People unnecessarily limit themselves, and then they try to limit you."

"I'm not learning what I need to know here," Han said. "I'm not the most patient person."

"Nor am I," Crow said. "But I have had to be incredibly patient for longer than you can even imagine." He thought a moment. "Who am I? I was once the Bayars' enemy. Their greatest rival."

By now it was clear that the only way Han was going to hear this story was in small bits and riddles. "And now you're not?" Han said.

Crow smiled faintly. "I suppose you would say I am a shade. A ghost of my former self. A remnant of who I used to be, made up of memory and emotion. The Bayars no longer perceive me as a threat. And yet"—he tapped his temple—"I have something they want very badly."

"Knowledge," Han guessed. "You know something they need to know."

"I know something they need to know, and I intend to use it to destroy them," Crow said matter-of-factly. "That is the reason for my existence."

Han was lost. "When you say you are a ghost of your former

self, what does that mean, exactly?"

Crow's image shimmered, dissolved, and then reassembled itself. "This is all that remains of me," he said. "I am an illusion. I exist in your head, Alister. And in Aediion, the meeting place of wizards. Not in the world you consider real."

"You're saying you're . . . dead?" Han stared at Crow. "That doesn't make sense." At least, it didn't fit in very well with what he'd been taught at temple. But then he'd never claimed to be a theologian.

Crow shrugged. "What is death? The loss of a body? The loss of the animating spark? If that's the case, I am dead.

"Or is life the persistence of memory and emotion, volition and desire?" Crow went on, as if in a debate with himself. "If that's the case, I am very much alive."

"But you have no body," Han said.

Crow smiled. "Precisely. I have no corporeal body, nothing beyond what I conjure up in Aediion. And a body is required in order to get things done in the real world. A body is necessary in order to take revenge on the Bayars. Specifically, a wizard's body, since that would allow me to use my considerable knowledge of magic."

"And that's where I came in," Han said. "I could provide the flash you needed."

"That's where you came in." Crow eyed Han critically, head cocked. "You seemed perfect. You are extremely powerful— surprisingly so. You'd had little to no training, which made you vulnerable to my influence and eager to spend time with me. You hated the Bayars, and, given your tawdry background, I assumed that you were ruthless and unprincipled. All good."

"All good?" Han asked, rolling his eyes. This was a bit more honesty than he needed.

Crow nodded. "At first I was able to take control of you fairly easily, particularly when you were actively using your amulet. I even provided support at times, when you seemed in danger of being prematurely killed."

"You mean the thorn hedge, when we were chased across the border into Delphi," Han said. "And when we escaped from Prince Gerard at Ardenscourt." Han had immolated several of Montaigne's soldiers with seemingly little participation on his own part.

"Yes," Crow said. "But eventually, as you became more adept, you put up rudimentary barriers that kept me out. Very frustrating. I looked for a way back in."

"And then I came to Aediion," Han said.

"To my delight, you did." Crow threw him a sidelong glance. "In Aediion, you were still vulnerable to whatever illusion I conjured up. I could still get into your mind. We could have actual conversations, and I could teach you. That opened a realm of possibilities."

"But . . ." Han frowned. "There were still times, even after we began meeting, that you possessed me in real life, right?" he said. He'd found himself on the upper floors of the Bayar Library amid old dusty books. He'd discovered a map of Gray Lady and a list of incantations in his pocket. Scribbled notes that were now tucked away in his saddlebags. "I kept losing big chunks of time on the days we met."

"At the end of our tutoring sessions, when you were nearly drained of magic, the barriers came down. I could take possession of you and cross over with you when you left the dreamworld," Crow said, without a trace of apology.

"Is that why you worked me so hard?" Han asked. "To wear me down so you could seize control?"

"Well, that and, of course, we had considerable work to do," Crow said. He shrugged. "Unfortunately, you were useless for magical tasks in your depleted condition, or I might have gone after the Bayars then and there. But it did allow me to get out into the world."

It gave Han the prickly shivers to imagine Crow inhabiting his body. "Yet you chose to spend your time in a dusty old library," Han said.

Crow frowned at Han, looking dismayed. "You remember that?"

"You left me in the wrong place a few times," Han said. "In the stacks."

"I had only a brief window of time before your amulet was drained completely," Crow said. "Several times we ran out before I could return you to where you were supposed to be."

"Well, I thought I was losing my mind," Han said. "What were you looking for?"

"I was only trying to stay ahead of you," Crow said, biting his lip and shifting his gaze away. "You are a challenging student, Alister, always asking questions and demanding answers."

"I don't believe you," Han said. "I think you were working your own plan. Were you maybe looking for a way to seize control of me permanently?"

Crow's eyes glittered, signifying that Han had hit on the truth. "That would have been perfect. But impossible, it seems." Crow closed his eyes, as if reliving it. "Can you imagine it, Alister? Can you imagine what it was like for a shade like me to experience the world again through all of your senses—vision and touch, and smell and taste and hearing?"

"I wouldn't have gone to the library, I'll tell you that," Han said.

Crow laughed. "I like you, Alister. All of this would have been easier if you were unlikable. And stupid. You would have been considerably more tractable."

"Tractable gets you nothing," Han said, feeling like a country boy at market. Crow had dumped so much on him that he couldn't quite see where the holes were. Questions rattled around in his brain.

"So. I have been uncommonly frank with you," Crow said, interrupting his thoughts. "Now, tell me: why did you come back? Shall I assume that you still want something from me?"

"I'm on my way back to the Fells to go up against the Bayars and maybe the entire Wizard Council," Han said.

"All by yourself? That seems ambitious even for you," Crow said dryly. "What, exactly, do you hope to accomplish? Beyond flinging your life away."

Han knew he had to give a reason that the cynical Crow would understand. A reason that would make Crow his ally, for now, anyway.

"The Bayars want to put Micah Bayar on the Gray Wolf throne," Han said. "I'm not going to let that happen."

"Mmm. The Bayars are nothing if not persistent," Crow murmured. "It's a pity young Bayar didn't die in Aediion." He paused, peering at Han through narrowed eyes to see if he'd felt the poke. "What is it between *you* and the Bayars? What did they do to you?"

"They murdered my mother and sister a year ago," Han said. "They were all the family I had. And, recently, there was a girl, Rebecca. My . . . ah . . . tutor. She's disappeared, and the Bayars are responsible. I think they did it to get back at me."

Crow looked into Han's eyes. "You poor bastard," he said, shaking his head. "You're in love with her, aren't you?"

Damn my readable Aediion face, Han thought, scowling.

Crow laughed. "Let me give you a piece of advice—don't go to war over a girl. It's not worth it. Falling in love turns wise men into fools."

"I didn't come to you for advice," Han said. "I came to you for firepower. The odds are against me. Even if you help me."

"You're coming back to me for help after what happened the last time?" Crow raised his eyebrows. "I thought you were smarter than that."

"Everything is a risk," Han said. "There's a chance you'll betray me again, but now I'm on the watch, so you're less likely to be able to do any real damage. The risk from the Bayars, on the other hand, is real and imminent."

Crow stood, legs slightly apart, head tilted, regarding Han as if he'd never really seen him before. "My, my, Alister, such big words. This young woman, this teacher of yours, she *has* polished you up, hasn't she?"

Rebecca. Han's gut twisted. In return, he'd likely gotten her killed.

"What's underneath is still the same," Han said. "I'm going to get what I want and nobody is going to get in my way. Including you. We do this thing my way or you're out. Take or leave."

"All right," Crow said. "We'll do things your way. But I *will* give you advice, and you can choose to use it or ignore it."

"Fair enough," Han said, his questions rekindling in his mind. "But first, I need to know—what happened between *you* and the Bayars, and when did it happen? Where have you been in the meantime? And how did you happen to choose me?"

"Does any of that really matter?" Crow said, turning away so Han couldn't read his expression. "This is an alliance of convenience, nothing more. Isn't that enough?"

"I've learned that whatever you don't want to talk about is the thing I want to know," Han said, thinking, If I know the *why*, if I know what drives you, I can better predict when I'll get the blade in the back.

"As I said, if I tell you the truth, you won't believe me." Crow paced back and forth, his image rippling again, which Han had come to recognize as a sign of agitation. Was it such a horrible memory that Crow couldn't stand to surface it?

"Try me," Han said, as Crow continued to pace. "Come on. At least tell me a really good lie; you might convince me."

"It doesn't matter to you what happened," Crow said. "It was long before you were born."

You're not even that old, Han thought, then remembered that Crow could be any age.

"Nothing you say can possibly shock me," Han said. "But nothing happens until I know what your story is."

Crow finally swung around to face Han. A bitter smile twisted his features. "We'll see," he said. "We'll see just how foolhardy you are." His image changed a little, sharpened, came into focus.

His hair remained fair, glittering, framing refined blueblood features—eyes the color of mountain asters and a good-humored mouth. As before, he looked to be only a few years older than Han.

His clothing had become more elaborate—a finely cut coat in satin and brocade, oddly old-fashioned, its champagne color a few shades darker than his hair. He was brilliant with power—handsome as a fancy on the make.

"You've asked what I really look like," Crow said, turning in a little circle, extending his arms. "Feast your eyes. This is how I looked when I went up against the Bayars."

The wizard stoles around his neck bore images of ravens, and his coat was embroidered with a device—a twined serpent and staff, angled through a crown engraved with wolves.

The device was familiar—where had Han seen it before?

"It was an exciting and dangerous time," Crow said. "I was young and powerful, and I competed with the Bayars in every arena—politically, magically, and in"—here he stumbled over the words a bit—"in all manner of relationships. Just as it seemed that I had beaten them for good, I was betrayed, and the Bayars captured me. When that happened, I took refuge in the amulet I carried for so long."

Han tapped his amulet with his forefinger. "You're saying you hid in a *jinxpiece*?"

Crow smiled. "Immediate disbelief, as I anticipated. I so enjoy being right all the time. As I told you, I was an innovative user of magic. I hoped that the amulet would end up in friendly hands. Unfortunately, the Bayars realized that the key to everything they desired lay in the flashpiece. Though they have been trying to extract its secrets for more than a thousand years, they've been spectacularly unsuccessful."

Han struggled to assemble the bits Crow had given him. It was like working a puzzle that doesn't reveal its meaning until the last piece is in place.

Except the image that was forming was impossible.

As if Crow had read Han's mind, an amulet appeared at Crow's neck, hanging from a heavy gold chain—the mirror image of Han's serpent amulet.

"I am the original owner of the amulet you carry now," Crow said. "I had it custom made for me when I was about your age. I needed something powerful enough to conjure magic the world had never seen before. There is not another like it in the world."

Han stood frozen, each word he might have spoken stillborn on his tongue.

"After Hanalea betrayed me, I dared not reveal myself to the Bayars," Crow said. "So I've been lying imprisoned for a millennium. When the amulet came into your hands, I seized the opportunity. Naturally, I have done my best to make sure they don't recover it."

Han looked down at his amulet, tracing the serpent head with his fingers. He looked back up at Crow, his mind traveling to the end of that road. "You can't be serious," he whispered. "That can't be true."

Crow still smiled, but his blue eyes were hard as glacier ice. "My name was Alger Waterlow," he said, caressing the serpent flashpiece. "The last wizard king of the Fells."

Han stared at Crow, speechless, his mind frothing like a potion made with incompatible ingredients.

Crow inclined his head. "You look suitably stricken, Alister. I'll leave you with that, then, and give you time to think it through before you do or say anything rash. I am, as you've no doubt figured out, always here and always available. Come back to Aediion when you are ready to partner with me. If that should ever happen."

He gazed at Han for another long moment, searching Han's face as if hoping Han might stay with him. Then he blinked out like a fivepenny candle.

CHAPTER THREE

BAD NEWS AND GOOD NEWS

During the long journey from Fetters Ford to Delphi, Raisa managed to forget, now and then, that she was furious.

Furious with Gerard Montaigne, the monster who held her friends in his grasp.

Furious with those at home who were conspiring to steal her birthright, by murder or other means.

Furious with Captain Edon Byrne, who seemed willing to sacrifice his own son for the Gray Wolf line.

Furious most of all with herself. Had she not left the queendom nearly a year ago, none of this would have happened.

But it's not easy to remain angry while falling asleep in the saddle. Raisa would startle awake to find Captain Byrne's hand on her back, preventing her from toppling to the ground. "Eat something, Your Highness," he would say, handing her a sack of dried fruit and nuts. "Eating will help keep you awake."

She would accept it without thinking, without remembering

that she hadn't forgiven him. By the time she remembered, he'd have spurred his horse forward or dropped back behind her, too far away for easy speech. She wasn't speaking to him either, not unless absolutely necessary, since there was no predicting what might come out of her mouth.

Byrne drove them on like a man possessed—Raisa suspected that he'd have ordered them to ride all night if the horses could have stood it. As it was, they rose before light and rode long past dark—even though the days were growing longer as the fields greened around them and the lower slopes of the northern mountains lost their snowy cloaks.

Byrne had chosen to travel east, through northern Arden, and not directly north, as Raisa had thought to do. His reasoning was simple: "If Lord Bayar knows you were in Fetters Ford, he'll expect you to enter the queendom via the West Wall. We need to do the unexpected."

Arden's forces had been drawn south, to fortify the border between Arden and Tamron, as Gerard's sole surviving brother, King Geoff, awaited the results of the siege of Tamron Court. The countryside lay eerily quiet, as if the entire realm were holding its breath.

They couldn't ride through the rough in the dark, so they chanced the Delphi Road through northern Arden, skirting the mountains, meaning to cross the lower Spirits via Marisa Pines Pass.

Raisa understood that speed was of the essence. There was no point in undertaking a long, arduous, dangerous journey through Arden and Tamron only to arrive home and find that her sister Mellony had been named princess heir in her place.

Besides, Captain Byrne wouldn't want to spend any more

time with an angry, moody, downhearted princess than he had to. And he was no doubt worried about Raisa's mother, Marianna, the queen he was blood-sworn to serve and protect.

Raisa worried about her mother, too. Worry squeezed her insides like a too-tight corset.

Long days on horseback allowed far too much time for thinking. Raisa's mind traveled faster than the horses—all the way to Fellsmarch, to the fairy castle on an island in the Dyrnnewater, to her mother's privy chamber, where plans were no doubt being laid to take away Raisa's throne.

An image of her mother and Lord Bayar came to her—their heads together over some critical document, Marianna's hair like pale, beaten gold of the purest kind, the High Wizard's silver and black as wood ashes.

When Raisa was at court, she and her mother had been like fire and ice, each intent on changing the form and nature of the other. Now Raisa hoped they could complement each other, each draw on the other's strengths, become an alloy of steel, if only her mother would give her the chance.

Mellony couldn't do it: she was only thirteen, and Mellony and Marianna were too much alike.

"Mother, please," Raisa whispered. "Please wait for me."

In her blackest hours, Raisa knew that it was all her fault—the crisis at home, the invasion of Tamron, and what would surely happen to Amon Byrne and the other cadets when Gerard Montaigne breached the walls of Tamron Court. If not for her, Edon Byrne would be home, where he belonged, looking after the queen, and Amon would be commander of his class at Oden's Ford.

She'd lost Han Alister, too—their budding romance had been

yanked out by the roots. He was the only sweetheart she'd ever had who hadn't any agenda beyond that of young lovers everywhere. Even though they had no future together, he'd left a huge hole in her heart.

It seemed that everything she touched turned to sand. Everything she cared about slipped through her fingers.

In her dispirited state, she closed her ears to the reasonable voice that said, *You'd never have loved Han Alister if you hadn't left the Fells. Or gotten to know Hallie or Talia or Pearlie. Or learned what it meant to be a soldier. If you survive, you'll be a better queen for it.*

She nurtured her anger, fed it and indulged it, because it was her best alternative to despair.

She had to hope that Gerard Montaigne was still occupied to the west, keeping Tamron Court under siege. If the city hadn't surrendered, the prince of Arden wouldn't know she'd escaped. And as long as the city resisted, Amon would live.

Some pieces on her mental game board were still unaccounted for—Micah Bayar and his sister Fiona, for instance. She'd last seen them on the border between Tamron and Arden, during the battle between Tamron's brigade and Montaigne's much larger army. Had they escaped as well? Or had they died in the first skirmish of an undeclared war?

Raisa balled her fists inside her gloves, cranky as a badger with its foot in a trap. The Queen's Guard learned to tiptoe around her lest they get an undeserved tongue-lashing.

The landscape grew lovelier as they left the sodden plains of Tamron behind and climbed into the foothills. Cypress turned to maple and oak, brilliant with spring foliage, and then to aspen and pine.

They spent the night in Delphi, the city-state between Arden and the Fells that supplied coal, iron, and steel to all the nations of the Seven Realms. The city seethed with refugees from Arden and Tamron, since only fools and desperate people would venture into the pass when snows still howled around the peaks and piled up in the high valleys.

Byrne took Ghost to a horse trader and swapped him for a sturdy mountain pony, better suited for travel through the pass in this season. The trader was so astonished at the bargain she'd made, she threw in a fine clan-made saddle and bridle with silver fittings.

Raisa's new pony was a shaggy dappled gray mare with a white mane and tail. Raisa promptly renamed her Switcher, as had become her custom. She'd changed horses too many times in the past six months, and this way it was easier to remember.

That night, Raisa slept alone in a lumpy bed in a room rented to all eleven of them at the outrageous price of a crown a head. Her guard sprawled on the floor all around her like a litter of overgrown puppies. They were older than she, but not by much.

Some lay fast asleep, snoring and mumbling in their dreams. She envied their ability to drop off as soon as they stopped moving. Others played at cards or read by candles purchased for another crown apiece. If Raisa even went to the privy, Captain Byrne sent an escort along. She was never sure if this was to protect her or to prevent her running off. When she asked him, he replied, "To protect you, Your Highness. Of course."

They left long before dawn the next morning, while stars still pricked the sky. Byrne hoped to make it through the pass by nightfall. In summer, that would be a challenging and arduous journey. In winter or spring, unlikely. Possibly foolhardy.

Above Delphi, the paved road became wheel-rutted dirt, and finally little more than a game trail, hedged on both sides by great granite boulders, the way so narrow, only one rider could pass between. Before long, patches of snow appeared in the shaded areas to either side of the trail. By midday, the ground was covered, and they traveled over packed snow and ice. By afternoon, the trail was drifted over in places where the wind swirled through.

Snow sifted down on them from junipers that overhung the trail, perfuming the air with their sharp, sweet scent. The forest would break the wind, at least, until they climbed above the tree line.

A storm the night before had glazed each twig and branch with ice, and they glittered in the sunlight as the breeze stirred them. The tracks of snowshoe hares and other small game crisscrossed the trail. Raisa flexed her fingers in her gloves, wondering if she should string the bow Byrne had given her, which she carried in her saddle boot.

They'd probably prefer she be unarmed, given that she was angry enough to shoot someone.

She had missed riding the mountain trails of the Fells more than she'd realized. In Oden's Ford, she'd been consumed by work, with little time for pleasure riding. Her equestrian classes reflected the flatland style of warfare. Flatland cadets rode across a broad, featureless landscape in precise formation, wheeling their horses like so many deadly court dancers, bristling with weapons.

Raisa urged Switcher to greater speed, her lighter weight allowing her to outpace her guard. Up, up, up they climbed, splashing through rippling sunlight and shadow, icy evergreen branches whipping across her face, her breath pluming out and crystallizing in her hair and on her wool hat.

Raisa crested the upslope and reined in her mare.

The Spirit Mountains spread before her across a wide valley, fully visible for the first time: rank upon rank of peaks shrouded in snow and cloud. Green spires of fir and brilliant birch smudged the lower slopes. The cool blue of shadow on snow filled the valleys where the sun had not yet penetrated. Frowning gray granite summits were concealed, then revealed by streaming mist. The cold voice of the Spirits called to her, and something within her answered.

This was the dwelling place of her ancestors, blood and bone of the upland queens. And, somewhere ahead, the city of Fellsmarch lay hidden in the Vale. Somewhere ahead, her mother waited—the mother who might be planning to disinherit her.

Switcher stood splay-legged and breathing hard, despite Raisa's slight weight. "I'm sorry," she murmured, stroking the mare's neck, knowing they had an even tougher road ahead of them. The southernmost Queen peaks were gentle, ancient matriarchs ground down by the witch winds that stormed down out of the north after solstice. These mountains were so old, their names had been forgotten.

But ahead lay brooding Hanalea, greatest and most terrible of all. Plumes of steam rose from the hot springs, geysers, and mudpots that dotted her shoulders where the fiery Beneath broke through the thin crust of the earth. Her name would never be forgotten, not as long as her people remembered the Breaking, and observed the Næming.

To the south and west lay Tamron Court, where Amon Byrne was trapped by Montaigne's army. Further east was Oden's Ford, where Raisa had left Han Alister without saying good-bye.

Once again, the pain settled beneath her breastbone, squeezing off her breath. Not grief, exactly, but . . . well, yes, grief for the words that would never be spoken, for a love that would never be consummated, and for a friend whose life was in desperate peril.

Maybe it was better that way. Better for Han, at least. Assuming Raisa survived, she was destined for a political marriage. Han had already lost his family and most of his friends. Further involvement in the treacherous politics of the Gray Wolf court would likely get him killed. He'd been doing well at the academy in Oden's Ford. Better that he stay there and forget about her.

Maybe he already had.

Gripping the reins hard, she stared straight ahead, drawing deep breaths, biting her lower lip, no longer seeing what lay before her.

As her guard surrounded her, she heard the creak of saddle leather, the rattle of hooves against rock, the soft greetings of horses. She breathed in the scent of damp wool and soldiers too long on the road.

"Your Highness."

Raisa flinched, still staring straight ahead.

"Your Highness, please," Byrne said. "I wish you would not insist on racing so far ahead."

This time, she twisted in her saddle, looking into his windburnt face, now etched with concern.

"I thought you said we were in a hurry," Raisa said.

"Aye. We are. But you should be riding in the middle of the triple, not breaking trail out in front. We cannot protect you if you ride out of sight of us."

"Am I a prisoner who must be watched constantly?" Unable to control the quaver in her voice, she clapped her mouth shut and stared down at the ground.

Byrne gazed at her for a long moment, then turned in his saddle, waving the others back with his gloved hand, clearly preferring that they not overhear this conversation. "Take fifteen to rest the horses before we push on," he called.

He dismounted, dropping his reins so his horse could lip at the sparse vegetation. Raisa dismounted also, taking shelter from the wind between the two horses.

"We are here to serve and protect you, Your Highness, not confine you," Byrne said. The gray eyes reproached her.

Raisa knew she was being unreasonable, but she couldn't help herself. She couldn't even trust herself to reply. Instead, she yanked her gloves off with her teeth. Working quickly, before her hands went numb, she tucked in the ends of frosted hair that had been ripped free by the wind. The skin on her cheeks and hands was already chapped, despite the layers of lanolin cream she applied morning and night.

"The Queen's Guard serves the queen and the princess heir and the Gray Wolf line," Byrne persisted, squinting into the distance, hunching his broad shoulders against the raw wind.

"And if our interests diverge?" Raisa dabbed at her eyes, hoping the cold would explain her sniffling.

To this the captain made no answer, for there was none. Picking a fight with Captain Byrne was as unrewarding as assaulting a brick wall. He stood, solid and unmovable, while you skinned your own nose.

"Perhaps we should talk about what happens when we arrive," Byrne suggested, still graciously averting his eyes.

Raisa nodded, pulling her gloves back on. That seemed to be a safe topic, at least—her arrival in the Fells. Since it was beginning to seem like it would actually happen.

"I'll stay a night, at least, at Marisa Pines Camp, until I know if it's safe to go down into the city," Raisa said. That, of course, presented its own risks, if what her mother had believed was true—that the Demonai clan favored setting Marianna aside and putting Raisa on the throne instead. Raisa was suddenly glad they'd decided to take the eastern route, rather than traveling past Demonai Camp. Except . . .

"Was my father in residence in the palace when you left, or at Demonai?" Raisa asked. "I'll want to meet with him as soon as we arrive." Raisa's father was a clan trader, and patriarch of Demonai Camp. He split his time between the city, the highland camps, and trading expeditions throughout the Seven Realms. He would fill her in on the latest news.

"The royal consort was staying at Kendall House," Byrne said. "Or at least he was when I left Fellsmarch three weeks ago."

Kendall House, Raisa thought, frowning, wishing he were lodged in the palace. Kendall House was an elaborate mansion within the castle close. It represented a kind of way station in her mother's affections—not exiled entirely, but not admitted to full intimacy, either.

Raisa's father, Averill Lightfoot, Lord Demonai, was a steadying influence on her mother, when she let him get close enough.

A counterpoint to Lord Bayar's influence.

"What about the Demonai warriors?" Raisa said. "What have you heard from them?"

Byrne shrugged. "I don't have the connections to the clans that you and your father do." He paused. "Rightly or wrongly, the Demonai seem convinced that Marianna intends to set you aside. I think we can assume that they are preparing for war."

Raisa drew her cloak more closely about her. The sun passed behind a cloud, and suddenly the wind seemed more cutting.

This exchange seemed to remind Byrne of the urgency of their mission. "We'd best be on our way so we can make use of the light." He laced his fingers, offering Raisa a boost up, and this time she accepted.

CHAPTER FOUR
A WELCOME
HOME

By late day, they were still climbing toward Marisa Pines Pass, the great southwestern gateway into the Fells. To the east, the blue sky turned indigo, and a few stars appeared, low on the horizon. But Byrne had his eye on a streak of gray cloud to the northwest. "Blood of the demon," he muttered. "More snow. And it'll be here before morning. That's all we need—to be held up by a storm." He scanned the tops of the trees, judging the wind speed and direction. "There's no way we'll make it through the pass tonight, so we'd better be under cover when it hits."

They increased their pace, making for a way house Byrne knew of at the southern end of the pass that would provide shelter against wind and drifting snow. Raisa rode in a kind of frozen stupor, her hood pulled low over her face, drawing what heat she could from Switcher.

The wind began to rise long before they reached their destination, swirling the fine, powdery snow up from the ground, raking it free from the trees and flinging it into their faces. Soon it was full dark, and then darker than that, as the racing clouds devoured the stars. They never saw the rising moon. It began to snow, lightly at first, and then more heavily, tiny ice pellets that stung their exposed skin and increased their misery.

In Oden's Ford, Raisa had never needed anything heavier than kidskin gloves. She tucked first one hand, then the other under her cloak, guiding Switcher with her knees alone. But Byrne, who did not miss much, handed her a pair of long woolen riding gloves with deerskin palms. Clanwork, no doubt. Raisa pulled them on gratefully.

The horses were now mere shades in the swirling darkness. Byrne strung a rope between them so they would not lose each other. He seemed to find his way by instinct. They had no choice but to go on—they had to find shelter from the growing storm.

It was oddly reminiscent of the day the previous spring when Raisa, her mother, her sister Mellony, Byrne, and Lord Bayar had gone hunting in the foothills. A forest fire had rushed down from the mountains, and they'd taken refuge in a canyon. They'd ridden, roped together, through the smoke and ash, scarcely able to see the horse in front. Then, it had been blistering hot, the air too thick to breathe. Now the air seemed too thin, lacking sustenance, crackling in their noses. It was numbingly cold.

Last spring, the wizards Lord Bayar and Micah, and Micah's cousins, the Mander brothers, had saved their lives, magically putting the fire out.

Had it really been less than a year ago?

Switcher plowed forward doggedly in the gelding's wake, her nose and mane crusted with ice, her flanks steaming in the frigid air. The snow was so powdery fine and deep that it seemed at times the horses were swimming, flank high in a milk-white ocean.

Finally, amazingly, they broke out of the trees and into a small clearing in the shelter of a vertical rock wall. Crouched against the rock face was a sturdy wooden building with a stone chimney and a shake roof layered over with snow. And next to it, a crude lean-to for the horses. Raisa's mare slowed to a stop of her own accord, as if sensing that relief was at hand. Scrubbing snow from her eyelashes, Raisa stared dumbly at the buildings, afraid they would disappear as quickly as they had appeared.

All around her, the relieved guards were dismounting, shaking off the accumulated snow, and leading their horses toward shelter.

Switcher stamped her foot impatiently, but Raisa made no move to dismount. She squinted at the cabin, thinking there was something out of order about the scene before her. She caught the faint scent of wood smoke, though the air was so cold as to be almost painful to breathe.

And then she saw them. Out of the swirling white, they loped toward her, faces and ruffs crusted with snow, eyes blazing out a warning. Wolves, what seemed like dozens of wolves, the forest boiling with gray-and-white bodies that poured into the clearing, led by the familiar gray she-wolf with gray eyes.

They were her ancestors, the Gray Wolf queens. A warning that the line was in danger.

Still mounted, Byrne edged his gelding up beside her. "Your Highness? Shall I help you down?" The captain was fixed on her, his head tilted as if he were about to ask another question.

She put one hand on his arm to stay him, and with the other

pointed toward the cabin. Her teeth were chattering so hard she could scarcely get the words out. "Byrne. No snow . . . the chimney . . . in front of the door."

He followed her gaze, took it in quickly. No smoke curled from the chimney, but the snow had melted for a distance all around it. The snow drifted undisturbed against the cabin, but it was gone from in front of the door. Meaning someone was inside, or nearby. Only, no one would willingly leave shelter in such a storm. Nor put out his fire, either, unless he was trying to hide his presence.

Byrne shouted a warning as the first crossbows sounded from the surrounding woods. The soldiers on the ground looked up in surprise. Some of them fell where they stood, their black blood steaming as it splattered into the snow. A few managed to scramble back onto their horses, spurring them into the trees, wrestling weapons out of their saddle boots, struggling with gloved hands to string their bows. But not many.

Raisa sat frozen, watching all this as if it were a drama and she a spectator, until Byrne pushed her head down with his gloved hand. "Lie flat and follow me!" he growled, demonstrating by leaning close into his horse's neck and slamming his heels into the gelding's sides. They twisted and turned as they crossed the clearing, Byrne leading the way. Raisa flinched as something whined close to her ear, burning the skin at the back of her neck. She pressed her face into Switcher's neck, her heart clamoring in fear.

As they reached the first of the trees, a large shape materialized out of the swirling flakes, a man on foot swinging a great sword. Switcher screamed and reared back, and the blade missed taking off Raisa's head and bit into the mare's shoulder. Raisa caught a glimpse of a grinning, bearded face as the man reached for her, grabbing a fistful of cloak.

Their eyes met, and a look of startled recognition passed across the man's scar-puckered face. He looked oddly familiar to Raisa, too.

There was no time to dwell on it. Raisa twisted Switcher's head around, stood in her stirrups, and slammed her boot into the attacker's chin. His head snapped back and he disappeared from view as they charged on into the darkness.

The sounds of fighting faded behind them, but Byrne pushed the exhausted horses forward relentlessly. The wind howled, and the swirling flakes reduced the world around them to the space of a few yards, broken by the gray skeletons of trees. Off to the left and right, Raisa could see gray bodies loping through the trees, easily keeping pace with them. So they were still in grave danger.

Raisa prayed. "Sweet Lady in chains, deliver us," she whispered. It was odd how an attempt on her life could snap her out of her funk.

The weather was a blessing and a curse. It fought them every step of the way, yet between the wind and snow, all traces of their trail would be obliterated within moments of their passing. As the snow deepened, their forward progress slowed as the horses plunged forward through mammoth drifts. Switcher plowed along behind Byrne's gelding, her head at the other horse's flank.

Finally, Switcher's slow plodding stopped. Raisa straightened and pushed back her hood. Byrne had reined in. He peered into the darkness on all sides, listening with his head cocked. Finally he nodded as if satisfied, and turned off the invisible trail into the deep snow to the left, floundering through drifts that were chest high on the horses in some places.

They ended in a grove of snow-covered pines whose weeping branches brushed the ground on all sides. Byrne dismounted on the lee side of one of the great trees and motioned for Raisa to do the same. Sliding her travel bag over her shoulder, she attempted to do so, but found her frozen limbs would no longer obey her commands. Murmuring an apology, Byrne slid his gauntleted arms under her and lifted her off her horse. Using his shoulder, he bulled his way through the drooping branches and into the shelter of the tree.

There, in the pine-scented darkness, it seemed almost temperate, the unrelenting shriek of the wind muted by thick branches with their layering of snow. Byrne set Raisa down on a carpet of pine needles.

"I'll see to the horses," he said, and shoved back outside.

Raisa looked around. No wolves in evidence. So they were safe—temporarily, at least.

Resisting the temptation to curl up and go to sleep, she tugged off her gloves and boots and began working her fingers and toes, conscious of the risk of frostbite. The pain as the blood returned was stunning. Using a fallen branch, she swept a small space clean of pine needles and debris, then centered it with a pile of dry twigs and a bit of fireweed. Reaching into the traveler's bag, she pulled out flint and iron. By the time Byrne returned with the saddlebags and an armful of weapons, she had a hot, smokeless fire going, and was hanging her socks and gloves to dry.

"Were you able to find shelter for the horses?" she asked, sitting back on her heels.

He knelt, pushing the bags into a dry corner. "Aye, I hobbled them out of the wind, under another overhang. Gave them plenty of grain, but we'll need to melt some snow to—"

"Bones!" Raisa said, sitting up straight. "How is Switcher's shoulder? I'm sorry. I meant to look at it."

"It's not too bad," Byrne said. "I cleaned it out some, but she wasn't very patient with me. I'll take another look when it's light out."

"Thank you, Captain," Raisa said. "I should have seen to it myself." After an awkward pause, she added, "And thank you for saving my life. Again."

"I'd rather you held off on thanking me, Your Highness," Byrne said dryly. "We're sheltering under a tree in the middle of a blizzard. And if we get out of this, there are lots of other ways to die between here and the capital."

The Byrnes were pessimistic sorts.

"All right," she said briskly. "Consider my thanks withdrawn. In the meantime, give me your wet things, and I'll hang those as well. In the off chance we survive the night, we don't want to wear wet again tomorrow, with the temperature dropping."

Byrne shook his head, the corners of his mouth twitching. "Forgive me, Your Highness," he said. "I had forgotten how capable you are."

"I spent three years with the Demonai," she said. "They travel light. If you don't pull your weight, you're left in camp with the toddlers and old people."

"Some would prefer to stay in camp than ride with the Demonai," Byrne said. He yanked off his gloves and handed them across to Raisa. Pulling off his boots, he peeled off his socks also

Raisa noticed, however, that he replaced them with dry socks from the saddlebags and thrust his feet back into his boots. Obviously, the captain did not mean to be surprised bootless.

Raisa hesitated, rubbing and stretching her recently freed toes, then followed his example. As she leaned forward to lace up her boots, Byrne suddenly gripped her shoulder. The presumption was so out of character that she looked up, startled.

Byrne swore softly. "Blood and bones! You're wounded! Why didn't you say anything? What happened?"

Raisa reached up and fingered the wound on her neck, which she had completely forgotten. Her hand came away sticky. "A near miss is all, Captain. It's not serious."

"I'll be the judge of that," he growled. "I'd better take a look. Assassins sometimes daub their arrow points with poison." With that, he pressed his lips together as if he'd said too much. He turned her so the heat of the fire was on her back, brushed aside her hair, and poked at the back of her neck with thick fingers. "How d'you feel? Any dizziness, double vision, creeping numbness?"

Raisa shuddered. Given time, she was sure she could conjure any of those symptoms. "Do you know who they were?" she demanded. "You seem to have your suspicions."

"Valefolk, from what I could tell. Not clan. But I didn't get a good look at them." Byrne produced a small iron pot, which he filled with snow and set to heat on the fire. "I don't see any signs of poison, Your Highness. But we'll wash it out good, just the same, and apply a poultice to draw it out, and then—"

"You said *assassins*, Captain," Raisa snapped, interrupting the medical report.

Byrne released a long breath. "I don't know for sure," he admitted. "But I think that's what they were. Highwaymen don't come up here. The clan wouldn't stand for it. Besides, there aren't enough travelers this time of year to keep 'em in business, not a band that size. Highwaymen wouldn't attack a triple of soldiers. We don't carry much money, and there's easier meat and better weather downslope. They were well fed, well mounted, and well armed. I believe they were expecting us."

Byrne leaned over the fire, and the flames illuminated the grim planes of his face. "If I'm right, they're still looking for us, or will be when the weather clears. And they have the advantage of knowing where we're headed."

The water had heated to Byrne's satisfaction, so he lifted the pot off the flame with a heavy stick. He dropped several clean rags into the water, let them steep for a few minutes, and lifted one out with the same stick. When it was cool enough to handle, he squeezed out the excess water and applied it to the back of Raisa's neck.

"Ow!" she hissed, startled by the heat. "Sorry," she added, gritting her teeth. Byrne ignored the complaint, kneading her skin and scrubbing away the blood that emerged. He exchanged the bloody cloths twice more, then emptied a pouch of vegetable matter into the water remaining in the pot. Their sanctuary filled with a pungent scent. Snakebite root, Raisa thought. Used to draw poisons of all kinds.

Byrne thrust his stick into the pot and lifted a steaming mass of stinking root. Allowing the excess water to drip away, he dumped it onto a clean square of cloth he'd spread over the pine needles. Folding the cloth over, he pressed out the excess water.

Byrne plastered it over the back of Raisa's neck. It stung at first, but then felt soothing. He finished by wrapping the whole mess over with linen. "There. We'll leave that in place for a few hours, then see how it looks."

Raisa swiped futilely at a trickle of water running down her back.

Byrne scrubbed out the pot with snow, then refilled it and set it on the fire to melt. "I'll take water out to the horses and have another look around," he said.

"Will the rest of your triple be able to find us here, do you think? Should we wait for them once the weather clears?"

Byrne shook his head. "We'd better hope they don't find us, because if they can find us, so can those that ambushed us." He busied himself packing up his medical kit, avoiding her eyes. "We'd better go forward on our own. Any survivors . . . that are able . . . will continue the fight and delay them. We're seriously overmatched, so we'd best avoid them if we can. Two will be harder to spot in these mountains than a triple."

And then she understood. No one else survived, she thought. Their orders were to stand and fight, once she was away, even though they were outnumbered.

"They're all *dead*?" she said. She thought of them, tumbled all around her on the floor of her room in Delphi. "But . . . they were so young, most of them," she whispered.

"This is our job, Your Highness." Byrne lifted his wineskin, sloshing it gently as if to judge the contents, and offered it to Raisa, who shook her head.

She dug the heels of her hands into her temples, wishing she could grind away the guilt. "No," she whispered, half to herself.

"I will not allow my best soldiers to be wasted like this."

"We've not much in the way of food and supplies," Byrne said, as if she hadn't spoken. Obviously, Raisa wasn't going to be allowed any time for hand-wringing. "Just what you and I were carrying. Our best bet is to get through the pass and push on to Marisa Pines Camp as quickly as we can."

And that is just what those hunting us will expect us to do, Raisa thought.

"Now, about weaponry," Byrne said. "As I recall, you are a fair shot with a bow." He put his hand on Raisa's bow, which was laid out next to him.

Raisa nodded. It was no time for false modesty. "I'm good with a bow, though I've not tried that one. It seems a good size and weight for me, though."

"Are you any good with a sword?"

"I . . . Amon's worked me hard at swords these past months," Raisa said. "But it's not my strong suit."

"Try this one." He extended his sword toward her, hilt-first.

Raisa stood, gripping the hilt with both hands. It was fashioned to represent the Sword of Hanalea, the signia of the Queen's Guard. The cross-guard was cast in heavy metal, to resemble the rippling tresses of the Lady, and the pommel was the figure of the Lady herself.

It was nearly too heavy for her to lift, even with both hands. Shaking her head ruefully, she handed it back and sat down again. "I'm much safer with this in your hands than in mine. It's lovely, though. The workmanship is exquisite. Is this a family heirloom?"

Byrne cleared his throat. "The queen—your mother—had it made for me when I . . . at the time of her coronation. When I was made captain. Marianna said it signifies that I hold Hanalea's true line in my hands."

His face, weathered by decades of pain, revealed more than he probably intended.

Raisa stared at the captain, her mouth slack with surprise. Byrne looked away quickly, as if he hoped to extinguish that knowledge in her eyes.

He's in love with her, Raisa thought. I've been stupid blind not to see it.

Raisa recalled what her mother had said when she'd explained why there could never be anything between Raisa and Amon.

He's a soldier, the queen had said, *and his father's a soldier, and his father . . . That's all they'll ever be.*

Raisa had come close to making the same mistake herself—about her mother's captain. She'd thought of Edon Byrne as steady, calm, capable, and practical above all else. Not a romantic bone in his body. The Captain Byrne she knew was bluntly honest, not a keeper of secrets.

She'd been wrong about that. She'd been wrong about so many things.

You've lived your life with a broken heart, Raisa thought, staring at Byrne. So why did you have to break my heart, too?

And before she knew what she was doing, she was speaking aloud. "Why did you do it?" she said softly. "Why did you take Amon away from me?"

"Your Highness," he said. His expression, his posture, the way he flexed his hands—it all told her to back off. "I don't know what you mean."

"I am not going to keep quiet about this just to make it easier on everyone," Raisa said. "You are stuck here with me, so you may as well talk about it."

Byrne came forward on his knees and lifted the pot off the flame. "I'd better go out and water the horses," he said.

"I'll still be here when you get back," she said. "We can talk now or after."

He sighed noisily and set the pot on the fire. Then sat back on his heels. "You are talking about my choosing of Corporal Byrne as your captain, I suppose?" he said.

"I am perfectly satisfied with Amon as my captain," Raisa said. "I am talking about the linking, or—or the binding, or whatever you call it." She shuddered, recalling how a simple kiss between them had caused Amon excruciating pain. When Byrne said nothing, she added, "Why was that necessary? And why has it been such a big secret?"

This is why it's a secret, Byrne's expression said. This conversation.

"All of the captains are bound to their queens," Byrne said finally. "It's been that way since the Breaking."

"Did you really think it was necessary to bind Amon to me?" Raisa lifted her hands, palms up. "We've been friends since childhood."

"I did it for the line," Byrne said, looking into her eyes unapologetically. "I did not do it to keep you away from my son. Or my son away from you."

"Are you sure?" Raisa felt her mean streak surfacing. She wanted to hurt Byrne to make up for what had been stolen from her. "Are you sure that you weren't jealous because I loved Amon, while . . . while . . ."

Byrne continued to look at her, waiting, and she trailed off. No. She couldn't go there. She wouldn't go there.

"The linkage protects the line," Byrne said, when it was clear she wouldn't go on. "Amon is the best choice to serve as your captain. If it served the line for you to . . . be together, the linkage would not interfere."

"*Really*," Raisa said. "Where is that written? Where's the rule book on all this? I just blunder along, thinking I'm free to make choices, and then I find out they've been made for me."

Byrne inclined his head, acknowledging this, then looked up at her again.

"Where does it tell me what I'm supposed to do now?" she whispered, blinking back tears.

Byrne produced a handkerchief from somewhere and handed it to her. "You serve," he said. "You find happiness where you can. In love or not, you find a way to continue the line."

Just as he had done.

And just like that, Raisa's resentment faded, leaving a dull ache, like the muscle memory of an old injury. She realized that her bitterness had become a habit, that somewhere along the line, she'd accepted that she and Amon would never be together as lovers. That she needed friends as much, or even more, right now.

And then what had she done? She'd fallen for Han Alister— someone else she couldn't have, in a marriage, anyway.

"None of us are free to follow our hearts," she said. "Not really. Is that what you're saying?"

He shook his head. "No one can stop you from loving some- one," he said.

Raisa dabbed at her eyes. "I thought that, for me, it would be different, that I would find a way to make it happen. That I would marry for love." She cleared her throat and straightened her shoulders. "Now I know," she said, "like every other Gray Wolf queen, I will settle for a political marriage to someone I don't love."

Byrne half smiled. "Somehow I don't think you will settle, Your Highness."

I can always emulate Marianna, Raisa thought. And find love outside of marriage. She'd never forgiven her mother for not loving her father more. Now, belatedly, Raisa was beginning to realize that choices are not always as black-and-white as they seem.

Impulsively, Raisa leaned forward and gripped Byrne's calloused hands. "How is she doing, Captain? The queen, I mean?"

He looked down at their joined hands, and up into her face. "My Lady, I don't think—"

"You are linked to her. You must know something of her state of mind."

Byrne grimaced as though she'd strayed onto a forbidden subject, a topic too intimate for discussion. Like love.

"Your Highness, it's not my place to guess what—"

"If I'm going to help her once I return to the capital, I need to know," Raisa said bluntly.

Byrne looked at Raisa, almost defensively. "It's not as if I can read her mind."

Raisa nodded. "I know." She paused. "I just wish I understood her better. She never shared a lot with me, growing up, about herself. We are so different. I don't even look much like her."

He shook his head. "No, you favor your father more. Though she is tall, she has always seemed delicate to me, like . . . like maiden's kiss." Maiden's kiss was a spring flower that bloomed for a day and shriveled at a touch.

"Her Majesty has been melancholy lately," Byrne went on. "And no wonder. There is constant pressure from the Spirit clans, from the High Wizard and the Wizard Council. That, along with your absence . . ." His voice trailed off. "I did not want to leave her at this time."

"It's my fault you had to leave her, Captain," Raisa said, again feeling the crush of guilt.

"If I were assigning blame, Your Highness, I would not begin with you." Byrne plunked his saddlebags down in front of Raisa. "What food I have is in there. We'd better eat, then get some sleep so we can move when the storm is over."

He stood, lifting the pot of water, and ducked out through the branches to water the horses.

By the time he returned, Raisa had rummaged through his saddlebags, pulled out a loaf of bread and a wedge of cheese, and set them out on cloths. Byrne divided the cheese with his belt dagger and handed half to her, then carved off thick slices of bread. When the food was gone, he slapped the blade thoughtfully across his palm.

"Do you carry a dagger, Your Highness?"

Raisa nodded. "I do, as a rule, but Micah and Fiona took mine."

"Then take this one." He wiped the blade on his breeches, returned the blade to a sheath at his waist, then unbuckled the belt, handing the whole package to her. Raisa slid the blade free, turning it so it caught the light. It was of the same make and design as the Lady sword, with the image of Hanalea worked into the hilt.

"I can't take this!" she protested. "It belongs in your family."

"I've not much use for it, in fact," Byrne replied. "If I let an enemy get close enough to need it, I deserve what I get." He raised his hand to forestall further protest. "At least carry it until we reach Fellsmarch." He yawned. "We're not going anywhere until this storm goes south, so we may as well get some sleep." He unrolled his blankets in front of the makeshift entrance and slid under them.

Raisa crawled into her own bedroll, which was laid close to the fire. She set the knife in its sheath by her left hand. Their frail shelter trembled under the assault of the witch wind, and snow sifted down through the branches. "I'll pray to the Maker that the storm moves on," Raisa said sleepily.

"Be careful what you pray for, Your Highness," Byrne said, his face turned away from her so she couldn't see his expression. "We could use a little wind to move the snow around. We'll be easier to track when the weather clears."

CHAPTER FIVE
OLD ENEMIES

The wind began to dwindle sometime before dawn. Raisa awoke to the sudden quiet and the realization that Edon Byrne was missing. She sat up, shivering, scrubbing the sleep from her eyes with the heels of her hands. Byrne's blankets were rolled and tied, and a pot of tea steamed over the rekindled fire. A breakfast of more bread and cheese was laid out just outside the fire ring. The message was obvious: Byrne meant to make an early start.

Raisa stood and stretched, gingerly massaging her hip bones and backside. She had too little padding to enjoy sleeping on the ground. Unwinding the linen from around her neck, she scraped the poultice free, hoping Byrne wouldn't insist on replacing it. She ate quickly, washing the dry breakfast down with tea, then began layering on clothing. Her socks and gloves were dry, but stiff and uncomfortable.

When she stepped outside, carrying their remaining gear, she was confronted with one of those transformations that are common in the mountains. Stars glittered over the peaks to the west. Where the thick pines blocked the wind, the ground was covered with a thick layer of new snow, pristine and virginal, in some places drifted higher than Raisa's head. More exposed areas were scoured clean, with the wind still teasing the snow free and spinning it off into the darkness. Although it was still dark and very cold, the coming day promised to be a fair one.

"Good morning, Your Highness." Raisa spun around. It was Byrne, leading their horses, both already saddled. Switcher was fighting the bit, ears laid back, protesting the early start. "We can hope our assailants are sleeping in, but I think it wise to travel as far as we can under cover of darkness."

Raisa nodded. She stroked the mare's neck, making soothing noises, examining the gash in the beast's shoulder. Byrne was right: it looked superficial. Strapping her bedroll and saddlebags behind her saddle, she swung up onto Switcher's back, every muscle screaming a protest.

It was slow going. This climb to the pass would have been difficult in good weather with fresh mounts. The footing was treacherous, with hazards and obstacles concealed by the drifts. At times they waded through snow that reached the horses' chests. Where space permitted, they left the trail and walked under the trees to either side. The snow wasn't as deep in the forest, and they would be less visible to anyone who might be watching from a distance. But once the sun spilled over the eastern escarpment, Raisa felt terribly exposed: a dark insect climbing a white wall of snow.

At least they had a clear view of their back trail. Raisa couldn't help looking over her shoulder, expecting at any moment to see a crowd of riders coming fast. But she and Byrne climbed all morning with no sign of pursuit, and Raisa relaxed fractionally. If they could reach Marisa Pines Camp, the clans could provide an escort the rest of the way.

They took their midday meal in the saddle, dismounting only to walk beside the horses where it was steepest, to rest them a bit. The sun shone down from a brilliant blue sky, kindling the ice that coated rock and pine branches. When they were still several miles below the notch, Byrne turned aside into a copse of trees. Raisa followed automatically, reining in when he did.

"Here's where it gets dangerous," he said.

"What do you mean?" Raisa looked about, blinking as her eyes adjusted to the gloom under the pines. Here and there, glittering shafts of sunlight penetrated all the way to the ground. Switcher dropped her head and nibbled hopefully at the pine branches within reach.

"There are many ways to get to the pass, but only one way through. And no cover for the last couple of miles, since we'll be above the tree line."

Branches stirred above their heads, and snow sifted down. Raisa raked it out of her collar. "They can't possibly have caught up with us, could they?" Would anyone who was not fleeing for his life have braved the storm so long, or pressed on before daybreak?

"Anything's possible."

Raisa waited, and when Byrne did not speak, she said, impatiently, "Well, if they're coming, it doesn't do us any good to wait for them here, does it?"

He grinned. "A fair hit, Your Highness. And well deserved."

He paused, as if debating whether to go on. He stroked the gelding's neck, murmuring soft endearments, then said to Raisa, "You're different from Queen Marianna, if I may say so."

"So I've been told," Raisa replied dryly. "Usually in the midst of a scolding."

"Meaning no disrespect to your mother, I think it's a good thing."

Raisa flinched in surprise. This was most unexpected, coming from a man who was clearly devoted to Marianna. "What do you mean?"

Byrne cleared his throat. "I told you she was frail and beautiful, like maiden's kiss. You're more like juniper. You seem to thrive in the worst weather, and I'd guess you'd be impossible to uproot once you've set yourself."

"You're saying I'm tough, prickly, and stubborn." She'd heard that often enough, most recently from her teachers at Oden's Ford.

"Aye, but because you're small, they'll underestimate you. And that's not a bad thing, in these dangerous times. Keep 'em guessing, is my advice, and you'll survive in the capital."

Raisa smiled, knowing she was being paid a compliment. "Thank you, Captain. But first, I have to survive the afternoon."

"Look you, if there's trouble, you lay down on that horse and ride for the notch and don't look back. I'll follow after as soon as I can."

Right. Just like the rest of the triple.

In response, Raisa set her heels hard in Switcher's sides. The startled mare tossed her head and stumbled forward, out of the grove of trees and back onto the trail.

The brief winter's day was failing when they passed the tree line. Long blue shadows extended before them as the sun declined behind the West Wall. Out of cover of the trees, the wind daggered right through Raisa. She leaned forward, as if by doing so she could urge the mare along faster. Byrne took the lead most of the time, breaking trail. On this last long push to the top, they simply made all the speed they could.

As they neared the notch, the snow cover dwindled, scoured away by the relentless wind. The sun plunged behind the West Wall. The stone escarpment flamed momentarily, then night fell with the suddenness of the high country.

Finally, there was no more trail above them, only a long steep slope behind them. On either side, great granite slabs framed Marisa Pines Pass. At its narrowest, it was no wider than a horse trail. It was said that, years ago, a small band of Demonai warriors had held a thousand southern soldiers in the pass.

"Wait here," Byrne ordered. Raisa did as she was told, while Byrne rode on at a quick walk to scout the pass ahead. Raisa shivered, even though the great stones blocked the rising wind. Moments later, Byrne returned, appearing nearly silently out of the gloom. "Come on."

They rode ahead slowly, single file, through the narrow waist of the pass. Raisa squinted up at the sheer walls on either side, the slice of sky between. Beyond, the way broadened into what would be a lovely alpine meadow in summertime, now hidden under a shroud of snow. The moon was already rising. As it cleared the mountains to the east, the meadow was flooded with a silver brilliance, as cold and pure and unforgiving as any breath of mountain air. She felt the prickle of magic all around her.

They were home.

Somewhere behind her, a wolf howled, its voice raking up gooseflesh on the back of her neck. Ahead and to the right, its packmate answered, its voice a cold, heartless note in the dark.

Raisa's heart began to hammer.

Byrne was just ahead and to the right, horse and rider a dark silhouette against the shield of the moon. He half turned to face her, as if to inquire what the matter was.

And then she heard it, like a bad memory from the night before, the sound of crossbows, the thwack of bolts hitting home. Byrne's body shuddered with the impact of multiple blows. The gelding reared nervously, shaking his head, then screamed as he, too, was struck. Byrne clung for an instant like a thistle to his back, then toppled sideways from the saddle.

"BYRNE!" Raisa's scream reverberated in the small canyon. Heedless of the volleys of arrows that hissed past her and clattered against rock, she spurred Switcher forward to where her captain lay on his back in the snow. Sliding from the saddle, she knelt next to him, lifting his head. His body bristled with shafts, and one transfixed his throat. He tried to speak, but produced only a gush of blood. Lifting one arm, he weakly waved her off. Only the confusion and the wildly plunging horses had saved her thus far.

Someone grabbed her by the hair and yanked her upright. A gauntleted arm circled her waist and dragged her off her feet, shoving her belly-down across the saddle in front of him. Her captor kept her pinned in place with one arm while he spurred his mount to a gallop.

With the horror of Byrne's murder and the helpless jouncing

against the horse's back and the kaleidoscopic view of the ground, Raisa nearly lost the contents of her stomach. *No!* she said furiously to herself. *I'll find a way to make the bastards pay if it's the last thing I do!* She concentrated on that thought, and made what plans she could.

The scent of pine and a reduction in the force of the wind told her they'd reentered the forest. *Which side of the pass?* she wondered. Her captor slowed his horse to a walk, apparently looking for some landmark. Finally he grunted in satisfaction and turned to the left. Another hundred yards, and he yanked on the reins, bringing the horse to a halt. He slid out of the saddle, then dragged Raisa down also, setting her on her feet, but keeping one beefy hand on her shoulder. She swung around to look at him.

She took in the stringy brown hair, the cruel slash of a mouth, the tobacco-spit eyes. He was the same soldier who had gashed Switcher's shoulder, but this time she recognized him.

Blood of the demon! Raisa thought. Can things get any worse?

One side of his face was puckered and scarred, evidence of a serious burn.

Raisa had been responsible for that.

He was clad in what looked like army-issue winter garb, but there was no signia on it anywhere. A discolored stubble covered the lower half of his face, lorded over by a broken nose.

Raisa knew where and how it had been broken.

Mac Gillen, she thought, and all the hope drained out of her. She'd last seen Gillen at Southbridge Guardhouse, when she'd rescued members of the Raggers street gang from the dungeons where he'd been torturing them. She was the one who'd smashed a burning torch into his face. The other gang members had beaten him badly, payback for the treatment they'd received at his hands.

His belly cascaded over his sword belt, but Raisa had no illusions. He'd be all muscle underneath. He smelled of horse and sweat and general poor hygiene. He grinned wolfishly, revealing intermittent teeth stained with kafta nut in a jaw swollen and discolored where her boot had connected the night before.

Raisa looked about. They stood in front of a kind of rude cave, created where two slabs of rock leaned together. His horse was an upland breed, shaggy and wiry enough to negotiate mountain trails. Standard issue for the Queen's Guard.

A dozen wolves sat on their haunches in a semicircle around them, whining uneasily.

Gillen stared at her expectantly, waiting for her to speak. Raisa said nothing, knowing that nothing she said could possibly do her any good.

Finally, Gillen couldn't stand it any longer. "You wondering why you an't dead yet, girlie?" he said, scratching his privates.

None of the possibilities that came to mind were appealing. Raisa stood, feet spread slightly apart, and said nothing.

"I'm curious, y'see," Gillen said. "That's why I carried you off. I wanted to ask a few questions—just you and me." He took a step toward her, and she took one back. "We was told the Princess Raisa would be riding through here. But the only girlie that's come through here is you." He lifted his hands, palms up, in mock confusion. "The thing is, I know you, but you wasn't no princess when we met before."

Raisa shook her head. "You're mistaken," she said. "We've never met."

"You sure?" he said, crowding her back toward the entrance to the cave. "Maybe I looked different when you saw me before."

The gray wolves swarmed in around them, growling and snapping their jaws.

Right. I'm in danger, Raisa thought. Like I couldn't figure that out on my own.

"You sure your name an't Rebecca? Rebecca, sister to Sarie, the Ragmarket streetrat?" He pressed his palm against his ruined cheek. "The Rebecca what did this to me?"

Raisa continued to back away, shaking her head.

"You know, the girlies don't like me so well as they did," Gillen said, "with my face all scarred up like this."

You couldn't have been all that charming before, Raisa thought, but didn't say it aloud.

"I'm not who you think I am," she said. "Surely you can see that." She'd decided it was best not to be Rebecca just now. The only thing she could do was deny it, and keep denying it.

"You do talk different than before," Gillen said. He gave her a push, and she stumbled backward, barely keeping her feet. "You're like a whole different person, know what I mean?"

The wolves set up a chorus of yips.

Raisa glared at them. Either shut up or attack, she thought. Make yourselves useful.

"So what were you doing in Southbridge, Your Highness?" Gillen breathed, his hand closing around her throat. He pushed her back against the rock slab, pinning her. "You go down there to see how the other half lives? You got a soft spot for streetrats, is that it? You one of those blueblood ladies likes to walk on the wild side?"

Raisa pulled at Gillen's hand, trying to release the pressure. "If I'm like a different person, maybe it's because I'm not who you think I am." It wasn't easy to force her voice past Gillen's grip on her throat.

Desperately, she sorted through the street moves that Amon had taught her. Gillen's clothing was heavy enough to deflect some of the body blows she knew. And anything she did, it would have to take him down for good. She'd find no escape or rescue in the middle of the woods. She couldn't risk making him angrier than he was.

All this thinking took no more than a fraction of a second. Time seemed to have slowed to a creep, as if to stretch out what little remained of her life.

"Our orders are to kill you, Your Highness, but there's no reason I have to do it right off," Gillen said, his foul breath washing over her face. "So long as you end up dead, it don't matter. I think you owe me for what you done, and I'm going to make you pay."

"Sir. Whoever you are. I am not without resources. If you free me unharmed, my family will make it worth your while," Raisa said.

Gillen released a loud bray of laughter. "Your family? How do you know they an't the ones that hired us?" He slammed her head against the rock to emphasize his point.

Stars circled in front of her eyes. Her pulse pounded in her ears, and a bitter, metallic taste swelled in the back of her throat.

"*Listen to me.* I don't have much money with me, but if you take me safely home, there's a reward in it for you. If you kill me, you won't have a moment's peace for the rest of your life."

He laughed. "I know better than to cross the one that hired me," he said. "I learned my lesson on that. I'll take my reward here and now."

"Who hired you?" Raisa asked, thinking maybe he'd actually tell her.

Gillen just shook his head, grinning.

"Well, whoever it was, he won't be happy when he finds out you killed the wrong person," Raisa said.

Gillen gazed at her, brows drawn together, and she could see the wheels turning behind the piggy eyes. "I'm gonna take my time on this, know what I mean? I don't want them others to come and interrupt." He turned to his horse, dug into his saddlebag, and pulled out a coil of cording.

"Come on." He shoved her roughly, sending her stumbling toward the cave. Another shove and she was inside, on her hands and knees, the rock and ice on the floor of the cave slicing into her palms. She quickly turned and gathered herself into a crouch. He loomed in the doorway, blotting out what little light there was.

"I'm going to tie you up and come back later," he said, walking toward her, slapping the coil of cord against his hip. "I want to give you time to think about what's gonna happen."

Raisa debated, her thoughts seeming to reverberate inside her skull. There was the unlikely chance she could get free before Gillen returned. There was also a chance she'd freeze to death before he came back.

Freezing to death wasn't a bad way to die. It seemed preferable to what Gillen had in mind.

But if she allowed herself to be bound up, she'd have given up any chance of fighting free. She was the descendant of Hanalea, the warrior queen. She would not die bound hand and foot in a cave. Or ravished and tortured to death by this traitorous lowlife.

She lifted both hands in appeal. "All . . . all right. Just don't hurt me."

Gillen focused on her left hand, on the heavy gold wolf ring on her forefinger. "Gimme that ring," he said. "I need something to take back, to prove you're dead."

Raisa pulled on the ring, struggling with it. "It's too tight," she said. "It won't come off."

"We'll see about that," Gillen said. "I'll cut it off if I have to." His hand snaked out, and he seized her left wrist, yanking at the ring with his right hand.

Raisa straightened her arm, allowing Byrne's dagger to fall free of her right sleeve. She had to catch it, and she did, gripping the Lady hilt. Gillen was focused on the ring, wrenching at it, swearing.

Raisa rammed the blade through soiled wool and the soft flesh of his belly, up under the rib cage, as far as it would go, until the crosspiece rested against his shirt.

He screeched and let go of her hand. He tried to shove back from her, but she followed, keeping pressure on the blade with both hands now, twisting it with all her strength, knowing she'd have one chance, and one chance only, to deliver a killing stroke. If he survived the first one, she'd live to regret it, but not for very long.

Mac Gillen's fist slammed into the side of her face and she flew backward, colliding with the stone wall of the cave. She lay there stunned for a few moments, swallowing blood from her bitten tongue, half expecting Gillen to come and finish her. But he didn't. Finally, she lifted herself upright, propping herself against the wall to keep from falling over.

Gillen still lived, though he probably wouldn't for long. The sergeant lay sprawled on his back on the floor of the cave, breathing wetly, an expression of sick bewilderment on his face, blood bubbling on his lips. He'd managed to yank out Raisa's dagger, and it lay next to him, caked with blood and dirt.

She recalled what Cuffs Alister had said a lifetime ago: *Next time you go to stab someone, do it quick. Don't study on it so long.*

He'd be proud, she thought. She hadn't hesitated with the blade, and she'd struck true. Was this progress—that a street killer would be proud of her?

And then she knelt on the floor of the cave and heaved out her midday meal. After, she cleaned out her mouth with a fistful of snow.

That's all right, she thought. Killing should never come easy, not even for a warrior princess.

Gillen finally lay quiet, his eyes wide and fixed.

Retrieving her dagger, Raisa wiped it clean in the snow at the cave's entrance. She restored it to its sheath and tucked it into her breeches. She forced herself to search Gillen, hoping for clues or proofs of who'd hired him, but found nothing of consequence. A purse with a few coppers and crowns, and a hip flask—that was it.

It was unlikely he'd be carrying that kind of evidence anyway. What did she expect, a death warrant from the queen her mother? A scribbled note from Gavan Bayar? These were the kinds of orders that were whispered in the dark corners of the world.

Her head pounded and her right eye would no longer open properly. She pressed a fistful of snow against the side of her face, hoping it would reduce the swelling. All the while she tried to ignore the small voice that whispered, What's the use? You may as well surrender. You are totally alone now, and these hills are filled with your enemies. What was it Byrne had said? Well fed, well mounted, and well armed. And you have a dagger against them.

Recalling Gillen's concern about being interrupted, she knew she had to go, and quickly. Their trail would be easy enough to follow. Gillen's comrades might arrive at any moment.

Gillen's horse waited outside, apparently a well-trained military mount. The gelding rolled his eyes at her approach, but did not protest when she searched through the saddlebags. He was even more cooperative when she fished out an apple and fed it to him, stroking his nose.

Gillen's gear included a large heavy sword in a scabbard, a crossbow and a quiver of bolts. A bedroll and a canvas tent. One entire saddlebag was packed with trail food, which would prove useful, assuming she lived long enough to get hungry.

She fingered the crossbow. Unlike Byrne's longbow, it required no great strength to draw it. A memory came back to her: her eight-year-old self trailing Amon to the archery field. She'd refused to leave the butts until he gave her a chance at the crossbow. At first, the quarrels had gone wide of the straw target, but her aim improved quickly. Amon had loaded the first few bolts for her, then shown her how to cock it herself, his patient hands over hers.

On her next name day, her father, Averill, had gifted her with a longbow, made to fit her size and strength. That was her preferred weapon, but her bow had been left in the pass.

Fitting her foot into the weapon's stirrup, she spanned it, grateful for the muscles her year at Oden's Ford had built. She clipped the bolt into its channel. She'd have one shot, at least.

Methodically, she adjusted the stirrups to her small frame, wanting to hurry, but making sure she did it right. Leading the gelding alongside a fallen tree, she used the trunk to vault aboard.

A glance at the sky told her that dawn was not far away. By then she needed to get a better fix on her location and find a hiding place. If she weren't already dead or in the enemy's hands.

CHAPTER SIX

SIMON SAYS

The day after his meeting with Crow, Han rode in a kind of worried stupor. His head ached and his stomach churned, like he'd been drinking stingo and chasing it with blue ruin.

He would have made an easy target, had any of his enemies happened by. Fortunately, most of his fellow travelers were refugees simply intent on making it to a place of shelter for the night. If he nearly rode over a few, well, they managed to get out of the way.

Could it possibly be true, what Crow claimed—that the infamous Demon King of the Fells had lain fallow in the serpent jinxpiece that Han now carried? That the powerful evil he represented had never gone out of the world?

Han had been overconfident—even smug about his ability to manage risk when it came to Crow. His theories had been true—as far as they went—but nothing had prepared him for this. How could it possibly be safe to partner up with the Demon King?

The mean streets of Ragmarket seemed friendly and welcoming, their dangers completely manageable, next to this.

All of Han's life, the specter of the Demon King had been used as a cautionary tale to frighten misbehaving children and would-be sinners. He had been the club held over everyone's head, the justification for a peculiar system of rules and boundaries restricting the queen, the Wizard Council, and the clans.

Alger Waterlow was the reason the clans kept wizards on such a tight leash; the reason their amulets and talismans were no longer permanent. He'd done more than anyone else to birth the Church of Malthus, with its interdiction of magic. He'd been the reason the Seven Realms had fractured into seven warring pieces.

He'd broken the world.

And there was that connection of blood. How diluted could that bloodline be if Han carried such a virulent strain of magic? What else had he inherited?

Demon-cursed, Han's mother had called him. And it turned out she was right.

Would it be better or worse if Crow knew they were related? If he knew that Han Alister, a streetlord and thief, was his descendent? If he knew how far the family fortunes had fallen?

How could it be a good thing to forge a link to Waterlow that could never be broken? It was one thing to be related to a Demon King who had died a thousand years ago, and whose tainted blood had been diluted by centuries of intermarriage. It was quite another for him to be resurrected and entwined in Han's life.

Then again, Han was beginning to question everything he'd always believed. Who was he to preach sermons, after all? If Alger Waterlow and the Bayars were enemies, who would he choose between them? And Lucius—Lucius Frowsley had been Waterlow's best friend—a thousand years ago. He'd believed in him. Defended him to Han.

It had been difficult enough to go back to Aediion. Now Han was more confused than ever.

He arrived in Fetters Ford in early afternoon, on an unusually warm early spring day. He made his usual rounds of inns and taverns, asking after Rebecca. In one called the Purple Heron, the taproom was deserted, save a sturdy-looking boy wiping down tables.

The boy looked up at Han's approach, his round face wary. "If you're hungry, we got a ham we can slice down, and the bread's fresh made," he said, swiping sweat from his face with his sleeve. "If you're looking for a hot supper, you'll have to wait."

"I'm looking for a girlie," Han said.

"We don't host that kind of trade," the boy said. "You might try Dogbottom's, down the high street."

Han shook his head. "I'm looking for a particular girlie," he said, wishing he had an image of Rebecca to show. "She's small, with green eyes and black hair, maybe chin-length." He stuck out his hand, indicating her height. "A mixed-blood. Pretty."

The server's head came up, and he glared at Han, his cheeks smudged pink. Then he turned away and resumed scrubbing like he meant to take the finish right off. "Don't remember nobody like that," he said.

Han stared at his broad back, made temporarily speechless by the server's reaction. "Ah. Are you sure? She might have been with two charmcasters, tall ones, a girlie and a boy, about our age."

"Nope." The boy flung down his rag and moved to the hearth. Snatching up the iron poker, he thrust it into the flames. "If you're not here for food and drink, you'd best move on."

Han threaded his way between the tables, moving in closer. "Could have been a few weeks ago," he persisted. "Are you sure you haven't—?"

With a roar, the boy wheeled around and charged at Han, wielding the heated poker.

Han danced aside, hooking his foot around the boy's ankle so he sprawled forward onto the stone floor, the poker pinwheeling across the room and clattering against the wall.

Han guessed this tavern boy hadn't been in many street fights.

In a heartbeat, Han had planted his knee above the server's tailbone and twisted his arm behind him until the boy cried out in pain.

"Twitch, and I'll break your arm," Han said through gritted teeth.

The boy said nothing, but he didn't move, either.

"Now, then," Han said softly. "Let's have the truth. Start with your name."

The server turned his head so Han could see one round eye. "S-Simon," he said. "It's Simon."

"All right, Simon," Han said. "Don't waste my time. What do you know? When was she here, and who with?"

Simon shook his head carefully. "Do what you want, but I'm not telling you nothing," he mumbled. "I'm not talking to any cutthroat, thieving highwayman."

Han took a deep breath, his pulse accelerating. Keeping

pressure on the arm, he put his free hand on Simon's shoulder, allowing unchanneled flash to trickle into the tavern boy.

Simon twitched. "Hey! What do you think you—?"

"Simon," Han said, lacing his speech with persuasion. "I don't want to hurt her. I only want to find her and keep her safe."

"You're—you're—you're . . ." And then he seemed to forget what he was about to say. Simon's visible eye was going droopy-lidded. "I don't know anything about any girlie. I don't trust you."

"There isn't much time," Han said. "She's in danger. You have to help me."

Tears pooled in Simon's eyes, spilling down his cheeks. "It's too late anyway. She's dead." He sniffled wetly. "It's your fault."

"What do you mean—she's dead?" Han demanded, louder than he'd intended.

"Ow!" Simon said, thrashing under Han's weight. "You're burning me."

Han let go of Simon's shoulder and gripped his amulet, channeling the power torrenting through him. He lowered his voice, but somehow it came out sounding deadlier than before. "I'm going to let you sit up," he said. "And then you're going to tell me what happened. *Right now.*"

Han sat back on his heels, one hand on his amulet. Simon sat up, facing him, his expression sullen and wary and frightened. Han reached out and gripped the boy's wrist and opened the flow of power.

Simon's eyes fastened on Han's face like he was witch-fixed as he stumbled into speech. "She stayed here three or four weeks. I could tell she was running from somebody, but it was like she was waiting for somebody, too—somebody to help her. She always wanted to know about who else was in the taproom. Now I know. She was running from *you*," Simon said bluntly, persuasion freeing his tongue.

Han said nothing, and Simon continued. "Two days ago, a group of rovers came in, and one of them—scruffy-looking, he was—he was bothering her, trying to buy her drinks and like that. Well, she'd have none of that. She told him off, then walked out in the stable yard, said she needed some air." Simon gulped in some air himself. "An' that's the last I saw of her. I know she didn't leave on her own. She left her things in her room, but her horse was gone, and them rovers that was bothering her, too."

"What kind of rovers?" Han said. "Were they charmcasters? Soldiers?"

"I don't know," Simon said. "Could've been soldiers. Lots of sell-swords come and go these days, most not wearing colors. Not so many jinxfl—charmcasters. And the borderlands is full of thieves, murderers, and worse. These spoke Ardenine, but spent Fellsian coin."

"Did she give a name?" Han persisted.

"Brianna. It was Lady Brianna. A trader." Simon swiped at his nose.

Brianna. Well, Rebecca would have reason not to give her real name if she thought the Bayars were still after her.

"Describe her again," Han said.

"She had copperhead blood," Simon said, "but still you could tell she was a lady—not the kind that usually dines in taverns. She was gracious and kind—always a good word for . . . for anybody."

Simon was smitten—any fool could tell. But Han knew there was something Simon wasn't saying.

"What else?" Han said, trickling more power into Simon. "What happened? Why do you think she's dead?"

"Th—there was two other Tamron ladies were going to travel with her. Bluebloods. They followed her outside. We found them in the yard—stabbed to death and robbed. I'm guessing 'twas the same bunch."

Han's hopes turned to lead inside him. Was it possible Rebecca had come all this way on her own, only to be murdered or kidnapped by bully ruffins?

"But you didn't find Lady Brianna's body?" Without meaning to, Han tightened his grip on the boy's arm.

Simon shook his head, his lip quivering. "N-no, but—there was blood everywhere. And she wouldn't just *leave*, would she? Not without a good-bye. Not without her belongings."

"Where are they now? Her belongings, I mean."

Simon pressed his lips together and hung his head.

"Tell me," Han said, beginning to lose patience.

"They're in my room, but I didn't *steal* them, if that's what you're thinking," Simon added defensively. "I put them away for safekeeping. In case she came back."

Only, Simon didn't expect her to come back. Han could see it in his eyes.

"Show me," Han growled, knowing Simon wasn't at fault, but somehow unable to apologize.

Simon led Han back to a cubbyhole-size room behind the fireplace that might once have been the woodbin. The furnishings consisted of a pallet on the floor, a wooden trunk, and a small, sad shrine in the corner consisting of candles, flowers, and the missing girl's belongings.

Simon pointed to the shrine. "There. That's them."

Han knelt next to it and sorted through the muddle. There wasn't much—a few articles of clothing that seemed too big for Rebecca, and fancier than anything he'd ever seen her wear. Nothing looked familiar. But then, she'd left her belongings behind when she disappeared from Oden's Ford.

Her horse was gone, Simon had said. So maybe she was still alive. It was the best clue he'd had so far. The only clue. If it was really her.

"What kind of horse did she ride?" Han asked.

"A flatland stallion," Simon said. "A gray."

A stallion. Traders rode ponies, as a rule. Someone else had seen a girlie matching Rebecca's description riding a gray. But Rebecca had kept an upland pony cross in Oden's Ford. A mare that had disappeared along with her.

If she'd been carried off alive by someone other than the Bayars, there was no telling where they'd gone.

Nothing fit together. Frustration boiled inside him, but there was nothing to do but press on.

Han finally arrived in Delphi in early afternoon. The city was, if anything, more crowded than he remembered. Now there were refugees from Tamron as well as Arden.

At least these were problems he didn't have to solve. There was little news from the Fells, save the old story that the princess heir was still missing and that her younger sister might be made heir in her place. Of greatest interest to Delphi were the threats from the "copperhead savages" that they would close the border and interrupt trade between Delphi and Fellsmarch if the princess were set aside.

Han bypassed the Mug and Mutton, where he'd met up with Cat and outsharped the needle point. Had it been less than a year ago? He hoped Cat and Dancer were still walking out, immersed in their summer studies, far from the turmoil of his life.

He paid top-shelf prices for room and board at another inn, and replenished his supplies, enough to get him to Marisa Pines Camp, anyway. He wondered if the matriarch Willo Watersong would be there.

He regretted their strained parting when he left for Oden's Ford. Yes, she had lied to him, she'd conspired with those who meant to use him. In a way it was a relief to learn that she wasn't perfect. Maybe the hardest lesson Han had learned was that nobody is purely bad or good. Everybody seemed to be a mixture of both.

Han meant to set out for Marisa Pines Pass the next morning, but a spring storm came howling down from the north. A foot of snow fell in Delphi, and the livery man said that meant three or four feet would have fallen in the pass, and only an idiot would try to make it through before the weather settled.

Han knew about spring storms in the mountains, so he delayed a day. He spent that time walking from inn to inn to stable, asking if anyone had seen a green-eyed girlie traveling with two charmcasters. Or a pack of rovers. Or a girlie on her own. One tavern maid recalled a pair of charmcasters resembling Micah and Fiona passing through some weeks before. Nobody recalled anyone resembling Rebecca, with or without rovers.

She's not dead, Han repeated to himself over and over. Delphi is a madhouse. It's not surprising she wouldn't be remembered. When had she become so important to him?

He paid the stableman for extra grain rations for Ragger, and the pony stuffed himself.

"Don't get used to the soft life," Han murmured, more to himself than to the rugged pony. He bought himself a pair of snowshoes at the market in Delphi, gritting his teeth at the price.

He left Delphi before dawn the day after the storm, a day that promised to be brilliantly clear. He'd debated waiting another day, letting other travelers break trail for him through the pass. But more bad weather was closing in, another early spring storm, and he decided he'd better travel while he could. By the time that weather hit, he hoped to be snug in Marisa Pines.

CHAPTER SEVEN

THE LADY SWORD

The crossing into the Fells was anticlimactic, compared to last time. Han kept hold of his amulet, his hand stuffed into his coat as if for warmth. A bundled-up bluejacket pried himself out of his warm guardhouse to give Han the once-over and wave him on. It seemed that Fellsian eyes were turned inward now, focusing on the drama surrounding the princesses. No one seemed to care if a lone rider crossed into the north.

Han was oddly disappointed. He'd almost hoped for a confrontation, like any sword-dangler wanting to try out his shiny new weapons.

Ragger was downright frisky as they began the gentle climb that led to the pass, crow-hopping and tossing his head, trying to wrench the reins out of Han's hands.

"Better save your strength," Han said. "You'll be complaining before long."

It was the same road he'd traveled with Dancer eight months

before, transformed by the recent snowfall. It was hard to say how much had fallen. In some places the wind had piled it into drifts higher than Han's mounted height. Other places were scoured clean, down to bare rock. Once the sun rose, light glittered on the peaks, setting every twig and icy rock face aflame.

Han hadn't much experience traveling in early spring in the mountains. He'd spent his summers in the mountain camps, his winters running the streets of Fellsmarch. As they climbed, the temperature dropped, the clear sky seeming to suck up the heat of Han's body, no matter how many clothes he layered on. He drew heat from his amulet, using bits of flash to warm his hands and frozen face.

Even in summer, the weather in the mountains was changeable and treacherous, but Han was surprised how much the deep snow slowed him down. The road became a trail, threading between great blocks of stone that blocked the wind and drifting snow, at least.

It wasn't long before Ragger stopped his prancing and dancing and bore down for the long haul, laying his ears back along his head. Han rested him frequently, graining him at every stop from an already dwindling supply.

It was past midday when Han came on a clan way house, called Way Camp, which lay a few hundred yards off the main road. He and Dancer had stayed there on their way south back in autumn. Han turned off the road toward the camp, thinking he could rest Ragger under shelter this time.

Han was tempted to stay the night. The Demonai often stocked the way camps with food and other supplies, especially this time of year. Han had chosen to travel light since he'd assumed he'd reach Marisa Pines by nightfall.

But if they stayed, they might be overtaken by the next storm, and then there was no telling how long they'd be stranded there. He decided that if the camp were provisioned, they'd stay and weather the storm under shelter. Otherwise, they'd push on through the pass, hoping to beat the snow.

When they reached the clearing, Han recognized the small cabin and attached lean-to for horses, layered with snow. Ragger went balky at the edge of the trees. He skidded to a stop, tossing his head, nostrils flaring as if picking some dangersome scent out of the razor-sharp air.

That was when Han noticed the bodies.

There were eight or ten scattered in bunches, like they'd gone down fighting together. Snow shrouded them in a rumpled coverlet as if the Maker had tried to put them to rest.

Easing his bow from his saddle boot, Han fumbled with the bowstring with half-frozen fingers, drew an arrow from his quiver, and nocked it, all the while scanning the camp for signs of life.

Nothing—no disturbance in the pristine snow cover. The snow frosted the corpses, unmelted, so the bodies were cold. This killing had happened at least a day ago.

It reminded Han of the time he'd passed through a dark cemetery in Ragmarket after the resurrection men had been at work. He'd realized to his horror that he was surrounded by linen-wrapped corpses, spilled everywhere on the ground, shallow graves yawning beside them. He'd fled the burying ground, screaming. He'd been seven years old at the time, the same age as his sister Mari when she burned to death.

When Ragger finally settled, Han heeled him into a walk,

circling the clearing, staying within the fringe of trees, alert for any movement in the surrounding forest. The cabin seemed deserted. The snow billowed up against the door undisturbed.

Han dismounted and led Ragger forward. Keeping hold of the reins, he knelt next to the first body, brushing away the snow.

It was a tall, sturdy girlie, a little older than Han. She had the look of a sword-dangler, though she wore no emblem of allegiance. Her coat was crusted with frozen blood, and a crossbow bolt centered her chest.

Could she be a mercenary come up from the south? Had she run into a Demonai scouting party? No, the Demonai used longbows as a rule, and black-fletched arrows.

Ragger's head came up and he whinnied out a challenge. Han swiveled on his knees, aiming his arrow into the woods in the direction the horse was pointing.

A riderless bay horse stood at the edge of the trees, ears pricked forward, watching them.

Han lowered his bow. Once he'd assured himself the horse was on his own, he called out softly, "You there. Where's your owner?"

The horse staggered toward them, nearly going down, and that was when Han noticed the bolts feathering the gelding's shoulder and neck. He was sturdy, standard Fellsian military issue, with a shaggy winter coat. He was fully tacked—obviously a casualty of the recent battle, or ambush, or whatever it was.

When the horse came within reach, Han held out his hand and the gelding lipped at it. There was a carry bag slung over the saddle, and Han lifted it down, murmuring soothingly to the badly wounded animal.

Han poked through the contents of the bag—a soldier's kit. In a side pocket was a pay voucher from the Queen's Guard of the Fells, made out to one Ginny Foster, Private.

What were bluejackets doing out here in the middle of a storm, all out of uniform?

Han made a quick circuit of the killing field, clearing snow away from two or three more bodies. All were dressed in nondescript traveling garb, most young.

Whose side were they on? Who had killed them? Had any of them escaped? And where were the killers now?

It didn't seem wise to linger here, even though the battle was long over. If the killers were still in the area, they might return to this shelter when the new storm hit.

Han came up alongside the injured horse. It stood, head down, breathing hard. It would probably go down for good after a day or two of suffering.

"Hey, now," he said, reaching around under the bay's neck, probing with his fingers, finding the hot vein, gripping his amulet with his other hand.

"It's all right," he whispered, following with one of the deadly charms Crow had taught him.

The bay went down easily, but Han still shivered. It was the second time he'd killed with magic, the first he'd killed intentionally. Maybe it would get easier with time.

Han took a quick look inside the cabin, finding nothing of value except a sack of frozen oats in the lean-to, which he took.

Mounting up again, Han pulled his serpent amulet free, letting it rest on the outside of his coat. He slid his bow into his saddle boot, within easy reach, though he hoped the raiders or invaders or whoever they were had moved on.

For the rest of the afternoon, Han climbed as the sun descended toward the West Wall. As he approached the pass, he saw that others had come this way since the storm. Though the trail was drifted over in spots, elsewhere the snow was beaten down, pockmarked with hoofprints.

Han pressed on cautiously, acutely aware that anyone ahead of him could look back down the mountain and see him crawling up the slope behind them. In fair weather, he'd have given the strangers plenty of time to put distance between them, but a scrim of cloud had appeared on the horizon. He had no choice. The next storm was closing in, and there was no other path through this side of the West Wall.

As he passed through the narrowest part of the pass, his nerves screamed and his skin prickled. He knew it was a prime place for an ambush. Magic or not, a bolt between his shoulder blades would take him down quick.

Arrows were faster than jinxes—isn't that what he'd told Micah Bayar a century ago?

He navigated the pass unmolested, pausing a moment at the highest point to scan the long descent in front of him. The snow was scuffed up and tumbled about, and it had happened recently. Something lay across the trail just ahead, black against the snow.

It was another body, bristling with arrows. A fresher kill, and clean of snow, so it must have happened since the storm.

Han sat motionless for a long moment, his eyes searching the downslope ahead of him. He scanned the masses of stone to either side of the trail, in case archers waited to ambush him there. The wind pitched fine snow into his face, stinging like glittery ground glass.

He was getting much too close to this action. He had no intention of dying here, within a day of his destination. But he couldn't stay here either, not with bad weather coming.

He nudged Ragger forward at a slow walk, murmuring reassurances he didn't believe himself. He rode up alongside the body and sat looking down at him.

The man lay on his face, arms stretched out ahead of him as if he hoped he could still go forward. Blood spattered the snow all around him. He was tall, broad-shouldered, dressed like the dead soldiers back at Way House. Whoever had attacked him meant to make sure of him—Han counted eight arrows sticking out of him before he left off numbering them.

The snow surrounding the body was trampled down, bootprints and hoofprints of at least a dozen riders. Han examined the tracks descending toward Marisa Pines Camp. They'd left at a dead run. Afraid they'd be caught? Or still chasing someone?

Was this one last straggler from the attack at Way Camp? Why had they been so eager to finish him off? It was almost as if this man was such a dangerous person that they wanted to kill him extra dead.

Robbers or southern renegades wouldn't worry about one survivor, would they? Soldiers never carried much money, not even right after payday. In Ragmarket, everybody knew they were not worth slide-hand, let alone a hard rush.

Anyway, they'd left Ginny Foster's pay voucher behind.

It didn't make sense—unless they'd served as guard to something valuable—trade goods, maybe. Maybe whoever had attacked them didn't want anyone carrying tales back to the capital.

Wary as he was of being ambushed, Han would have ridden on by, except that he saw something glittering in the snow next to the dead soldier.

Taking a quick look around, Han dismounted and knelt next to the body. It was a sword, lying half under the dead man.

Made itchy by the notion of stealing from the dead, Han gently turned the body over, freeing the sword.

It was a beautiful piece, the hilt and cross-guard worked in gold, in the form of a lady with flowing hair.

His attackers must've been in a real hurry, to leave it behind.

No simple soldier carried a blade like this. It was the kind of movable that was handed down in blueblood families. Could this man be a noble in disguise?

He studied the man's face for clues. He was older than the others he'd seen—of middle age, with graying hair in a military cut, his gray eyes staring out accusingly. There was something familiar about that face, about those gray eyes.

Han shivered, making the Maker's sign, as if someone had walked over his own grave. Ah, Alister, he thought, shaking his head. You're likely going all romantic about a thief and his stolen sword.

With his thumb and forefinger, Han gently closed the soldier's eyes. The body was still faintly warm, and hadn't stiffened up completely. He lifted the soldier's hands and pressed them together across his chest. Then sat back, staring, his heart thumping.

The soldier wore a heavy gold ring on his right hand, engraved with circling wolves.

He'd seen rings like that before.

A memory came back to him: Rebecca's Corporal Byrne smashing him up against a wall in Oden's Ford, his hand in a choke hold around his neck, demanding to know where Rebecca was.

When Byrne had released him, Han had noticed the ring he wore. Wolves. Just like this one. Just like the ring Rebecca Morley had worn. At the time, Han had thought maybe she and her corporal had exchanged love tokens.

Now when he looked into the dead man's face, he saw a reflection of the younger Byrne—the same gray eyes, the same bone structure. This was Corporal Byrne's father. It had to be.

"Blood and bones," Han said. The knowledge birthed more questions than it answered.

The elder Byrne was captain of the bluejackets. Han recalled that day in Southbridge when the younger Byrne had saved him from a beating by Mac Gillen, a brutal sergeant in the guard.

Maybe you're the son of the commander, and maybe you go to the academy. That don't mean nothin', Gillen had sneered.

The dead soldiers—they were bluejackets for sure, then. Members of the Queen's Guard traveling without uniforms.

So somebody had murdered a party of bluejackets in Marisa Pines Pass? But why? And who? Only the Demonai came to mind—if tensions between the clans and the Valefolk had erupted into conflict—but the Demonai warriors didn't use crossbows.

And why would the guard ride unbadged? They must have crossed the border at Marisa Pines Pass. Were they coming back from some secret mission in the south?

Han didn't know much about military matters, but he'd thought the Highlander army was supposed to handle spats across borders. Not the Queen's Guard, who were more like bodyguards or constables. Their natural enemies were thieves, assassins, and other city criminals who would never attack soldiers traveling in a pack.

Whoever it was, whatever their purpose, it wasn't Han's fight. He had no use for bluejackets. They'd killed his mother and sister, had burned them to death in a stable. They'd hunted Han relentlessly for murders he didn't commit. He didn't owe them anything. He told himself this while he tried to put poor dead Ginny Foster out of his mind. While he tried to ignore Captain Byrne's body lying in the middle of the trail.

Han and Amon Byrne had had their differences, mostly over Rebecca, but Byrne the Younger had stuck up for Han when nobody else did. Corporal Byrne seemed to have scruples at a time when scruples were scarce.

Han considered the blade, thinking he should leave it with Byrne, lay it next to him or press it into his hands. It seemed to belong with him, somehow.

But if he left it there, the next traveler through the pass would just take it and sell it in the markets.

I should take this to *lytling* Byrne, Han thought. He should have it—and the ring—along with the story of how his father had died.

Carefully, he slipped the gold ring off Byrne's finger and tucked it into his purse.

That done, Han knew he'd better be on his way. He felt exposed, perched on high ground as he was. Danger thickened the air in the pass, making it hard to breathe.

But somehow it didn't seem right to leave without some sort of ceremony.

Captain Byrne had died fighting. What did a person do for a soldier? After a moment's thought, Han drew his own knife and put it between the dead man's hands, the hilt pointing toward his head. He wasn't much for praying, but he bowed his head over the body and commended Captain Byrne to the Maker and the Lady.

Han carried the sword back to Ragger, who was looking on disapprovingly. He slid the blade into his saddle boot next to his longbow and mounted up, thinking his home country was shaping up to be more dangersome than foreign places had ever been.

CHAPTER EIGHT

ENDINGS AND BEGINNINGS

Raisa found her hiding place at daybreak in a small ravine a few hundred yards off the main trail down into Marisa Pines Camp. There the trail ran over solid rock, and the wind had swept it clean of snow, making it hard for anyone following to tell where she'd turned off. After she stowed Gillen's gelding at the head of the ravine, she went back with a pine bough and did her best to brush away the tracks leading away from the road.

She fed and watered the horse, but left him saddled and ready to ride. She built a fire under an overhang, and huddled next to it, eating Gillen's hardtack and sausage.

This might be your last meal, she thought, recalling all the elaborate banquets she'd attended at Fellsmarch Castle.

In fact, she was ravenous, and it tasted wonderful. She loved eating while breathing in the cold clear air, and being alive. She'd never really appreciated it before.

She'd learned so much in the past year—would it all go to waste now?

I'm only sixteen, she thought. I've got plans.

If she died in the mountains, Han Alister would never know what had happened to her.

And Amon. He was still alive—he had to be. She could feel energy singing along the connection between them. He would know she was in danger. He'd be frantic to get to her.

"I'm sorry," she whispered. "I'm so sorry about your father. Stay alive and hurry home. I need you more than ever now."

It was tempting to press on when safety seemed within her grasp. Marisa Pines Camp was an easy day's ride away, if the weather stayed clear. She was tempted to make a run for it, to trust that she could evade her would-be assassins a little while longer.

But they would be waiting for her somewhere along the trail. They knew exactly where she was going, and they would bend all their efforts toward preventing her safe arrival. It was a bright sunny winter day. Everywhere she went she left tracks over the virgin snow cover. Each time she broke out of the trees she'd be visible for miles, a dark spot on white. Better to wait for the cover of darkness and then proceed cautiously, creeping off-trail whenever she could. Perhaps one person, alone in the dark, could slide through the traps they'd no doubt laid for her.

Sometimes inaction demanded more strength from a person than action.

She tried to look ahead, tried to convince herself she would make it to safety, that all of this struggle would not be in vain. She was determined to stay alive, to take vengeance on those who had murdered Edon Byrne. Who had tried their best to murder her.

At Marisa Pines, she could finally rest under the protection of the clans, and properly mourn those who had paid for her passage with their lives. Once there, she could send word to her mother the queen about the attack in the pass and the loss of her captain.

It was a grave attack on the queen's authority. Maybe it would wake Queen Marianna to the real dangers circling the Gray Wolf throne. Perhaps Marianna would be willing to travel to Demonai Camp, as Elena had suggested, and allow clan healers to verify whether the High Wizard was still bound to the queen. They could determine how much damage Gavan Bayar had done and find a way to undo it.

If Raisa survived, she swore that she would bend all her efforts to helping her mother win this most important of battles. They would join together—mother and daughter, queen and princess heir. If Marianna would allow that, after Raisa's year in exile.

They represented the Gray Wolf line—and nothing could stand against them.

Even Mellony could have a role to play. Raisa would seek out her younger sister, would quit seeing her only as a rival for power and her mother's affections.

A brush with death could be the midwife to wisdom and good intentions. She prayed she would live long enough to carry them out.

Thus resolved, Raisa curled up next to the fire. She should sleep—she would need to be clearheaded tonight.

But sleep was long in coming. Danger pressed in on her from all sides. It weighed her down, flattening her against the ground. Several times, her eyes flew open when some small sound startled her.

When she finally fell asleep, she dreamed a series of vivid scenes, like fever dreams, or the images in a clan memory stone.

She lay next to Han Alister on the roof of the Bayar Library at Oden's Ford, her head pillowed on his shoulder. Fireworks burst overhead, raining flame down on them. Suddenly, he rolled over, pressing her onto the roof tiles, his knife at her throat. "What are the rules for walking out?" he demanded. "Who can you kiss, and how often, and who starts?"

"I don't *know*," she said. "I don't *know* the rules."

And he looked at her with those riveting blue eyes, brushed her cheek with his hot fingers, and whispered, "What are you afraid of? Thieves or wizards?"

The scene dissolved, and she was a small child again, cuddled on her mother's lap. Marianna read through a picture book while Raisa tangled her fingers in her mother's glittering hair.

After that, she dreamed of a long-ago picnic on Hanalea. Her mother pelted her father with hard rolls when he teased her. "Next time I'll choose a wife whose aim is not so good," Averill said, laughing.

The scene shifted. Marianna sat next to the pompous Duke of Chalk Cliffs, who thought himself quite the ladies' man. The duke chattered on and on about his hunting lodge in the Heartfangs and how she should come visit. Marianna looked down the long table to where Raisa sat, and raised an eyebrow, her mouth quirking in a half-smile. Her mother could say more with one small gesture, one shift in expression, than Speaker Redfern in an hour-long sermon.

Finally, Raisa, Mellony, Marianna, and Averill snuggled together in a sleigh, riding out at solstice to see the fireworks.

Marianna's cheeks were rosy with the cold, and she laughed like a young girl. Raisa sat between her parents, holding their hands, the link between them. It made her feel cozier than the fur throws tucked in around them.

There followed more visions, new and unfamiliar. Not her own memories, then. Clairvoyance? Foretelling? Or the recent past?

Her mother knelt in the Cathedral Temple, head bowed, hands clasped in front of her, tears running down her face. Speaker Jemson knelt next to her, one hand on her shoulder, speaking softly. Marianna was nodding, she was speaking, too, but Raisa could not make out the words.

Marianna at her desk in her privy chamber, scrawling words across a page, spattering ink in her haste. Speaker Jemson and Magret stood by as witnesses. The queen signed her name, blew on the page to dry the ink, rolled and tied it, and handed it to Jemson.

Queen Marianna stood on her balcony in her tower bedroom, looking out over the city, her hands resting on the stone railing. The city sparkled under a light blanket of snow, the spring bulbs poking through. It was late afternoon, and the sun was descending, casting long blue shadows wherever it could slide between the buildings.

Beyond the castle close, children played in the park, and Marianna watched them in their brilliant colors spin and collide and pop up again, the sound of their laughter carrying in the softening spring air. Marianna smiled to see them, tucking her hands under her arms to warm them.

The queen heard another sound, this time behind her, and she started to turn.

"Mother!" Raisa jackknifed to a sitting position, suddenly wide awake, her heart flailing painfully in her chest. She'd slept the whole day through, and it was nearly dusk. The fire had long since died, and what heat the spring sun had provided was rapidly dissipating. Gillen's horse looked at her, snorting clouds of vapor.

Her cry seemed to echo, reverberating among the peaks, the tombs of the dead queens all around her. At first it was *Mother!* and then it seemed to change to *Marianna!* Repeated over and over and over until it faded to silence.

"Mother," Raisa repeated, softly this time, and yet still the mountains heard. They took up the refrain again. *Marianna!* Only this time they named off the line of queens.

Marianna ana'*Lissa* ana'*Theraise* ana'. . . and so on, all the way back to Hanalea. The names echoed and clamored through the mountains like the tolling of a great bell. There had been thirty-two queens in the millennium since Hanalea healed the Breaking. The mountains named them all.

Raisa had always felt embedded, safe in these mountains, connected to the future and the past. Now she felt like a loose thread dangling, the entire web threatening to unravel. Or like a sapling ripped out of the soil and left to die. She closed her eyes, sending up a wordless prayer.

When she opened her eyes, she was ringed by wolves, larger than any she had ever seen before. Gray wolves in all the colors that gray can be. Their eyes were blue and green and golden and black.

"Go away," she whispered, putting up her hands for defense. "Leave me alone."

One wolf padded forward, stepping lightly over the snow, regarding Raisa with wise gray eyes. The others parted to give her room.

"Greetings, Raisa *ana'*Marianna," the wolf said. "We are your sisters, the Gray Wolf queens." The she-wolf sat down, curling her fluffy tail around her feet. "Isn't it a shame," she said, cocking her head, "that we become queens only in the pain of losing our mothers?"

"I need to rest," Raisa said. "I have a long way to go tomorrow." She drew her knees up, wrapping her arms around them. "I've had enough dreams for one night."

"And we as queens birth our successors only in the pain of our own deaths," a green-eyed wolf said, as if Raisa hadn't spoken. "But the knowledge that our daughters follow us eases our passage."

The gray-eyed wolf nudged Raisa's knee with her nose. "You are not alone. If you concentrate, you can feel the connection all the way back through the Gray Wolf line."

"We serve as advisers to the reigning queens," the green-eyed wolf said, "only when the situation is dire. Like now."

"Well, I've been seeing you for months," Raisa said, shivering. "Why haven't you spoken to me before?"

"Your mother could no longer hear us," the green-eyed wolf said. "That's why we came to you."

"Althea," the gray-eyed wolf said reprovingly.

"Well, it's true," Althea said. "Raisa may as well know. The Bayar blocked up Queen Marianna's ears so she could not hear our warnings."

"Why should I listen to you?" Raisa said. "You might be

hallucinations, or demons conjured by my enemies. Or a bad dream," she said hopefully.

"You must listen to us," the gray-eyed wolf said. "You have many enemies. Unless you take action, they will destroy the Gray Wolf line."

"That's why I'm going home," Raisa said. "To help my mother the queen. For too long we have not heard each other."

The wind stirred the treetops, whispering, *Marianna*.

The wolves stirred, too, looking at each other, snapping their jaws and whining.

"The line now hangs by a thread," the gray-eyed wolf said. "And you are that thread, Raisa *ana'*Marianna."

It was so close to her thoughts that Raisa shivered again.

"My mother and I are in danger," Raisa said. "Is that what you're saying?"

"Beware of someone who pretends to be a friend," Althea said. "Look close to home for your enemies."

"Why is prophesy always so bloody cryptic?" Raisa said. "Why can't you just flat-out tell me what's going on?"

The wolves rose, as if at a common signal.

"This is the message we bring you, Raisa *ana'*Marianna, descendent of the queens of the Seven Realms," Althea said. "You must fight for the throne. You must fight for the Gray Wolf line. You must not allow yourself to be ensnared as Marianna was. The future of the realm balances on a knife's edge." She bowed her head and turned away, moving off at a trot.

The others followed, all but the gray-eyed wolf. She tilted her head, regarding Raisa thoughtfully, as if taking her measure. Raisa thought she saw sympathy in the she-wolf's eyes.

"Raisa *ana'*Marianna, my sisters speak the truth, but it is incomplete. Do not make the mistakes that I made. Choose your friends carefully. Never forget that two threads spun together are stronger than one of double thickness."

"My mother and I," Raisa whispered. "Is that what you mean?"

The she-wolf glanced over her shoulder, as if worried about being overheard by her sister queens, then turned back to Raisa. "Know that sometimes you must choose duty over love. Do not forget duty. But choose love when you can."

Raisa stared at her. "Who are you?" she whispered.

"I am Hanalea *ana'*Maria, who shattered the world."

"But . . ." As Raisa groped for words, Hanalea bowed her head and turned away. She broke into a lope, ears back, tail streaming behind her, disappearing into the shadows under the trees.

Raisa opened her eyes again. She lay on her back, staring up at the treetops. The cold and wet had seeped through her coat. Snow sifted down on her as the wind stirred the branches.

Marianna, they whispered.

She sat up, her head still clouded by the remnants of dreams, a knot of dread in her middle.

So it was a dream. But what did it mean, this twilight visitation? Was it a nightmare born of worry? A premonition of something that might occur? An obscure parable symbolizing something completely different?

It was said that the Gray Wolf queens had the gift of prophesy, but she'd never seen it in her mother, Marianna. Was this how the messages came—from gray wolves in a dream?

Or perhaps it was just that—a dream. The remnant and consequence of a tragic day.

Could she trust in a tradition of magic that seemed to have gone dormant—relics of a past when wizards behaved, amulets lasted forever, and queens knew what they were doing.

What would she find when she returned to Fellsmarch? What was the danger so potent that the wolves had issued this warning?

She had to know. She had to know now.

She scrambled to her feet. As she did so, she saw that the snow all around her campsite was pocked with pawprints the size of luncheon plates.

Wolfprints.

Bloody bones, she thought. Maybe she was losing her mind.

"I'm sorry," she whispered to Gillen's horse, who'd stood saddled all this time. He'd managed to scrape his back against a tree, knocking the saddle askew. She released the bit long enough to feed and water him again, then tightened the girth and mounted up.

When she emerged from the dark narrow canyon, more day-light remained than she expected. The last rays of the sun reflected back from the snow, illuminating the road before her. She looked up and down the trail, then turned north, toward Marisa Pines Camp.

Raisa walked the gelding off the trail when she could, though it made for slower going, hoping it would prevent her being spotted by anyone looking down from above. She kept Gillen's cocked crossbow next to her, knowing that her one shot was unlikely to save her.

It was all she could do to keep the gelding reined in, when what she wanted to do was break into a gallop, to race all the way to safety. Occasionally she stopped and listened, hearing only the movement of branches overhead and the hiss of snow on snow.

Those hunting her would be proceeding cautiously also, not wanting to miss her in their haste. Or maybe they had set a trap and were sitting like spiders, waiting for her to fall into it.

She did her best to stay alert to her surroundings, to live outside of her head. She couldn't afford to dwell on all the decisions that had brought her to this place, where life and death intersected. Her future—her life depended on this small space of time on this narrow road that led from Delphi, through Marisa Pines Pass, and down to the camp.

Where are the Demonai? she thought. Why couldn't they be patrolling this stretch of road?

Raisa eased her white-knuckled grip on the reins as the light dwindled. Perhaps she could move a little faster now, at least until the moon rose. But the lack of light made traveling off-trail more dangerous. If her horse sprained his leg, she was done. So she risked the trail more often, making better speed in places where the trees closed overhead and hid her from prying eyes.

How many of them were out there, she wondered. How many had died at the hands of her guard? Would they split up or stay together? Would some ride the trail, hoping to overtake or intercept her, while others lay hidden along the way?

Raisa scanned the forward trail, trying to spot likely ambushes, but the darkness hid them as well as it hid her. Ahead, the trail threaded through a narrow gorge, running alongside the frozen-over stream at the bottom. She could see tracks—evidence that horses had passed this way since the storm.

She told herself that just because horses had passed this way didn't mean they were still here. Anyway, there was no other way through. Keeping close to the canyon wall, lying flat so she wouldn't be silhouetted against the entrance, she walked the gelding into the gorge.

The element of surprise was what saved her. The men waiting in the canyon had likely been waiting for hours with nobody to kill, and so were less alert than they might have been.

Halfway through the gorge, Raisa saw a flicker of movement against the opposite canyon wall. A horse whinnied a greeting, and Gillen's horse answered.

Boots scraped against rock as soldiers scrambled for the weapons they'd laid aside.

She drove her heels against the gelding's sides, and he spurted forward. Behind her, somebody swore a Northern oath. A shout went up, clamoring against stone.

As they exploded from the mouth of the canyon, Raisa urged her horse to even greater speed. They flew down the narrow corridor between the trees, risking life and limb in the near-darkness. Behind her, she could hear the rattle of hooves on stone evolve into the thunder of pursuit.

The gelding seemed eager to run after his long night hobbled in one spot, and Raisa gave him his head. Trees blurred by, the wind of their passing fierce against her face. She might end up thrown over a precipice, but she'd be dead if they were overtaken anyway.

She considered her chances of making it all the way to Marisa Pines Camp ahead of her pursuers. Her gelding was fresh, and she was lightweight compared to those chasing her. But she didn't know the trail, and she didn't know whether they'd laid other traps for her. Anyone could hear them coming a mile away.

They broke out of the trees and crossed a broad meadow. Hearing crossbows behind her, she ripped back and forth across the meadow, something the Demonai had taught her. The bolts hissed past, none coming close. But her zigzag pattern slowed her down, and when she looked back, the assassins had gained on her.

Once again, she regained the shelter of the trees, but couldn't seem to open more space between her and the riders behind her. At a rough count, there seemed to be a half dozen.

To either side she saw wolves loping through the woods, ears back, legs extending and bunching, easily keeping pace.

Couldn't you cross in front of them, scare their horses or something? she thought.

Foam flew from the gelding's mouth, and his pace dwindled a bit. How long could he keep going? The other horses had to be tiring as well. More so than hers.

They funneled between two great slabs of rock into another canyon.

Blood and bones! Up ahead, two riders on either side of the trail angled forward to block her way, crossbows dangling loosely in their hands, grinning.

Raisa looked wildly to either side. The canyon was narrow here, and there was no way to ride around them. She heard shouts of victory from the riders behind her when they saw that she was trapped between them.

Anger sparked within her. These were cowards and traitors, attacking her eight on one.

She wrestled Gillen's heavy sword free of its scabbard. Extending it ahead of her like a pike, she drove her heels into the gelding's sides.

"For Hanalea the Warrior!" she shouted, barreling forward, straight at the riders in her way. The grins fell from their faces, replaced by surprise and panic. They wrenched at their horses' reins, trying to drag their mounts out of the way.

The sword point drove into the neck of one of the horses as Raisa thundered by. The horse screamed, and Raisa let go immediately to avoid being dragged from her own mount.

A crossbow sounded at close range, and something slammed into her upper back, pitching her to the ground. She landed flat on her face, and the gelding came and stood over her, dripping foam on her neck. She pushed to her feet, trying to ignore the pulsing pain in her back and the numbness and tingling in her left arm.

The other assassins were bottled up behind the two who'd ambushed her, but they'd be on top of her in no time. Reaching for the pommel of the saddle, Raisa tried to remount but found her arm nearly useless, the pain too stunning to manage it. Instead, she hooked down the crossbow and raced in among the tumble of rocks at one end of the canyon. She began to climb, her breath hissing between her teeth, tears running down her face. Whenever she stretched and moved and reached up, the bolt in her back shifted and the wound blazed with pain and her head swam.

She was putting off the inevitable, but she was too angry to care. To be taken so close to her destination by the traitors who'd murdered Edon Byrne was unacceptable. The only way to avenge his death was to survive, but just now that was looking less and less possible.

She climbed until she could climb no further, then wedged

herself into a crevice. She set her crossbow next to her right side, her Lady dagger on her left. They could pry her out like a mollusk from the cliffs along the Indio. She'd make them pay a small price, at least.

Did they know she was wounded? Maybe not.

She felt blood trickling down her back from the entry point under her left shoulder blade. Oddly, the pain in her back was diminishing, replaced by a spreading numbness. Had the point damaged a nerve?

She heard someone shouting from below, someone she couldn't see.

"Let's not prolong this. You'll never get away on foot. Surrender now, and you'll not be harmed. Resist, and I make no guarantees."

Right, Raisa thought. We do have our faults, but stupidity doesn't run in the Gray Wolf line. She made no response.

After a long moment, she heard the officer shouting out orders. The men would be spreading out, searching the canyon. She heard rock clattering on rock, men swearing, the sound of them climbing all around her.

Then, across the canyon, one of the renegade soldiers came into view, hoisting himself onto a small ledge. Straightening, he looked around. When he saw Raisa, he grinned, crooking a finger at her.

"Merkle!" he shouted, looking back the way he'd come. "Up here! She's—"

Raisa lifted the crossbow and shot him through the mid chest, as she'd been taught. He stumbled backward, disappearing from sight. She heard the others shouting when he hit the ground.

That might slow them down a bit, anyway, she thought. She felt peculiar, her thoughts tangled and slow. Her lips and tongue were numb, and she could no longer feel her fingers on her left hand.

She blinked away a double image, and then she knew. Poison. The arrow point was daubed with poison.

Eight on one isn't enough, then, she thought. No. We have to use poison. So much for notions of fair play. If she'd had any to start with.

Her stubborn confidence drained away. How could she fight poison? It would be plant-based, likely of clan make. The clans produced some remarkable poisons.

She'd bled a lot at first, but she no longer felt blood trickling down her back. Was that good or bad? If she kept bleeding, might she bleed out some of the poison?

It was potent, all right. Her vision blurred and rippled, and her muscles twitched. The rocks around her shivered and quaked. Wolves moved like shadows through the darkness, whining, pressing their warm bodies against her as if somehow they could keep her in the world.

She could only hope she'd be dead before they found her.

Now she heard more commotion down below, men shouting at each other. What was that all about?

Time passed—in her muddled state, she wasn't sure how much. She thought they would have found her by now. It had gone quiet in the canyon.

She fingered the Lady knife. *When someone comes, you stick them. When someone comes, you stick them.* Raisa repeated it over and over so she wouldn't forget.

Amon always said that was the purpose of weapons practice—
to train the muscles and nerves so that in a fight they do what
they're supposed to do without conscious thought.

She heard Amon's voice in her head, low and desperate. *Rai.
Don't you die. Don't you die on me, Rai. Stay alive. Stay alive. Stay
alive.*

Her hand fluttered helplessly. *I'm sorry. I'm sorry. I did my best.*

Most of all, she regretted her parting with Han. There was so
much she'd wanted to say to him, confess to him. She'd wanted to
create a truth between them to replace the lies. Now he'd likely
never know what had happened to her. How she really felt about
him. Who she really was.

She tried to fix on Han's face, to hold it in her mind—the
brilliant blue eyes under fair brows, the oddly aristocratic nose,
the pale scar jagging down one side.

Tiny pebbles cascaded past her, pinging on rock. Someone
was coming, climbing down from above. Her hand scrabbled
through the dirt and closed on her dagger.

CHAPTER NINE

A HUNT INTERRUPTED

Sometimes a descent is trickier than the climb. Ragger wanted to move faster on the downhill side of the pass—not a good idea where snowdrifts concealed imperfections in the trail that ranged from small ravines to major boulders.

The beaten-down trail continued. The horsemen seemed to be traveling at a breakneck speed. Some of them split off into the surrounding woods, while others continued on. Were they still chasing someone? Or splitting up so they'd be harder to track themselves?

Finally the trail dropped below the tree line, and the relentless wind abated somewhat. Han was grateful and apprehensive at the same time. The pine forest closing in tight around him made him jumpy.

He came up on a small rise overlooking a series of ridges that sloped away to the Vale, like waves on a frozen sea. He'd have to find a camping place soon, despite his worries about weather.

Clouds piled up to the north, but the sun still glittered over the horizon, streaming over the razor-sharp western peaks. The wrinkles in the landscape cast long blue shadows over the snow. It was already dark in the canyons. The firs had faded to black smudges in the shadows of the peaks.

Han heard the sounds of the chase before he saw the hunters. A trick of the landscape amplified sound so it reverberated up from below: the clatter of hooves over rock, men shouting to one another, even the thwack of crossbows.

It must be the raiding party whose tracks he'd been following all day—the ones who'd killed Captain Byrne and the other blue-jackets. He'd guessed right—they'd been on the hunt, and now they must have flushed their quarry.

Was it one last surviving bluejacket? They couldn't let even one win free?

Fighting off the voice that said, *Not your business, Alister*, Han edged Ragger forward until he could look down over the valley below. It was deep and bowl-shaped, dropping to an iced-over streambed at the bottom. It had burned over at some time in the recent past, so it was relatively clear of trees.

As he watched, a single horse and rider emerged from the trees and galloped across the clearing, the rider practically horizontal in the saddle. She was a woman, by the size of her, dressed like the dead soldiers and riding a similar horse. She stuck to its back like a burr, and horse and rider zigzagged across the clearing, confounding the aim of the archers behind.

Six more riders appeared, perhaps a hundred yards behind the girlie, baying like hounds on the scent of blood. The crossbows sounded again, and bolts arced overhead and slammed into the ground all around the girlie and her horse before they disappeared into the forest on the far side.

Han watched, transfixed, until they were lost in the trees. The sounds of the chase diminished until the clearing was once again quiet and empty, save the bolts that stood quivering, black against the snow, evidence that it hadn't been a dream.

Ragger snorted impatiently and tossed his head. Han spoke to the gelding, absently soothing him as he tried to make sense of what he'd just seen.

Those in pursuit rode upland military horses with shaggy winter coats. They had the look of unbadged bluejackets, too— carefully nondescript. They'd be trying to prevent the girlie from reaching safety in Marisa Pines, just a few miles away.

They were aiming to kill, six on one. The bluejacket girlie rode like a clan warrior, but there was no way she'd escape. It was a private life-and-death contest that had nothing to do with him.

He told himself he should ride on, grateful that the chase would keep them occupied while he took a different path.

But what had he told Rebecca when she'd asked what he meant to do when he returned to the Fells?

I'm tired of people in power picking on the weak. I'm going to help them.

Han didn't know the story behind what he'd seen. Still, whoever she was, he had a greater stake in helping that girlie in a six-on-one fight than in shilling for a queen he hated.

It sort of related to why he was here. Byrne had been captain of the Queen's Guard, and father to the intensely honest Amon Byrne, and this girlie was all that remained of his company. And Amon Byrne had been a friend and commander to Rebecca.

Without a conscious plan, he heeled Ragger into motion, skidding sideways down the slope to where he could follow after. He started out careful, but soon found himself driving his heels into Ragger's sides, afraid he would arrive too late.

The chase came to an abrupt end a mile farther down the trail in a small glen littered with broken rock. Han could hear men shouting to each other. Looping Ragger's reins over a laurel bush, Han dismounted and pulled down his longbow and a sheaf of arrows. He scrambled up the side of the canyon, over ice and rock, and then forward until he could look down into the ravine, squinting to make the most of the failing light.

The fugitive's riderless horse stood to one side, head down, sides heaving, coat steaming in the frigid air. At first Han thought he was too late, that the girlie was taken. But the hunters dismounted all in a blood frenzy, loading their crossbows and drawing their blades. Apparently they'd brought their quarry to bay. Perhaps the horse had stumbled, and she'd been thrown.

Or maybe she'd been ambushed. On recounting, now there were at least eight men in the canyon.

One of the men raised a fist, signaling the others to wait. Cupping his hands around his mouth, he shouted into the blind end of the glen. "Let's not prolong this. You'll never get away on foot. Surrender now, and you'll not be harmed. Resist, and I make no guarantees."

Ha, Han thought. The girlie saw what happened to her friends. She'd be a fool to take that offer.

The man waited. There was no answer save the rattle of frozen leaf in the wind. He shrugged and nodded to his men. They swarmed forward into the rock debris at the end of the ravine, thrusting their blades into the underbrush, poking into crevices and behind boulders, wading through snowdrifts to their waists, working their way ever higher on the canyon walls.

Suddenly, a soldier on one of the ledges across the canyon from Han shouted something, then staggered, stumbled, and fell, screaming, arms windmilling wildly. He landed on his back on a slab of rock on the floor of the canyon. One of his comrades scrambled over the rocks to where he lay.

"Corporal Merkle!" he shouted, his voice shrill with indignation. "The bloody bitch put an arrow in Jarvit."

Corporal? Han thought. They *are* military, just as I thought. Why would they attack Byrne's company? Shouldn't they be on the same side?

The hunters now looked more like the hunted, muttering to each other, swiveling their heads, scanning the rock walls of the canyon and huddling low to present a smaller target. They seemed more than willing to allow somebody else the glory of finding the hidden archer.

Merkle swore and jabbed a finger toward the right rear of the canyon. "The bolt had to come from somewhere over there," he snarled. "She's just a chit of a girl, you cowards!"

"She kilt Lieutenant Gillen a'ready," Merkle's friend whined. "I'm just sayin' she's more dangersome than you think."

Han's head came up in surprise. Gillen? Mac Gillen? If the girlie had really killed Gillen, that was a service worth rewarding. *Any enemy of Mac Gillen is a friend of mine.*

The soldiers stood, still grumbling, shooting glances up at the wall of the canyon where the girlie must lay hidden. They seemed to have little appetite for this job.

"You did for Captain Byrne, didn't you?" Merkle sneered. "You're in too deep to back out now. She gets away, you're in a world of trouble."

With black looks at their corporal, the soldiers resumed their search, albeit more cautiously this time.

So it was true. Gillen and a group of renegades had murdered their commander, and all of those traveling with him. Likely, Byrne had been the real target, and now they wanted to finish the job so no one would go back carrying tales.

Han made his decision.

Circling the rim of the canyon, he took up a position opposite the corner where the girl must lay hidden, closest to Corporal Merkle.

He'd need no magic for this job.

Han fitted an arrow to the bowstring, drew it back to his ear, and released. At that close distance, the shaft from his longbow spun Merkle half around before he toppled facedown in the snow.

Han was moving before the officer hit the ground. Shouts went up from the men below, echoing against stone. If he could draw the bastards away, perhaps the girl could find a way out of the canyon and escape. But with the loss of Merkle, the men in the canyon couldn't seem to organize a pursuit or retreat. They milled about, brandishing hand weapons and launching a few belated arrows toward Han's former position.

Han chose another target and loosed. Ran a little farther and loosed again. Two for two. Bedlam ensued. Three of the remaining four soldiers scrambled for their horses, while the fourth fell dead with an arrow in his eye. Han shot the last three in various stages of mounting their horses.

"Guess you're not used to targets that shoot back," Han said. He waited a few moments to see if there was anyone he'd overlooked. One of the fallen soldiers shoved to his knees and crawled painfully toward a bay gelding that stood nearby. Han's arrow had caught the bluejacket just beneath the rib cage, and he left a smear of blood on the snow as he crept forward, one hand extended in a pleading manner. The bay stood, tossing his head, rolling his eyes, warily watching the wounded man's approach.

Nocking another arrow, but keeping the tension off the string, Han descended toward him, leaping lightly from ledge to ledge, until he was perhaps a dozen yards above him. Taking his time, he set his feet, drew back the string, aimed carefully.

The soldier wheezed a greeting to the bay, and the horse extended his head toward him, snorting curiously. Lunging forward, he got a grip on the stirrup. Laboriously, he began to haul himself to his feet.

Han's arrow went clean through the back of his neck, and the man died without another sound.

Slinging his bow over his shoulder, Han circled around to just above where he assumed the girlie must be hiding. "Hey, there! Are you all right?" he called.

There was no answer.

"They're gone." He peered into the canyon, trying to spot her on a ledge lower down. "You're safe now. I . . . ah . . . chased them off."

Still no answer. Then again, why should she trust him?

Swearing softly to himself, he dropped over the edge and half slid, half scrambled down the slope, clutching at juniper to slow his descent, flaying his fingers in the process. On a narrow ledge, a man's height above the floor of the canyon, he found a large puddle of blood, purple-red in the snow. Ice crystals were already forming around the edges. Next to the puddle was the fletched end of a crossbow bolt. She must have broken it off.

No.

"Where are you? I know you're hurt. Please. Let me help you." Han knelt, scanning the ground. A scattering of crimson drops led him back into the underbrush.

"I'm coming," he called. "Don't shoot me."

Sliding the longbow from his shoulder, he set it down. Cautiously, he pulled the branches aside, crawling forward on hands and knees, kindling a wizard light on the tips of his fingers to show the way.

She was wedged into a crevice in the rocks, knees drawn up under her chin, a knife resting across her knees, the useless crossbow by her side. She was very still, scarcely breathing, like an animal that hides in the open. Had the light not caught the blade, he might have missed her. But when he got too close, she waved the knife. "Stay back," she whispered. "Leave me alone. I'm warning you." She swallowed, licked her lips, lifted her chin stubbornly. "Come any closer and I'll cut your throat."

It was Rebecca Morley.

"Rebecca?" Han whispered, amazed relief warring with dismay. He sat back on his heels, his mind churning. His eyes fastened on her knife. Its design mimicked the sword he'd taken from Captain Byrne. The knife was probably his too.

How had she ended up with Captain Byrne? Could Byrne's bluejackets have been the "rovers" Simon saw in Fetters Ford? But what would they be doing there?

"Rebecca." Han leaned forward, extending his hand, and she raised the fancy knife again, looking wild-eyed. "Don't you know me? It's Han."

Han realized that he looked like no one's hero. After weeks on the road, he was shaggy and stubble-faced, lean and grubby. He knew that he too was out of place, probably the last person she'd expect to see.

But still recognizable, right? After all, he'd recognized her.

"It's all right," he whispered, unconvincing even to his own ears. "I won't hurt you."

She waved a hand dismissively to show she didn't believe him. She was in bad shape. The snow around her was spattered with blood. One side of her face was purple with bruises, as if she'd been beaten. The other was bloodless and pale. Her hair was shorter than he remembered—it had been cropped since he'd last seen her.

The green eyes were cloudy and confused, the hand holding the blade tremoring.

"What have they done to you?" he murmured, fighting down nausea and fury. She was a blueblood, after all. It wasn't supposed to work like this.

His mind raced. Had she escaped from the Bayars? Had the Byrnes rescued her? Had Amon Byrne been among the dead at Way Camp and he hadn't noticed? Or was Corporal Byrne out in the woods somewhere, dead or wounded?

But Byrne had said he was traveling straight north, entering the Fells through West Gate.

Would Micah Bayar go to this extreme to take revenge on Han? Would they send a triple of bluejackets out to murder a young girl? Or, as he'd guessed, had the real target been Captain Byrne, and Rebecca just happened to be there?

Where had she learned to ride like that? Not in less than a year at Oden's Ford.

With so many missing pieces, this puzzle was still impossible to put together.

Taking a deep breath, he leaned forward, looking into her green eyes, speaking soothing nonsense. "What is it with you, Rebecca? Seems like you're always waving a blade in my face. You any better with a knife these days?" And like that. She narrowed her eyes, frowning as though he were speaking a foreign language.

He'd always had quick hands. In a moment he had the knife away from her. He tucked it under his belt, while she struggled to reach it, calling him amazingly vile names. "Don't worry," he breathed. "I won't lose it. I have it right here." Prying her out of her hole, he gathered her into his arms, trapping her hands so she couldn't reach for the knife or scratch out his eyes.

She flinched at his touch, eyes going wide with shock. A moment's struggle, more a clash of wills than anything else, and then she settled, eyes wide and fixed on his face, trembling like an animal in a trap.

"I'm a wizard, remember?" he said, still running on like a clock wound too tight. "Remember when you told me all about wizard kisses? Wizard kisses sizzle, you said. It's not so bad when you get used to it." This brought no response, and he expected none. He kept talking like a Mad Tom, though, the one way he could think of to keep her in the world.

"Let's go down and see Ragger. I've got some supplies in my

saddlebags. We'll try to find out where all this blood is coming from."

She weighed nothing, but still it was awkward climbing downslope over boulders and ledges in the dark with Rebecca in his arms, afraid he would fall and do further damage. Her breath hissed out, and he knew he was hurting her. At one point she began to struggle, and it was all he could do not to pitch forward and tumble all the way to the bottom.

When he reached the canyon floor, he whistled for Ragger. To his amazement, the gelding came, though he snorted at all the blood and bodies lying about.

One-handed, Han untied his blanket roll and dropped it in a spot next to the canyon wall where the snow had been scoured away by the wind. He set Rebecca down atop it and wrestled off her coat. By then, despite his patter, she'd drifted into unconsciousness, lashes dark against bloodless skin. So pale, he pressed his fingers under her chin to feel her pulse and make sure she still lived.

As he worked, Han sorted through his worries. He didn't know how many assassins there were to begin with, and whether more might show up at any moment. But he was more worried Rebecca might bleed to death before they made it to Marisa Pines.

Using her knife, he cut the bloody shirt away. Supporting her with one arm, he looked her over. The rose tattoo below her collarbone shone bloodred against her pallor.

She'd taken an arrow beneath her left shoulder blade. It must have knocked her off her horse. She'd managed to break off the shaft close to the skin, but the tip was deep inside.

The wound had quit bleeding. The flesh had swollen up around the shaft, closing it off. She might be bleeding inside, though. He laid his ear against her breast, her skin soft against his bristled cheek. Her breathing sounded normal, not wet, at least, and there was no evidence of air coming through the wound. So perhaps the lung had been spared. She hadn't bled out all that much. The wound looked survivable if he could get her to a healer.

But something wasn't right. She seemed muddy and confused, almost like the wound had begun to fester. Could she be in shock from loss of blood? She was a small person, after all.

He studied the flesh about the arrow shaft, pressing his fingers against the wound. Rebecca moaned and tried to shift away. Taking hold of his amulet, he sent a whisper of power in, exploring. It disappeared immediately. He tried again, and the same thing happened. A third time, stronger than ever, and power hissed off his fingers like smoke in a strong wind.

What the . . . ? It was like something was sucking up the power before it could take effect. But he'd never noticed anything magical about Rebecca before.

It reminded him of the silver cuffs he'd worn until Elena *Cennestre* took them off eight months ago. The clans had fastened them around his wrists when he was just a baby. They were like magical darbies—handcuffs of sorts. They suppressed his magic and prevented others from using their magic on him.

Several times, charmcasters had tried flaming him, or spelling him, and the cuffs had sucked the power away. Just like this.

He'd never tried spelling Rebecca before, save for a little wizardly leakage, but . . .

Frantically, Han searched her for something—an amulet, a token—anything that could be interfering with the magic. When he picked up her right hand, the gold wolf ring on her forefinger felt blazing hot.

"Hmm," he said, examining the ring. It was the one that matched Captain Byrne's, tucked away in his purse. And the one Corporal Byrne was likely still wearing.

Clanwork, they must be, since they were magical.

"Where did you get this?" he murmured. Gritting his teeth against the heat, Han tugged at the ring, finally managing to wrench it off her finger. "Sorry," he said. Carefully, he tucked it into his purse next to Byrne's. "I'll give it back, I promise," he said.

Once again, he pressed his fingers against the wound, sending power in, a diagnostic he'd learned in Master Leontus's healing class. There was an unnatural cold all around the shaft, and it was spreading. It was too soon for it to be infection. Infection was hot anyway, right?

Poison. Likely a clan brew. They were widely available from clan traders and in the markets.

Han swore, feeling cheated—like all his hard work had been for nothing.

It was well that Rebecca had bled some, or she'd be dead already. If Merkle and his cronies had known she was wounded, they could have ridden away and left her to die without a worry.

Han knew one thing—there was nothing he could do for her here. He might be gifted, but he was no healer. He had to get her into more capable hands, and quickly. And that meant

Marisa Pincs. He had to hope that Willo was there. If she wasn't, Rebecca would die.

Likely, she'd die anyway.

Fetching an old woolen shirt from his saddlebag, he dropped it over her head, without bothering to put her arms into the sleeves. It was huge on her, reaching to her knees, but it would keep her warm, at least.

He thought of constructing a litter, but knew that would take too much time. They'd have to ride double. The trip would be hard on her, perhaps fatal, but he had no choice. The bile rose in his throat, and he swallowed it down.

He would not lose her. He refused. He prayed to the Maker. *Just let something work out for once. Let me save someone before this war begins.*

It occurred to him that maybe his prayers were like curses— they simply drew the attention of vengeful gods.

Despite the urgency he felt, he took the time to put Rebecca's horse and one of the assassins' mounts onto a lead line. The horses were clues—evidence of the crime that had been committed. He pushed away the thought that Rebecca wouldn't be able to tell what had happened because she'd be dead.

It was just as well Rebecca was light, or he wouldn't have been able to mount Ragger with her slung over his shoulder. Once seated, he managed to turn her so she sat astride, leaning back against him, head tucked under his chin, one of his arms curled about her body to keep her from sliding from the saddle. The bow was in its boot at his knee, but it would do him no good riding double as they were. He'd be nearly helpless if they came under attack. He touched his amulet, reassuring himself.

He hoped the heat of his body would help. Hoped Willo was at Marisa Pines and not visiting one of the other camps. Hoped they wouldn't meet any more assassins along the way.

Hoped he would not have to hold Rebecca Morley as she died.

CHAPTER TEN
THE PRICE OF HEALING

By now it was completely dark. The birds had quit their evensong and it would be hours before the moon rose behind a layer of cloud. It was unnaturally quiet, as if the world was holding its breath, waiting to see how it would all come out. The only sound was the crunch of Ragger's hooves on snow.

Han wanted to slam his heels into Ragger's sides and propel him into a gallop that would take him to Marisa Pines Camp in a hurry.

There was such a tiny chance of success, all the odds stacked against them. If they went too slowly, Rebecca would die. If they went too fast, and Ragger broke a leg, Rebecca would die. If they ran into more assassins, Rebecca would die.

Rebecca lay mostly quiet in his arms, moaning now and then when he jostled her, otherwise exhibiting no signs of awareness. He sensed she was moving farther and farther away from him, retreating from the poison into some interior sanctuary from which she might not return.

Han struggled to remember Master Leontus's lectures on healing, the recitations he'd drowsed through. I'll never have need of that, Han had thought. I'm being trained to kill people, not heal them. He'd thought everyone he'd ever want to heal was already dead.

He'd been wrong.

Han concentrated. Bits and pieces came back to him. Leontus marching up and down the classroom, Adam's apple bobbing wildly as he attempted to convince his skeptical audience of students to consider healing as a vocation.

Gifted healers work by taking on the illnesses and injuries of their patients. This involves considerable pain, suffering, and expenditure of power.

Healers search out discordance in the bodies of their clients. They create order out of chaos, protecting body and spirit from toxins.

It's important that healers set boundaries during the healing process. You are of no help to your patient if you yourself succumb.

Healers are teachers as well as therapists. They teach their clients to fight back.

Healers are braver than the most valorous warrior, because they make themselves vulnerable. They open channels between them and those they treat.

Leontus was a wire-haired zealot preaching to the unconverted, and students made fun of him each time he turned his back.

Han recalled only remnants of charms—both to help the patient and protect the healer. He spoke them aloud, hoping he could recapture them that way.

Rebecca stiffened against him, then trembled as a seizure rolled through her body. Once again, Han pressed his fingers against the wound, sending power in. The area around the wound had gone icy.

The poison was doing its work. Han knew she would not make it to Marisa Pines.

Ragger lurched forward, responding to the sudden grip of Han's knees. Making soothing noises at the gelding, Han opened his coat and shirt, ignoring the rapidly dropping temperature. Lifting Rebecca's shirt, he pulled her body tight against his bare chest, wrapping his coat around her to hold the heat in.

Gripping his amulet, he whispered the opening charm for healing. Then he tentatively reached out for her with his mind. That much, he remembered—how to get hold of the thoughts of others for a purpose.

He'd halfheartedly participated in the exercises in class. They'd paired off, and . . .

The channel opened, and he was through. She was cold, so cold, the poisoned wound like an open window that drew the heat and life of her body away.

Healers nudged the patient, convincing them to fight back. Shivering, he burrowed deeper, cautiously making his way toward the spark of life that smoldered at her center.

Come on, Rebecca. Fight back. Don't go down on the bricks for them. Stick with me. Don't give in. Don't let them win.

It was as if he'd wandered into a cold cave without a map, bumping into memories and emotions in the dark. Images slid through his mind, from a different life—much of which made no sense to him. A vast expanse of water—an ocean he'd never seen. A pair of red dancing shoes. Opulent palace interiors. An emerald necklace in the shape of a serpent. A view of Fellsmarch at night through a wall of glass, the wizard lamps pricking out the streets below.

And people: Amon Byrne in a fancy dress uniform, standing at rigid attention in an entryway. Averill Lightfoot Demonai, his face softened by an affection meant for someone else.

Lord Demonai? Rebecca knows Lord Demonai?

Well, she is of clan blood.

An elegant blond-haired lady cradling a newborn baby, singing a lullaby in a high, clear voice. Micah Bayar, clad in black and white, extending his hands, the black eyes glittering with lust and triumph.

No. Han turned away from that one to see himself, in the upstairs room at the Turtle, holding the music box he'd given Rebecca. And now, there he was, very close, leaning down for a kiss, his eyes blue flecked with gold. It was a peculiar inside-out feeling to experience this from the other side.

Han swam in a sea of emotions—bone-deep guilt. A longing for home. An aching sense of loss that was not his own. Anger and betrayal and fear.

Now she *was* fighting back, fiercely, with what little strength she had left. But she was fighting *him*. She saw his presence as a threat, not a help. Maybe she didn't want him finding out her secrets.

"Hey, now, save your strength," he whispered. "I won't intrude where I'm not wanted."

So he turned his attention to the wound. Maybe there was a way he could detoxify the poison, or drive it out of her body. But he just didn't know enough.

Well. If he couldn't rid her of the poison, maybe he could keep it at bay, keep it from killing her before they reached Marisa Pines. And so he dug in, throwing up barricades between the poison and the life force in her.

Minutes passed, and the poison halted its spread. It stayed, quarantined in the flesh surrounding the wound.

It was not without a cost. Rebecca might be protected from the poison, but now he himself was vulnerable to it, despite his much larger body size. Soon he was reeling in the saddle, head pounding, chilled and nauseated. Ragger snorted and danced, wary of the muddled stranger on his back. If they'd come upon more assassins, there was no way Han could have mounted a defense.

He was a stranger in enemy territory, and instinct told him to hide his serpent amulet from view. He poked it under his shirt, out of sight, so it rested against his skin. He pulled out the lone hunter piece Dancer had made, and displayed it on the outside.

But he slid his hand under his shirt and kept hold of the flash that had once belonged to the Demon King.

Time passed. The shadows of the trees shortened, then lengthened again. The snow came, falling softly all around them, shrouding the hard edges of the world. Somehow, he drank the rest of his water. The last drops burned like flames down his throat. Hot was cold and cold was hot—an apparent side effect of the poison.

He kept one hand fastened on the serpent amulet, the other pressed Rebecca close. His amulet flamed and cooled in his hand. Power flowed from the amulet, through Han, into Rebecca. Where Han had been hot, and Rebecca cold, now it was reversed.

She blazed against the frozen skin of his chest. Ragger chose his own way now, the reins slack over the pommel of the saddle.

Han heard a familiar voice in his head, persistent, unrelenting, badgering him.

Alister. What are you doing? Stop! Let the girl go. You'll ruin everything. You're killing yourself. After all the time I've invested in you, you are not allowed to destroy yourself.

Shut up, Crow, Han thought. I know what I'm doing.

Other voices joined in. This one sounded like Corporal Byrne. *Stay alive, Rai. Stay alive. Stay alive until I come. Don't give up.*

Rai?

Han was seeing things now, so maybe he was hearing things too. The landscape flickered and crawled in his peripheral vision. Wolves. Gray wolves flanked them to either side, weaving through curtains of snow. The wolves turned into fine blueblood ladies, their skirts sliding over the snow. Then back to wolves. He tried to ignore them, to pretend they weren't there. But it seemed almost like they were helping, keeping them moving in the right direction. An escort of sorts, through the blinding snow.

He made a plan, practiced what he would say like a small child might. If he practiced it enough, engraved it into his mind, he still might remember even if he was out of his head. Any delay might be fatal to Rebecca.

Find Willo Watersong. We need Willo. The girl is poisoned.

He stared down at the snow, thinking that it would refresh his burning throat, but he couldn't figure out how to get to it.

He became oddly conscious of his breathing, focused on it, convinced that if he didn't remember to breathe, he would simply stop.

Breathe.

He tilted his head back, and snowflakes sizzled on his tongue like sparks. The forest around him rippled and quaked, the colors running down like paint on a canvas. Or fireworks. He remembered something about fireworks and rooftops and hope.

Leaves glittered in the sunlight.

Sunlight. The sun was up. The snow had stopped. Or was it just another hallucination?

Breathe.

With an odd clarity, he noticed that the fresh snow on the trail had been churned by many horses. Plumes of steam rose around him, and the stink of sulfur and wood smoke intruded into his clouded mind. He just couldn't remember why it was important.

Looking down, he saw with some surprise that there was a girl in his arms, dark head drooping against his shoulder, cheeks flushed with the cold, lips slightly parted in sleep. He squinted at her. What was her name again?

He brushed her cheek with a trembling forefinger. Her face was black and blue where someone had hurt her, but she was alive. He released a long breath of relief as tears ran down his face. He must have slept and dreamed she was dead.

He was so focused on solving this puzzle that he was surprised when Ragger came to an abrupt halt. He looked up to see a small child standing in the middle of the trail in deerskin leggings and tunic. He blinked, and then there were two, no four.

"He's hurt!" one said, in Clan.

"So is she!"

"Who are they?"

He heard dogs barking and more excited chatter. A wave of dizziness rolled over him, then the voices of a gathering crowd.

"Willo," he whispered. "Need Willo."

Then three Demonai warriors stepped out onto the trail between Han and the small pack of children and dogs. They were armed with longbows, arrows nocked, but aimed at the ground, dressed in the sunlight and shadow Demonai clothing. The tallest warrior reached up, grabbing for Ragger's bridle, but Ragger showed his teeth and reared up, nearly dumping Han and the girl onto the ground. The Demonai backed off quickly.

"Stay off," Han said, his mouth and tongue so numb he was scarcely understandable. "Get out of my way."

"What have you done to that girl, jinxflinger?" the Demonai demanded. "Let her go."

What he was saying didn't make sense, but Han was too far gone to sort it out. He had a plan. He'd practiced it all the way there, repeated the message over and over in his mind.

"Willo," he croaked. "Need Willo. The girl is poisoned."

Rebecca's head drooped like a flower on a long stem, her face buried against his coat.

The Demonai raised their bows. "Keep your hands where we can see them," the tall warrior said. "Let the girl go."

"Can't," Han whispered. "She'll die. Where's Willo?"

The warriors looked at one another as if this were a hard question.

"Where is Willo?" Han shouted, losing patience. "The girl is dying. Tell me where she is or I'll ride right over you."

The children broke and ran toward camp as if chased by demons.

"Give her to us," the tall warrior said. "We'll take her to Willo."

Han shook his head stubbornly. He had a plan, and this wasn't it. "Where's Willo?"

The warriors exchanged glances again.

"This way," one of the Demonai said. "Follow us." Two of them began walking down the trail ahead away from Han, while the tall one stood aside, his bow slack in his hands.

Han urged Ragger forward at a walk. They walked past the tall warrior. In his peripheral vision, Han saw the warrior raise his bow, take careful aim. But Han's muddled mind could not process this, could not divine the significance.

"No!" someone shouted. "Stop! Don't shoot! It's Hunts Alone!"

Han looked up to see Willo flying toward them, moccasins flashing in and out of the snow, hair streaming out behind her. She wore white—full skirts, a long deerskin tunic overtop, not even a coat.

Huh, Han thought hazily. White was the color of mourning in the camps. Had somebody died?

She was trailed by a dozen young children.

Han's vision swam, and Willo became a smear of motion. He swayed, shaking his head to clear it, and then she was right in front of him.

Willo extended her hand and took hold of Ragger's bridle, murmuring a greeting to him. Instead of laying back his ears and baring his teeth, the gelding snuffled gently at her hand.

Willo looked up at Han. "What's the matter, Hunts Alone?" she asked. "What's happened?"

Beyond her, like an echo, he could hear the children chattering in Clan.

"It's Hunts Alone!"

"Hunts Alone? He looks different."

"His hair's the same."

"What's that he's got around his neck?"

"Is he sick?"

"Who's that girl?"

Willo put her hand on his arm, and power flowed into him, steadying him, clearing his head enough to speak.

Han forced the words past his numb lips. "This girl's been poisoned, Willo. An arrow-point daub, and the tip's still in her."

"Whose?" She snapped out the question, but he understood.

"Not . . . not clan. S . . . soldiers. Upland soldiers, I believe. I don't know what poisons they use."

"Who is she?" Willo asked, craning her neck, trying to get a look at Rebecca's face.

"R–Rebecca Morley. She lives in the Vale, but she has clan blood." Maybe Willo wouldn't treat a flatlander.

The matriarch kept her hand on his arm. Han had the odd sense that her touch was all that was keeping him upright. She was looking at him oddly. "Did you take an arrow also?"

He shook his head. "I . . . I tried to save her. But I'm no healer."

"You used high magic?"

Han nodded. "I tried." He waved his hand dispiritedly. "Didn't work. I . . ."

Han felt the flow of energy change, filling some void within him. "Oh," Willo breathed, her eyes going wide and pooling with tears. "Oh, Hunts Alone . . ." Her voice broke.

"I'm sorry," he said. Saliva seemed to be building up in his mouth, and he had no way to swallow it. His body no longer reliably followed his commands.

Breathe.

"Will you give the girl to me?" she said. "Will you let me try?"

He nodded, dizzy with relief. "Please, Willo. Please. Save her. It doesn't matter . . . what happens to me."

"Release her," Willo said. "Let go of your amulet and release her to me."

In his head, Han could hear Crow shouting in his ear. He ignored it. He released his death grip on the amulet.

Willo extended her arms, and Han leaned forward, easing the girl into them. Willo looked down into Rebecca's face and gasped, going pale under her bronze skin. "Blood of Hanalea!" she whispered.

Han went cold with dread. Was she dead? Was Rebecca already dead? Was he too late after all? Had he carried a dead body all the way to Marisa Pines?

Willo looked up at the gawking Demonai. "Bring Hunts Alone to the Matriarch Lodge," she ordered. "Quickly now. And find Elena *Cennestre.* I need help."

"Willo!" Han called, but she was already away, striding toward the lodge with Rebecca limp in her arms. The bowmen gripped his arms, pulling him from his horse, and though he tried, he couldn't keep his seat, and he fell forward into blackness.

CHAPTER ELEVEN

SECRETS REVEALED

Raisa woke to the sound of women's voices and the aroma of food cooking slow. For a while she only listened and breathed, afraid to open her eyes. Her entire body tingled and burned, as if pins and needles were being driven into her skin. It was much like the sensation of blood returning to fingers and toes after a day out in the cold. Hearing, smell, touch, taste: each was exquisitely sensitive to her surroundings. Even the quiet conversation clamored in her ears.

The women spoke the upland dialect. She heard other familiar sounds: the whirr of a spinning wheel, the thump of the overhead beater on a loom, the hiss of flames on the nearby hearth. Raisa knew where she was before she opened her eyes—in one of the upland clan lodges.

She lay sprawled on her stomach on a deep feather bed under a light blanket, her sleeping bench close to the fire. She wore a loose garment, a white flax tunic that tied at the neck. A dull pain in her back drew her attention, insistent as a toothache. Gingerly, she slid her hand into her neckline and explored the area with her fingers, encountering layers of bandages.

She must be at Marisa Pines. How had she come there? It was like opening a book at random, or walking into the middle of a scene in a play without knowing what had come before.

It didn't matter, she thought, closing her eyes. All would be well now. She could finally rest after her long struggle to stay alive. Somebody else could take responsibility. She would tell her mother what had happened, and Marianna and Averill would do something about it. With that reassuring thought, she drifted back into a more peaceful sleep.

When she woke again, it was late afternoon or early evening. Light leaked in around the doors and windows, but lanterns had already been kindled against the encroaching darkness.

A disturbing image surfaced: Captain Byrne on his face in the trail, his blood black against snow, his back bristling with arrows.

Other memories elbowed forward. Mac Gillen, the renegade officer who'd carried her off, had, in a peculiar twist of fate, saved her life. She'd killed him and had taken his horse. But they'd waited for her at the pass and chased her down the long slope into a canyon, until a bolt had flung her from her horse. She'd managed to kill one more, but the poison was spreading, she was growing weak, and they were closing in. And then . . .

When she closed her eyes, she saw a familiar face, lit by torchlight, sculpted by pain, a landscape of high cheekbones, long straight nose, intense blue eyes, framed by fair hair.

Han Alister. He'd intruded into her personal nightmare somehow. It didn't make any sense. She'd left Han back in Oden's Ford.

As far as she knew, he was still there, thinking she'd abandoned him.

She shivered, remembering the burn of his hands against the cold, spreading stain of poison, and the power that bled into her, thawing the frozen places.

She'd fought with him. She'd tried to escape into oblivion, but he'd followed her, breached her defenses, and . . . and what? They'd intertwined, joined together like fire and ice, and he'd sheltered her from the insidious cold.

She'd never felt safer—she'd never felt more alive than when she lay dying in Han Alister's arms.

There was something—something about her ring. He'd taken her ring from her. She lifted her hands, and the wolf ring was right where it belonged, on the forefinger of her right hand.

So maybe it *had* been a dream, she thought, disappointed. She'd meant to die with his face before her, and she'd hallucinated the rest.

That should have been reassuring, but all she knew was that now she felt empty. Bereft. Alone as she'd never been before. There was something else—something lurking in the back of her mind. Something she didn't want to remember.

Raisa pushed up on her elbows, suddenly aware of a raging thirst and a crashingly bad headache. The women by the fire must have been watching, because two of them rose, setting aside their needlework, and came and knelt next to the pallet.

One of them was her grandmother, Elena Demonai, Matriarch of Demonai Camp. The other was Willo Watersong, healer and Matriarch of Marisa Pines Camp. Raisa had met her at the renamings and other feast days during her time fostering at Demonai.

Both women were dressed in white—white woolen shawls and white-cured deerskin shirts and long full skirts. Worry shivered down Raisa's backbone. White was the color of mourning among the clans.

"Granddaughter, it's good to see you open your eyes," Elena said. "You've slept for three days."

Willo inclined her head and made the sign of the Maker. "Briar Rose, welcome to our fire. Please share all that we have." The upland greeting to the guest.

"I'm thirsty," Raisa whispered.

Willo maneuvered Raisa into a sitting position, supporting her with an arm about her shoulders. Elena raised a cup of water to Raisa's lips.

She took a long swallow. It burned her lips and tongue and scalded her throat, bringing tears to her eyes. She shook her head, refusing more. "It's too hot!"

Willo and Elena looked at each other, and both nodded.

"It's the poison," Willo said. "It confuses the nerves in those who survive. Hot things seem cold, and cold hot. Some say it's like being set aflame."

"Do you know what it is? The poison, I mean." Raisa looked from Willo to Elena.

"It's made from tree fungus," Willo said. "It grows on the north side of slopes. We use it sometimes to harvest fish for smoking."

Elena offered the cup again, and Raisa did her best to drink, ignoring her reverberating nerves. Afterward, she ran her tongue experimentally over her lips, and was surprised to find them unblistered. "How long . . . how long does this last?"

Willo shrugged. "Hard to say. Most don't survive."

Elena set aside the cup when it was clear that Raisa would drink no more. Her grandmother, who was always so calm, seemed twitchy and nervous.

"Let me take a look at your wound, as long as you're awake," Willo suggested. "I've packed it with snakebite root, though it's a bit late to draw the poison."

Obediently, Raisa lay down on her stomach, cradling her face on her arms. Willo drew up her shirt and cut the bandage away from her wound. Elena fetched a pot of hot water from the fire.

"Can you tell us what happened?" Elena asked, sitting down next to her again. Her grandmother was always one to go straight to the point. "Who attacked you?"

"Only if you feel up to talking about it, Your Highness," Willo murmured.

Raisa fought back a prickle of unease. This was her grandmother, after all, and Willo was known throughout the Spirits as a gifted healer. Surely she could trust them. She'd always felt safe and cared for in the upland camps, away from the politics at court.

Yet she felt besieged by enemies—so much of what she had once believed had turned out to be false.

"Those who attacked me were renegade members of the Queen's Guard," Raisa said finally. "The only one of them I knew was Mac Gillen, and he is dead." She drew a sharp breath, gritting her teeth as Willo scraped the poultice away from her wound. "This is the second time my own guard has betrayed me. They came after us before, on the way to Oden's Ford. That was Gillen's doing too, though he wasn't actually there."

Elena nodded. "Nightwalker said as much."

The Demonai warrior, Reid Nightwalker, had rescued Raisa and her escort from Gillen's renegade guards.

"Last time, they seemed to want to take me alive. This time, they obviously meant to kill me." So what had changed in the interim?

Willo plastered more snakebite root over the wound. It was gloppy and unpleasant, but felt faintly warm. Which meant it was probably cold.

"Captain Byrne is dead," Raisa went on. "He died defending me in the pass. I believe the rest of our party was killed at Way Camp, or thereabouts. We need to send someone to collect their bodies."

Elena nodded as if this were old news. "Nightwalker and a party of warriors retraced your trail back as far as the pass." She paused. "He'd just returned from the city when you came here. Nightwalker was so worried about you—but he was also furious. He only left your side because he intended to hunt down and . . . *question* . . . those who attacked you." Elena's face hardened, eyes glittering. "But he was too late. He found Captain Byrne and several groups of unbadged soldiers dead. Some killed with crossbows, others with a longbow."

"A longbow?" Raisa mumbled into her pillowed arms. "I remember crossbows, but I don't remember anyone shooting with a longbow." All dead, she thought. Well, maybe that explained the mourning dress. Except . . . Raisa twisted her head, trying to look up at them. "Have you sent word to my mother? Does she know about Captain Byrne? Is she on her way here?"

Willo's hands stopped moving for a long moment, and she and Elena exchanged glances again.

"We don't know, granddaughter," Elena said. "We sent a messenger to Fellsmarch, and we've not heard back."

"You've not heard back in *three days*?" Raisa's voice rose. It's been three days, she thought. Why haven't you come? The memory of the wolf dream crashed in on her again. She didn't want to speak about it, because saying it aloud would make it real.

"Something's happened," Raisa said. "Something's wrong. She would answer. She couldn't ignore this. She wouldn't."

"Nightwalker left for Fellsmarch yesterday, to speak directly to your father," Elena said. Her fingers twisted in her skirts. "The speakers say that . . ." Willo shook her head quickly, and Elena didn't finish.

"We'll just have to wait to hear from the Vale," Willo said. Raisa could feel the power in Willo's hands soothing her, making her sleepy. "It should be soon."

Raisa closed her eyes and breathed out slowly, trying to relax under Willo's hands. But new questions kept bubbling up as she sorted out what she did and didn't know. "How . . . how did I get here? I was wounded, and they were coming for me, and—I don't remember."

"Hunts Alone brought you here," Willo said.

Raisa searched her memory. "Hunts Alone? Who's that?"

"Well." Willo hesitated. "Perhaps you know him by his Vale name—Hanson Alister."

It hadn't been a dream, then. Han Alister had come to her in the middle of the Spirit Mountains. Han Alister had saved her life.

How did all of these people get tangled up together?

"Briar Rose?" Willo prompted, when Raisa didn't say anything.

"Why would Han Alister have a clan name?" Raisa blurted.

"He's Valeborn and a wizard besides."

Elena cleared her throat. "I did not realize that you two had met." She didn't sound happy that they had. "He seemed confused—or maybe delirious. He called you Rebecca."

"I went by that name in Oden's Ford," Raisa said. "We were in school together there. He didn't know who I really was."

But now he would find out. He probably already knew.

Raisa's stomach clenched miserably. She'd wanted to tell him herself—to explain. She didn't want him to hear it from somebody else.

Elena leaned forward, fingering her Demonai amulet. "Was Hunts Alone one of those who attacked you?"

"Why would he attack me?" Raisa asked irritably.

"No one thinks Hunts Alone attacked the princess heir except you and Nightwalker," Willo said, scowling at Elena. "Sit up, Your Highness."

Willo helped her sit up again. Raisa felt as weak as a day-old kitten.

"The jinxflinger had my granddaughter's talisman ring in his possession," Elena said defensively. "And Hanalea's Sword, and the ring that belonged to Captain Byrne." She turned to Raisa, as if looking for allies. "And we still don't know how Hunts Al . . . how Alister came to find you."

"However he found her, Hunts Alone saved her life," Willo said, reordering Raisa's hair with her fingers. "He had to remove the talisman ring in order to do it."

Raisa wasn't following this conversation at all. "But there were eight of them," she blurted out. "Eight men attacking me. What happened to them? How did he get me away from them?

Did they leave me for dead or . . ."

"We just don't know," Elena said, sliding a look at Willo. "That's just it—everyone is dead, and there are too many unanswered questions."

"Well, what does Han—what does Alister say about it?" Raisa asked impatiently. It was like the two matriarchs were being confusing on purpose.

Willo shook her head. "He has been too ill. We've been unable to question him."

"He's *ill*?" Raisa leaned forward. "Was he injured? What happened? *Where is he?*" Every answer seemed to spawn more questions.

"Hunts Alone knew you had been poisoned," Willo said. "He used high magic to save your life. Wizard healers treat patients by taking on the injuries of their patients. It's a risky business, and Hunts Alone is relatively untutored." She looked at Elena, and her gaze hardened. "He should not have been put into this position. He should not be here at all. He's had only a few months of training."

A tension crackled between the two women that Raisa had never seen before.

"No," Raisa whispered, shaking her head. "He should never have risked it if he didn't know what he was doing."

But neither woman seemed to hear. They were focused on each other.

"It was his duty to save her life, if indeed he did," Elena said, returning Willo's glare.

Raisa looked from one to the other. "What do you mean, it was his duty?"

They both looked at her, mouths clamped shut, as if wishing they could call the words back.

There was something in Willo's face—some secret she did not want to reveal. She cut her eyes to Elena as if to say, *This is your fault. You tell her.*

"Hunts Alone is sworn to serve the clans and the Gray Wolf line," Elena said.

"What?" Raisa headache was growing worse with every revelation. Her sleepiness had fled, despite Willo's efforts. "What are you talking about? Han hates the Gray Wolf line."

Elena raised her eyebrows and looked at Willo, as if to say, *Ha!* Willo rolled her eyes and bent her head over her bandages.

None of this made any sense. Han Alister blamed the queen, her mother, for the deaths of his mother and sister. Why would he sign on in their service?

As Willo wound a bandage around Raisa's middle, Raisa caught hold of her wrist. "Somebody had better tell me what's going on," she said, glaring at the two matriarchs.

Willo turned her head and looked pointedly at Elena. It was still her turn, apparently.

"Marisa Pines and Demonai Camp agreed to fund Alister's schooling at Oden's Ford in exchange for his future service," Elena said, shrugging.

"The clans are training a *wizard*?" Raisa wondered if it were possible she was still dreaming. "But that . . . but that . . ."

"It's complicated, granddaughter," Elena said, patting her knee. "Perhaps we can discuss this further when you—"

"Then why isn't he at school, if you're sponsoring him?" Raisa asked. "Why did he come back here?"

"This is, it seems, the *future*," Willo said, biting off each word. "The Demonai called him home. He was not allowed to finish his course work, nor serve an apprenticeship." She wrapped a wide piece of linen over Raisa's shoulder and around her waist, tying it off neatly.

Elena stood then, and strode back and forth, talking with her hands as usual, directing her arguments at Willo.

"Willo Watersong, the attack on the princess heir more than justifies our decision to bring Alister back. If what you say is true, and he did save her life, this single act has repaid our investment twice over. It was worth it."

"Do you think it was worth it to him?" Willo whispered.

"Where is he?" Raisa demanded, struggling to rise from her pallet. "Where is Han? I want to see him."

"Granddaughter . . ." Elena said, furrowing her brow. "You should rest now. I'm afraid this has been—"

"No!" Raisa said, louder than she'd intended. "If I've been sleeping three days, then four days have passed since somebody tried to kill me. I want straight answers to my questions, and I want to see the person that you say saved my life. I want to see what price he's paid for it."

"If you insist," Elena said, her face tight with disapproval.

Willo helped Raisa to her feet, keeping one hand clamped around her elbow. "He's in the next room," Willo said. The Matriarch Lodge had several sleeping chambers walled off with curtains, where patients could stay under the watchful eye of the healer.

Willo pulled aside the deerskin drape and they ducked through. Elena remained in the common room, as if Han's ailment might be catching.

A ceramic stove glowed in the center of the room, kept stoked by two apprentices, a boy and girl a little older than Raisa. A stub of sweetwood smoldered in a burner, and one of the apprentices waved the smoke toward their patient with a large fan.

Han Alister lay on a pallet close to the fire, smothered in blankets, his face pale and glistening with sweat in the firelight. His hair was damp, plastered down on his head, and he twitched and trembled under the blankets, mumbling and muttering to himself.

"Sweet Lady!" Raisa said, looking down at him. The skin seemed tightly stretched across his bones. Usually he blazed with life. Now it looked as though the vital essence had been wrung from him. Tears stung her eyes. She sank to her knees next to the sleeping bench and gently raked strands of golden hair from his forehead.

Don't you die. Don't you dare. I forbid it.

As if Han Alister had ever listened to anything she said.

Raisa swallowed hard and looked up at Willo, who was looking down at her, eyes narrowed, lips pursed thoughtfully. "Isn't it too hot in here? He's sweating."

"We are drawing the poison out of him," Willo said, "with heat and smoke and purgatives. Because there is no entry point, we can't use snakebite root, the way we have with you. We've taken him to the healer's spring also, but the heat is nearly intolerable to him, and he fights us. Last time, he nearly drowned Bright Hand." Willo nodded toward one of the apprentices, a boy about Raisa's age. "I imagine the poison has affected him the same as you—it has confounded his senses."

Raisa imagined being dipped in a hot spring just now, and shuddered.

"He's been having seizures," Willo went on, "but that seems to be easing off some." She turned to her apprentice. "Bright Hand, has Hunts Alone eaten? Has he drunk anything?"

The apprentice shook his head. "We've tried. He refuses. He's been confused."

Even if he lives, what if he never recovers his wits? Raisa thought.

"Shouldn't you—shouldn't you try a wizard healer?" she asked. "There might be something that could be done for him with high magic."

Willo nodded, seeming unoffended. "I agree. We don't know much about high magic and charmcasters. They usually refuse to allow us to treat them. But who could we trust from Fellsmarch? We could fetch someone from the academy at Oden's Ford, but I believe Hunts Alone will either recover or die before someone could make it there and back."

Raisa took Han's hand. Power buzzed weakly through his fingers, a faint shadow of his usual leakage. Which made her think.

She lifted the blanket that was drawn up to his chin, and peeked underneath. Then looked up at Willo.

"Where is his amulet?" Raisa asked.

"He carried two," Willo said. "I hid them away before the Demonai could take them from him." She reached underneath his pallet and pulled out a deerskin pouch. "I didn't want anything to happen to them."

Raisa weighed the pouch in her hand, then untied the strings and dumped the contents onto the coverlet next to Han. There were, indeed, two amulets—one the serpent amulet she remembered, the other unfamiliar—a bow hunter carved out of gemstone.

"Mother Elena made the Lone Hunter amulet for him," Willo said. "This other one—I've never seen it before."

"He wore the serpent amulet at Oden's Ford," Raisa said, remembering how it had reacted to her the last time she'd touched it. "Maybe one of the masters there gave it to him." She bit her lip, looking down at it. "I don't really know anything about it," she admitted. "But I think it might help him, to have it on. It might keep his magic from leaking away."

Willo glanced toward the common room, then looked back at Raisa, put her finger to her lips, and nodded.

Raisa lifted the serpent amulet by its chain, careful not to touch it directly. She and Willo stripped back Han's blanket, and Raisa carefully unbuttoned the heavy wool shirt he wore underneath.

Unfastening the clasp on the chain, she lowered the amulet until it rested on his bare chest. Immediately, it began to glow, as if in greeting.

What if it does more harm than good? Raisa thought. Amulets draw away power, don't they? But they also store power and provide it to wizards who need it.

Would there be any left after he'd used it to heal her?

Pushing his damp hair out of the way, she fastened the clasp and tucked the chain under the collar of his shirt. Taking his hand, she poked it up under the loose shirt and closed the fingers around the amulet. Then she slid the blanket back up to his chin.

Still on her knees, Raisa looked up at Willo. "Oh, Willo," she whispered, stroking Han's cheek, stubbled with a shadow of reddish beard. "This is all my fault."

The healer smiled, tears standing in her dark eyes. "Really?

I was thinking that it was all *my* fault."

"I remember . . . something of what he did to heal me," Raisa said. "I know I fought him. I have so many secrets. I tried to keep him out. He didn't save me because I am the heir to the Gray Wolf throne. He . . ." Her voice broke.

Willo put her hand on Raisa's shoulder, and power trickled in. "Heart's ease, Your Highness," she said. "You don't have to explain anything to me."

"If you . . . if you think I can be of any help," Raisa whispered, "I would be willing to sit with him, or take over the fans, or . . ."

"Thank you, Your Highness, but perhaps you'd better rest another day or two before you take on the role of healer's apprentice." Willo took Raisa's arm and helped her to her feet. "Let's get you back to bed."

As they shuffled toward the entrance, Raisa heard voices in the next room. They ducked through the deerskin curtain to find three new arrivals in the Matriarch Lodge.

It was Raisa's father, Averill. And Amon Byrne.

Amon! Raisa's heart lurched in relief.

Amon's eyes fixed on Raisa immediately, raking her from her tousled head, over her knee-length shift, to her feet in their ridiculous heavy wool socks. He closed his eyes and lifted his face toward the sky as if sending up a prayer of thanksgiving. Then fixed his eyes back on her as if to make sure she didn't disappear on him.

Amon looked awful. He might have come straight from hell to the Matriarch Lodge, with the memory of that place still engraved on his face. He looked years older, and yet dreadfully young. The gray eyes were clouded with pain and grief, and his face was layered with weariness under a stubble of beard.

"Sweet Lady of Grace," Raisa whispered. "Thank the Maker you're safe."

She wanted to throw her arms around him, to tell him how sorry she was, to tell him how his father saved her life, to tell him that none of this was his fault. She wanted to ask him a thousand questions. She wished she could banish everyone else from the room.

"Corporal Byrne," she whispered, her voice still hoarse from the effects of the toxin. "I'm afraid I have bad news."

She took a faltering step toward Amon, stumbled, and would have fallen, save that Averill leaped forward and caught her in his arms.

"He already knows, Briar Rose," her father said. "Nightwalker brought us the news."

"Nightwalker?" Raisa looked past Averill, toward the door. "Is he . . . ?"

"He stayed on, in the city, to . . . to . . ." Averill's voice broke, and he cradled her close, kissing the top of her head as if she were a young child. "Thank the Maker you are alive. You have no idea what I . . . When Nightwalker told us what had happened, that you were badly wounded, I was afraid we had lost you too."

For a long moment, Raisa allowed herself to be Averill's daughter, to slide her arms around her father and press her face into his leather shirt. To rest there a moment, safe.

I'm finally home, she thought. Things have to get better from here on.

Averill set her down on her feet, carefully, as if she might break, keeping one arm around her shoulders for support.

"Corporal Byrne," Raisa said, struggling for calm composure. "Your father was one of the bravest and wisest men I have ever met, and he was so proud of you—justifiably so."

"Your Highness," Amon said. "I am so sorry. I should have been there. It should have been me."

"No," she said, raising her hand to stay him as tears streamed down her face. "Had you been there, I would have lost you too, and I could not bear that, to lose both of you." She faltered, trying to regain control of her voice. "As it is, it is a grave loss to the line, and to me, personally."

Amon nodded once, looking straight ahead, his eyes pooling with unshed tears. A muscle moved in his jaw, and she knew he was clenching his teeth. "Thank you, Your Highness," he managed to say. He swallowed hard.

Raisa mopped at her face with her sleeve. It's all right to cry, she told herself. Soldiers and queens are allowed to cry, aren't they?

She was half Demonai. Demonai don't cry.

"Captain Byrne and his triple were not the only heroes," Raisa continued, determined to shape the telling of this story before it got away from her. "After I was wounded, Han Alister risked his own life to save mine." She paused, watching their faces closely. "I understand that some of you know him as Hunts Alone."

Averill glanced at Elena, raising an eyebrow. Elena nodded, her lips pressed tightly together.

"Alister's here?" Amon said. His gray eyes searched the room.

Raisa tilted her head toward the back room. "He's in there, fighting for his life."

"Blood of the demon!" Amon took a step toward the partition. "Was he wounded? What did he . . . ?"

"There's more news, daughter," Averill said quickly, a warning in his voice. "More news that cannot wait."

Raisa turned around and looked up into her father's haggard features, newly engraved with loss and grief—yes, and fear. For once, her father's trader face betrayed him.

"Lightfoot," Elena said. "What is it? What's happened?"

Averill put his hands on Raisa's shoulders and looked down into her face. "She's gone, Briar Rose," he said. "Your mother—Queen Marianna—she is dead."

CHAPTER TWELVE
BEQUEST

Raisa twisted away from her father's touch, shaking her head.

"No," she snapped. "That can't be. That's not possible." Her eyes searched the faces around her, looking for reassurance, finding none. Willo's expression said that this news was not unexpected, that it confirmed her worst fears. Raisa could tell that her grandmother, Elena, was already strategizing, turning this over in her mind, assessing what this might mean to the Spirit clans—the Demonai, specifically.

Averill looked as if he wished he could somehow shield Raisa from this news and all its implications. He was widower and parent, both, in that moment.

"Oh," Raisa said, her voice trembling, "this is a dark season."

Elena Demonai dropped to her knees and bowed her gray head. "Long life to Raisa *ana*'Marianna, named Briar Rose in the uplands, Gray Wolf Queen of the Fells."

Amon drew his sword. He fell to his knees in front of Raisa, laying the blade at her feet. "My sword and my life in your service, Your Highness."

Like a stand of lodgepole pines in a gale, they all went down, leaving Raisa standing alone.

That's the way it's going to be, she thought. There's no shelter for me—not from any of this. I'll stand alone the rest of my life. She stood, fists clenched, head bowed, allowing a shuddering sob to pass through her body as her dreams of a reconciliation with her mother collapsed into dust.

Flower Moon came up behind her with a cushioned chair. Bright Hand brought a fur throw, and Raisa wrapped it around herself gratefully, wishing she could pull it over her head and hide. Wishing she could be alone with her grief. Successor queens traditionally retreated to the temple for three full days of mourning before assuming their duties.

But, no. That was not possible—not now. Even though her insides ground together like shards of shattered glass.

She gestured at the people on the floor. "Please," she said. "Get up. Or sit down. Make yourselves comfortable." She blotted tears from her face with the heels of both hands. "Tell me what happened. Tell me everything."

"Briar Rose . . ." Averill stopped and swallowed hard, glancing around the common room. "We don't need to do this now—in public. Your mother—"

"My mother is dead, and I feel like I'm hanging by a thread. I need you to tell me everything—what you know, and what you only suspect. Then we'll decide what to do, and if we can allow time for mourning."

Her father blinked at her. Took a second look. Then inclined his head in assent.

The apprentices brought in cushions to sit on, and Raisa managed to get everyone off their knees. Amon sat at her right-hand side, Willo on her left. Averill and Elena sat cross-legged in front of her.

Willo spoke to Bright Hand, who brought a cup of steaming tea to Raisa. She sipped at it, trying to ignore the cross signals her nerves were sending her, feeling strength coursing through her.

Willo put her hand on Raisa's shoulder, and the healer's touch calmed her and cleared her head. Raisa closed her eyes, wishing she could sink into the sleep of forgetting.

One thought was uppermost in her mind: *This is all my fault.*

"How did it happen?" Raisa said, opening her eyes. "And when?"

"She fell from the Queen's Tower four days ago," Averill said, looking down at his hands. "In the early evening. She fell from her balcony, landed in the courtyard, and was killed."

Raisa thought back. That would have been the night the wolves appeared to her. The night eight renegade guardsmen did their best to kill her. The night after Edon Byrne died. It was too much of a coincidence. The events were linked—they must be.

She remembered Althea's words: *The Bayar blocked up Queen Marianna's ears so she could not hear our warnings.* And now she will pay the price.

Willo stroked Raisa's hair, gesturing for more tea. "You were both in the city at the time?" Willo asked, looking from Amon to Averill.

Averill nodded. "Corporal Byrne had just arrived from the

West Wall with the news that Briar Rose had disappeared from Oden's Ford."

"I knew you were in the north, with . . . with my father, trying to get home," Amon said, looking at Raisa. "I knew you were in danger, but still alive. So Lord Demonai and I met with Nightwalker to strategize. To discuss whether to send a guard to meet you."

"Nightwalker was there too?" Raisa looked from her father to Amon. She knew that Nightwalker rarely descended into the Vale if he had a choice.

Averill nodded. "He's been there, off and on, for two months. I asked him to come and attend me, with a handful of Demonai warriors." He hesitated, as if not wanting to introduce more trouble into the present disaster. "Tensions have been running high with the Wizard Council, and I needed a guard I could trust."

The implications of this settled like a heavy wet cloak, adding to Raisa's misery. The queen's consort and the Wizard Council had clashed for as long as she could remember, but the former Demonai warrior Averill Lightfoot had never felt the need for a handpicked guard before.

"We decided Nightwalker should go to Marisa Pines Camp to see if there'd been any word of you. He'd already gone when . . . when word came of Marianna's death."

"Did anyone see it happen?" Elena asked.

Averill shook his head. "The queen was resting in her bedchamber," he said. "When Magret went in to wake her for dinner, her bed was empty, and the doors to the balcony stood open. Magret looked off the terrace and saw . . . she saw Marianna lying on the pavers below."

Raisa fought to drive that image from her mind. "Magret?" She looked from Averill to Amon. "Magret Gray was attending the queen?"

Averill nodded. "Marianna had requested her specifically in recent weeks. She seemed more at ease with Magret than with anyone else."

Raisa's dream came back to her, the one in which Queen Marianna stood on her terrace. She heard a noise and turned. . . .

"Was Magret in the outer chamber the entire time?" Raisa whispered.

Averill shook his head. "She divided her time between the Princess Mellony and Queen Marianna. Since Marianna was asleep, she was attending the princess."

"And the Queen's Guard? Where were they?" Elena demanded.

"They were outside her door the entire time," Averill said. He paused, glancing at Amon. "That's what they say, at least."

"Who was on duty?" Raisa asked. "Are they . . . are they trustworthy?"

Clearing his throat, Amon named them off, a half dozen guards, none of whom Raisa knew. "I know three of them," Amon said, as if reading her thoughts. "The ones I know are good soldiers. And loyal."

"Loyal or not, how difficult would it be for a wizard to get past them?" Elena said. "You should be asking where the Bayars were during that time."

Willo's hand tightened on Raisa's shoulder. "Elena," she said. "We don't need to—"

"All right—where *were* they?" Raisa asked, wrapping the furs more closely around her. "Does anyone know? Have Micah and Fiona returned from the flatlands?"

Averill nodded. "They returned at least a week ago, though they stayed holed up in the Bayar compound on Gray Lady until the past few days. Lord Bayar has been in frequent meetings at the Council House. That's where he was the night Queen Marianna died—if you are willing to take his word for it, that is. No one else was there as witness, save other members of the council."

"And no one—no one saw the queen's body in the courtyard before Magret raised the alarm?" Raisa asked.

Averill shook his head. "The balcony overlooks the queen's private gardens," he said. "Marianna wasn't fond of gardens, so she never spent much time there. Only her gardeners would have reason to enter."

Raisa shivered. How long had her mother lain there, helpless and broken and alone, before she died? *I should have been there,* she thought miserably. *She shouldn't have been alone with this.*

"Magret Gray was the first . . . was the first to see to the queen?" Raisa asked. Averill nodded.

"Have you spoken with Maiden Gray?" Elena asked. "What does she say?"

"That is why I took so long to bring the news," Averill said. "I would have come sooner, but I didn't know that Briar Rose was at Marisa Pines until yesterday. I wanted to . . . gather as much information as I could before I came."

Before evidence could be destroyed or covered up, was the implication.

"I hope you are being careful, Lightfoot," Elena said. "If it *was* murder, the perpetrators wouldn't hesitate to kill a troublesome consort, too."

"Don't worry about me," Averill said, managing a faint smile.

"What did she say?" Elena asked. "Was there any sign that there was more to it than a fall from a balcony?"

Averill shook his head. "No obvious sign. It appeared Marianna was killed by the fall and not by anything else."

Would a wizard's touch have left traces behind? The trauma of the fall could have covered over any subtle signs of foul play. Or a wizard could have clouded Marianna's mind and made her think she could fly. Or planted the impulse to kill herself.

"However," Averill continued, "the queen had this in her fist." He drew a small pouch from his pocket and emptied the contents into his hand. It was a length of heavy gold chain, the links twisted and broken at either end. It was fine work—clan made, no doubt.

It was the kind of chain often used to carry amulets and talismans.

"Magret found it," Averill said, "when she was preparing Marianna's body."

Elena reached her hand toward it, her face grim and hard. She poked the chain with her forefinger. "So. It seems that the queen's murderers left clues behind."

"We don't know there was a murder, Elena," Willo said. "Not for sure." She turned to Averill. "Did they find anything else?" she asked. "Anything else that would help us?"

Averill shook his head.

"Let's think about this," Raisa said, her voice low and wooden. "What if someone pushed my mother off her terrace? And what if she reached out and grabbed the chain around the killer's neck, trying to save herself? And when she fell, it broke."

"That's plausible," Averill said. "I must admit, that's what I thought too."

"But it's not enough, that it's plausible," Willo said. "We still have no proof that—"

"It was the Bayars and their allies," Elena said. "You know it was. Who else stood to gain from the queen's death? Nightwalker is ready to go to war, and I don't blame him. The Demonai will not continue to stand by and see the Næming violated without retaliating."

Raisa fought down the voice in her head, the Demonai voice that said, *Yes! Go to war against my mother's murderers. Shed their blood as they shed hers.*

"You need better proof if you launch a war in the Fells," she said wearily. "The Bayars are guilty of plenty, but we don't know that they had a hand in this. I will maintain a rule of law, even if it's inconvenient."

"It's the rule of law that has brought us here," Elena said, fingering her braids. "It seems that those who follow the law become victims."

"And those who do not follow the law become tyrants," Raisa said. "No one has more reason to demand revenge than me. But it's the Queen's Guard's responsibility to bring my mother's killer to justice. If there is a killer."

"Where was the Guard when Queen Marianna was murdered?" Elena said. "Captain Byrne was dying in Marisa Pines Pass, and Corporal Byrne was in the flatlands. Who was in charge of keeping the queen safe?"

There was dead silence for a long moment. Amon sat up straighter, fixing his gray eyes on Elena, the fingers of his right hand beating a tattoo on his thigh. Raisa knew that he was furious, but doubted that anyone could tell who didn't know him as well as she did.

These are the people I am going to have to manage, Raisa thought, if I am to succeed as queen.

"Elena *Cennestre*," she said. "That's enough. I would ask you to remember that ten members of my guard gave their lives in Marisa Pines Pass for my sake." At least anger and frustration were potent distracters from the grief that threatened to overwhelm her.

"Forgive me, Granddaughter," Elena said. "I apologize for my blunt words. I mean no disrespect to the Guard, or to you, Corporal Byrne." She looked at Amon, who nodded fractionally. "I still believe that we Demonai can contribute more. You need more protection in these times than your Guard can offer. We would like to help."

"I will keep that in mind, Grandmother," Raisa murmured.

"Has anyone searched the queen's rooms?" Elena asked, looking at Amon and Averill. "If the broken chain carried an amulet, it might have fallen to the floor."

"We did search the queen's bedchamber and the—the area around her body," Amon said, licking his lips and glancing at Raisa. "It's always possible they may have missed something."

"We will search her bedchamber and her garden again, thoroughly," Averill said. "I'll return to the city tonight and enlist the rest of the Demonai."

"Where . . . where is my mother now?" Raisa asked, hoping it wasn't a cold place. Marianna had always hated the cold.

"She lies in state in the Cathedral Temple," Averill said, "in

Speaker Jemson's care. Once the speakers divine her final resting place in the Spirits, we will arrange for her burial."

"What about Mellony?" Raisa asked, suddenly seized with the urge to see her sister. "Where is she? And . . . how is she, do you know?"

Averill shook his head. "She is being held closely in Fellsmarch Castle, for her own safety, it is said. She is fragile, as you know, and distraught, of course, about her mother. They were so close. . . ." His voice trailed off, and Raisa knew he wished he could take the words back.

She had caught the implication, of course—Marianna and Mellony were close, as Raisa and her mother were not.

"I was not able to speak with Mellony in private," Averill went on, "much as I tried. She is surrounded by armies of guards and ladies-in-waiting, and the Bayars are constantly with her."

"The Bayars? Which Bayars?" Elena demanded.

"All of them. Gavan Bayar, Micah, Fiona, and Lady Bayar," Averill said. He paused. "As consort, I don't have the authority to send them away. They're like attack dogs surrounding a pretty pet. I expect an announcement of Mellony's betrothal to Micah any day now, though I'm guessing they would delay any wedding plans until after Mellony's coronation. Just to be sure."

Raisa nearly dropped her tea. She leaned forward. "What? What do you mean?"

Averill looked at Willo and Elena, almost accusingly. "She doesn't know?"

"Briar Rose is just out of her sickbed today," Willo said. "It seemed wise to allow her to gain strength before we told her."

Elena nodded. "We didn't see any reason to bring it up

now. As long as Marianna was alive and healthy, it seemed . . . premature."

"Tell me," Raisa said through stiff lips, knowing matters were about to get even worse.

"The queen meant well," Averill said. "Despite your differences, she wanted to protect your right to the throne. You must know that, Briar Rose."

"Will someone please tell me what's happened with the succession?" Raisa said, gripping the arms of the chair to keep from springing to her feet.

"Queen Marianna was under tremendous pressure from both the Wizard Council and her own council of nobles," Averill said. "You had disappeared, and she did not want to mention your letter for fear of putting you in danger."

Raisa looked up and met Amon's eyes, saw the question in them—*what letter?* She shifted her gaze back to Averill.

"But in the last few months, Marianna drew courage from somewhere," Averill said. "Perhaps she knew in her heart of hearts she was being deceived, was being spelled by the High Wizard. She dismissed Speaker Redfern and brought Speaker Jemson to the Cathedral Temple. He has been a great source of strength to her, but a source of pressure also. As you know, he is committed to the Old Faith, to the restrictions put in place after the Breaking, and to the integrity of the Gray Wolf line."

Averill loved her, Raisa thought. He's always loved her. Even with everything that's happened to divide them. What a pity she never loved him back.

So many regrets. So many lost opportunities.

"Lord Bayar kept after the queen," Averill continued, "telling her that if something happened to her, there would be a vacuum of power, that there could be a civil war, that we could be invaded from the south. Most members of the Queen's Council supported Bayar."

Bright Hand approached with the teapot, and Raisa impatiently waved him away. "So?"

"So two weeks ago Marianna announced a change in the succession," Averill said heavily. "She maintained you as princess heir, but added a provision that allowed Mellony to be crowned queen if Marianna herself were to pass away and you had not returned."

Raisa stared at her father as the implications of this soaked in.

"She meant to protect your claim while addressing the concerns about a vacuum of power," Averill said quietly. "I believe that she knew you were best suited to succeed her. She was trying to satisfy the Spirit clans, the Wizard Council, the speakers, and the Council of Nobles."

"Blood of the demon," Raisa whispered. "She tried to please everyone, and maybe signed her own death warrant." She pressed her fingertips against her temples. Her head pounded, as if thoughts and revelations were banging on the inside of her skull.

"Here's a theory," she said through her fingers. "Micah and Fiona returned home and told their father that I'd left Oden's Ford and might be on my way back. That forced Bayar's hand. He couldn't take the risk that I'd show up and ruin everything. So he murdered the queen, my mother, and set a trap for me. If I stayed in the south, Mellony would have been crowned and married to Micah. Even if I showed up later, they'd have time to dig in so they'd be impossible to dislodge. If I were stubborn enough to stay and fight, they would have found a way to do away with me then. But, naturally, the best outcome was to make sure I'd never come back."

"We have no proof of that, Briar Rose," Willo said softly.

Raisa shook her head. "Just humor me here. If I were dead and there was no alternative, the clans would have to accept Mellony. So the Wizard Council probably assumed it was a good bet to proceed."

"Your Highness, we would never—" Elena began.

"What choice would you have?" Raisa interrupted. "Who else would you get? My cousin Missy Hakkam?" Raisa shuddered. "Mellony would be the only surviving heir to the Gray Wolf line."

They'd been outfoxed all along the way. They'd underestimated the ruthlessness of their enemies. If not for Edon Byrne and Hanson Alister, they would have won already.

They they they, Raisa thought. I have to be careful. As Willo says, we have no proof it was the Bayars. Not yet.

But who else could it be? Who else had an interest in seeing Mellony on the throne? Or was there another motivation she wasn't seeing? Did she have enemies of her own? Gerard Montaigne, for instance. He would benefit from a vacuum of power in the Fells.

And if it was the Bayars, which Bayars? Was Micah involved?

Into the charged silence, Raisa said, "What are people saying? In the palace and in the streets?"

"There is some gossip," Averill said. He stopped, searching Raisa's face for permission to go on. "There is talk within the close, Your Highness, that the queen took her own life," he said.

"There is talk that she had been drinking to excess. This talk is widespread and persistent."

I wonder how that got started, Raisa thought bitterly. Listen and learn. Show any sign of weakness, and your enemies will pounce.

"And . . . outside the close?" Raisa asked.

"People are worried," Averill said. "They know that you are missing, and they wonder what will happen now. They don't know anything about Mellony, while you have considerable support among the working classes. Because of the Briar Rose Ministry."

A worrisome thought crowded to the front of Raisa's mind. "Who else knows I'm alive?" she asked, looking around the circle. "You sent word to my father. Was the Guard notified, or the Council of Nobles, or . . ."

"I told no one in the capital about the attack," Averill said. "So whoever was behind it is probably wondering what happened. And worrying that you might suddenly surface."

"People in camp are talking," Willo said, "even though I rushed you into Matriarch Lodge as soon as I recognized you. You arrived in the middle of the day, after all, and the Demonai nearly shot Hunts Alone when he brought you in." She passed a weary hand over her forehead. "There are rumors going around, but only my apprentices know who you really are."

"Well," Raisa said, "I hope we can keep it within the camp until we— Bones!" She slammed her fist into her other palm as a thought struck her. "This won't work if any of those who tried to kill me returned to Fellsmarch saying that I got away. If they did, they'll be on the watch for me to return to the city."

"Let's hope that Hunts Alone is well enough to answer questions in a day or two," Willo said.

Han. A wave of weariness and despair washed over Raisa, and she leaned back and closed her eyes.

"Your Highness," Willo said. "You must rest. All of these problems will still be here tomorrow."

Raisa nodded, wishing it were not so. Wishing she could go to sleep and wake up to a world with her mother still in it. A world where she would be safe and protected for a little while longer.

CHAPTER THIRTEEN
WALKING
WOUNDED

The others dispersed to various lodges for the night. Willo slept on a cot in Han's room, in case he needed anything. Amon would have bedded down in his clothes in front of the door to the common room where Raisa slept, but Willo had the apprentices set up a cot for him.

Weary as she was, Raisa couldn't seem to get comfortable. Her back ached despite the willow bark tea she'd taken for pain. Every time she closed her eyes, scenes from the past intruded, actions she wished she could remake with the wisdom of hindsight. She lay on her stomach, tears dampening her pillow, a vast aching hollow in her middle.

She heard Amon tossing and turning on his cot by the door.

Guilt and grief thickened the air, smothering her, making it difficult to breathe. No. She could not—she would not allow Amon to torment himself.

She sat up, easing her back against the wall, wary of pressing on her wound. "Amon?" she whispered. "Are you awake?"

His answer came back through the darkness. "Yes. Do you need something?"

"Come sit with me? Please?"

She heard the creak of his cot as he sat up, putting his feet on the floor. He padded over and sat down on the cot next to her. It sagged under his weight. "Are you all right? Do you want me to call Willo?"

Raisa shook her head. "Neither of us is sleeping, and we're both hurting, and I really, really want to talk to you."

"Are you sure you're up to it?" Amon asked. "Willo said you should rest."

"I think talking would do me more good." Raisa patted the bed next to her. "Here. Lean against the wall."

Amon slid toward the head of the cot and arranged himself next to her, trying to get comfortable in the narrow space.

She took his hand, cradling it between her own. "Just stop it," she said. "Stop blaming yourself."

For a long moment he said nothing, a dark silhouette in the light from the window. Then, "What makes you think I'm blaming myself?"

He was still a terrible liar.

"Because I know you. If anyone's to blame for all of this, it's me."

He raked his free hand through his hair. "Why would you blame yourself? None of this is your fault."

"Not my fault? Where do I start?" Raisa bit her lip. "If I hadn't left the Fells, none of this would have happened. My mother would still be alive, and your father, and all the guards who died defending me." She shuddered. "If I had stayed home, maybe we could have worked out our differences."

Amon thought this over. She appreciated the fact that he didn't come back with an immediate denial. "Well," he said, "you had no way of knowing how it would come out."

"*You* had no way of knowing," Raisa said. "I'm supposed to have the gift of prophesy. Why couldn't I have seen how it would end?"

"Prophesy never seems to work that way," Amon said. "Even when people see the future, they don't understand it, or they don't believe it, or they close their eyes to it."

They sat in silence for a few minutes. Then Amon said, "I've been wondering this ever since you disappeared from Oden's Ford. What happened? Was it Micah?"

"Lord Bayar sent four assassins to Oden's Ford to murder me. Micah offered me an alternative—marry him instead. So I agreed."

Understanding dawned in Amon's gray eyes. "So *Micah* was the one that killed the assassins?"

Raisa nodded.

"Ah," Amon said. "That's one mystery solved. We couldn't figure that out—who would have killed them with wizardry."

"Well," Raisa said, leaning against him, "I managed to kill one on my own." It all seemed so long ago, on the far shore of a turbulent sea of events. "We were on our way north when we ran into Gerard Montaigne's army on its way into Tamron. A Tamric patrol showed up, and I escaped in the confusion."

"I knew you had gone north, I could feel it," Amon said. "Since you were spotted during the skirmish, I thought you'd likely gone to Tamron Court."

She shook her head. "I decided to go on home since I was halfway there."

"I should have kept a closer eye on you at Oden's Ford," Amon said. "We knew you'd eventually run into the Bayars."

Raisa shook her head. "No. Stop. That was my fault too. It was my letter to my mother that gave me away." She swiped away a tear that had somehow leaked out.

"What letter? The one your father mentioned?"

"I persuaded Hallie to carry a letter from me to Queen Marianna, via my father," Raisa said. "I wanted her to know why I left, and that I was coming back. I should have known the Bayars would be watching everyone close to me in case I tried to get in contact. That's how they found out I was at Oden's Ford. It wasn't a random sighting at all." She swallowed hard. "And it may have been my letter that caused her to change the succession the way she did."

"Well." Amon considered this. "Maybe otherwise she'd have disinherited you entirely."

"But she might still be alive," Raisa said.

"But for how long?" Amon said. "Once Mellony was set to inherit, they'd want to make it happen and put Micah on the throne."

Long enough for me to see her again, Raisa thought.

They sat in silence for a while. Finally Raisa spoke.

"Your turn. I thought . . . When your father told me you were in Tamron Court, and Montaigne had the city under siege, I was afraid I'd never see you again."

He squeezed her hand, but said nothing.

"So what happened?" Raisa said. "Captain Byrne said you

intentionally gave out the story that I was in the city in order to keep Montaigne occupied."

Amon grunted.

"Weren't you afraid of what Prince Gerard would do when he found out you'd fooled him?" Raisa said.

Amon shrugged, looking down at their joined hands.

"Will you say something, please?" Raisa said, exasperated. "What were you thinking? How did you get away?"

He sighed heavily. "Just be glad you weren't there, Rai," he said. "Gerard is a monster, but the royal family of Tamron isn't much better. Those Tomlins spend most of their time plotting against each other. When all else fails, they resort to poison. During the siege, the entire city was starving, but King Markus hosted a feast every night inside the palace. He was furious when Queen Marianna wouldn't send an army to drive off Montaigne—even though he'd lied to her. He threatened to kill off the Gray Wolves, one each day, ending with me, if the Fells didn't respond."

Raisa's mouth went dry. "What? How could he possibly blame you if . . . ?"

"Don't try to apply logic to what he does," Amon said. After a thick pause, he added, "Wode Mara was the first."

Raisa stiffened and sat upright. "Wode? He's . . . he's *dead*?"

Amon nodded, twisting the gold wolf ring on his finger. "And don't ask me how he died, because I'm not going to tell you."

Wode was a red-haired cadet, with a broad, pleasant, perpetually sunburned face. He had a girl back in Chalk Cliffs, and was saving up to marry her.

"That's not possible," Raisa whispered.

"I thought I would have to kill Markus myself, but Liam Tomlin beat me to it. He and his sister poisoned him."

"Liam? Poisoned his father?" Raisa recalled Liam and his sister, the Princess Marina, at her name day party—both tall, graceful charmers, with soft curls and strong noses. And a way with poison, apparently.

I'm not ready to be queen, Raisa thought, shuddering. I'm not ready to go up against all these ruthless people. I'm not ready to play this high-stakes game as ruler of the Fells.

"Liam was crowned king, but he didn't get to enjoy it for very long," Amon said. "Montaigne breached the walls two days later. And after that . . . after that it was a massacre." Amon closed his eyes, the lashes dark against his pale cheeks.

"How did you get away?" Raisa asked. "And—and what about the rest of the Gray Wolves?"

"Tamron is soft, and the Ardenines know it," Amon said. "They aren't used to fighting for their lives. The Ardenines were focused on two things—capturing you and the Tomlins, and stealing everything that wasn't bolted down. They slaughtered everyone who got in the way." Amon passed his hand over his face as if to wipe the memory away.

"So we each killed an Ardenine soldier of the right size, and stole the uniforms. We've all been to the academy; we speak the language well enough to pass. We sieved through the lines while they were otherwise occupied. We went northeast to Swansea because we knew the roads to Fetters Ford and Oden's Ford would be closely watched.

"But the worst part—the worst part was, I knew you were in trouble. I knew you were in danger, I knew you were dying, and

I couldn't get to you." He swallowed hard. "I couldn't reach you. You can't imagine . . . what that was like." His voice shook.

Raisa recalled Amon's voice in her head. *Don't you die, Rai, don't you give in.*

"I think that your father had a premonition," Raisa said. "It was almost like he knew what would be demanded of him, and he made the sacrifice."

"It should have been me," Amon said, blotting his eyes with his sleeve. "I am your captain. I am responsible for your safety."

"You are responsible for the Gray Wolf line, remember? The line comes first, not the individual queen. Your father saved the line. I *need* you, Amon. I need a captain. If I'm going to build a queendom out of this mess, I need one person I can trust. I need you to be alive, understand?"

Raisa leaned her head against Amon's shoulder again. Neither of them said anything for a long while.

"Where is the Wolfpack?" Raisa said. *What's left of them*, she added silently.

"Right now they're assigned to the Queen's Guard in the capital," Amon said. "Awaiting orders. I'm hoping they can give us early warning of any plans afoot from the other side."

"If they are planning Mellony's coronation," Raisa said, "what will they do for a captain of the Queen's Guard?"

"Hmm," Amon said, frowning, "I hadn't thought of that. The knowledge about the linking has been kept within our family and the speakers of the temple. Mellony won't know about it, and the Bayars won't know, either."

"It's always been a Byrne," Raisa said. "They'll want everything to seem as normal as possible. They won't want to provide any excuse to question the succession. Beyond what's already there, I mean."

Amon turned his head to look at her. "What are you saying?"

"I'm saying don't be surprised if they offer you the job," Raisa said. "If it gets that far."

"No." Amon shook his head. "There's no way they would want me next to Mellony. They'll choose someone more malleable."

"We'll see," Raisa said. "They won't know you're already named as my captain. They're used to working around your father. You're young, and they don't know how capable you are."

"Like I would ever agree to that," Amon said, sitting up straighter. "Serve as captain to your sister at the request of my father's murderers."

"Amon." Raisa put her hand on his arm. "You're not supposed to know any of that. When they ask, be ready to say yes."

"What?" He stared at her.

"If you say no, that will tell them everything they need to know. They'll know whose side you're on. They'll suspect I'm alive, or at least that you know more than you're saying. It will be your death warrant."

"That wouldn't ever work," Amon said, stubborn resistance on his face.

"I didn't tell you to actually *serve*," Raisa said softly. "Just say yes when they ask, all right? Practice until you're good at it."

"Hmmmph," he said, not making any promises. After a pause, he said, "How did you get away? After my father was killed, I mean?"

"After your father went down, Mac Gillen dragged me off

so he could see to me personally. That probably saved my life. I killed him with your father's dagger, took his horse, and made a run for it, hoping to make Marisa Pines before they caught up with me. After I was hit, I crawled in among some rocks. When I realized that the arrow was poisoned, I knew I was done for." She tried to keep her voice matter-of-fact, the story brief and to the point. The guilt Amon carried was heavy enough as it was.

"That's the last I remember. I guess we'll have to ask Han Alister the rest of it. Apparently, he showed up out of nowhere, saved my life with high magic, and brought me here to Marisa Pines." She sighed. "Elena and Nightwalker don't seem to believe that story."

Amon cleared his throat. "When you disappeared from Oden's Ford, Alister and I—we talked some. I don't know what to make of him. I don't know what drives him, and I don't exactly trust him, but . . ." He hesitated, but his relentless honesty drove him on. "He told me he was traveling back to the Fells to look for you. He'd go via Marisa Pines Pass, and I'd take the western route. So that explains how he came to be there."

"I don't know what will happen when he finds out who I really am," Raisa said. "If he even survives." She shivered, and Amon put his arm around her, drawing her into his steady warmth.

"It's that bad?"

Raisa nodded. "He looked . . . he looked awful, Amon. Willo doesn't know if he'll . . . She's worried about him. My mother died, and I never got to tell her that I loved her, that I finally understood—just a little, anyway. If Han dies too, I don't know what I'll do."

She was weeping again, surrendering to grief and pain and fear. "I lied to him, Amon. Day after day after day. I pretended to be someone I wasn't. I allowed him to get close to me, knowing that we had no future together."

"You had no choice," Amon said.

"I could have trusted him," Raisa said. "Now he's going to question everything. He's going to think that everything— everything was a lie."

"How do you know what *his* intentions were?" Amon said, blunt as always. "He has a reputation in Ragmarket, you know."

Raisa hesitated, unsure whether to go forward. "It's hard to explain—my memory is so jumbled. But when he healed me, it was like he opened up to me. Like he had no secrets. Like I got to know him in a way that . . ." She trailed off, taking in Amon's pained expression.

"He is a wizard, Rai," Amon said. "Remember that."

Raisa nodded, straightening, blotting at her eyes. "I'll remember," she said, recalling Althea's warning: *You must not allow yourself to be ensnared as Marianna was.* "Anyway. What's done is done. I should have been there for my mother, but I wasn't. I should have died in the canyon, but I didn't. In a way, this is a new beginning. We have to put all these regrets behind us and look ahead. We can't spend energy on what might have been. If we do, our enemies will eat us alive."

She looked up at Amon hopefully. "We can't change the past, but we can shape the future."

And as she said it, she realized that it applied to more than politics.

She'd spent the past year yearning for Amon Byrne, agonizing over what would never be between them, immersed in regret. She'd pushed the issue in ways that were unfair to both of them.

She remembered what Edon Byrne had told her, with the authority of someone who knew what it was to sacrifice love to duty.

You serve, he'd said. *You find happiness where you can. In love or not, you find a way to continue the line.*

She loved Amon Byrne; some part of her would love him all her life. But the way she'd handled it had prevented her from enjoying what she could have with him. He was her very best friend—had always been her very best friend.

And she needed friends more than ever now.

They slept side by side that night, arms wrapped around each other, as they had a hundred times as children. They were two wounded people—new orphans cut loose and lonely, and they needed each other.

The magical barrier between captain and queen never interfered.

CHAPTER FOURTEEN

WORD GAMES

Han had slept in the Matriarch Lodge at Marisa Pines Camp nearly every summer of his life. The sounds and smells seeped into his pores, they soothed him, and had made him feel safe in a way he'd never felt at home.

Now he was back here again, but this time, every sensation was painfully amplified. The pressure of a blanket on his skin was excruciating, the voices in the room clamored in his ears, he was hot, he was cold, his skin prickled and burned as if a thousand biting insects feasted on him. His eyelids felt like sandpaper, scratching his eyes. He wanted to shed his skin like a snake.

When they took his amulet, they'd ripped out his heart, leaving a gaping hole where the magic poured out. Whenever people came near him, they hurt him, poured boiling water into his mouth, shredded his tender skin with hard, rough hands. They tried to boil him alive and freeze him to death by turns. He fought back. He tried to strike out at them whenever they came near, so they mostly kept their distance.

When he thought he would drown in his own saliva, they turned him over and let it run out of his mouth. Several times his entire body seized up, going rigid for minutes at a time. All of his muscles ached for hours after the spasms passed.

When he opened his eyes and saw Willo, he fixed on her face and tried to speak, to plead with her not to let them torment him anymore. But his words never made it past his lips.

Finally, they gave him back his amulet. It rested on his chest like a warm fire, just the right temperature, and he held on to it with both hands. It was his tether to the world. It kept him grounded, kept the flash circulating instead of leaking away. Now he heard a familiar voice speaking in his head, unexpectedly kind and soothing.

Well, now, Alister, you've managed to survive in spite of yourself. There is a god that looks after fools, apparently.

Crow? Nah. Not possible.

Han tried to remember how he'd come to be at Marisa Pines. What had happened? Had he caught Mari's fever again? There were some fevers that came back over and over.

They kept pestering him with food and drink.

And then he opened his eyes and found himself staring into Rebecca Morley's face. She was waist-deep in water, hair plastered down, and steam rising all around her, like one of those fish-maidens in stories who ask riddles, and if you get the answers wrong they try to drown you. Rebecca had hold of his ankles, and Willo and somebody else held his arms, and they were lowering him into a freezing hot spring.

He didn't have any clothes on, but he was too muddleheaded to worry about it.

Another time, he woke on dry land. Rebecca had some porridge on a spoon and was trying to wedge it into his mouth. Her hand trembled and tears stood in her eyes.

Well, if it means that much to you, he thought.

He opened his lips but kept his teeth sealed together in case it was blistering hot, but it was all right, and he opened his mouth farther, and she smiled like they'd done something fabulous together. She slid an arm around his shoulders, and Willo came in on the other side, and they managed to raise him up so he could drink without drowning. Rebecca put a cup to his lips. It was lukewarm tea, and he managed to keep it from pouring out the corner of his mouth, which had been a problem lately.

He was embarrassed to have Rebecca Morley feeding him like a weanling. But her touch soothed him. It was good to rest in her arms.

There was something he should remember about Rebecca Morley. Something had happened. Wasn't she hurt? Hadn't she died? Just now she looked better than him—dressed in a clan tunic embroidered over with gray wolves—too fancy to be wearing in a sickroom.

He reached up and wiped away her tears with his thumb, but she just made more. And that was all he remembered for a long time.

The next time he awoke, he found his amulet warm and humming. He looked up and there was Fire Dancer sitting next to his sleeping bench. Dancer had his hand on Han's amulet, feeding it power while it fed power to Han.

"What are you doing?" Han whispered. He was a little amazed when the words came out and Dancer heard and understood them.

"I've been lending you power over the past few days," Dancer said. "You seem to use yours up as soon as it appears. It's one way I can help you heal yourself without getting poisoned."

"Oh." Han considered this. The flash trickled in like rum brandy, and he felt better than he had in a long while. "Do I have to give it back?"

Dancer laughed, though there were worry lines around his eyes. "We'll see. Maybe I'll be low one of these days and you can help me out."

Han felt more alert, his mind clearer, too, than it had been. And he was ravenous, even though his mouth tasted like a stable that needed mucking out.

"Do you know—is there anything to eat around here?" he asked.

Dancer grinned. "Please. You know there's never anything to eat in my mother's house."

A young man with a healer's amulet appeared out of nowhere with a bowl of stew, a jug, and a cup. He set the food on a bench next to the bed and backed away, making sure not to get too close to Han.

"Have I got something catching?" Han asked as the healer retreated.

"You've been rough on Willo's apprentices, I hear," Dancer said. "You're lucky anyone's willing to come within arm's length."

Han sat up, propping against the wall. Dancer unstoppered the jug and poured him some upland tea.

"Don't get used to being waited on," Dancer warned, going back to stoking his amulet. "It's almost over." He wore clan garb—leggings and a deerskin tunic beaded in Willo's distinctive designs, his amulet tucked discreetly underneath.

"You mean to tell me they let two wizards back into Marisa Pines Camp?" Han said. "The Demonai must be going into spasms."

Dancer laughed again, and Han was pleased that he'd said something that made sense. Something funny, in fact. His brain felt like one of those lacy cheeses they sold at Southbridge Market sometimes—full of big holes in places where he used to know things.

Han's attention was diverted as someone pushed through the curtain from the next room.

It was Cat Tyburn.

"Hayden! You should see the blades they got in the market here," she said. "But they're all a bunch of copperhead thieves, the iron they want for a . . ." She abruptly stopped speaking when she saw Han sitting up.

She dropped to her knees next to his sleeping bench, staring narrow-eyed into his face. "Cuffs! You awake? You an't still crazy sick? I was beginning to think you was a Mad Tom for good."

Cat and Dancer were supposed to be at Oden's Ford. What were they doing here? Cat especially. She hated the clans, didn't she?

"What are you doing here?" he said aloud. "You're supposed to be at school."

"Me and Dancer came here to beat you senseless for running off without telling anyone where you were going," Cat said. "We thought it would make more of an impression if we waited 'til you woke up."

"We weren't that far behind you," Dancer said. "Bird finally told me where you'd gone, and why, about a week after you left." Anger passed across his face like a cloud shadow over a field.

Hmmm, Han thought. Why *had* he come? And then he remembered: to find Rebecca Morley.

He fastened on that. Where was Rebecca? How had he come to be here? What had happened? How long had he been lying here? That was one of the holes.

"Four days," Dancer said, as if he'd read his mind. "A lot has happened. A lot has changed." He studied Han's face to assess how clearheaded he was. "That's why I wanted to stoke you up. There's a lot of pressure from . . . well, from everyone."

"Pressure?" Han reached for the jug of tea, missing it on his first pass. He still felt tingly all over, his fingers fat and clumsy, though they looked their regular size. Concentrating, he reached again, took hold of the jug, unstoppered it, and poured, while Dancer watched, hands extended to catch it if Han dropped it.

"The queen is dead," Dancer said. "Maybe murdered. She fell from the Queen's Tower a week ago."

Han blinked at him. Thought for a moment. "M–Marianna? That's her name, right?" He looked up at Dancer for confirmation.

Dancer nodded.

"So. Guess I'm a little late." Maybe he was out of a job. Maybe he could go back to Oden's Ford and continue his schooling. The thought cheered him.

But then he remembered the princess heir. "So, there's a new queen, right?" he said, frowning.

"Well, that's the problem," Dancer said. "The new queen hasn't been crowned yet. It's likely to come to a fight between the two princesses, Raisa and Mellony."

That was the name. Raisa. She was the one that had given money to Jemson's Temple School. He didn't know anything about the other one.

And then another memory trickled back. Captain Byrne, shot full of arrows.

"Captain Byrne is dead too," Han said. Could Byrne's death and the queen's be connected? "Did you know? He died in Marisa Pines Pass."

Dancer nodded. "I know. They brought Byrne's body back, and the Demonai hosted an ábeornan ceremony last night, a funeral pyre. They honored him as a fallen warrior. Very unusual to honor a flatlander like that."

More memories. Rebecca Morley racing for her life. The ambush in the canyon. The poison daub.

Han gripped Dancer's sleeve and spit it out before it faded again. "Byrne and Rebecca were traveling together, in a party of bluejackets, when they were attacked. As far as I know, she's the only one that survived."

A memory came back to him—a bone-deep connection, a shared memory, a linkage that bolted them, soul to soul, while he struggled to keep her alive. And wolves—gray wolves like wraiths, passing in and out of the trees.

But had she survived? She'd been near death when they arrived. But he thought he remembered something about Rebecca and porridge.

"Rebecca! Where is she?" Han asked.

"That's what I wanted to talk to you about. Rebecca Morley," Dancer said, glancing toward the door like he was afraid they would be interrupted. "There's something you should know."

Fear prickled at the back of Han's neck. He scanned Dancer's face, looking for clues and fearing the worst. "She's not dead. I could have sworn she came in to see me. She seemed all right then. She even tried to feed me something."

Was it possible all of his efforts went for nothing?

Dancer was shaking his head. "No, she's well, getting better every day. She had a nasty wound in her back, but you took the brunt of the poison, so she's recovering faster. She's coming in to talk to you, in fact. I just wanted to warn you that—"

He looked up, startled, as the drapery at the entrance was twitched aside and Rebecca slipped through the opening.

She wore full clan skirts that fell nearly to her ankles, tooled and studded leather boots, and a loose linen overshirt embroidered around the neckline and tied at the waist with a handwoven purple sash. Around her neck she wore a necklace of roses and thorns in gold, and her dark hair framed her green eyes like a soft, shiny cap.

She was a feast for the eyes, even in Han's present debilitated state.

Han looked down at himself, thinking he could use some cleaning up.

Hey, now, he thought. She's the reason you look and feel like you've been run over by a muckwagon in Pinbury Alley. But looking at her, seeing her alive and looking so well—it was all worth it. He'd do it all over again.

"Han," she said, stopping just inside the door as if unsure of her welcome. "May I come in?"

"It depends," Han said, trying to gather his wits. "Last time I saw you, I believe you tried to cut my heart out."

"Last time I saw *you*, I believe you spit porridge on me," she shot back. Then she flinched, probably remembering that she was the ultimate cause of the porridge spitting.

She tried for a smile, but her face looked pinched and ashen, nervous even, and her eyes avoided his. "Do you feel up to talking for a few minutes?"

Han shrugged, looking around the room. "I got no—I have no plans, as far as I know." It seemed like a long time ago that she was his tutor and he was a student of pretty speech, but he couldn't break himself of the habit of correcting himself in her presence.

Rebecca looked at Dancer and Cat. "Could you give us a few minutes?"

Cat didn't want to leave, Han could tell. But Dancer took her elbow and firmly ushered her out of the room.

Rebecca plunked down on a chair next to his sleeping bench. She was very pale, and her nose was pink, her lashes clumped together as if she'd been crying.

"I am . . . so relieved to see you looking so well," she said, smoothing her skirts with her hands. Her eyes flicked up to his face. "You are feeling better, I hope?" she said in a rush.

He studied on it. Even though Dancer had left off stoking his amulet, he felt restored, comfortable, happy, almost sleepy.

His luck had finally changed. Rebecca was alive. He was alive. They were together. That was all that mattered.

"I'm good," he said, smiling up at her. "Though I guess I'm in no hurry to suck up more of that poison any time soon."

"Nor I," she said, shaking her head. "Did you have that—that reaction where water felt boiling hot? And where you . . . where you . . ."

"Where you felt like you had the night itches?" She nodded, her cheeks stained pink, and Han rolled his eyes. "I swear I must've had every possible symptom." He frowned at her. "Didn't you try to drown me once?"

"Well, we were trying to sweat out the poison, and so we took you to the healer's spring. . . ." Her voice trailed off when she saw he was teasing.

"I was so worried about you," she went on. "I don't think I could have endured it if you had been . . . permanently. . . If you had . . ." She stopped and breathed out, gripping the arms of the chair. "Anyway, I wanted to thank you for saving my life. Whatever happens, however we go forward, I will never forget your service to me."

Service? She seems different, Han thought. Oddly formal. Nervous and ill at ease. "Captain Byrne is dead," he said. "Did you know? I found him in Marisa Pines Pass, shot full of arrows."

She nodded. "Yes, I know. I saw . . . I saw it happen. We've fetched back his body. Maybe . . . maybe Dancer told you?"

He nodded. "I have his sword. Or at least I did when I arrived. It's fancywork. I thought maybe Corporal Byrne would want it."

"That's thoughtful of you," Rebecca said. "I know he will want it." She rushed ahead. "He's here, you know. Corporal Byrne. He's just outside. He asked to speak with you when I'm . . . when I'm finished. He'll want to ask you questions, and to . . . to thank you."

Maybe that's why she's so twitchy, Han thought. Last time

they were all together, Han had jumped out Rebecca's bedroom window so Amon Byrne wouldn't run him through with his much plainer sword.

Rebecca seemed to have something important to say to him, but couldn't quite spit it out. So she asked him a question.

"I wanted to ask you how it happened that you saved my life," she said. "I don't really remember much, and people have been asking . . . lots of questions."

"When you disappeared from Oden's Ford, I headed for Marisa Pines Pass, looking for you, asking about you all along the way." Han paused, waiting for the holes to fill in. "In Fetters Ford, this innkeeper's boy remembered someone that looked like you—but said your name was Brianna and you'd been murdered by rovers."

"Ah," Rebecca said, nodding. "Simon."

"There was nothing else until, north of Delphi, I saw where some bluejackets had been killed at Way Camp. They were out of uniform, but they carried bluejacket gear and papers. It must have happened in the middle of the snowstorm." He looked at her, and she nodded but didn't volunteer more. "Then, farther on, I found Captain Byrne's body in the pass. I couldn't make sense of it. They were all done by crossbows, not clan arrows. I couldn't figure out what had happened, who was fighting who, and why."

Rebecca plucked at the folds in her skirt, straightening the fabric.

Han continued on. "After I came through the pass, I heard horses coming, what sounded like a hunt going on. I saw them chasing you, shooting at you, though I didn't recognize you at the time." He rubbed his chin. "I decided to follow along and see if I could help you."

Rebecca looked up, tilting her head. "Really? If you didn't know me, what made you decide to intervene?" She waved her hand. "After all, I could have been a criminal being chased by the Queen's Guard."

"It was six on one," Han said, thinking, This shouldn't be that hard to figure out. "Eight on one at the end. From your size, I guessed you were a woman or a child—and you weren't shooting back. Plus, they were out of uniform—for all I knew, they were bully ruffins.

"Even if they'd been badged up and wearing their blue jackets, it just seemed unfair to me. I didn't know the background, but I can't believe it's in the queen's interest to send eight men out to kill a girlie like you." He looked at Rebecca very directly. "And if the queen approves of that, there's something wrong with her."

Rebecca got that slapped look she wore sometimes.

Han ran back over what he'd said. No, it all made sense, and nothing offensive that he could see.

"S—so, what happened then?" Rebecca croaked.

"By the time I caught up with you, you were holed up in the canyon and they were closing in on you." Han took a long drink of tea. His mouth was still wicked dry.

"It wasn't until I pried you out of your hidey-hole that I realized it was you. I couldn't figure out what you were doing there. Once I took a look at your wound, I realized the arrow was a poison daub, and—"

"Wait a minute," Rebecca said, putting up her hand. "What happened to the men who ambushed me?"

Han hesitated, wondering what she would think of him, then shrugged. "I killed them."

Rebecca stared at him as if waiting for the rest of the story. "All of them? None of them got away?"

He nodded, beginning to wonder why she was so hungry for details. Was she vengeful, or bloodthirsty, or scared they'd come back? "I didn't have much choice."

"You killed eight men all by yourself?"

"Well," Han said patiently, "I took them by surprise."

"Did you . . . did you use magic?"

He shook his head. "There wasn't any reason to. My bow was good enough." When she said nothing, he added, "One of my teachers says that the most important thing a wizard needs to learn is when not to use flash. Otherwise, you'll be caught without when you really do need it. You conserve it, you save it, and when you do need it, you use only as much as necessary."

He stopped, knowing that was too much information. Why would she be interested in what Crow had to say?

"So, what happened after you killed them?" Rebecca prompted. She still seemed to be wrestling with the notion that he'd put eight men down on their backs with a longbow.

"I knew my only chance of saving you was to bring you to Marisa Pines Camp and to hope that Willo was here."

"Right. You knew Marisa Pines," Rebecca said, her brow furrowed. "Willo said you'd fostered here every summer?"

Han nodded wearily. It was so good to see her—he was desperate to stay awake and enjoy it—but all of this talking was wearing him out.

"But you were the one who saved my life," she said. "You

used high magic. That's what Willo said."

"Well. I realized that if I didn't do something, you'd be dead before we got here." He grimaced. "So it's a good thing I didn't use up my flash hushing those ruffins or we'd both be dead."

"You nearly died as it is," Rebecca said, taking both his hands. "I am so, so sorry. So sorry for everything." Her expression said she was sorry for things he didn't even know about yet.

It was almost like she was worried he'd think badly of her. Did she think he resented the fact that he'd nearly died saving her life?

It was worth it, he thought. He gripped her hands, pulled her face down close, and kissed her, long and slow, savoring it, despite his frayed nerves. She broke it off before he did, pulling back, her face pale, her green eyes large and haunted.

Maybe it was the aftereffects of the poison, but he found himself saying something he'd never ever said to any girlie ever before. "I love you, Rebecca. And I'm not sorry. I would do it all over again, even knowing the cost of it. I couldn't face losing you."

Rebecca's reaction to this was peculiar, to say the least. She reared back, looking almost panicked. She was the one so good with words, but now she was stammering and stumbling like her tongue was tangled up.

"I think you're supposed to say you love me too," he said finally. "Just so you know, for next time."

"I do," she said, her cheeks bright with embarrassment. "I do love you." She said it quick, but it was still too late.

After an awkward silence, Han cleared his throat. "So, Rebecca," he said, "what's your story? Why did you disappear from Oden's Ford? And who were those riders and why were they after you? Was it because you saw them murder Captain Byrne and they didn't want you telling tales?"

Rebecca took a deep breath, seeming to brace herself. "Micah Bayar kidnapped me from Oden's Ford," she said. "He said he'd kill me if I didn't go along."

"Bayar," Han murmured. It confirmed what he had suspected all along. "I knew it. Do you . . . did it have to do with the fact that we'd been walking out?"

Rebecca shook her head, looking surprised. "No. It's . . . it's a long story, but it's something between me and Micah. Nothing to do with you."

"Something between you and Bayar?" Rebecca nodded. Han didn't much like that. "Then who were the riders who came after you?"

"They were renegade members of the Queen's Guard," she said. "One of them, at least, you know. Sergeant Gillen."

Han frowned, puzzled. "I don't remember seeing Gillen. . . ."

"I killed him myself," she said. "When I escaped from them the first time."

Right. They'd said as much, there in the canyon. He'd known she had starch—he'd known it since she'd rescued the Raggers from the Southbridge Guardhouse. But still.

"I was the one they were really after," Rebecca went on. "They killed Captain Byrne—they killed everyone to get to me."

"Why would they be after you?" Han said, mystified. "I mean, they went to a lot of trouble, didn't they? There couldn't be much swag in it. They didn't even spoil the bodies, not that I could tell."

"My real name is not Rebecca Morley," she said, lifting

her chin and looking him straight in the eye, almost defiantly. "The first time I ever used that name was the day we met, at Southbridge Temple. I had gone down there to see Speaker Jemson about providing funds for his ministry. Amon—Corporal Byrne—suggested that if I were going to walk through Ragmarket and Southbridge, I should do so in disguise."

Han was a long step behind. "You were going to give money to the Temple School? Since when does a tutor make that kind of iron?"

"I lied to you when I told you I was a tutor," Rebecca said.

"So you never worked for the Bayars?"

Rebecca shook her head. "My family is quite wealthy, although I don't have ready access to the money." She paused. "Or I didn't, at least," she added, almost to herself.

So she was more than just an upstairs servant. She'd been a true gilt-edged lady slumming in Ragmarket? Was that what she was saying?

Apprehension roiled Han's stomach. He knew something about gilt-edged ladies and what they expected from him.

"When you abducted me from the temple, I didn't want you to know who I really was," she went on. "So I kept on with the pretense. I didn't know you—but I'd heard that you were a thief and a ruthless killer."

She paused, and Han wondered if she was thinking about the eight bluejackets he'd just done.

"I never had the chance to tell you the truth, even after I went into the Southbridge Guardhouse after the Raggers. I didn't want anyone to trace what happened back to me. Anyway, I never thought I'd see you again." Rebecca looked down at her hands.

It was a peculiar conversation. Emotion crackled in the air, much more than seemed called for. Rebecca was practically down on her knees apologizing for lying to a former street thief about whether she was a little rich or a lot rich.

"Well," Han said cautiously, "I guess I knew, going in, you were a blueblood. To someone like me, nearly everyone is."

Now that Rebecca had begun this story, she seemed determined to finish it. "When I went to Oden's Ford, I was running away from a forced marriage, and I didn't want my mother to find me. Rebecca Morley had served me well before, so I used the name again."

Han's neck and shoulders prickled. This story was familiar. Where had he heard it before—a story about a blueblood running away from a marriage?

"Who were you running from?" Han asked, his mouth dryer than ever. "Why were those bluejackets trying to kill you? If you're not Rebecca Morley, then who are you?"

Leaning forward, she gripped his right hand and looked into his eyes. "I ran away to avoid marrying Micah Bayar," she said. "My mother, the queen, insisted." Turning his hand palm-up, she dropped a coin into it.

He looked down at it—a girlie coin, the familiar portrait in profile glittering in the light from the lanterns. He looked up at Rebecca, down at the coin, and the holes filled in. Why hadn't he seen it before?

It was like she thought if she fed him poison in little bites, it'd be easier to swallow.

"My real name is Raisa," she said. "Raisa *ana*'Marianna, soon to be Queen of the Fells."

CHAPTER FIFTEEN
THE PRICE OF DECEPTION

It seemed to Raisa that time slowed to a crawl. Han looked down at the crown coin, then back up at Raisa. He extended his forefinger, tracing her profile, then shook his head.

Raisa cradled Han's hands in hers, holding her breath. She didn't know what reaction to expect—anger, revulsion, cold disdain, disappointment, disgust. He'd made it clear enough what he thought of queens and their kind.

He looked up, his blue eyes meeting hers directly, and there was her answer. Betrayal. His eyes were filled with betrayal, anger, and loss. It was all she could do not to look away. She forced herself to hold his gaze. She owed him that.

Han gently pulled his hands free, leaned back, and closed his eyes. "No," he said, lacing his fingers across his middle. "That's not true. It can't be." His voice tremored slightly.

"I'm sorry," Raisa said. "I'm sorry I lied to you, and I'm sorry it has to come out now, in this way."

Han didn't open his eyes.

"I didn't want to burden you now, when you're still recovering," she said. "It's not right, and it's not fair. But I knew if I didn't tell you, someone else would, and I wanted to do it myself."

Han said nothing. He kept his eyes closed, the lashes dark against skin as pale and hard as We'enhaven marble, flawed only by the ragged knife scar over his right eye.

"This doesn't have to—to change things between us," Raisa said. "I mean, of course it will change *some* things, but . . ."

Han opened his eyes. When he spoke, his voice was low and deadly cold. "What kind of a fool do you take me for?"

There was something frightening in his face. Something that said she was the enemy now, and he would never trust her again.

Raisa shook her head. "I don't take you for a fool," she said. "I know that you—"

"Do you think I don't know how the world works?" he said. "Do you think I don't know how it is between people like you and people like me? D'you think I've never been with a blueblood girlie before?" He snorted. "They used to come down to Ragmarket looking for adventure. Looking for a quick tumble with someone who wouldn't complicate their lives in the long run."

"That's not how I look at you at all," Raisa said, stung.

"Or maybe I'm part of your, what do you call it, your *ministry*," he said bitterly. "A bit of personal hands-on charity. A chance to raise up the unwashed and ignorant. . . ."

"*You* came to *me*, as I recall," Raisa retorted, unable to help herself. "I wasn't looking for a job. You asked me to tutor you, and I agreed."

"Trust me to pick a princess out of everyone in Oden's Ford," Han said. "I do have an eye. I always could spot a heavy purse in the street." He unconsciously fingered his wrists as if the cuffs were still there. "It must have been amusing for you to hear me prattle on like a love-struck fancy. How do I say this—poor Alister is getting above himself."

"I am not laughing at you," Raisa said. "How could I? I care about you. I—"

"You care about your pony too," Han said. "Your pony provides a useful service." He closed his eyes again, as if he couldn't bear to look on her anymore.

Raisa couldn't seem to find the right words, the right thing to say. If there even was a right thing. Han Alister always had a way of making her lose her footing. Now the raw grief over her recent losses and her guilt over lying to him rendered her inarticulate, stopped up the speech that usually came so easily to her. And so what she said only made things worse.

"I can certainly understand if you're . . . if you're angry. I know that you blame the Queen's Guard and—and Queen Marianna for what happened to your family. Maybe me as well. I wish there were some way to bring them back. But I can't. I'd do almost anything not to have to confess this to you. You must feel that your trust has been violated."

Han opened his eyes and looked at her without moving any other part of his body. "Your mother is dead," he said. A statement.

"Yes," Raisa said.

"Good," he said, closing his eyes again.

They flew open again when Amon Byrne spoke from the doorway.

"Your . . . Rai . . . ah . . . would now be convenient?"

As he stumbled over her name, Raisa realized Amon didn't know if she'd told Han her true identity.

Amon's eyes shifted from Raisa to Han. He'd wanted to come with her when she'd told him she meant to tell Han Alister the truth.

I need to face him on my own, she'd said. *There are some things you can't protect me from.*

"He knows," Raisa said, twisting her hands in her lap. "So it's all right with me, but . . . Corporal Byrne wanted to speak with you, remember?" she said to Han. "Is that all right, or would you rather do it another time?"

Han scowled, and she thought he would refuse. After a long moment, he sighed, sitting up straighter. "Now is as good a time as any," he said.

Obviously, speaking with Amon was preferable to continuing to converse with her.

Amon came and stood at Han's bedside, shifting from one foot to the other. "Are you feeling better?" he asked.

"Sit down, Corporal Byrne," Han said, squinting up at him. "You're making me edgy, looming over me like a snub-devil bawler." The pain, betrayal, and vulnerability were gone. Replaced by his street face.

Raisa wondered if he were using the thief-lord patter flash on purpose, to needle her.

"Sit here, Amon," Raisa said quickly, getting up from her chair and retreating a few paces away. "I insist."

Amon sat, resting his hands on his knees. "I wanted to thank you for risking your life to save the Princess Raisa," he said.

"Just so you know," Han said, brushing his hand over his face, "I didn't actually set out to save a princess."

"I know," Amon said. "And I apologize for lying to you. We felt it was necessary for Her Highness's safety."

"Well," Han said, "it explains a lot. All this time, I was feeling sorry for you, having a flirt for a sweetheart. And here it turns out it was strictly business between the two of you."

His chilly blue-eyed gaze flicked from Amon to Raisa, and something about the mocking way he said it told Raisa that he didn't believe that at all. That he was smart enough to know their relationship was more tangled than that.

"Yes," Amon said, swallowing hard. "Strictly business." He kept staring at Han, his brows drawn together like he was puzzled about something. "There's something about you that's . . . that reminds me of . . ." He looked at Raisa, then shook his head, dismissing it.

"I hoped you could tell me more about my father's death," Amon went on. "The— Her Highness has told me what she knows."

Han's mocking expression faded, his features softened. "Captain Byrne was a brave man," he said. "And fair. My father was a soldier too. I don't remember much about him, but I'd like to think he was like your da." He paused as if gathering his thoughts. "I don't know that I can help much. Captain Byrne was already dead when I came along, and his killers had gone after—had gone. But I have something for you."

He turned a peeved expression on Raisa, as if aggravated that he was forced to speak with her. "Do you know what they did with my gear?"

"It's over here," Raisa said. She crossed to the outside wall, grateful for something to do.

Kneeling, she sorted through Han's belongings, and rose, cradling a deerskin bundle in her arms. "Was this what you wanted?"

Han nodded. "There should be a ring, too," he said. "In my purse."

Raisa handed the purse and the bundle to him.

Han fished in the purse and came up with the wolf ring. He looked up at Amon. "I took these because I was afraid someone else coming through the pass would steal them," he said, as if he thought he had to defend robbing Captain Byrne's body. "I hoped I might have the chance to give them to you."

He handed both the ring and the bundle over to Amon, who carefully unwrapped it, sliding the sword free.

Amon lifted the sword, turning it so the light reflected off the blade. It was the Sword of Hanalea, and it matched the dagger that Byrne had given Raisa.

Amon looked up at Han. "I know this sword," he said, his voice thick with emotion. "Queen Marianna gave it to my father. It was one of his most cherished possessions. I . . . it seems I need to thank you again."

Han waved off Amon's thanks. "Well, good. You can make use of it, then. Never learned to do much with a sword myself. Smaller blades are more my style, the kind you can hide." He fingered his sleeve to demonstrate, then dropped his hands into his lap.

"What about those that did the killing?" Amon said. "Do you know if—"

"All dead," Han said, meeting Amon's gaze without apology. "I hope that helps."

Amon nodded, looking relieved. "It does. It might keep the Princess Raisa safe a little longer."

Han shrugged his shoulders. "So. I'm sorry for your loss. The world can't afford to lose men like your father." He extended his hand, and Amon gripped it.

Well, at least *they're* getting along better, Raisa thought.

They all looked up at the sound of a disturbance in the outer room: a clamor of clan voices, Dancer's rising in protest.

"No! Don't go in there. Briar Rose is speaking with—"

Two people burst into the room without announcing themselves—Elena *Cennestre* and Averill Demonai. Trailed by Willo, Dancer, and Cat.

After a perfunctory nod at Raisa, Elena and Averill came and stood over Han, staring down at him as if he were an exotic specimen. He sat up a little straighter, arranging his bedclothes around himself. Raisa knew he felt vulnerable, pounded by her confession and now surrounded by his masters, the powerful clan royalty. She wished she could send them away, tell them to return in a week when he'd had time to recover.

But she couldn't. Events were bearing down on them relentlessly.

Willo must have felt the same, because she stood at a little distance, arms folded, looking like she wanted to expel the visitors, too.

"Well?" Elena said, looking at Fire Dancer and raising her eyebrows, gesturing toward Han. "Did it work? Will he be up to casting charms in the next few days?"

Dancer went still for a long moment, then sighed as if this were a question he didn't want to answer in front of Han. "It helped," he said finally. "I've been feeding Hunts Alone's amulet for two days. I think he is feeling better. Aren't you?" He looked at Han for corroboration, trying to include him in the conversation.

Han looked from Dancer to Elena, his expression momentarily perplexed. Then it cleared once again to a blank, flat expression. He slid his hand under his shirt and fingered his amulet, whether for comfort or possible defense, Raisa wasn't sure.

He said nothing.

Averill put his hand on Elena's arm and shook his head. "Elena *Cennestre*, please." He turned to Han and bowed, bringing his fist to his forehead, a clan greeting. "Hunts Alone, welcome to our hearth. Please share our fire and all that we have." He paused. "It is good to see you are feeling better," he said. "Because of your illness, I have not had the opportunity to thank you for saving my daughter's life. I owe you a debt of gratitude."

"We are eager to hear your story," Elena said. "If what Willo Watersong believes is true, it seems our investment in you has paid off."

"Has it?" Han said, looking from one to the other. "Then why don't we call it evens."

"This was just one battle," Elena said quickly. "The war is just beginning."

"Our immediate challenge is this," Averill said. "It is likely that those who tried to murder Queen Raisa will try again as soon as they realize they were unsuccessful. This is a very danger-ous time, from now through the coronation."

"The coronation?" Han looked over at Raisa, no trace of emo-tion on his face. "Oh. I get it. So she's not really the queen yet."

"She *is* the queen of the Fells," Elena said, glaring at Han, "by the rules of the Næming. But if she dies, the crown passes to her sister, Mellony. The queen's enemies believe Briar Rose is dead already. So those who tried to kill her will likely try to crown Mellony."

Han poured himself more tea. "So maybe Queen Raisa had better hurry back to the palace before they change the monograms on the silver."

"I agree," Raisa said. "I need to return to Fellsmarch before these plans get any further along."

Averill shook his head. "To be honest, based on what I have observed, it will be difficult to assure your safety if you return to the Vale now."

"Is it really that bad?" Raisa looked from her father to Elena. "I'm not a coward," she said. "I don't mean to hide out in the mountains while they crown my sister in my place."

"No one who knows you would call you a coward," Averill said. "But the reality is, your enemies have had nearly a year in which to grow their power unhindered. They've put allies and henchmen into positions of trust—in the Guard, in the army, in the palace. We will have to proceed carefully."

"Carefully, yes," Raisa said. "But I need to stand up to these people. It was running away that created this situation in the first place."

Averill put his hands on her shoulders and looked into her eyes. "Briar Rose, I've already lost Marianna. I don't want to lose you too."

"What happens next?" Han asked loudly, like he was impatient with this father-daughter heart-to-heart.

Averill turned back to Han. "The speakers have chosen

Queen Marianna's final resting place here in the Spirits, and the peak will be renamed to honor her. The coronation will be held after the queen's entombment. According to the recently revised provisions of the succession, Mellony will be crowned if Raisa is still missing at the time of the coronation."

He squatted to put his face at the same level as Han's. As a trader, persuasion was his specialty. "We need to let everyone know that the true heir has returned to the Fells. She needs to be seen and recognized by the people, by the Council of Nobles and the Wizard Council, so no one can claim otherwise. And we need to accomplish this without getting her killed." He smiled grimly. "It won't be easy. We'll all need to work together."

"The Princess Mellony is, for all intents and purposes, in the custody of our enemies," Elena put in. "The palace is under their control as well. So it will be difficult for Briar Rose to return there now."

"As consort to the late queen and father of the princesses, I am on the Council of Regents," Averill said. "But I'm just one voice. Lord Bayar is pressing for Mellony's coronation, sooner rather than later."

"What's the plan, then?" Han asked. He seemed to be making a point of ignoring Raisa.

"That is where we are hoping that you and Fire Dancer can help us," Averill said. "There was a time that the Demonai were more conversant with charmcaster talents, charms, and capabilities. Some of that knowledge has been lost. Perhaps we can discuss this over the next few days and arrive at a plan of action."

Han drew his knees up under the covers and wrapped his arms around them.

He's so young, Raisa thought. He's only—what—seventeen? Why is he having to make these kinds of decisions? Why am I?

She thought back to a scant ten months ago, when her biggest dilemmas revolved around whether to wear black or white or purple to the Bayars' name day party.

I was born to this, though, she thought. He has no money on the table. Except his own life.

"Where will the coronation be?" Han asked.

"Traditionally, it is held in the Cathedral Temple," Averill said. "It will be best if we can keep Raisa's presence here a secret until that time."

"I will attend my mother's memorial services and burial," Raisa announced.

Han's gaze brushed over her, then away again.

Averill winced. "Briar Rose, I know that you want to honor your mother," he began. "But it's just too dangerous. I know that she will understand if you—"

"Father, I have not been allowed to bathe and dress her body," Raisa said bitterly. "Nor hold vigil over her bier in the temple. I mean to be by her side as she greets our ancestors, the Gray Wolf queens. She will speak to them on my behalf, and introduce me as her successor. It is part of the ritual. It is part of the process that makes me queen."

Tears ran down Raisa's cheeks, and she blotted at them with the back of her hand. She'd kept her tears in check all through her conversation with Han. Now she was ambushed by grief and regret once again.

"There is so much I would like to say to her—that I wish I had said to her before," she said. "We parted in anger, and now that will never be resolved." She fisted her hands and extended to her full height. "You would demand to be there, Father, if you were me. The entire Wizard Council wouldn't keep you away. I will not have her committed to the flame without seeing her."

Raisa's father and grandmother looked at each other, seeming at a loss for how to handle their uncooperative queen-to-be.

"Why don't we make our final decision once we have an idea what the charmcasters can do," Elena said. She looked at Han. "Nightwalker will be back this afternoon. We'll meet after dinner tonight to determine whether—"

"Then you had better go and let this charmcaster rest," Willo said, nodding at Han. "Else you may be handling this problem all on your own."

"When is the burial?" Han asked abruptly.

"The burial service is scheduled for Sunday," Averill said. "Three days from now."

"I'm riding down to Fellsmarch today," Amon said. "I'm taking my father's ashes back to the capital to arrange for his burial. I'll speak with my cadets and find out the news. If you wait until tomorrow afternoon, I'll have more information."

Raisa glanced at him, surprised. She hadn't realized he planned to leave again so soon. "I would also like to attend Captain Byrne's memorial," she said.

"Perhaps you will," Amon said. "Please. Just give me until tomorrow."

"What will you say about your father's death?" Averill asked him, his face sympathetic. The elder Byrne and Averill had been friends, even though they had both been in love with Marianna. Relationships were complicated at court, but Averill the trader was a master at handling those complications.

"He and his triple were apparently attacked by a band of southern mercenaries on their way back to the capital," Amon said. "Everyone was killed."

"I'll ride down to the city with you," Averill said. "The Council of Regents is meeting tomorrow morning and I will need to be there to support you."

Elena nodded. "Thank you, Corporal Byrne. Take care along the way, both of you. We'll meet tomorrow afternoon, then." She sighed. "I wish things were different, Willo," she said softly, as close as she would get to an apology. "I wish we didn't have to fight wizards at a time when we are mourning so many losses."

Averill and Elena walked out together. Willo turned and looked pointedly at the rest of them, tapping her moccasined foot.

Dancer raised his hand. "Mother. Just give me a few minutes with Hunts Alone," he said. "Then I'll go." He sat down in the chair next to Han's bed, the one Amon had vacated.

"I'll stay too," Cat Tyburn said, settling in by the hearth. Raisa had almost forgotten she was there.

"Han," Raisa said softly. He didn't look up. "I just want you to know that—"

But he shook his head, raising both hands, palms out, as if pushing her out the door.

Raisa didn't want to go. She didn't want to leave Han with that awful, blank, lonely look on his face. But she, of everyone, had done the most to put it there.

She shrugged into her jacket in the outer room and walked out into the glittering sunlight with Amon. It had snowed again overnight, and she had to lift her skirts to keep them from dragging in the snow where it hadn't yet been beaten down.

"I feel sorry for Alister," Amon said. "I never thought I'd say that, but I do. There's a lot of pressure on him to come up with a plan. And if anything goes wrong, you know it'll be his fault."

Amon took Raisa's arm, pointing her back in the direction of the common lodge. "When I return from the city, I'll meet with him again to see how we can work together to keep you safe." They took a half dozen more steps, and he said, "It would be easier if you didn't attend your mother's memorial."

"I know. But I have to." She paused. "I wish you didn't have to ride down to Fellsmarch. Those who tried to kill me would likely seize any opportunity to make you disappear too. After everything that's happened, I don't want to let anyone I love out of my sight."

Amon's stride faltered. "That goes both ways, Rai," he said. "I'm responsible for your safety. But I can't do my job well if I'm constantly chained to your hip."

He looked ahead and made a face. Well, it was just a drawing together of eyebrows and a tightening of the lips, but Raisa knew Amon very well.

"Look who's here," he said. "No doubt you'll be in good hands now."

The market square was crowded with people. A group of riders was dismounting in front of the common lodge, surrounded by the usual gaggle of children and curiosity-seekers. Raisa recognized their horses—the best mountain ponies the clans could provide—and their distinctive winter travel garb. The unlidded eye glittered at their necks.

Demonai, Raisa thought, picking out Reid Nightwalker's tall frame among them. So these must be the warriors quartered in Fellsmarch, who had served as guard to her father.

Reid walked toward them, having handed off his horse to one of his comrades, a girl Raisa recognized as Digging Bird. She had been with the party of Demonai warriors that had rescued Raisa and Amon from Robbie Sloat and his renegade guards back the past summer. Now Digging Bird wore a Demonai amulet too.

"Your Highness!" Nightwalker said, in Clan, his relieved smile softening the honed planes of his face. "Or should I say, Your Majesty. I am relieved to see you up and walking around."

He bent his knee before Raisa, bringing his fist to his forehead, clan style. "The Demonai are ready to serve you, Briar Rose," he said, raising his head to look at her. "We will fight relentlessly against those who tried to murder you and who continue to endanger the realm." Clan always sounded more formal than Common.

Nightwalker came back to his feet, graceful as any predator. His braids glittered with owl feathers and bits of silver, and his jacket and leggings were embroidered over with subtle Demonai symbols. His winter travel cloak was sunlight and shadow on snow—nearly invisible in the forest.

One braid per wizard killed—that was the old rule of the Demonai. Most still went braided, centuries after the wizard wars supposedly ended.

"Good you're back from the city," Raisa said to Nightwalker. "I'm told it's a dangerous place these days."

The Demonai warrior shrugged. "I can look after myself," he said. "Even though there is no safety for uplanders anywhere within the Fells anymore." Reaching out, he put his fingers under Raisa's chin and tilted her face up, examining the fading bruises on her cheekbone. "Of course, I don't need to tell *you* that," he said. "When I saw what had been done to you, I wanted to lead a party of warriors onto Gray Lady and rid ourselves of this infestation of wizards for good." His voice shook a little, and it appeared to take some effort to regain his composure.

"We have to resist a rush to judgment," Raisa said. "While it's tempting to blame my mother's death on the gifted, we need better evidence before we—"

"We *do* have better evidence," Nightwalker interrupted. "We've learned something more about the queen's death."

Raisa gripped his arm. "What is it? What did you find out?"

Nightwalker shook his head, grimacing. "I should not have spoken prior to our meeting. It's actually Lord Averill's and Night Bird's news to share."

"Night Bird?"

Nightwalker nodded toward the warrior Raisa knew as Digging Bird, who was striding toward them from the pony corrals, a frown on her face. "Night Bird is her Demonai name," he said.

When Night Bird drew closer, her eyes fixed on Raisa, then went wide in recognition and surprise. The new warrior dropped to one knee before Raisa, her soft curls flopping forward as she bowed her head and brought her fist to her forehead. "Your Highness. I am sorry. I did not recognize you at first."

"Night Bird, I haven't forgotten your brave service at the turning of the leaves," Raisa said. "The Demonai warriors saved my life that day, and you played a major part."

Night Bird came back to her feet, seeming eager to escape the attention she was getting. "I am honored that you remember me." She shifted her eyes away and bit her lip, her cheeks pink under her coppery skin. "Please accept my condolences at the loss of your mother the queen." She seemed badly rattled for one who was usually so self-assured.

Raisa inclined her head. "Thank you. Congratulations on being named to the Demonai. In these dangerous times, I'm grateful to have warriors like yourself that I can trust."

Night Bird raised both hands as if to ward off the compliment. She looked almost stricken. "Thank you, Your Highness," she whispered through stiff lips.

Ah, Raisa thought. She's probably heard that Nightwalker and I have a history together, and she's wondering what my return will mean to their relationship. Though she had better get used to it. Nightwalker has been making history for years, throughout the uplands.

"Speaking of dangerous times," Nightwalker said, breaking into Raisa's thoughts, "Elena *Cennestre* tells me that Fire Dancer is here at Marisa Pines. Is that a good idea—to host two jinxflingers in camp at once? Especially given all that's happened already. I understood that Dancer was to stay in the flatlands and continue his studies when Hunts Alone returned home."

"I can't speak to that since I've just heard about this plan for the Demonai to train up wizards," Raisa said dryly.

"It was Lightfoot and Elena *Cennestre*," Nightwalker said. "They did it without my knowledge. I found out about it only by chance. Briar Rose, it is risky to recruit jinxflingers to fight jinxflingers. Fire Dancer should adhere to the bargain that was struck."

"My cousin Dancer is Marisa Pines bred," Night Bird said. "And that is the extent of his obligation."

Startled, Raisa and Nightwalker swiveled to face her.

"As son of the matriarch, Willo Watersong, Dancer doesn't answer to Elena *Cennestre* or Lord Averill," Bird went on. "Unlike Hunts Alone, he made no bargain with the Demonai. Although he's agreed to work with us, he does so on his own terms. When Fire Dancer learned that Hunts Alone had been recalled to the Fells, nothing I said could keep him in the flatlands."

"Then you should not have told Fire Dancer that Hunts Alone had been recalled," Nightwalker said, lips tightening in annoyance. "I still don't understand why you did that."

"I have known Fire Dancer since we were *lytlings*," Night Bird said, putting her hand on Nightwalker's arm. "I trust him. He is someone that we want to have on our side."

The girl *is* different than last time I saw her, Raisa thought. She's less bedazzled by Nightwalker. She's speaking up more.

"Under the terms of the Næming, wizards are not allowed in the Spirits," Nightwalker said. "It is an accommodation to have them here at all."

"Even though Hunts Alone saved my life?" Raisa said.

Nightwalker rolled his eyes. "If it's even true, then the jinx-flinger is merely keeping his end of the bargain."

"What do you mean *if it's true*?" Raisa shivered and pulled her jacket closer around her shoulders.

"Don't you think it's an odd coincidence that he just happened along when you were under attack?" Nightwalker said. "It's almost as if it had been planned that way. And what better way to win your trust?"

"What are you saying?" Raisa knew perfectly well what he was saying, but she wanted him to articulate it clearly.

"Is it really believable that he could pluck you away from a crowd of assassins and emerge unscathed himself?" Nightwalker shrugged as if to say, Believe what you will, but . . .

"He wasn't unscathed," Raisa retorted. "He used high magic to turn the poison. He's been deathly ill for days from the effects of it."

"Hunts Alone is ill?" Night Bird looked from Raisa to Nightwalker. "You didn't tell me that."

"There's not a mark on him, Elena says," Nightwalker said. "It's some mysterious jinxflinger illness, supposedly caused by the fact that he healed Briar Rose. It would be easy enough to fake."

"Perhaps you should speak to Willo, then," Raisa said acidly. "And explain to her how Hunts Alone fooled her so adeptly."

"I'm not saying he's lying." Nightwalker raised both hands. "I'm just saying it's a *possibility*. We should be wary of jinxflinger lies, especially given what's happened to the queen."

Amon spoke up for the first time. "Alister's illness seems authentic enough to me," he said. "It's my guess that he would be more than happy to leave the queen's service and have nothing to do with the fight that's coming. Those of us who are concerned about the safety of the Gray Wolf line will do everything in our power to make sure that doesn't happen."

"He stays," Nightwalker said, as if Han might try to weasel out of his obligation. "He doesn't have a choice. Now that we've trained him, he's committed to fight with us against the Wizard Council."

"There's always a choice," Amon said. "Alister goes his own

way. Don't underestimate him." He turned to Raisa and inclined his head. "By your leave, Your Highness. I'd best be going if I'm to be back by tomorrow afternoon."

Raisa nodded distractedly, and he walked away.

Nightwalker looked after him, frowning, then turned to Night Bird, his expression softening. "Night Bird, please see whether our quarters are assigned in the visitors' lodge and arrange for the ponies to be grained tonight. And, one more thing." He leaned close, speaking softly so Raisa couldn't hear. He smiled at Night Bird, and she smiled back, then walked away, a bounce in her step.

Well, she's still somewhat bedazzled, Raisa amended.

Nightwalker waited until she was beyond overhearing distance, then said to Raisa, "Corporal Byrne seems to believe Hunts Alone's story," he said.

Raisa had been surprised by Amon's defense of Han, but endeavored not to show it. "His father was murdered by the men who attacked me," she said. "If Corporal Byrne is convinced that Han is telling the truth, perhaps that should be evidence enough for you."

"Please don't be angry, Your Highness," Nightwalker said, smiling ruefully. "You know I have no love for wizards. I was raised to mistrust them, and nothing they've done while you've been away has allayed that mistrust. The situation has gone from bad to worse. No doubt you've heard that Queen Marianna changed the succession and set you aside."

"Well," Raisa said, her heart contracting painfully, "not exactly."

Nightwalker hesitated. "It is not proper or safe to speak ill of the dead, but I believe that was her intention. Perhaps she couldn't help herself—she was under the Bayar's influence. Or perhaps she was looking for an heir that looked more like a flatlander."

Raisa came up on her toes, seizing hold of the front of Nightwalker's coat, pulling his face down toward her. "You have no right to say that," she said fiercely, tears stinging her eyes. "You have no idea what my mother's intentions were."

Nightwalker reared back a little, focusing on Raisa's face as if truly seeing her for the first time. For a long moment, they stared at each other, Demonai warrior and princess heir.

"Briar Rose," he said finally. "Again, I am sorry. It seems that I have misjudged your feelings about the queen, especially after what happened a year ago. I need to listen more before I speak. This has been a difficult season for all of us."

"That's something we can agree on," Raisa said, releasing her hold on Nightwalker's front.

Nightwalker still seemed eager to explain himself. "You see, in recent months, there have been multiple jinxflinger raids on our villages on the lower slopes."

"Why would charmcasters attack the villages?" Raisa asked.

"The clans have cut off trade in magical objects—amulets, talismans, and the like," Nightwalker said, with grim satisfaction. "Our Demonai metalworkers no longer make them, having shifted production to other goods. Given their other actions, no doubt the wizards are preparing for war against us. They are hoping to spoil the villages and come away with enough magical weaponry to fill their armories."

"The villages wouldn't keep amulets on hand, would they?" Raisa asked. "What would they do with them? They're traded mostly at Marisa Pines."

"The jinxflingers don't know that," Nightwalker said. "There have been more and more incursions into the Spirits, more and more pressure from them. Lord Averill and I are endeavoring to provide better protection to the villages, but the Demonai are spread thin. So you can imagine how I felt when I heard about the attack on you. I'm sorry, Briar Rose, but I'm not in the mood to believe pretty words from jinxflingers."

"Has my father brought these issues up with the Queen's Council?" Raisa asked.

Nightwalker nodded. "Repeatedly. Lord Bayar excuses violations of the Næming, saying that the Spirit clans must resume production of flashcraft and make it freely available. He claims that under the circumstances bad jinxflinger behavior is understandable."

"Have the Demonai considered a compromise?" Raisa said. "Could you make some less-powerful amulets available to them?"

"Not when they are conspiring against you," Nightwalker said. "The last thing we want to do is arm our enemies prior to a war."

Once again, Raisa felt the crush of responsibility.

"I am sorry," Nightwalker said. "You have troubles enough to think about. All will be well—you'll see. I am glad you are recovering, and it is a relief to have you back in the mountain home. I'm looking forward to getting reacquainted." He brushed his knuckles lightly across her cheek, his eyes searching her face. "It's good to see you in clan garb again. It suits you."

"You're looking well also," Raisa replied. And it was true: Reid Nightwalker Demonai always turned heads when he walked through camp.

He smiled, meeting Raisa's eyes. "Right now, I'd better go and find Elena *Cennestre*." He paused. "Where will you eat tonight, Your Highness? Will you be at the visitors' hearth or . . . ?"

"I'll probably stay at Willo's hearth," Raisa said. "I'm still under her care, strictly speaking."

"So you are staying in the Matriarch Lodge?" When Raisa nodded, he said, "I will come to dinner, then. I would like to ask Willo about some treatments for laminitis in our ponies."

"Well, then, perhaps I will see you later," Raisa said.

She watched him walk away, toward the visitors' lodge, feeling as if she had a dozen fellscats on leashes snarling and snapping and going in different directions.

CHAPTER SIXTEEN

A WAY
FORWARD

Han waited until everyone else was gone, then said to Dancer, "Didn't you hear Willo? I need my rest." He closed his eyes and folded his hands across his chest, assuming a sleeping position.

"Hunts Alone," Dancer said. "Let me explain about Elena *Cennestre*."

"There's nothing to say," Han replied without opening his eyes. "Good the two of you were able to work out a plan to fix me up and get me back in fighting shape."

"We didn't work out a plan," Dancer said. "Willo was the one who suggested I might be able to help you heal by using flash. You and I both know Elena Demonai will bleed us dry if that's what it takes to keep wizards off the throne in Fellsmarch. She won't wait until you're healthy and fit to go forward. You can't go up against the Bayars in a depleted state."

Han said nothing.

"There's one thing Elena and I agree on—we don't want to

see wizard kings," Dancer went on, "especially not the Bayars. I'd
be willing to stand in for you, but I can't do what you do. We
took the same classes, and I've worked hard all year, but you've
gone beyond me. I'd like to think it's your amulet, but I don't
think so." He hesitated. "I think it's what you've learned from
Crow. And the way you're made."

"What makes you think I've gone beyond you?" Han said,
scrunching down in the bed. "If I have, it's likely because you've
been focusing on flash metalsmithing."

"I'm not being modest." Dancer shrugged. "We have different skills. I'm getting better and better at making tools, but that
won't help in the middle of a firefight." When Han said nothing,
he added, "You saved the Princess Raisa's life. I couldn't have
done that."

"It wasn't because I knew what I was doing," Han said.

"Even more impressive."

"And it wasn't because she's a princess," Han went on, slitting
his eyes and squinting at Dancer through his lashes.

Dancer brought up both hands. "I know."

"I hate bluebloods like her," Han said. "They put on Ragmarket clothes and go slumwalking, but underneath they're still
wearing We'enhaven lace and Tamron silk. For them it's an *experience*, like holding séances or smoking razorleaf. And when they
get back to the palace, they shed their slum clothes and climb into
the bath and wash you right off."

Han forced an image of Rebecca/Queen Raisa in her bath to
the back of his mind. He stowed it away with the image of Raisa
in We'enhaven lace and Tamron silk smallclothes.

"I tried to tell you not to get tangled up with her," Cat

said, startling him. Han had forgotten she was there. When Han frowned at her, she added, "You know. Back in Ragmarket."

"I'm not tangled up with her," Han said.

"Huh." Cat drew out a small blade—it looked like a new one—and began flipping and catching it.

Wishing Cat wasn't there to hear and comment, Han turned back to Dancer. "The thing is, it doesn't change them. They just keep going on being bluebloods. They think we're amusing, like monkeys in a traveling show. We're something to do for a day or two, when things slow down at the palace. Something to talk about at parties."

Han unstoppered the tea and took a long drink right from the jug. No point in working on his manners now.

Though he hadn't been doing it for her anyway. He'd been doing it for himself. Hadn't he?

"Eventually, they leave for good," he said, setting the jug down. "They don't care if they leave holes behind."

"You're the one who always leaves," Cat said. "Is that it?"

"It's not that," Han said. "She used me."

"How did she use you?" Dancer said. "By tutoring you? By kissing you? By—"

"Cuffs Alister pining after a princess," Cat interrupted. "Everybody always said you was ambitious."

"Cat," Dancer said, shaking his head.

Quit running on, Alister, Han thought. It wasn't like they'd walked out together. Much. Some shared kisses, some embraces, that was it. She'd never made him any promises. Except the implied promise—to be the person she claimed to be. To trust him enough to tell him the truth.

"She lied to me," Han said finally. "Everything between us was a lie."

"Good you never lied to her," Dancer said. "You told her exactly what you were doing there, and who was paying for your schooling, and what was expected of you after." Dancer raised an eyebrow.

"At least I never pretended to be anything other than what I am," Han said. "Girlies know what they're getting with me, so they can take or leave."

"Is that what you think?" Cat said, fists on hips, eyes narrowed. "Do you think it's that easy? It don't matter what a sweetheart says to you, it's what you believe." She paused, and added softly, "It's what you hope for."

That was exactly it—hope. Rebecca Morley had been the first good thing, the first true thing in his life since Mari had died. She represented possibilities; something he could aspire to. Something he might dream on—a future. Even though no promises had been made between them.

Unbidden and unwanted, a memory surfaced from that day in Oden's Ford when Han and the girl he knew as Rebecca had decided to walk out together. What she said that day came back to him, a warning that he only now understood.

I will hurt you too, even if I don't mean to. I'm not the girl you think I am. And you will remember this conversation and wish that you'd listened to me. How can you want this if you know from the beginning that it will end badly?

He'd been furious when he thought the Bayars had stolen his future from him. And then it turned out that his hopes were built on scummer and sand.

Now he knew that he had no future with Rebecca Morley. Rebecca Morley didn't exist.

He felt like a fool, like the victim of a cruel hoax. And he hated feeling like a fool.

She's tough for a blueblood, he'd thought, a lifetime ago. *Maybe tough enough to be with me.* He hadn't considered that he might not be tough enough to be with her.

"I like her," Dancer volunteered, as if he'd been following Han's thoughts. When Han glared at him, he shrugged. "I can't help it. I admit, I don't know her as well as you do. But we could do worse in a queen, and I think that's what we have to focus on. She has backbone—more than Marianna, I think."

"So the Fells has gained a better queen, while I've lost a . . . friend that I trusted," Han said, his voice low and bitter.

"From what I've seen, she cares about you, in spite of everything," Dancer said. "She just lost her mother, yet she's been looking after you every day since she left her own bed."

"I am *interesting*, no doubt," Han said, mimicking a blueblood tone. "Streetlord turned wizard. How *intriguing*. I *must* tell all my blueblood ladies. Maybe we can share around. I hear these gutter-bred tatterdemalions are lusty between the sheets."

Cat snorted, rolling her eyes, and Dancer laughed too. "Does she know you're very distant relatives?" he asked. "Hundredth cousins, or something?"

Han considered this. He didn't know what had been said out of his hearing, but Raisa hadn't mentioned it during the big reveal. Elena *Cennestre* and the others wouldn't be eager to highlight the fact that he himself carried Hanalea's blood. That he, in fact, might have a tenuous claim to the throne.

Hmmm. His mind raced off in extravagant directions. Ambitious directions, as Cat would say.

"What does he mean, you're related?" Cat asked, pulling Han back to the conversation. "Does he mean related to the queen?"

Han shook his head. "Never mind. It's nothing. We're probably all related to the queen."

"Anyway," Dancer said, "my thinking is this: I don't want us to die in a war between the clans and the Wizard Council. The only way to avoid a war is to keep the Wizard Council from using force to get what they want. That's going to be hard to do."

He flexed his hands. "They're probably feeling powerful right now, if what we think is true. They likely killed the queen, they think they killed the princess heir, and they're about to put their own candidate on the throne and marry her to a wizard. That will start a war with the clans for sure. We have to convince them to back off. The only way to do that is to persuade them that we have more firepower than they do."

Han was impressed with Dancer's reasoning. And ashamed. Given his feelings of betrayal, his impulse had been to do the minimum to keep his end of a bad bargain. It was no swag out of his pocket if Mellony ended up on the throne in the end. And a wizard king? He had no desire to see Micah Bayar as king of the Fells, but maybe it wasn't his business. Han had no business swimming in the blueblood lake anyway.

That's your problem, isn't it, Alister? Han thought. You thought *you* were the player. You thought you were the street-smart gang lord who knew how to take a warm mark. Who knew how to stare down a rival and take care of his own.

You just found out you were playing for the small bits. You

found out there are smarter, more ruthless streetlords in the world.

Han was badly wounded—in all ways. And his instinct was to withdraw from the cause of that pain.

He looked up at Dancer, who met his eyes directly. Cat and Dancer hadn't needed to return from Oden's Ford. They could have stayed there, snug and safe, while the Fells disintegrated into civil war. And once the war began, it was likely invaders would be up from the south to split the spoils. If things had been bad in Ragmarket and Southbridge before, what would it be like in the middle of a war? And if the Bayars won, how long would he, Han Alister, last?

He'd thought he had no money on the table, but he did, in fact.

As if he'd overheard Han's thoughts, Dancer said, "I will not let Lord Bayar win this. I'll die before I let that happen, and not because I've made any bargain with the Demonai. I'd like to have you with me in this fight, but if need be, I'll go it alone." Dancer's blue eyes burned with an intensity Han had never seen before.

"You won't be alone," Cat said, putting her hand on Dancer's arm. "Whatever Cuffs decides to do."

Han didn't have to play for Rebecca Morley, who'd gammoned him and lied to him, used him and made a fool of him. He could do it for pride, for reputation, for payback, and for Cat and Dancer, who would die alongside him if they didn't win.

He'd do it for himself while he licked his wounds and decided how to go forward from here. It would give him time to sort out his feelings about Rebecca. *Raisa*, he corrected himself. Avoiding her wouldn't help. He needed time with her, one-on-one. Time to figure out who she really was, and whether she'd been playing him for real.

Only this time he'd be more careful about giving his heart.

Han sighed. "All right," he said. "I'm in. All the way. I'm still angry, but I'm done sulking."

They nodded solemnly, eyes averted, as if not wanting to cause him further embarrassment.

"Cat," Han said. "Are you still crewing for me?"

Cat eyed him suspiciously, then nodded. "I swore to you, didn't I?"

"Good. Corporal Byrne and Averill Demonai are riding back to Fellsmarch this afternoon. I want you to go with them."

Cat's looked from Dancer to Han. "What? You want me to go off with a bluejacket and a copperhead? What do you take me for?"

"Do you want to help me or not? Remember what I said? That you couldn't just do the jobs you liked?"

Cat nodded grudgingly. "I remember. But who's going to keep an eye on you up here?" She swept her hand wide. "I don't trust any of them."

"I don't have people to spare. You know the city, and I need eyes and ears there." When Cat still looked uncertain, he added, "I wouldn't send you if it wasn't for a reason. I want you to go back to Ragmarket and get set up there again, like you said."

"What do you mean, get set up?" Cat asked.

"See if the clamor's died down. It should have—the Bayars have other worries, and last they knew I was in Oden's Ford. I know you said all the Raggers are dead, but see if somebody didn't get overlooked, if you can get a crew together again."

Cat stared at him. "What kind of crew do you want? Rushers or slide-handers or lock-charmers or runners or what?"

"I need rum divers and dubbers, girlies and coves that can amuse the law. More important, I want quality, people we can trust—just a handful's enough to start." He jerked his chin toward his pile of belongings. "Take my purse and give whacks out of that. I expect we'll be in the city inside of a week."

Cat sorted through his things and held up his purse. "You sure you want me to take all of this?"

Han nodded. "The clans'll be good for more."

"You want me to say who's streetlord?"

Han thought a moment. "Tell them my street name's the Demon King. Here. I'll show you the gang sign." Cat handed him a charred stick from the hearth, and Han scratched out a symbol on the hearthstone—a vertical line with a zigzag across it. "Call it the staff and flash," he said. "Say I've got uptown connections but nasty enemies," he went on. "Tell them not to come in if they're quivery."

"Got it," Cat said.

"Now, here's the first thing I want you to do." He paused, staring at the hangings dividing the sickroom from the common room. Had he seen them twitch?

Bones. He should have put up magical barriers, but that hadn't occurred to him, here in the camp. In his current condition he wasn't sure that was even possible.

He motioned to Dancer, nodding toward the divider. Dancer silently rose, crossed to the divider, and yanked the curtains aside.

The common room was empty.

"Maybe I'm still a little whimsy-headed," Han said, "but

come in closer." Lowering his voice further, he said, "Cat, tell everybody on both sides of the river that the bluebloods mean to take the throne away from the Briar Rose. Tell them to come to the queen's funeral and let the gentry know what they think of that. Do you think you can get that done before the queen's burial on Sunday?"

Cat nodded.

"And you be careful yourself. If it's still hot, lay low. I don't want to lose you. I'll see you at the memorial and we'll go from there." Han tipped his head toward the door. "Better go or you'll miss Corporal Byrne."

Dancer walked Cat to the door. They stood there for a long moment, whispering together. Dancer reached out and brushed back a stray lock of Cat's hair. Then they embraced, Cat coming up on her toes as they kissed.

Envy shivered through Han. How long, he wondered, before he could fill the gaping hollow in his middle where his hopes had lived?

He shook it off, trying to focus on making plans. He'd meet with Raisa and the clan royalty tomorrow. And tomorrow night he'd visit Crow for a heart-to-heart.

CHAPTER SEVENTEEN
THE GAMES
BEGIN

Amon Byrne preferred the most dangerous roads in the Seven Realms to navigating the even more dangerous political mazes at court. He was not blessed with the ability to lie easily and glibly, to beguile others with his wit and persuasion. He was not adept at the kind of speech that prettied up ugly things—the kind that convinced others to act against their own interests.

Most of the time, it didn't bother him. He had confidence in his other talents. He'd worked hard at developing his strengths so that he could put them at the disposal of his queen and country. Most of the time he managed to avoid getting into jams he had to talk his way out of.

But now he was confronted with a situation that would require a complex stint of lying to an audience that knew varying bits of the truth.

He waited in the anteroom outside the queen's audience chamber. He'd spent his boyhood in the castle close, so the surroundings were familiar. The politics were not. It had taken most of the morning to determine who could grant the permission he requested. The court being between queens, the government was in turmoil.

Amon touched the wolf ring on his right hand, which had become a habit. It settled him.

The chamberlain poked his head out of the doorway. "Corporal Byrne?" he said. "They are ready for you."

When Amon walked into the familiar audience chamber, he saw that the queen's throne had been draped with black. He was glad to see that nobody was sitting on it. Yet.

They'd set up a kind of alternate arrangement at the other end of the room, a rather elaborate raised chair with other chairs clustered around it on a riser. This would be the Council of Regents, made up of Gavan Bayar, the High Wizard; Bron Klemath, General of the Highlander Army; Lassiter Hakkam, the head of the Council of Nobles; Raisa's father, Averill Demonai, representing the Spirit clans; and Roff Jemson, now speaker of the Cathedral Temple.

The side walls of the audience chamber were lined with blue-jacketed guards, most of whom Amon didn't know. That was alarming. With a jolt, he realized that, as Raisa's captain of the Guard, he actually commanded them, but right now they seemed more of a threat than a support. He hadn't been gone from the capital so long that there should have been such a dramatic turn-over of palace guards.

Posted closest to the council members was sharp-featured Mason Fallon, with his ink-black hair and permanent beard shadow. Amon didn't know Fallon well, but he'd never trusted him. Now Fallon wore a corporal's scarf. When had that happened, and who had authorized it?

Amon was cheered by the sight of Jemson. There was one friendly face, at least, besides Averill. Jemson had presided over the ceremony that had linked Amon and Raisa as captain and queen-to-be, before they'd left for Oden's Ford. So the speaker was keeping secrets of his own.

Sitting on a level with the council members was Micah Bayar, who had no official role and shouldn't have been there. Was he there by his father's choice? Or by Mellony's?

Amon scanned the others. He'd never been fond of Klemath, and Klemath had no love for the Byrnes. There was a natural competition between the elite Queen's Guard and the regular army, and Amon's father, Edon Byrne, had made no secret of his opinion that the army should rely less on mercenaries and more on native soldiers. And recently, it seemed that Klemath had allied himself with the Wizard Council on many issues.

Klemath had set his sons, Keith and Kip, after Raisa, hoping to rise by marrying into royalty. Now he might be hoping for a match with Mellony, assuming the Bayars had kept him in the dark about their marriage plans.

Lassiter Hakkam was as slick as most nobles, dressed in expensive clothes in the latest style. He was clever, but in Amon's opinion, not particularly smart. Hakkam was uncle to Raisa, father to Melissa and Jon. They'd never had much use for Amon, since he was a commoner.

Gavan Bayar wore black wizard robes, his stoles draped over his shoulders, embroidered with the familiar Bayar falcons, his amulet in prominent display overtop. He looked down at Amon, his gaze sharp and calculating, as if Amon were a haunch of roast meat he was prepared to carve.

Micah mirrored his father, in black robes and falcon stoles, his skin chalky against his black mane of hair. He leaned forward almost eagerly, black eyes fixed on Amon as if he thought Amon might bring important news.

Averill was finely dressed in trader style, his Demonai talisman a challenge to the Bayars and their wizard amulets. He wore white, the mourning color of the Spirit clans. This made him stand out against the others like a dove amid crows.

Amon couldn't help thinking that those in mourning black resembled a flock of carrion birds ready to pick over his bones.

The Bayars bracketed Raisa's sister, Princess Mellony, who occupied the ornate chair at the center. Though they hadn't dared to actually seat her on the throne, they might as well have. She was already taller than Raisa, but she looked to Amon's eyes like a little girl in a big chair.

Mellony had always been frillier than Raisa, even when they were small. But the gown she wore today was intended to make her look older, to make her fit the role that some intended her to play.

To look like a queen of marriagcable age.

She's thirteen, he thought. Almost fourteen. Her gown was of mourning black and simply cut, showing off her fair skin and blond hair. The tip of her nose was faintly pink under the powder, and her eyes showed evidence of weeping. Today, dressed and made up as she was, she looked to be sixteen. Queen Marianna's diamonds sparkled at her neck and wrists.

She's already dressing the part, Amon thought bitterly. He'd always thought of Mellony as lightweight and insubstantial, but . . . was it possible she'd played a role in clearing the path to the throne?

Stop it, he said to himself. You're biased. You always will be in favor of Raisa. Mellony had always been close to her mother. It made sense that she'd want to wear the queen's jewels now.

Amon came forward and knelt before Mellony, bringing his fist to his chest. "Your Highness," he said. "Please accept my con-dolences for your loss, a loss we share as a nation in mourning."

That wasn't bad, he thought. He'd rehearsed it all morning.

"And accept my sympathy for your loss also, Corporal Byrne," Mellony said, in a clear, high voice. "A loss we feel almost as keenly as you do. This is a dreadful time, is it not?" She gestured with a glittery hand for him to rise. "Please. Sit. The Byrnes are our friends and loyal servants. They are welcome to sit in our presence."

Amon guessed that someone must have coached her on the royal "we."

A chair was produced for Amon, and he settled into it awk-wardly. Since he was off the dais, everyone was still looking down at him.

"Welcome back to court, Corporal Byrne," Lord Bayar said. "I was surprised to hear that you'd returned to the Fells. I had thought you were still at the academy. How did you come to hear of your father's death?"

"I was, in fact, already en route, Lord Bayar," Amon said. "My father had asked me to delay my schooling and return home, given the situation here. I only wish I had come sooner."

"The situation here?" Bayar asked. "What, specifically, do you mean? Did you have a particular reason for concern?" He paused. "A concern about the queen, perhaps?"

Amon wasn't sure where this was going, but he could feel danger thickening the air, and hear the throb of his heartbeat in his ears.

"We were concerned about Gerard Montaigne's activities in Tamron," Amon said. "He has a very large army. Once he stabilizes his hold on Tamron, we're guessing he might come north."

It seemed this wasn't the answer Bayar expected. He gazed at Amon, unblinking, for a long moment, then nodded, seeming pleased. "Precisely. Naturally, we share your concern."

General Klemath leaned forward. "I'm surprised that your father felt it necessary to call you home for that reason. Protection of our borders is the responsibility of the army. With the help of the Council of Wizards, of course."

"Aye," Amon said. "But if Montaigne comes north, our place is here. The royal family will need extra protection so the army can focus on its job." He paused. "I see that Micah has returned home early as well. Perhaps for the same reason?" He gazed at Micah, hoping his face didn't betray him. At least the two of them—maybe Lord Bayar as well—knew Micah had kidnapped Raisa from Oden's Ford and come north with her, only to lose her along the way.

With any luck, the Bayars didn't know he knew.

"I returned because I believed that at this point in time, I could be helpful here," Micah said. "And because there were some, here at court, that I missed." He smiled at Princess Mellony, and she blushed and lowered her eyes.

Once again, suspicion pinged at Amon.

"I'd hoped to find the Princess Raisa here when I returned," Amon said. "Has there been any word from her?"

"No," Micah said. "The princess heir is still missing." He looked at his father as he said it, his expression unreadable.

"Surely there has been some news of her whereabouts," Amon persisted, watching Micah's face. "I've been away at Oden's Ford, but I assumed that—"

"There has been no trace or word of the princess heir since she fled the queendom in the autumn," Lord Bayar said. His gaze flicked to Micah—a warning. Micah's lips tightened, and he said nothing.

So that was to be the story. Neither Queen Marianna nor the Bayars had told Mellony that her sister had been located in Oden's Ford. They wouldn't mention that Micah and Fiona had lost Raisa in Tamron while bringing her back to Fellsmarch. It would be easier to set her aside if she hadn't been seen or heard from since she disappeared nearly a year ago.

Amon looked from father to son, wondering what Micah had told his father about Raisa. Micah lifted his chin and returned Amon's gaze, as if daring him to say more. He must suspect that Amon had helped Raisa flee to Oden's Ford, that they'd been together there. But any admission of that would expose them both to charges of treason, and Micah knew it.

"Oh, I miss Raisa!" Mellony said, swiping at her eyes. "Now more than ever, we should be together. We have sent birds and messengers all over the Seven Realms," she added, her voice trembling. "I know my sister would be here for our mother's funeral if she could be." She drew in a shuddering breath. "I do fear the worst."

The Seven Realms are at war, Amon thought. Communication is disrupted. How could you think that Raisa would receive a message even if you sent it? But he didn't say that aloud. He knew he was on precarious ground. If he left Raisa's enemies with the impression that he would not play along, he would never make it out of the city alive.

"How long have you been back, Corporal Byrne?" Lord Bayar asked, fingering the elaborate ring he wore on his right hand.

Amon heard a trap in the question, but wasn't sure which way to step to avoid it. "I arrived in Fellsmarch a few days ago from the West Wall," he said. "I was here when word came about my father. I immediately left for Marisa Pines Camp."

"The Demonai found Captain Byrne's party in the pass. All dead," Averill said.

"All dead?" Mellony blurted. "What about the brigands who attacked him? Do we know who they were?"

"No, Your Highness," Amon said, excruciatingly aware of the Bayars to either side of the princess. He kept his eyes downcast, knowing his limitations as a liar.

"It's unlikely we will ever know exactly what happened, since his entire party was killed," Lord Averill said. "His attackers have probably already crossed back into Tamron."

"I hope that we in the Guard can work with General Klemath to fortify our borders against further encroachments from the south," Amon said. He looked to the general, and received a chilly nod in return.

"If his murderers are identified, we will show no mercy," Princess Mellony said fiercely.

"Have you considered the possibility that the Demonai themselves may be to blame?" Lord Bayar asked, as if Averill were not sitting there. "Relationships with the copperheads have been strained of late. There are some who suspect that they may have had a hand in the Princess Raisa's disappearance."

Careful, now, Amon thought. He glanced at Averill Demonai, whose trader face slipped a little.

"That seems unlikely, sir," Amon said, turning back to Lord Bayar. "My father and the other guards were killed with crossbow bolts and blades. Not Demonai weapons."

"Anyone can pick up a crossbow," Lord Bayar said.

"The strained relations you mention are a direct consequence of jinxflinger incursions into the Spirit Mountains and attacks on our upland villages," Averill said. "While the Demonai have ample cause to move against wizards, it is difficult to fathom what motive the Demonai would have to murder Captain Byrne and his party. In fact, the Demonai honored Captain Byrne last night at Marisa Pines with a warrior service. That is extraordinarily rare, given that he was a Valesman."

"I've not seen proof that wizards are responsible for the attacks you keep complaining about," Lord Bayar said. "Nor convincing evidence that they've actually happened. We in the Wizard Council suspect that they are simply an excuse to continue the interdiction on flashcrafting."

Both Averill and Bayar were like actors speaking lines for their audience and not to each other.

Lord Bayar waited, and when Averill said nothing, he changed the subject. "I think we can agree that Captain Byrne was a brave and capable commander. Still, it's unfortunate that he left the queen unprotected, seemingly at a critical time." Bayar straightened his stoles. "I've not yet heard a good explanation for his leaving court."

Amon stiffened but, of course, had no answer for Lord Bayar, since he couldn't very well tell the High Wizard that his father had gone south to help smuggle the princess heir back into the queendom; that Byrne had hoped Raisa's presence would help strengthen Marianna against the influence of the High Wizard.

Averill gazed coldly at Bayar. "I have complete confidence that whatever Captain Byrne was doing, it was in service to the Gray Wolf line," he said.

"We will probably never know exactly what happened," Mellony said, breaking into the argument. "I'm sure this is a difficult subject for Corporal Byrne, with his father not yet buried." She leaned forward. "I was told you had a boon to ask, Corporal Byrne. Please, speak freely."

She's generous, Amon thought. Now that the crown is within her grasp.

Gavan Bayar sat forward, his hand on his amulet, eyeing him like he might strike him dead if he said the wrong thing.

"I do have a request," Amon said. "It is unusual, but I hoped that you might grant it in light of my father's long service to Queen Marianna."

"Anything," Mellony said quickly, then wilted under Lord Bayar's glare. "If we possibly can, Corporal Byrne, we shall," she amended.

"I would like to ask that my father's ashes be buried near his liege queen, on Marianna Peak," Amon said. At Mellony's puzzled expression, he rushed on, "Not—not beside her or anything. Perhaps somewhere nearby, maybe at the foot of her tomb, somewhere he can continue to watch over her in death as he did in life."

"Oh!" Mellony rose in a swish of silk, hands clasped in front of her, the tears pooling in her eyes. "Oh, that's so romantic. To think of Captain Byrne watching over his queen forever."

"Don't you Byrnes have a tomb in the Cathedral Temple?" Lord Bayar said, seemingly unmoved by romance. "Wouldn't it be more proper to bury your father next to your mother?"

"Aye, Lord Bayar, it would seem so," Amon said, looking the wizard in the eyes. "But my mother would understand. She knew when she married my father of the special bond between queen and captain. A bond that goes from life to death."

Lord Bayar scowled. Amon guessed that the High Wizard instinctively wanted to deny the request, but could think of no good reason to do so. "Speaker Jemson," Bayar said. "You will oversee Her Majesty's memorial service. You are in charge of maintaining the old traditions. Doesn't this seem ... disrespectful?"

Jemson templed his fingers together and considered this, his expression solemn. "I am well aware of the bond between queens and captains," he said finally, his face betraying nothing. "I would have no objection if that is what both families desire."

"Lord Demonai?" Lord Bayar turned to Averill. "As consort to the queen, I would think you might question the propriety of—"

"I am not at all threatened by Captain Byrne's ashes, Lord Bayar," Averill said. "I have never had reason to question Captain Byrne's loyalty nor the nature of his regard for the queen." The look he leveled at Gavan Bayar could have frozen the Dyrnnewater.

Mellony smiled damply. "I think my mother, the queen, would be pleased to know that her captain sleeps nearby," she said, sitting again.

Micah covered her hand with his own, leaned over and whispered something in her ear. She blushed and whispered something back.

"Thank you, Your Highness," Amon said, trying to ignore the display. He wanted nothing more than to get out of there. He much preferred the mean streets of Southbridge to the connivery at court. He'd gotten what he wanted, after all—a chance to survey the burial site ahead of time and an excuse to be in the thick of things at the memorial.

"With your permission, then, Speaker Jemson and I will walk the burial site later today and make a decision about my father's rites and the placement of his grave." Amon rose and bowed. "If I may, I'll take my leave."

"Not so fast," Lord Bayar said.

Amon froze in place, not looking up.

"Corporal Byrne, the Council of Regents must request a little more of your time," the High Wizard said. "Please, sit."

CHAPTER EIGHTEEN

A WEB OF LIES

Amon sat down again, endeavoring to keep his face as blank as new snow while his heart hammered under his uniform coat. He looked up and met the High Wizard's cold blue eyes.

"While it is difficult to look beyond our recent losses and Queen Marianna's burial, we must consider the issue of the coronation," Bayar said.

"The coronation, sir?" Amon said. He glanced at Princess Mellony, then back at Lord Bayar.

"As you astutely pointed out, our enemies are gathering to the south," Lord Bayar said. "Have you heard the news? Tamron Court has fallen to Gerard Montaigne."

Amon shook his head. "No," he said, pretending surprised dismay. "I hadn't heard that."

"We cannot afford to leave our throne unoccupied for long," Bayar said. "It will be perceived as a power vacuum that our enemies to the south will be only too happy to fill. Montaigne may decide that it's easier to conquer the Fells than to continue fighting against his brothers."

"I can see where that might happen," Amon said truthfully.

"Given the princess heir's extended absence, Queen Marianna made a difficult decision," Lord Bayar said. "She modified the succession, recognizing that the Princess Raisa might never return home. She named the Princess Mellony her successor in the event that . . . that the throne became vacant and the Princess Raisa could not be located," he finished delicately. He shook his head. "None of us ever anticipated that this alternate plan would ever be needed."

"Raisa may still return," Mellony said, a faint protest. "I don't want anyone to think that we're setting her aside."

"That is exactly what people will think, daughter, the Demonai in particular," Averill said. "That is one reason I voted against it on the council."

"This is difficult for the Princess Mellony to accept," Lord Hakkam said, speaking up for the first time. "But, in recognition of the current crisis in Arden and Tamron, the Council of Regents has determined that if the Princess Raisa does not return for Queen Marianna's memorial service, we must proceed with Princess Mellony's coronation."

Amon wished he could watch all the faces at once so as not to miss anything. He looked first at Speaker Jemson. The speaker's face was smooth and untroubled. He was a smart man. He probably knew the price of resistance as well as Amon.

Mellony somehow managed to look both guilty and thrilled. Unconsciously, she reached down and stroked Micah's hair as if it were a talisman. She'd never hoped to be queen, Amon thought.

She likes the idea. And she knows in her secret heart that it will win her Micah.

"Is it really so urgent?" Amon said finally, trying to sound as if this were interesting news that had little to do with him. "It seems like you have a little time before Montaigne regroups. The siege of Tamron Court must have taken a toll. And if he wants to march through the mountains, he'll have to wait for better weather. As far as I know, he has no experience with mountain warfare."

"And yet you just said that you returned home because of the risk Montaigne poses," Lord Bayar said, pouncing on Amon's words like a trout on a fly. *You can't have it both ways*, his expression said. "I don't think it's wise to underestimate Montaigne. Look what happened to the Tomlins."

"I can see why you would not want to leave the throne vacant for long," Amon said. "But what happens if the Princess Raisa returns at a later time?" He could feel Micah Bayar's black-eyed gaze on him.

Lord Hakkam shrugged. "There is no provision to . . . rearrange matters should that happen," he said. "You must admit, it was irresponsible of her to run off like that, without a word to anyone."

That was either brave or foolhardy on Hakkam's part, to call the princess heir of the realm irresponsible. Still, Amon could see how the nobility would take a dim view of Raisa's disappearance. They'd not been told that it had been precipitated by the prospect of a forced marriage to a wizard. They'd likely been told that Raisa'd had a spat with the queen and stormed off in a huff. The Gray Wolf line was known to be headstrong. Look at Hanalea.

Amon knew that was all he could do, to try to raise a doubt, to try to slow things down. But why would they tell Amon Byrne about their plans for the coronation? Unless—if Raisa still lived, and Amon knew where she was, they would expect him to rush back and tell her. And that might flush their quarry before she could cause real trouble.

So he sat, saying nothing, waiting to be dismissed, wondering what to say to Raisa, and how to prevent his own headstrong queen from doing something foolhardy.

"Queen Mellony will need a captain of her guard," Lord Bayar said, wrenching him back to the present.

Oh.

Queen Mellony. The sound of it made Amon's skin itch.

"Aye," he said, nodding sagely. "That's so." He knew he sounded like a dolt, but he wasn't going to make the offer. His mind worked furiously. Raisa had been right, as she usually was about political matters. *Say yes*, she'd said. *Say yes, or it will be your death warrant.*

"I would be honored, Corporal Byrne, if you would consent to be captain of my guard," Mellony said, smiling at him.

Amon was glad Raisa had warned him, glad he hadn't been blindsided. The Bayars knew that the Byrnes stood in the way of their complete control over their chosen queen. So why would they go along with the selection of a Byrne as captain?

Raisa had suggested one reason: the Bayars knew the elevation of Mellony to the throne would be controversial. They would want to add any legitimacy to it that they could. If a Byrne consented to be captain, as tradition demanded, that would make her more credible.

The second possibility was that they really took him to be a fool.

The third possibility was that they wanted to keep him close and under their watch so they could handle him if he showed any signs of being uncooperative.

It was hard to keep in the front of his mind who knew what secrets.

Amon realized he was thinking on it too long, when they were all waiting for his response.

"I—I'm flattered, Your Highness," Amon said. "But surprised as well. Though I've been nearly four years at Oden's Ford, I'm still a cadet. I'm just eighteen. I would have expected you to choose someone with more schooling and experience."

"Come, now," General Klemath snapped. "You can't be that surprised. It's always been a Byrne, ever since the Breaking."

He doesn't seem happy about it, either, Amon thought. Perhaps he thought one of his idiot sons would be tapped for the post.

"We believe that character and bloodlines are more important than training and experience," Mellony said, smiling.

"Unless you prefer we name your sister Lydia or your brother Ira," Lord Bayar said.

Bones, Amon thought. He was surprised Lord Bayar knew he had a sister and brother. He didn't like that he knew it. Naming Lydia was a possible out for them. She was an artist, without training as a soldier. Although still a Byrne, she would be less of an obstacle to Bayar ambition. It would put Lydia in danger and would not offer much protection to the queen.

And Ira was eleven years old. He wouldn't go to the academy for two more years.

"General Klemath, you are right," Amon said. "I should have anticipated it. It's just—things are shifting so quickly, it's hard to keep up. I expected to have years in the Guard to prepare. With the tragic loss of the queen, and then the loss of my father—it will just take a while to get used to the idea, I guess."

Bayar's expression said *Don't take too long.*

"Corporal Byrne," Mellony said. "We have this in common: we are both thrust into roles we never expected. We can learn together, you and I."

Amon nodded. "I hadn't thought of it that way."

That's exactly what we don't need, Amon thought. A young, malleable, inexperienced queen and a green captain of the guard.

"So you agree?" Mellony said, leaning forward eagerly, the child unwilling to be denied.

Amon inclined his head. "Yes," he said. "I would be honored to serve as Captain of the Queen's Guard, Your Highness." After all, he already was, in fact.

Lord Bayar studied him for a long moment, then nodded, seeming satisfied. "Good." He looked at Speaker Jemson. "Isn't there some sort of religious ceremony?" he said, with clear disinterest. "Will you be handling that?"

Speaker Jemson nodded. "Typically, it takes place at the time of the coronation," he said. "I will prepare for that, along with the rest."

Jemson is a fair liar, for a dedicate, Amon thought.

"Thank you, Corporal Byrne," Lord Bayar said, dismissing him. "This Regent's Council meeting is adjourned."

Amon rose and backed away, bowing, but they were no longer paying attention to him. Mellony climbed down from her high chair and stood, chatting animatedly with Micah. As Amon watched, the young wizard slid an arm around Mellony's shoulders and drew her in for a kiss.

Amon didn't look forward to sharing all this news with Raisa.

"Corporal." Amon flinched and looked up to find Jemson next to him. "I am riding up to Marianna Peak now to observe the preparations. Why don't you come along? We can make some decisions and you can get the lay of the land."

"Yes, thank you, I will," Amon said, yanking his attention away from Mellony and Micah.

Speaker Jemson followed his gaze. "It seems we have our work cut out for us, doesn't it?"

Amon had to agree.

By the end of the day, Amon was physically and mentally exhausted. The Gray Wolves had accompanied Amon and Jemson to Marianna Peak, since Amon meant to use them as part of the honor guard for his father. Whatever the final plan, he wanted soldiers on hand he could trust during the memorial. His Wolves were all native-born, except for Pearlie Greenholt, who had come north with Talia, leaving her post as weapons master at Wien House. She had taken Wode's place in Amon's triple after Wode was killed in Tamron.

They walked the burial ground, and Amon took notes and made sketches. His father's urn would not take much space, so there was no need to chop a deep grave out of the still-frozen ground. He spoke to the stone carvers about an appropriate monument. All the while, he racked his brain, looking for a safe way to bring Raisa in and out of the site without exposing her to those who would be eager to finish the job they'd started.

When they returned to Fellsmarch, Amon debriefed his

Wolfpack again, giving them preliminary instructions for the day of the memorial. They wouldn't know about the Princess Raisa until the very last minute. He trusted his Wolves, but the fewer who knew, the less chance word would leak out.

He left the urn containing his father's ashes with Speaker Jemson. It would rest in state in the Cathedral Temple until the memorial service, when Amon and his Wolves would accompany it to the burial site.

He managed a late dinner with his brother Ira and his sister Lydia and her family. Three years older than Amon, Lydia was recently married and expecting a child. She and her husband, Donnell Graves, a merchant, had rented a home within the castle close, since many of her painting commissions came from the wealthy nobility who lived in the area. With their father gone, Ira would move in with Lydia until it was time for him to leave for the academy.

Lydia would have preferred to bury their father next to their mother in the Byrne tomb in the cathedral close, but it would not be the first time she had sacrificed her desires to the good of queen and realm.

There was much to talk about—memories and grief to share—and they were reluctant to let him go. As a result, it was quite late when Amon fetched his horse from the barracks stable for the long ride back to Marisa Pines. As he led the gelding through the stable doors into the courtyard, he saw movement in the shadows next to the building.

Amon assumed it was one of his fellow guards, staying late from the previous shift or early for the next. "Who goes there?" he called softly.

But the tall spare figure who stepped into the light was not one of the Queen's Guard.

"What are you doing here?" Amon asked, sliding his sword free, but keeping it pointed toward the ground.

Micah Bayar came forward, hands raised, palms out, to show that he was not touching his amulet. "Relax, Corporal Byrne, I mean you no harm. I just wanted to talk to you."

"That's a shame, Bayar, because I don't want to talk to you," Amon said, sorting through what he did and didn't know, and what he could and couldn't admit to. "Have you been waiting for me all this time?"

Micah nodded. "I looked for you at the barracks, but it seems you aren't staying here." He paused. When Amon said nothing, he said impatiently, "Why aren't you in the barracks? Where are you staying?"

"It's crowded in the barracks. Too many new faces. And it's none of your business where I'm staying." Amon wanted to mount up, but he knew that would make him vulnerable to a magical attack. "Now, if there's nothing else . . . ?"

Micah stepped into the gateway leading out of the courtyard, blocking the way. "I want to know if you've heard from the Princess Raisa, and if you know where she is."

"The Princess Raisa?" Amon assumed a perplexed expression. "How would I know where she is? You heard what I said at the Council of Regents meeting. I've been at Oden's Ford all this while, same as you."

Micah's eyes narrowed. "Don't lie to me. I know you took her to Oden's Ford. I know you had her hidden away there."

Amon snorted. "Let me get this straight: you think the princess heir of the realm ran away with a fourth-year cadet and has been living at a military academy for nearly a year?" Some devil within him made him add, "Why would she do such a thing . . . unless she was absolutely desperate to get away?"

Micah scowled at the dig. "I know she was at Oden's Ford because I saw her," he said.

"If you say so," Amon said. "Then maybe she's still there. Unless you know something I don't." He paused, wondering if Micah would actually confess to kidnapping Raisa. When Micah said nothing, Amon added, "Why do you care where she is? Looks to me like you're . . . ah . . . *supporting* the Princess Mellony." Amon raised an eyebrow.

"If the Princess Raisa is still alive, she should be crowned queen," Micah said.

Amon eyed Micah, trying to read his face in the inconsistent light. "Well, now, Bayar," he said. "You finally hit on something we can agree on."

"If you know where she is, you need to get word to her," Micah continued. "She has to be at Queen Marianna's funeral. Once Mellony is crowned, it will be too late."

"I didn't hear you speaking up at the Council of Regents," Amon said. "Seems to me that's who you should be talking to. Not a lowly corporal in the guard."

You don't fool me, Amon thought. You just want to know where she is so you can finish the job you started. Still keeping one eye on the wizard, he swung up into his saddle and nudged his gelding into a walk, aiming straight at Micah.

Micah Bayar waited until the last possible moment, then stood aside and watched him go by.

CHAPTER NINETEEN
A CALCULATED RISK

The day after the newling queen's confession, Han asked Willo to move him into the visitors' lodge, where he'd have less supervision and more freedom of movement.

Willo disapproved. "You'll overtax yourself," she said. "At least here I can attend you and limit your visitors."

He could have said, "You're already letting in all the people I'd like to keep out." But that wasn't Willo's fault. "I don't need anyone attending me," he said. "And I'll get more rest away from all the comings and goings."

Willo sat down next to Han on the sleeping bench. "What are you going to do, Hunts Alone?" she said.

"Do?" Han rubbed the back of his neck. "About what?"

"About Briar Rose," she said.

"Who?" Han pretended not to understand. "Oh. The queenling. That girlie has more names than a Ragmarket fancy."

"Be careful, Hunts Alone," Willo said, her voice low and

urgent. She glanced around as if to make sure no one else was within hearing distance.

"I'm always careful," Han said. He couldn't help looking around as well.

"I mean it. If the Demonai realize you are in love with her, they will kill you."

"Who says I'm in love with her?" Han retorted, avoiding her eyes. "Where do you get that?"

"I saw what was in your face when you handed her down to me at trailside," Willo said. "I heard what you said. If I can see it, so can others. Never forget that Averill is Demonai first—and he's no fool. He will not hesitate to kill you if he has any inkling that your intentions are—"

"I don't *have* any intentions, all right?" Han growled. "Except for staying alive and getting out of this mess as soon as I can. That will be hard enough to bring off."

"I know you." Reaching up, Willo brushed a lock of hair from his eyes. "You will go after what you want, regardless of the risk. And you stand to lose everything."

I *have* lost everything, Han thought. Then he corrected himself. Every time I think I've lost everything, I find there's still something else to lose.

"Look," he said, "I'm not a fool, though I act the part sometimes. I have no illusions about what I mean to Her Highness. I know all about bluebloods, and she's worse than most. She's been lying to me from the day we met."

"You are wrong," Willo persisted. "She cares for you—she really does. And that increases the risk. There are some that will kill her too, if they realize how *much* she cares. The Briar Rose

261

represents hope for the upland tribes—a chance to finally put one of our own on the Gray Wolf throne. A chance to redress more than a thousand years of occupation by jinxflingers and rule by the Valedwellers. Believe me, there is no one more dangerous than one whose hopes have turned to despair."

She fell silent, smoothing the folds of her skirts. "The Wizard Council has hopes also—to regain the power they once held. As long as they believe that the Briar Rose can be a part of that plan, she stays alive. And you are definitely not a part of that plan."

Han ground the heels of his hands into his temples, wishing he could shut out Willo's gentle voice. When had she become such an expert in politics?

Willo put her hand on Han's shoulder, her touch easing the pounding in his head. "I know how to keep secrets to protect those I love. You must keep this secret too." She searched Han's face, her own drawn tight with worry. "Promise me you will."

I might as well be spitting into the wind as talking to Willo, Han thought. He put his hand on her arm. "I'll be careful," he said. "I know how to keep secrets." He paused, for a heartbeat. "And now I need some favors from you."

In the visitors' lodge, Han was granted one of the rooms reserved for important guests. It had a hearth of its own on the outside wall, and two sleeping benches, each wide enough for two, piled with blankets and fur throws.

He wished he had someone to share all this luxury with. His thoughts went unbidden to Rebecca. Raisa. This was new to him—this feeling like he'd had a limb hacked off.

Two of Willo's apprentices were assigned to feed and dose

him at regular intervals. But they knocked before they entered and peeked at him out of the corners of their eyes and acted like they thought he would flame them at the drop of a moccasin.

It was tiresome, but convenient at the same time.

Han wore Dancer's replica of his Hunts Alone amulet displayed on the outside of his clothing, the Demon King's amulet hidden underneath. The flash in the replica was a faint reflection of the original. Han worried that if Elena touched it, she would know it wasn't the one she made. But though the matriarch likely noticed he wore it, she showed little interest in it.

Dancer continued to use the original Hunts Alone amulet, though he kept it hidden while in camp. He seemed to have made his peace with the borrowed jinxpiece.

That evening, Han and Dancer walked back to the Matriarch Lodge for the promised strategy meeting with all the players and plotters. It was the first time Han had seen Raisa since her confession to him. When they entered the common room of the lodge, she was sitting cross-legged on the floor, engaged in animated conversation with Averill and Elena Demonai. Her father and grandmother, Han reminded himself.

Still, she looked up when Han entered as if she sensed his presence. Leaning forward, her hands pressed onto her leggings, she searched his face with a kind of mute appeal.

Han averted his eyes and found a seat on the floor on the far side of the room.

Amon Byrne and Averill Demonai reported on the news from the capital. If the Princess Raisa didn't show at the queen's burial, they'd put her little sister on the throne. So suddenly the discussion was not *if* she would attend but *how* she could do it safely.

So the Princess Raisa would get her way, as princesses usually do.

Reid Nightwalker Demonai and the newly minted Night Bird were there. Several times, Han felt the pressure of Bird's eyes on him. He pretended not to notice.

Nightwalker was another matter. Han could tell that his presence was like a tick under the Demonai warrior's skin. So Han made it a point to challenge his black stare every chance he got, like they were rival streetlords in the market.

The site for the memorial service lay on the south flank of the newly named Marianna Peak, north of the Vale. At least it was neutral ground; if anyone had an edge, it was the clans.

Han knew the place—he'd hunted the area with Dancer and Bird—though it had been a long time ago. The flatlanders called it Camelback Mountain. The clans had a more picturesque name for the double summit. Now both names would be discarded in favor of Marianna.

The memorial site was accessible from the mountains to the north, using a high pass between the twin summits. Though that would be hard going this early in spring.

"Before we go further," Averill Lightfoot said, glancing at Han and Dancer, "there is something else you should know."

All eyes turned to the Demonai patriarch.

"When I returned to the city yesterday, I asked the Demonai warriors assigned to my guard to search the queen's gardens again, to see if there were any clues that Queen Marianna's guard might have overlooked." To Amon, he added, "I'm not meaning to suggest that the guard's search was lacking in any way."

"No offense taken," Amon said evenly.

Averill nodded, then put his hand on Bird's shoulder. "Night Bird, can you show us what you found?"

Now everyone stared at Bird. She fumbled in her carry pouch and withdrew an object wrapped in deerskin. Coming forward onto her knees, she set it on the ground and unfolded the leather covering.

It was a wizard's amulet in an old-fashioned style—a tangle of branches and birds in white and yellow gold, some of its fine detail worn smooth with long use.

"And where did you find this?" Averill prompted.

"It was embedded in the rose briar below the queen's terrace," Bird said, sitting back on her heels, dropping her hands into her lap. Where once Han could have read Bird easily, now it was difficult to tell what she was thinking.

"Is this familiar to anyone?" Averill asked. "Does anyone know which jinxfl— which wizard carries an amulet like this?"

They all shook their heads. Han rolled his eyes. It wasn't surprising that none of them had seen it. Most of those present never interacted with wizards if they could help it.

Dancer extended his hand. "Could I take a look?"

Bird nodded, and Dancer lifted the amulet, cradling it between his hands, turning it to catch the torchlight. "This is an old piece," he said finally. "Though made since the Breaking. Nearly all the flash has been discharged. It's seen recent use." He looked up. "I'd guess that somebody's been seen using this, if we ask around."

"Who should we ask?" Nightwalker said. "The Wizard Council? Why would they tell us the truth?"

"We will ask the flashcrafters at Demonai Camp," Averill said.

"Perhaps someone remembers renewing the amulet in the past."

Han took the flashpiece from Dancer and weighed it on his palm. "It's hard to believe that a wizard would drop his amulet without noticing," he said, frowning. "Or leave it lay if he did."

He met Bird's eyes, and she looked down at her hands, embarrassed to be accusing wizards of a crime in his presence.

"If Queen Marianna ripped it off her attacker, and it fell into the garden below, maybe he couldn't retrieve it right then," Elena said, taking the amulet from Han. "Maybe someone was down there."

Raisa shook her head. "Averill said that nobody saw the queen fall, or found her until Magret missed her."

"It may not be positive proof," Nightwalker said, "but it supports what I've said all along—we should not be allying ourselves with wizards to fight wizards who may be implicated in Queen Marianna's death. It puts them in a difficult position—acting against their own kind." Several of the young Demonai warriors nodded in agreement.

"What do you suggest, Nightwalker?" Elena said, leaning forward.

Nightwalker looked around the circle as if searching out allies. "I suggest that we send a small band of Demonai into Fellsmarch tomorrow. Some of us are familiar with the city now, and Lightfoot can easily gain us access to the palace. We seize the Princess Mellony and carry her back to Demonai Camp. Once we have control of both princesses, the Wizard Council would have no option but to give in."

"Is that what you think?" Raisa said, her voice cold and brittle as river ice. "That you have control of *this* princess now? I am not a game piece or a strategic castle you are trying to breach."

That's where you're wrong, Han thought. Nightwalker thinks every girlie is a castle to be breached. Best to keep your drawbridge up.

But maybe she knew that already, since the princess heir had fostered at Demonai Camp. Han studied the two of them, wondering just how well they knew each other. Jealousy flamed within him. He knew what Nightwalker wanted—he could see it in his face.

With some effort, Han wrenched himself back to what Elena was saying.

"Nightwalker could have phrased that more appropriately, Granddaughter, but do not be too quick to dismiss his suggestion," Elena said. "It would put an end to any plan to crown Mellony in your place. And it would minimize the danger to you."

"I've already lost my mother," Raisa said. "I will not risk losing my sister as well. You should understand this, Elena *Cennestre*. Must I remind you that Mellony is your granddaughter, too. I will not be a party to any kidnapping. I have to think that we can come up with a better plan."

Nightwalker shrugged as if it didn't matter either way to him, but Han could tell his pride was wounded.

Much as Han hated to admit it, he agreed with Nightwalker about one thing—the time had come to quit sneaking around and do something dramatic.

Everyone had an idea of how to manage the memorial service. Lord Averill suggested that Raisa arrive at the funeral buried in the midst of a crew of Demonai warriors, display herself, and then return to Marisa Pines when the service was over. Elena offered powerful talismans that might protect the princess from magical attack by the Wizard Council. Everyone agreed that the element of surprise was key, that the safest thing was to whisk her in and out before the Wizard Council could organize some sort of attack.

Han was happy to let everyone else talk while he and Dancer examined Corporal Byrne's sketchy map of the burial area. He wanted to discuss all this with Dancer and come up with his own plan. But all of a sudden he heard his name and looked up to find everybody staring at them.

"What?" he said, irritated to be caught napping.

"We've run through all our ideas," Nightwalker said. "And we wondered what the charmcasters had to offer." The Demonai warrior looked from Han to Dancer, his expression alert and interested, but Han guessed that Nightwalker's expectations were low.

Han shrugged. "I don't think much of what you've come up with so far," he said.

Elena's lips tightened. "I see. Well, then. Perhaps you can tell us what *you* suggest."

Han glanced at Dancer. "Me and Fire Dancer need to talk it over," he said. "We'll tell you what we come up with tomorrow. But if the Princess Raisa is queen of the realm, then everybody, including her, ought to start acting like it."

"What do you mean?" Raisa said, sitting up very straight, her green eyes fixed on him in that unnerving way she had.

The problem wasn't Raisa, Han thought, recalling how she'd walked into Southbridge Guardhouse like a lioness to face off with Gillen. She was fearless. Too fearless, sometimes.

"I'm just a streetlord," Han said. "Or used to be. But you don't get to be streetlord by hiding in your crib."

"We understand that," Averill said, his voice edged with annoyance. "But there has already been one likely regicide, and at least one attempt on the princess heir. There is a very real danger that—"

"I *get* that," Han said. "Believe me. But, say I'm streetlord of Ragmarket. Even in Southbridge, I don't *sneak* around hoping nobody notices. No, I strut in like I own the place. I walk right down the Way. I have my Raggers with me—I'm not stupid—but the point is, my enemies should be worrying about themselves and what'll happen if they get in my way. They should be wondering about my plans and what I know and who I've got on my side.

"The Princess Raisa? This *is* her turf. They're the trespassers. If she comes off like she's scared of them, it's over. She's got to go back to Fellsmarch. She's got to move back into the old neighborhood and clean out the riffraff rivals. Long as she's up here, she's out of power."

"We're not really asking for political advice," Elena said, her black eyes narrowed. "We were more interested in what you had to offer in terms of charmcasting."

Raisa surged to her feet, looking around at the others. "He's right, though. I cannot rule from here. The longer I stay hidden, the more time my enemies have to dig in. We'll never dislodge them if we wait."

Averill rolled his eyes. "He's telling you to do what you've wanted to do all along," he said. "That doesn't make it the right thing to do."

"We cannot afford to lose you, Granddaughter," Elena said. "If the jinxflingers kill you too, the line will be broken."

"Then we make sure that doesn't happen," Raisa said, looking around the room.

"The Demonai will do our part," Nightwalker said. "But it's going to be more difficult for us to protect you in the city. Hunts Alone has no real stake in this. We do. We haven't seen anything from the jinxflingers to suggest they'll contribute at all."

"Dancer and I will meet with you tomorrow, Your Highness," Han said to Raisa, using the formal title on purpose. "Just the three of us. I'll tell you what we have in mind, and you say yes or no. You're the princess, so it's your call. What you need is some firepower—enough to scare off the Wizard Council so they leave you alone, for a while, anyway. What you want is to make show. We can help with that."

CHAPTER TWENTY
LUCIUS AND ALGER

Han asked Dancer to walk back with him to the visitors' lodge. When they emerged from the Matriarch Lodge, powdery snow swirled around their feet in little devil dances, and Han's nose crackled in the icy air. Even in spring, it was still plenty cold at this altitude once the sun went down.

The visitors' lodge was nestled in the pines a short distance from the rest of the camp. Han and Dancer were single-filing it on the path when Han heard a step behind them.

Whirling, he gripped his amulet and extended his hand, his fingers tingling with flash.

"It's just me, Hunts Alone," Bird said, raising her hands and backing away, eyes wide.

Han lowered his charmcasting hand. "You can't ambush me like that anymore," he said. "Not a good idea."

"I can see that." Bird attempted a smile. "You've never been easy to sneak up on, but now you're jumpy as a fellshare."

"That's how I stay alive," Han said. After an awkward pause, he said, "Did you want something?"

Bird glanced over her shoulder to verify that no one was within hearing distance. "I heard you were hurt, saving the queen's life," she said. "I wanted to see if you were all right."

"I've been better," Han said. "But I'm all right."

"Good," she said, glancing at Dancer, whose face offered no clues as to what he was thinking. "I'm glad to hear that." She paused, scuffing at some leaves with her moccasin. When Han said nothing, she continued. "I'm off duty tonight. Could we—could I share your hearth? I would like to talk to both of you."

"Did Nightwalker send you here?" Dancer asked. "Was there something he wanted you to tell us? Or something he wanted you to find out?"

Bird blinked at him. "No. I came on my own. Why would you—"

"We have plans," Han said. "Jinxflinger business. Sorry."

They circled around her and walked on. Han resisted looking back. He wasn't proud of what he'd said to Bird. It felt petty and mean. But he did have other plans—plans he couldn't share with her. And it *was* jinxflinger business.

Choose sides against a streetlord, and you pay a price.

The visitors' lodge was deserted. The other guests, like Averill, would be plotting long into the night. Han led Dancer into his room and shut the door.

Dancer rekindled the fire and laid on another stick of wood. "I'm glad to be back in the mountains," he said, shedding his warm coat. "It's good to be back at my mother's hearth." Sitting down on the rug, he leaned his back against the hearthstone.

Han eyed him curiously. "You seem different. Like you're easier with being a wizard here in camp."

Dancer shrugged. "My time in the flatlands opened my eyes. Here, people mistrust us for being wizards. Everywhere else, people mistrust me for being clan." He smiled at Han's puzzled expression. "It's taught me that the flaw is in them. Not me. When I first found out I was gifted, I felt ashamed, like it was a fault or a curse. I'd been taught all my life that it was. I would have done most anything to get rid of it. I wanted to kill my wizard father for inflicting it on me." He half smiled.

"But what I've come to realize is, it's not a curse. It is a gift. Like my mother's gift for healing. I can do things that others can't do. I refuse to apologize for it anymore."

Han found himself wishing he had the same clear-eyed view. Lately it seemed like all he did was react to others and their plans. He'd never get anywhere if he didn't know what he was after and where he wanted to go.

"Like I said, it's good to be here," Dancer went on, "but I would have liked to stay longer at the academy. I was making progress with Firesmith. I think he was flattered to have someone who was actually interested in metalcraft and flash. He gave me some of his rare books to bring along." Dancer paused. "But you didn't bring me back here to talk about my plans."

"Well, in a way I did. Partly. I'm trying to figure out what weapons we have going into this."

Dancer nodded. "I can add more flash capability to the amulet I made for you now, if you want," he said. "Still won't be as powerful as the one I'm using. Elena's. Or the one you took from the Bayars."

"No rush," Han said, touching his replica amulet. It brightened fractionally. "I'm not really using this anyway, except for show." He paused. "You don't have to keep using my old amulet, you know," he said. "You could have another one made specifically for you."

Dancer stroked the amulet Elena had made for Han—the one he'd been using since he lost his in Arden. "I'm used to it now. And it's loaded with power. No reason to make a change."

Han understood. Once linked with an amulet, it was painful to give it up.

"I have friends at Demonai Camp," Dancer went on. "Not warriors. Craftspeople. Depending on what happens with the coronation, I'd like to go over there if I can be spared."

"Isn't that dangerous, going to Demonai Camp?" Han said. "As a wizard?"

"Everything is dangerous," Dancer replied, shrugging. "Though it will be easier if you can keep Elena and Nightwalker away."

Han nodded. "I'll do my best to keep them busy keeping an eye on me." He paused. "I asked you to come because I have a confession to make—I met with Crow again, on my way here."

Swiveling away from Dancer's incredulous expression, Han filled a teapot from the water jug and set it on the hearth.

"You're not serious," Dancer said finally. "You do have a death wish, I believe."

"Everything is dangerous," Han said, cocking an eyebrow at Dancer. He sat down on the edge of his sleeping bench and pulled off his boots. "But I need your advice."

"Hmmm. Never go back?" Dancer rolled his eyes. "Somehow I don't think you'll take it."

"It's not as dangerous as you think," Han said. "As I told you before, Crow doesn't have any power of his own."

"Then how, exactly, does he get to Aediion?" Dancer said. "When almost nobody else can get there?"

"He uses mine. My flash. Without me, he can't do anything," Han said. "But he's incredibly knowledgeable about magic."

"Then who is he in real life?" Dancer persisted. "And why won't he agree to meet you on your home ground?"

"If you can believe what he says, he doesn't exist in real life," Han said, serving up his story in small bites. "He exists only in Aediion. He's a remnant of a wizard who lived long ago."

"A remnant?" Dancer said skeptically. "He's been in Aediion all this time? And he just happened to find you the first day you visited?" Dancer pulled free a lock of hair, combed it straight with his fingers, split it into sections, and started interlacing them to make a braid.

Han pulled the serpent amulet from under his shirt and tapped it with his first two fingers. "Not in Aediion. Here. He's been waiting here for a thousand years. In this amulet."

Dancer stared at the amulet. Then looked up at Han. "He's been hiding in an amulet? I know a lot about flashpieces, and I never heard of that." He bit off a piece of string from a bundle in his pocket. "There are lots of wizards in Oden's Ford," he said. "Even more in the Fells. Don't you think it's more likely Crow is one of them?" He finished one braid, wrapping the lower end with colorful thread, and began another.

Han spooned highland leaf into cups, then poured boiling water over it.

"And why won't he tell you who he is if he wants to partner with you?" Dancer continued.

"Originally he meant to *use* me—not partner with me," Han said. "But the talisman you made put a stop to that. So last time we met, he told me who he really is."

Dancer leaned forward. "And?"

Han took a breath and spit it out. "He claims he's Alger Waterlow. The last Wizard King of the Fells."

Dancer's hands stilled themselves, and he frowned. "So you're meeting with someone who claims to be the Demon King, who nearly destroyed the world."

Han nodded.

Dancer gazed at him, speechless, for what seemed like forever. "And you mean to keep meeting with him?" he said finally, shaking his head.

Han nodded again.

"I don't like it," Dancer said, with his usual gift for understatement. "Either he's lying, which is bad. Or he could be telling the truth, which is worse." He blew on his tea to cool it. "Much worse."

"I don't like it either," Han admitted. "But it's the only hand I have to play. That's why I asked you here—to get your opinion."

"How am I supposed to give you an opinion when I've never even met him?" Dancer said. He sipped his tea, brow furrowed. Then he thumped the mug down on the hearthstone. "That's it. I need to meet him and see for myself."

"Well . . ." Han thought about this. "He can't come here, so you'd need to go back to Aediion. And he'll be furious that I brought you along."

"Why is that?" Dancer said. "Why doesn't he want anyone else to see him? What is he hiding?"

"He says he knows secrets the Bayars are hot for. If they find out I can talk to him, we're done."

"That's convenient, don't you think?" Dancer snorted. "Why should you believe him, Hunts Alone? What has he ever done but try to use you to get what he wants?"

Dancer was right. In truth, since Rebecca had turned into Raisa, Han had lost faith in his own judgment. How could he have been so wrong about her? How could he have missed that he was walking out with a princess?

Why should Han be following other people's rules when they broke the rules themselves?

Dancer was his best friend and ally—it was time to begin treating him that way.

"All right," Han said. "Come with me to Aediion and meet him and tell me what you think. If he's lying, the two of us might outsmart an imposter. Besides, I've arranged to—" He stopped and cocked his head. "Someone's coming."

Immediately there came a tapping at the door. Han levered to his feet and crossed to the entrance.

It was Willo, with Lucius Frowsley in tow.

It had been nearly a year since Han had seen his former employer, but the thousand-year-old man had retained the veneer of polish he'd sported at their last meeting. His hair and beard were trimmed and in order, his clothing tidier and in better repair than in the past.

Lucius looks better off, and I'm probably worse off than before, Han thought. The recluse had been more than an employer—Han had trusted him. Until he'd found out that Lucius had known the truth of Han's magical heritage and had never told him. What other secrets was Lucius hiding?

One thing hadn't changed—the old man carried a bottle of product in one hand and a fistful of cups in the other.

"I sent a runner after Lucius, as you asked, Hunts Alone," Willo said, looking from Lucius to Han.

"Hello, Lucius," Han said, touching his arm to orient him.

"Boy!" Lucius closed his eyes and smiled. His face crinkled like well-weathered badlands, as if he were basking in the warmth of Han's presence.

"Is there anything else you need, Hunts Alone?" Willo asked. Han shook his head. "Thank you, Willo."

"Send word to me when he's ready to go," she said, turning away and slipping out of the visitors' lodge.

"I can't tell you how happy I am that you're still alive." Lucius raised the bottle and waggled it suggestively. "We have something to celebrate."

Lucius always had something to celebrate. Han ushered him toward the hearth, his hand on the blind man's elbow. "Here. Sit by the fire," he said. "Fire Dancer is here, too. Want tea?"

"Tea?" Making a disapproving face, Lucius settled onto the bench next to the hearth and carefully arranged his cups next to him. "I'd prefer something stronger."

"Let's stick with tea for now," Han said. He refilled his own and Dancer's cups and made more tea for Lucius. Closing Lucius's hands around the cup, Han made sure he had a good hold before he returned to his seat.

"So," Lucius said, setting the tea aside without tasting it, "tell me everything, boy. Tell me about Oden's Ford. My years at the academy were the best years of my life. Are the houses still fighting on Bridge Street?"

"Still fighting," Han said. "And the provosts are still rounding them up."

"Bloody provosts," Lucius muttered, his milky eyes fixed on some private memory. "Them and their curfews. Alger, he used to tweak their pointy noses, let me tell you. He was like a vapor, that boy. He went wherever he wanted, whenever he wanted, and nothing the provosts could do about it."

"That's who I wanted to talk to you about," Han said. "Alger."

"Alger?" Lucius's head jerked up, his expression wary. "What about him?"

"What he was like when you knew him?" Han said. "For instance, what did he look like?"

"Well. He was devilish handsome," Lucius said. "Blond hair and blue eyes the color of the Indio in midsummer. Ladies claimed you could drown in 'em. Well built he was, and he moved like a cat. I wasn't so bad in my day, but never could compete with Alger Waterlow when it came to the ladies." Lucius rubbed his nose with the heel of his hand.

"Me and Alger, we once spent a whole weekend in the women's dormitory at the Temple School. Bunch of dedicates decided against taking vows after that." Lucius grinned a gap-toothed grin, which faded quickly. "'Course all that catting around ended when he met Hanalea."

"How did he get along with the other students?" Han asked.

"There was just something about him," Lucius said. "Folks wanted to be with him. He'd draw you in. Soon as he'd walk into

279

a room he'd be the center of attention. Ever'body loved him."

Han rubbed his chin. He was supposed to believe that the flame-eyed Demon King of the stories was the bang-up cove of Oden's Ford?

"Ever'body loved him—'cept Kinley Bayar, that is," Lucius amended.

"Kinley Bayar?" Han asked. "Who's that?"

"Remember? He was the one was to marry Queen Hanalea."

"Oh. Right," Han said.

"They was like oil and water—Kinley and Alger. Kinley always wanted to be in charge. So did Alger—and whenever he and Kinley went head-to-head, Alger usually won, and Kinley couldn't abide losing."

"Have you ever been to Aediion?" Han asked abruptly.

"Aediion?" Lucius said, blinking at the rapid change of topic. "A' course. Plenty of times. That was our back-alley highway. Our secret meeting place, especially during the civil war."

Which made sense, if Crow was telling the truth.

"Dancer and I have been to Aediion, too," Han said. "I've met someone there who claims to be Alger Waterlow."

Lucius's dreamy expression slid away. "Alger? What are you talking about?" The old man leaned forward, agitated, his Adam's apple jumping as he swallowed.

"That's why I wanted to talk to you," Han said. "It doesn't seem possible, but that's what he claims, and he knows more about magic than anyone I've met."

"Alger," Lucius breathed. His burled hands scrabbled in his lap as if trying to gain a purchase on the idea. "Alger alive. Who would've thought?"

"Well, not exactly alive," Han said. "He claims he's been hidden in his old amulet all this time." Han touched the serpent flashpiece, then remembered that Lucius couldn't see it. "He describes himself as a remnant. Not a ghost, exactly, but . . . he can't exist in real life. Not as himself, anyway."

Lucius licked his lips, his face more pasty pale than usual. "You sure about that, boy? You sure he can't find a way?"

"Well." Han shrugged. "He says not."

"Anything's possible when it comes to Alger Waterlow," Lucius said. "If I'm alive, then he could be too. Did he say anything about me?" He pawed at Han's arm. "Did he say what he wants? *Tell me.*"

Han shook his head, worried the old man might have a stroke. "He hasn't said much about the past, except that he wants revenge on the Bayars. He seems . . . he seems bitter about what happened."

"He should be bitter," Lucius said. "He's got reason." Turning, he groped for his bottle and pulled the cork with his teeth. He splashed product into a cup, his hand shaking. Then drained it and poured again.

"He also seems to blame Hanalea," Han said. "For betraying him."

Lucius shook his head, eyes squeezed shut, his hands wrapped around his tin cup.

"But—is that even possible?" Han went on. "That he could last a thousand years hidden in an amulet? Based on what you know about magic, and what you knew about him?"

"You listen to me," Lucius said, his eyes popping open again. "I don't know how it could be done, but if anybody could do it, he could." He emptied his cup with one gulp and refilled it. "Sweet Thea of the mountains, Alger's come back."

"Whoa, now," Han said, putting his hand on the old man's arm. Lucius flinched, nearly spilling his drink. "I'm not absolutely sure it's him. It could be some kind of a trick. I was hoping you could tell me something—some question I could ask him that only he would know the answer to."

"Something Alger would know." Lucius frowned, blotting his forehead with his sleeve. "Let me think."

While he was thinking, Han rose and refilled their teacups. Except for Lucius's, which was still full.

"Here's two things," Lucius said abruptly. "Two things that only Alger would know. First, what was their secret meeting place—him and Hanalea's? And what did he give to her as a love token when they were betrothed?"

"All right," Han said, thinking Alger and Lucius must have been tight friends if Lucius knew those kinds of secrets. "What are the answers?"

"They used to meet in the conservatory at Fellsmarch Castle, right over Hanalea's bedchamber," Lucius said. "Maybe it's still there. There was a secret passage from her room to the garden."

"The conservatory," Han repeated. "And what did he give Hanalea?"

"It was a ring, moonstones and sapphires and pearls," Lucius said. "Because he only ever saw her by moonlight, he said. Hanalea wore it the rest of her life." He shuddered. "Imagine what it was like for him—trapped in that amulet while Hanalea grew old and died."

Strange, Han thought. It wasn't just that Lucius thought

Crow's story was possible—he seemed convinced already that it was true. Like he'd been waiting to hear it for a thousand years. Like it was inevitable.

"What are you going to do, boy?" Lucius asked, breaking into Han's thoughts.

"Me and Dancer are going to Aediion tonight," Han said. "I'm going to find out if he is who he says he is."

"Look," Dancer said. "Even if he is who he says he is, and even if Lucius is willing to vouch for him, how do we know we can trust him? A thousand years locked in an amulet can change a person. He may be planning to finish the job he started during the Breaking."

"Boy—does he know who you are?" Lucius asked. "Does he know you're his blood?"

"No," Han said. "He doesn't seem to know much that's happened while he was—ah—locked up." Han shrugged. "I didn't know whether to tell him or not."

"You should tell him," Lucius said. "He deserves to know that his line didn't die with him. That could make all the difference. He can help you. He'll want to help you. Believe me, you want him on your side."

The old man stood, grabbing up his bottle and cups. "Call Willo," he said. "I'm ready to go home." And he refused to say anything more.

CHAPTER TWENTY-ONE

BACK IN AEDIION

After Lucius left, Han asked Willo's healer apprentices to keep any other visitors away. He warned them that he and Dancer would be using dangerous, unstable magic, and laid magical barriers around the perimeter to prevent their being interrupted. Then he and Dancer sat down on adjacent sleeping benches in the corner of the room.

"You sure you want to do this?" Dancer said. "Lucius seemed to think that Alger Waterlow is capable of almost anything. He seems frightened of him, almost."

"In a way, it supports his story," Han said. "If we can believe Lucius, Alger was powerful enough to conceal himself in an amulet for a thousand years."

"Why would anyone want to do that?" Dancer said.

"Maybe if you were desperate for revenge," Han said. "Or willing to do whatever it takes to win." *Like me*, he added to himself.

They sat in silence for a moment, each alone with his own thoughts.

"Have you tried returning to Aediion?" Han asked. "Since that day in Gryphon's class?"

"No, I haven't," Dancer said, staring up at the ceiling. "I never saw much use in it, and after what happened to you the first time, I wasn't eager to try it again."

"We should go," Han said, after another long pause. "I can bring you along, or you can come on your own power."

"I'll come on my own," Dancer said. "That way I can leave on my own. Are you wearing your rowan talisman?" Dancer reached up and touched his own. He'd made one for himself after Han's had prevented Crow from possessing him.

Han nodded, opening his collar so Dancer could see. "Wait a few minutes before you follow me. I'll give Crow a bit of warning that you're coming." Han didn't know if that was a good or a bad idea, but it seemed only fair. "I don't think it really matters where we meet, as far as Crow is concerned. He's just always there, waiting. But let's you and me meet in Mystwerk Tower."

What if Crow doesn't show? Han thought. I'll look like a fool.

That was the least of his worries.

He lay back, closing his eyes, and spoke the familiar words that would let him pass through the portal. And opened his eyes to Mystwerk Tower.

Midnight. Moonlight shafted down from the windows, kindling the dust motes in the air.

Crow sat cross-legged on the floor in front of Han, dressed all in black, eyes closed, head bowed, his flax hair the only brilliant thing about him. If Han didn't know better, he'd have guessed he was either despondent or praying.

Han reorganized his clothes, ridding himself of the clan garb he'd been wearing and arraying himself in elegant flare, down to the glittering rings on his fingers. It had become his way of honoring Crow, of meeting him on his own turf.

Crow opened his eyes and blinked up at him. "Alister!" He scrambled to his feet, brushing at his somber clothing. Then glittered up a bit, sprouting rings and sequins and jewels, as if to present a more cheerful appearance. "You're alive!" He looked eagerly into Han's face, examining it for damage. "Are you . . . are you well? How are you feeling?"

Han shrugged, surprised at Crow's concern. "I'll live."

"It's true, then, that the Maker looks after fools," Crow said, sounding more like his usual self. "You nearly killed yourself healing that girl. You stripped your amulet and yourself. I thought you were dead. Why did you do it?"

Han didn't know how to answer that question, in the past or present tense. "She was important to me. I had to try to save her."

"Did she live?" Crow asked. "Was all that sacrifice worth it?"

"She's alive," Han said. "I haven't decided whether it was worth it or not."

Crow laughed, and it was unexpectedly charming. "You're learning, Alister. I told you not to go to war over a woman. Though you must be a foolhardy sort if you came back here."

"I'm still not convinced you're telling the truth," Han said. "I've asked someone to join us here. Someone I trust."

Crow's smile faded, replaced by irritation. "No. Absolutely

not. Our bargain was you come alone. No one else is supposed to know I even exist."

"Our bargain was you'd help me against the Bayars. Not treat me like a sweet mark. You've got no business squeaking about the rules now."

Crow began pacing back and forth. "I'm trying to protect you. The Bayars have been trying to pry me free of that amulet for a thousand years. If they find out that you can communicate with me, what do you think will happen to you? Do you look forward to hours of torture in the dungeon at Aerie House? I've been there, and, believe me, I have no desire to go back."

"When you meet my friend, you'll realize there's not much chance he'll cackle to the Bayars," Han said. "Or that they'd listen if he did. It's too late anyway, I—" As if he'd called Dancer by speaking of him, the air between them thickened and rippled, and Dancer appeared, clad in fine ceremonial clan garb.

Crow took two steps back, eyes wide, raising his arms in defense. Instinctively, Han stepped between Dancer and Crow. Dancer looked momentarily disoriented, then fixed his gaze on Crow.

"You're smaller than I expected," Dancer said, cocking his head. "And no flaming eyes."

Crow grew fractionally larger and more brilliant, like a peacock displaying his plumage, or a streetlord making show. "A *copperhead*? You brought a copperhead here to meet me?" Crow lowered his arms slowly, staring at Dancer like he was a demon himself. "No," he whispered, his brow furrowed. "That's not right. You're a *wizard* disguised as a copperhead."

Dancer fingered his talisman. "Of course I'm a wizard, or I wouldn't be here. I'm also clan."

"Hayden Fire Dancer, meet Alger Waterlow," Han said, rather formally.

Crow seemed as edgy as a cat in Ragmarket. "There's something about you," he whispered, his eyes riveted on Dancer. "Something . . . hidden. Something dangerous. Something you don't want anybody to see. Have we met before?"

Dancer shook his head. "This is only my second time in Aediion."

"We have some questions to ask *you*, all right?" Han said, beginning to lose patience.

"Questions?" Crow's gaze flickered to Han. "What questions?"

"You say you are Alger Waterlow, the last of the gifted kings. If so, then tell me where you used to meet Hanalea in secret, before you ran off together."

"That's no one's business but my own," Crow said, pressing his lips together as if he never meant to open them again.

"It's our business if we're going to partner up," Han said.

"Send the copperhead away," Crow said. "I've no desire to partner with him. Then we'll talk."

Han shook his head. "I want him here as witness. Otherwise, we're both out of here." It was street bravado. He couldn't let Crow know how desperate he was for his help.

Crow scowled and gave in. "Very well. Hanalea and I used to meet in the glass house at Fellsmarch Castle," he said. "There was a passage through the walls from her chambers."

"Glasshouse?" Han said uncertainly. Lucius had said the conservatory.

"The conservatory," Crow said, waving his hand. "It's like a glass garden."

Han struggled to keep his street face while his stomach lurched. Was it possible Crow was telling the truth?

"All right, then," Han said. "Sounds plausible. What did you give Hanalea as a handfast gift?"

Crow's eyes narrowed. "Who told you that?" he demanded. "Where is this coming from?"

Han hesitated a moment. "Do you remember Lucius Frowsley?"

Crow seemed lost. "Frowsley?" He shook his head. "I don't really. . ." He looked up. "Do you mean Lucas?" he said. "Lucas Fraser? He was in school with me at Mystwerk. He was my best friend. But that was a thousand years ago."

Han frowned. Had Lucius changed his name? "Maybe," Han said. "It's a long story, but he's still alive. He gave me these questions. And the answers."

"Lucas," Crow whispered, more to himself than to Han. "Is it possible? I'd nearly forgotten about . . . that. He was so eager to live forever, but I had no idea if—"

"Just answer the question, will you?" Han said.

Crow's brilliant eyes fixed on Han. "I gave Hanalea a ring— moonstones and pearls and sapphires. And she gave me a gold ring, engraved with her name on the inside, so I'd always have her against my skin." He laughed bitterly. "The Bayars took it from me, along with everything else."

"It's really true, then," Dancer said, his hand closing reflexively around his amulet. "You *are* the Demon King."

Crow turned toward Dancer. Then stumbled back a step as

289

recognition flooded into his face and fired in his eyes.

"Speaking of demons," Crow said, his voice low and dangerous. "I believe you have a demon's face." Springing forward, he smashed into Dancer as he had done when he'd taken possession of Micah in Aediion. But again he bounced back, driven off by the rowan talisman.

"You're a filthy Bayar!" Crow cried, rolling to his feet, his image rippling and fraying like a flag in the wind. "Did you think I wouldn't know you after all these years? Do you think I wouldn't recognize that Aerie House stench?" His voice trembled, his face twisting in revulsion.

Dancer just stood there as if frozen, saying nothing.

"I *told* you how important it was to keep my existence a secret, especially from the Bayars," Crow said to Han, his voice low and furious. "Now you've gambled away what little chance you had in the first place."

"You're mistaken," Han said, since Dancer still said nothing. "Use your eyes. Dancer's no Bayar. He's clan, raised at Marisa Pines. I've known him since we were *lytlings*."

"Kill him," Crow said through clenched teeth. "Kill him now or we'll all suffer the consequences."

"Why is it you're always trying to goad me into killing somebody?" Han demanded.

"You're a fool, Alister," Crow said. "And I was a fool to trust you." He sizzled out like a dying spark.

Han and Dancer both stared at the spot he'd vacated.

"I'm sorry, Hunts Alone," Dancer said, with a heavy sigh. "I hope I haven't ruined it for you. I know you were counting on his help."

"What got into him?" Han said. "Maybe you were right—a thousand years trapped in an amulet has made him crazy."

Dancer shook his head. "Or maybe he's good at spotting a Bayar, that's all," he said quietly. As Han watched, Dancer's clothes changed from clan leggings and shirt to wizard robes, the stoles emblazoned with the Stooping Falcon. His hair, however, was still braided and tied in clan fashion.

"My mother is clan, Hunts Alone," Dancer said. "Have you ever wondered who my father was?"

"Well, I heard the story, what Willo said at your naming," Han said, his voice trailing away.

"It was true, most of it," Dancer said. "Except the part where she claimed she didn't know who it was. Can you think of a wizard ruthless enough to come into the Spirits and attack a young woman in the forest like that?"

Han studied Dancer's features—the jarring blue eyes set into his bronzed face, the angular bone structure, the heavy dark brows. As understanding dawned, Han's throat constricted painfully, as if there were a large rock he was trying to swallow.

"The resemblance *is* rather striking once you know to look for it," Dancer said matter-of-factly.

"Hanalea's blood and bones," Han whispered, shaking his head. "Your father is Gavan Bayar." No wonder Dancer had viewed his gift as a curse.

"You don't know how tempting it's been to present myself to Micah and Fiona as their long-lost older brother," Dancer said. "Almost worth getting myself killed. For a time, that seemed like an easy way out. I'd step forward as a Bayar, and they would murder me."

Memories came back to Han—Dancer's furious reaction when they'd met Micah and his cousins on Hanalea. It had seemed so out of character at the time. Dancer's knowledge of wizards and their ways—uncommon among the Spirit clans. Micah's reaction to Dancer, each time they met . . .

"Do the Bayars know?" Han said.

Dancer shook his head, half smiling. "I think Micah sees his father in me. It's like he knows on some instinctive level, but he just can't bring himself to believe it. I've never met Lord Bayar. If *he* knew, I'd be dead already."

"What about the Demonai? Averill? Elena *Cennestre*? Do they know?"

Dancer shook his head. "If *they* knew, they'd have drowned me at birth. Willo and I are the only ones that knew. Now you. And Crow, unfortunately."

Han recalled when Willo had brought Dancer to the city, to Speaker Jemson, hoping to cure him of his cursed gift. She'd kept the secret for a lifetime, trying to find a place for the son she loved in a world at war with itself.

"Why didn't you tell me?" Han asked, his mind reeling.

"You're one to talk," Dancer arrowed back. "How many secrets have you kept from me?"

"I'm not criticizing you," Han said. "I'm just asking why."

"I didn't know myself, until I began to manifest," Dancer said. "After, I almost told you, several times. But I knew how you felt about the Bayars after what happened to your family. I didn't know how you would react. And now there's Cat. She hates the Bayars—they murdered all of her friends. And my mother—Willo—she made me swear never to tell." Dancer spoke matter-of-factly, looking directly into Han's eyes. "For a long time I didn't want anyone to know. But now—I'm glad you found out. I'm tired of acting like it's our fault. Like I'm ashamed of who I am. I can't control what other people do. But I can decide how I'm going to handle it."

Anger sparked in Han. Why should Dancer and Willo bear that burden—keeping their secret, always worrying it would come out, worrying what the Bayars would do if they knew.

"Does Willo have proof?" Han asked. "That it was Bayar, I mean."

"She still has the Bayar's ring," Dancer said. "When she found out she was with child, she hid the ring away and claimed she didn't know who the father was."

When Han opened his mouth to speak, Dancer raised a hand to stop him. "She was trying to protect me—from the Bayars and the Demonai. But once it was clear I was gifted, it became too big a secret to keep. I knew it would come out sooner or later."

"She should have named him," Han growled, "and brought him to justice."

"We may think so," Dancer said, nodding, "but she has a bone-deep fear of Bayar that she cannot shake. Being attacked so close to home destroyed her confidence. She has never felt completely safe since." He paused. "Bayar is going to pay for that."

Han put his hand on Dancer's shoulder, squeezing it. "You're my best friend," he said. "I don't care who your father was."

Dancer shrugged. "I hope Cat feels the same way. I'm going to tell her. I don't want to keep secrets from her, either. Not anymore." He fingered his amulet. "Let's not say anything to Willo—not until after the queen's funeral, anyway. She's worried enough as it is that I'm going. She doesn't want me anywhere near Bayar."

"That's up to you," Han said, still trying to get his head around this news. "It's your secret. But I think you should talk to her soon."

CHAPTER TWENTY-TWO

MAKING A
POINT

You have to trust Han Alister, Raisa told herself over and over. Even though he hates you now. You don't have a choice.

Well, in fact, she did have a choice. Lots of choices. She could go with the well-insulated sneak-in-and-out plan her father favored. Or the abduction plan Reid Nightwalker was pushing.

But she wanted to honor Han by trusting him, since she hadn't trusted him before. She only hoped she was making the right decision.

It didn't help that Nightwalker had made it abundantly plain that *he* didn't trust Han Alister, or his plan. Han had sketched it out the day before, in a brief businesslike meeting. Just the three of them, like he'd said. And Raisa had approved of it.

Then they had shared it with the others. Who *didn't* approve.

Nightwalker could be relentless. And persuasive. The sun wasn't even up, but he'd been distracting her for the last hour while she tried to get ready to travel to the memorial.

The topic was Han Alister and his plan.

"He's a jinxflinger," Nightwalker said. "How can you trust him to side with you against the Wizard Council?"

"Isn't that the idea?" Raisa said, rubbing her eyes. "Wasn't that why Elena *Cennestre* recruited him? He's supposed to be the secret weapon."

"I didn't say we shouldn't *use* him. I'm saying we shouldn't trust him with your life." Nightwalker leaned against the lodge-pole in the Matriarch Lodge, lithe and deadly as a fellscat. He'd dressed for battle, in the sunlight-and-shadow coat and leggings, his Demonai amulet glittering at his neck.

He didn't look droopy-eyed at all, though no doubt he'd been up half the night reinforcing his rights to the clan name, Night-walker. Raisa had seen him and Night Bird kissing good-bye outside the visitors' lodge at dawn when Raisa went out to the privy. So they were still together, apparently.

She forced her attention back to the present.

"Han hates the High Wizard," Raisa said. "I can't imagine him throwing in with them."

"That's what he's told *you*. But he has more in common with them than he does with any of us."

Raisa sat back on her heels, resting her hands on her thighs. "You're doing it again," she said. "Treating me like I'm stupid. I spent time with Alister at Oden's Ford. I know him better than you do. I know what I'm doing."

Nightwalker raised both hands. "Forgive me, Your Highness." He stopped and cleared his throat self-consciously. "It seems that I am always apologizing to you. I think I spend too much time with people who agree with me." He took a breath. "Despite my lack of diplomacy, it is not my intention to question your judgment. It is just that I'm concerned about your safety."

Raisa blinked at him, surprised. This was more introspection than she was used to from Nightwalker. But still—she wouldn't let him off that easily. "I suppose that's why you want to go to war against my sister. A princess of the blood. When you don't even know her intentions."

Nightwalker shook his head. "I only wanted to take her out of play. It would be safer for you, and safer for her as well."

"There's not going to be any fighting," Raisa said. "That will keep us all safe." She sorted through clothing, trying to figure out what she should wear that would send the right message to those assembled for her mother's memorial service.

No, she amended, pressing her fingertips against her brow. *What can I wear that will honor my mother and her legacy?*

She didn't have much to choose from—only what the clans had provided since her arrival. Everything else had been left behind, in Fellsmarch and Oden's Ford. She thought of the closets of elaborate dresses back in the capital and sighed.

You are a beggar of a queen, Raisa thought. Always guesting in someone else's house and wearing borrowed clothes.

She chose a gored clan skirt in boiled white wool and a beaded overtunic in lightweight suede and draped them over her sleeping bench. Willo had given her a fine white deerskin jacket with painted and embroidered Gray Wolf symbols on the back and sleeves. Clan mourning dress didn't mirror the dark weedy look of flatland funeral garb. It celebrated the lives of the dead and their connections with the living.

"Wait outside for me, please," Raisa said to Nightwalker, who seemed inclined to remain glued to her side until it was time to leave for Marianna Peak. Elena's orders, maybe, with two wizards in camp. Or was it his own inclination?

Nightwalker took hold of her elbows and drew her in for a lingering kiss. He smelled of leather and fresh air.

Raisa drew back a little reluctantly. He seemed eager to resume where they'd left off. She knew from experience that Reid Nightwalker could be a welcome distraction from all of her troubles, if she would let him. He could help her forget that Han Alister was treating her like poison.

"Nightwalker. Go. I need to dress. We'll be leaving soon."

The warrior's smoky-eyed smile made it plain that he'd gladly stay and supervise. But he ducked through the doorway into the outer room.

Raisa sighed. Whenever she was with Nightwalker, she felt under siege—personally and in all other ways. She needed to find a channel for his relentless intensity. He wore her out.

She missed Amon's steadiness. He had ridden back to Fellsmarch so he could accompany his father's ashes from the Cathedral Temple to their burying place. Averill was also back in the city and would travel to the memorial service with Marianna's bier. Raisa would have the Demonai with her, and Han Alister and Fire Dancer. That was all, and that would have to be enough. She hoped she could keep them from each other's throats.

Raisa was just pulling on her boots when she heard raised voices outside, what sounded like an argument. She poked her head through the curtains to find Han Alister and Reid Nightwalker circling each other like alpha wolves, hackles raised and nearly snarling.

Han was dressed more finely than she'd ever seen him, all in black with a pearl gray trim at the neck and on the sleeves. His shirt fit close to his body, showing off his distractingly lean, muscular frame. The Lone Hunter amulet glittered against the matte fabric, and the dark color set off his bright hair and blue eyes.

"What is going on?" she demanded, looking from one to the other.

"I told him he couldn't go in, that you were dressing. He's objecting," Nightwalker said, his posture one of barely contained violence.

"I just wanted to let you know that I was here," Han said, shifting his eyes to Raisa, then quickly back to Nightwalker. "I have work to do and not much time, if you don't want to be late for the ceremony."

"I'm ready," Raisa said, taking a deep breath.. "Let's begin."

Han looked pointedly at Nightwalker and jerked his head toward the door. "Out."

"I'm staying," Reid Demonai said, folding his arms and widening his stance as if he never intended to budge.

"We should do this in private, Your Highness," Han said. "If I'm going to protect you, the fewer who know what I'm up to, the better."

Han spoke to Raisa, ignoring Nightwalker. Well, Raisa thought, this is a welcome change. Ever since Raisa had confessed her true identity, Han hadn't spoken to her more often or at greater length than he had to. It was as if he had to pay a dear price for every word he spoke.

"I will not leave you alone with the princess heir," Nightwalker said. "It's too much of a risk, given the history of jinxflinger interference with our queens."

These two hate each other, Raisa thought, and it seems to go beyond the usual suspicion between wizard and clan. After all, Han should be comfortable with the Spirit clans. He'd fostered with them throughout his boyhood. He hadn't even been a wizard all that long.

A clearing of throats startled her. She looked up to find they were both looking at her, waiting for a decision.

"I've known Nightwalker for years," Raisa said to Han. "He's serving as part of my guard today. If he can be trusted with that, then surely—"

"I don't want him here, distracting me," Han said. "This is hard enough as is."

"So you admit it," Nightwalker said. "You don't know what you're doing."

"That's exactly the kind of flap-jawed, ignorant remark that I don't need while I'm working," Han said, looking at Raisa and raising his eyebrows as if to say, *See?*

"He stays," Raisa said, feeling like she was refereeing in the school yard. "But be quiet, Nightwalker, and allow Alister to do his work, or you're out."

Han jerked his chin at Nightwalker. "You. Sit in the corner and out of the way if you don't want to get splashed with magic."

Nightwalker scowled suspiciously but did as he was told.

Han circled around Raisa, appraising her. "Stand still," he warned her. "I'm going to have to touch you."

He sounded resigned to it, more than anything else.

Han slid his hand inside his coat, and Raisa knew he was gripping the serpent amulet. Maybe that was why he didn't want Nightwalker there. He didn't seem to want to display that amulet to anyone in the camps.

Raisa tensed up, her skin tingling in anticipation of the contact. His fingers hissed and fizzed as they brushed lightly against her head, her shoulders, the back of her neck, her waist. It reminded Raisa of the sculptor who'd struck her portrait for the crown coin, getting the feel of the clay before he shaped it.

Han stepped back and rubbed his chin, frowning. Then his expression cleared as he stared down at her hand. "Oh," he said. "You need to take off the talisman ring, or it won't work."

Raisa looked down at the wolf ring on her right hand.

"Your Highness, Elena Demonai gave you that ring for protection against jinxflinger charms," Nightwalker said. "Now would *not* be a good time to take it off. Not when you're going to be facing the most powerful jinxflingers in the Vale."

"Now would be a *very* good time to take it off," Han said. "If you want this plan to work."

"Forgetting about Alister and what he might be up to, that ring protects you if one of the wizards at the memorial decides to flame you," Nightwalker argued. "Without it, you'll be vulnerable." He paused, then murmured, not quite under his breath, "Unless that's the idea."

"She won't be vulnerable if you shut up and let me do my job," Han said, his hand still inside his neckline, his chin cocked up aggressively.

"Stop it," Raisa said. She slid the ring from her finger and tucked it into a pouch at her belt. "There. I'll have it right here in case I need it. You'd better hurry. It must be nearly time to leave."

This time was different. Han murmured charms as he circled around her, his face hard with concentration, his eyes fixed and focused internally. His fingers kindled little fires wherever he touched her. Raisa gasped as the magic slid under her skin, bringing the blood to the surface. She felt glowing and dizzy-headed, like she'd just stepped out of the sweat lodge at Demonai Camp.

Or like a lover after an episode of kissing.

Nightwalker watched from his corner, taut as a bowstring.

Then the wolves came. Singly and in pairs, they slid under the canvas dividers and through the walls, eye bright, tongues lolling, until a dozen were assembled, sitting on their haunches in a circle around them.

It reminded Raisa of the dream she'd had after Byrne was killed in Marisa Pines Pass—the visitation of the wolf queens on the night her mother died. There was gray-eyed Hanalea and green-eyed Althea. Sometimes, for a split second, she thought she saw the queens themselves.

Han glanced at the wolves, then back at Raisa. "Friends of yours?"

Raisa blinked at him. "You can see them?"

"I've been seeing them, off and on, since we—since I healed you," Han said. "I hoped they would come today. I don't know if this will work, but . . ." He extended his hands toward the wolf queens. Flame danced on his fingertips. Light arced from his hands to the wolves and back to him.

Hanalea tilted her head, gazing at Han with a wolfish grin.

Why would Han Alister see wolves? Raisa wondered. That

was a trait of the Gray Wolf line, linked to the gift of prophesy. It didn't make sense.

Must be some quirk of the healing process, she thought. Of their joining together.

The wolves closed their eyes and laid back their ears. Lifting their muzzles toward the sky, they began to howl, a mournful cry that raised the hair on Raisa's neck.

"Oh!" she said, shivering.

Nightwalker came upright, looking ready to spring. "What is it, Briar Rose? What did he do?"

"Your Highness, have you ever noticed how hard it is to concentrate and do things right when somebody's yammering in your ear?" Han said. "If this goes wrong, I'm just saying, I'm not the one to blame."

Despite his sardonic tone, sweat pebbled his forehead and dewed his upper lip, like he was expending considerable energy. Or was nervous about the outcome.

The wolves finished their dirge. Hanalea turned toward Raisa and dipped her head. The royal pack melted into shadow and dissipated.

Han withdrew his hand and stood, head down, taking quick shallow breaths like he'd run a great race. The Lone Hunter amulet underlit his face, creating shadows and highlighting planes. Sweat dripped off him, spotting the rug.

Raisa wrapped her arms around herself, gripping her elbows to either side. She still tingled all over, but that seemed to be the only lasting effect. "Was it . . . did it work?" she asked.

Han raised his head and blotted perspiration from his forehead with his sleeve. "We'll see soon enough."

Raisa saw the question on Nightwalker's face and decided to ask it herself, thinking she might actually get an answer. "What were you trying to do?"

"I was creating a sending."

"A sending? What's that?"

"A glamour. An image to use once we're on Marianna Peak. Something that will impress and confuse the Wizard Council and the rest of the bluebloods. Something that will make you a difficult target." Han glanced at Nightwalker. "Remember? I said I would create a magical distraction," he said, as if Nightwalker needed simple speech.

"Can I put my ring back on?" Raisa asked, pressing her fingers against her pouch.

Han frowned, biting his lower lip, then shook his head. "Better not. I think we have to keep the magical connection alive until after."

Elena poked her head through the doorway. "Are you ready? We must go, granddaughter."

Raisa would ride hidden amid the Demonai contingent escorting her grandmother to the queen's memorial.

Fire Dancer waited with the ponies. Han pulled him aside, leaned in, and murmured something in his ear. Dancer nodded, looking at Raisa.

Nightwalker came and draped a Demonai shadow cloak over Raisa's funeral garb, fastening it at the neck, and letting his hands linger on her shoulders.

The memorial for the queen was scheduled for late afternoon. Their journey would take them the better part of the day since they intended to keep to the mountains, circling around the

Vale from Marisa Pines, crossing the Dyrnnewater to the west of Fellsmarch, and coming at Marianna Peak from the northwest.

Elena and Willo rode alongside Raisa, while the Demonai warriors rode ahead and behind. Han and Dancer rode side-by-side, hands on their amulets, stoking them up for what lay ahead. Raisa wondered how much Han's had been drained by the creation of the "sending." She hoped it would be worth the cost.

Whenever Raisa looked at them, the two wizards had their heads together, talking quietly as they rode along. Dancer carried two large panniers on his pony, in addition to his bedroll.

It would be a cold, clear day in the mountains, perhaps a bit warmer downslope where the service would be. The stars blinked out to the east as the sun broke over the Spirits, spilling into the Vale below.

"Mother would love this day," Raisa said to Elena, squinting against the slanting light. "She loved the sun, even if she didn't love the cold."

"Mmm." Elena seemed preoccupied, no doubt worrying about her son, Averill.

Love makes you vulnerable, Raisa thought. And yet she'd always hoped for it.

They crossed the Dyrnnewater in early afternoon, on a high bridge over the river's foaming roar. Though they were too high to smell it, the water below carried with it all the filth and jetsam of the overcrowded capital to the east.

When I am queen . . . Raisa thought, as she had so many times before. And stopped.

I *am* queen.

They climbed high into the northern Spirits again, catching

glimpses of the greening Vale below. Raisa eagerly drank in views of the spires, domes, and turrets of faraway Fellsmarch. It glittered in the sunlight like a child's fairy city, the kind of place that disappeared when you came too close.

I'm coming home, she swore. Tonight, if I have my way.

Northwest of the Vale, they would leave the trail that overlooked it and strike north and east again, to come in behind Marianna and descend between her twin peaks. They paused at the joining of the trails to eat and rest the horses before the long climb ahead.

Leaving Switcher in the hands of Night Bird, Raisa walked a short distance through the trees to where she could take a last look into the Vale before they rounded the shoulder of the mountain and it disappeared from view.

The valley had come alive with people. Travelers clogged the roads, using conveyances appropriate to their stations. Some rode on fine horses, leaving the roads and cutting cross-country when they became impatient with their slow progress. Fine carriages competed for space with wagons packed with those who could spare a girlie for a ride. And some came afoot, even entire families, mothers and fathers carrying small children, scarves wrapped around their faces to turn the dust of the road.

They jammed the roads that descended from Fellsmarch, crossed the Vale, and climbed Marianna to the north. The citizens of Fellsmarch were turning out to say good-bye to their queen.

Raisa was touched and surprised. Marianna had not been popular, at least among the folk in the poorer neighborhoods of the capital. They had exploded in riots when it was rumored that the queen meant to set Raisa aside and name Mellony heir in her place.

"Sweet Martyred Lady," she whispered. "It looks like the entire city is on the move."

"Ragmarket and Southbridge, anyway. Plus all the bluebloods, of course."

Raisa flinched and turned. Han Alister stood next to her, looking down on the Vale. He could ghost about like any clan warrior.

He shaded his eyes, the wind ruffling his hair. "Maybe Westmarket, Roast Meat Hill, and the Bottoms, too."

"What do you mean?" she said. "How do you know?"

"I sent Cat Tyburn down to the city," Han said. "Told her to spread the word that the Princess Raisa would be here and might need an assist. That there were them that might try and take her throne away from her. Or hush her on the spot or slap her in darbies." He slid easily back into the thieves' cant she'd spent months tutoring him out of.

"What?" She tilted her head, looking up at him. "After we went to all this effort to keep my presence a secret, you spread it all over town?"

Han rubbed the back of his neck. "Do you think Lord Bayar listens to rumors from Ragmarket? Do you think the Council of Nobles meets in the Keg and Crown?" He laughed. "The Raggers and Southies are no danger to you unless you're carrying a fat purse through the streets. It's the bluebloods you got to watch out for. I hear they're rum liars and connivers." He looked straight at her, his blue eyes hard and brilliant as sapphires.

The pressure of his gaze was like a physical blow, but Raisa forced herself to stand her ground. "Han. I'm sorry I lied to you," she said, putting her hand on his arm. "If I had it to do over, I'd—"

"There are no do-overs, are there, Your Highness?" Han said.

"No," Raisa said, "but—"

"Anyway, don't worry about Ragmarket," Han said, stepping back, pulling free of her grasp. "It's the shoulder tap in the back hall of the palace you should worry about." He seemed determined not to get into the unfinished business between them.

"I know that," Raisa said, giving up. "Despite that, I plan to return to Fellsmarch Castle tonight, as queen-to-be."

Han glanced over his shoulder to where the Demonai were busy with the horses. "They're not going to be happy about that idea," he said. "'Specially Nightwalker. He can't control you down in the city."

"He doesn't control me now," Raisa snapped.

"He means to marry you," Han said, staring out over the valley. "Just so you know."

Raisa resisted the impulse to look back at Nightwalker. "What makes you think that?"

"He's not that hard to figure out." He lifted his chin, the angled light revealing a faint reddish stubble in profile.

Raisa wrenched her mind back to the conversation. "Well, if he wants to marry me, he'll have to stand in line," she said. "I'm sick and tired of being a means to an end."

Han turned to look at her, puzzlement flickering over his face. "A means to an end. You? What do you mean?"

"Everybody wants to marry the bloody throne. Nobody

would be interested if I lived in Ragmarket. I think I'll stay a maid."

"You have to marry, right? So you can assure a peaceful succession?" He'd resumed his carefully blank expression, but she noticed his hands were fisted at his sides.

"Like the one we're having right now?" She waited, and when he said nothing, went on. "I know you agree with me," Raisa said. "I need to get back to the palace immediately or chance losing the throne."

"And you're telling me this because . . . ?"

"I need your help. To return to Fellsmarch, I mean. I'll need protection."

Han shrugged. "Wasn't that the agreement? That I'd fight the Wizard Council on behalf of the clans and the true line of queens?" That detached, mocking tone was becoming annoyingly familiar.

I've hurt him, Raisa thought. I've hurt him badly, and violated his trust. Somehow I have to find a way to win it back. To win him back. To prove myself to him.

"I wasn't there when the agreement was made," Raisa said, looking into his eyes. "Anyway, that was between you and the clans. I know you're still resentful of the bargain you made— understandably. I don't need some grudging, halfhearted letter-of-the-law effort. That will get me killed."

"That'd be a shame," Han murmured. He paused, thinking, his fair brows drawn together. "Isn't that Corporal Byrne's job? Protecting you, I mean? You planning to make him Captain of the Queen's Guard?"

Raisa nodded. "He already is, in a way. I'll make it public at the coronation. But I'll need both of you," she said. "Even that might not be enough."

"What's in it for me?" Han asked, squinting into the distance. "I'm a sell–sword, after all. What are you offering in trade, since you seem intent on buying me all over again." His tone was light, but Raisa heard the trader underneath the words.

"What do you want?" Raisa asked.

Han pretended to study on it, but she suspected he had the answers ready. "Well, first off, I'll need a crib in the palace so I can keep an eye on you and everyone else. A nice place, mind you," he said, narrowing his eyes as if she might try to cheat him out of his due. "Big enough so guests can stay over. Adjoining your rooms."

"Adjoining my. . ." Raisa frowned. "No. That's not possible." Having a wizard next door was not a good idea. It had never been done. Even Gavan Bayar and Queen Marianna had kept a gallery between them.

Han raised his hands, palms up. "Do you want protection or not? Do you want me clear across the palace when you need me?" When she still hesitated, he added, "You asked what I wanted, remember? I won't take a job if I can't do it right. You know who'll get the blame if it goes wrong."

"All right," she said, wondering how Amon Byrne would react to this idea. "But no guests. Not right next door to my chambers." For security reasons, she told herself.

He smiled crookedly. "Your Highness, I have lots of friends who've never even been in a palace and—"

She held up her hand. "Never mind, Alister. I can tell this isn't going to work. I'll take my chances with—"

"You win," he interrupted, as if knowing he'd pushed too

far. "No guests—overnight, anyway."

She gazed into his face for a long moment, and he looked back steadily. "All right, then, so we are agreed. We—"

"Second, I'll need a monthly stipend," he said. "The clans are paying my living expenses, but I don't want to have to rely on that, in case they get aggravated with me. I got people to keep in the city, so—" He looked sideways at her, as if to assess the size of her purse. "Fifty girlies to start."

"Fifty girlies!" Raisa rolled her eyes. "Who are you keeping? A harem of fancy girls?" It wouldn't surprise her, given the stories she'd heard about the streetlord Cuffs Alister.

"It isn't your business what I do with the money," Han said. "You just have to decide whether it's worth it to you."

Raisa sighed. "All right. Fifty girlies. I'll speak with the steward when we—"

"Third, you need to keep teaching me manners," he broke in. "Protocol, dress, dancing, everything I need to know to be at court. Twice a week, an hour, minimum."

"Really?" Raisa raised an eyebrow. "Seems to me you're doing all right on your own—when you make the effort, that is. But if that's what you want, I will arrange for a tutor to—"

"No." He shook his head. "You. I want *you* to do it, just the two of us. It will give us a good excuse to meet in private on a regular basis." There was something in his gaze, something that suggested this was some kind of test that she needed to pass.

Raisa pressed her lips together to keep any words from spilling. And nodded her assent. Access was one of a monarch's favors to give away, and Han wanted guaranteed access on an ongoing basis. It was clever on his part.

"All right," she said. "There can't possibly be anything else."

"One last thing. I want you to name me to the Wizard Council," Han said.

Raisa stared at him. "What?"

"Back at Oden's Ford, when I asked about the council, you said that the queen appoints one member. That's what I want."

"I thought you hated the Wizard Council," Raisa said. "Why would you want to be a member?"

"Maybe I want to be a member of a club that would never let me in otherwise," Han said. "Just to give them the itches."

"Isn't that whom you're supposed to be fighting?" Raisa's voice rose.

Han put his finger to his lips. "Shhh. I'll be hacking at the council from the inside. But the Demonai won't understand. That's one reason I need a stipend from you."

"If they think you've turned, you'll be risking more than your income," Raisa said.

"I'll take that chance," Han said. "I'll be working for you, and you're the queen, right?"

Raisa rubbed her forehead. "Are you sure you're not a trader under the skin?" she asked.

"We're all traders in Ragmarket," Han said.

Raisa thought it over. Truth be told, she preferred Han Alister to most anyone else she could think of appointing to the council. He was likely less dangerous, since he had no preexisting alliances or family connections. And she couldn't imagine that he'd ever ally himself with the Bayars. "All right," Raisa said. "I'll appoint you to the Wizard Council."

Han spit in his palm and held out his hand.

Rolling her eyes, Raisa spit in her own palm and clasped his.

"Briar Rose?"

Raisa looked up, startled. Reid Nightwalker had approached without her noticing. His dark eyes flicked from Raisa to Han. "The horses are grained and rested and we're ready to go," he said, "It's another two hours to Marianna Peak."

Han smiled. "We're done," he said, and walked toward the horses with something of a swagger.

Reid stared after him.

Raisa wondered how much he had overheard.

She wondered if Han had intended that he overhear.

Who was the real player—her or Han Alister? And what was his game?

She was in over her head in so many ways. Vulnerable to him in so many ways.

I've got to get better at this, she thought, if I'm going to survive.

CHAPTER TWENTY-THREE

MAKING SHOW

It was midafternoon when they arrived on the north slope of Marianna, just below the joining of her twin peaks. The Demonai had sent several warriors ahead to scout the area and make sure the way was clear of unfriendly eyes.

Night Bird was one of them. She returned to say that the regular army had established a light perimeter to the north of the memorial site.

"They've posted soldiers upslope from the memorial site, but not many," she said. "Most have been sent downslope, since they seem more worried about threats from below. There is a huge crowd already gathered, and more coming all the time. The Queen's Guard has erected barricades around the memorial site itself, but the entire slope of Marianna is already packed with people."

"Really?" Elena said, her brow crinkling. "What kind of people? Soldiers, or . . ."

"Within the perimeter, it's jinxflingers and the Vale nobility and soldiers," Night Bird said. "Downslope, they're regular citizens. Not bluebloods, but tradespeople and laborers, line soldiers and scholars. Probably thieves and pickpockets, too. Thousands of people."

Raisa glanced at Han, who seemed totally focused on Night Bird. He wore his politely interested street face.

Night Bird continued her report. "I spoke with the corporal in charge of the Guard and told them that Elena *Cennestre* and a small party of clan royalty and Demonai warriors would be arriving soon from the north. I said that after the ceremony we'd be camping overnight on the north slope, then returning home tomorrow or the next day."

Strategically, that was a good place to be. The Demonai could place archers on the heights, and that would leave a back door open for a hasty retreat, if need be.

"Who was the corporal?" Raisa asked. "The one in charge?"

"Corporal Fallon," Bird replied. "Mason Fallon."

A cold rivulet of apprehension trickled between Raisa's shoulder blades. Someone else she didn't know, handpicked by her enemies. She was glad Amon would be there.

"What's the arrangement for the memorial?" Elena said.

"They've pitched several large pavilions around the queen's pyre," Night Bird said. "One flies the Gray Wolf banner, so it is likely the Princess Mellony is there. Another bears the Bayar pennant. A third carries the unlidded eye, though I didn't see Lord Demonai. The tomb is upslope from the memorial site, built into the side of the mountain. A number of people are milling around, making preparations."

"Did you see Corporal Byrne?" Raisa asked.

Bird shook her head. "He's escorting the queen's body. A smaller tomb for the late captain is to be built downslope from the queen's. I saw several flatland soldiers guarding the site."

So Captain Byrne *would* be buried near his queen, Raisa thought. In the arms of her mountain. And Amon was there, waiting for her. And the rest of the Gray Wolves—friends she hadn't seen since Oden's Ford. Friends she could depend on. She took a deep breath, releasing it slowly. Good.

"Fallon said that Speaker Jemson would conduct a brief service—first for Captain Byrne, and then for the queen. Then Queen Marianna's body will be committed to the flame, freeing her spirit to take up residence in the mountain. The High Wizard and a representative of the Council of Regents will also speak."

"But not the Princess Mellony?" Raisa asked.

Bird shook her head. "They say the princess is too grief-stricken to speak."

Or too intimidated by her keepers, Raisa thought grimly. If she would be queen, she needs to learn to speak up. Her people need to hear directly from her.

They set up a temporary camp under cover of the forest, then gathered one last time—Raisa, along with Reid Nightwalker Demonai, Willo Watersong, Elena *Cennestre*, Han Alister, and Fire Dancer.

"Briar Rose," Elena said. "I know that you want to be present for your mother's service. I still say it would be safest if you watch from the crest of the mountain. We could leave a party of warriors with you as guard. That way, you can see everything and yet be out of harm's way."

Raisa shook her head. "I will attend my mother's service," she said. "We have already discussed this."

Elena sighed and rubbed her chin. "I thought you would say that." She put a hand on Raisa's arm. "Then I beg of you. You are dressed like a Demonai. If you must descend to the tomb, then you're unlikely to be recognized if we ride as a group, with you hidden in our midst."

"Grandmother, I must participate in the service as the princess heir," Raisa said. "Before as many witnesses as possible, so that they cannot later deny that I have returned to the queendom. It's the only way to secure my succession to the throne."

"You cannot ascend the Gray Wolf throne if you are dead," Elena retorted. "We cannot protect you if you wade into a crowd. I know you are eager to prove that you are not a coward, but—"

"I'm not doing this to prove anything except my presence and intention to ascend to the throne," Raisa said. "I am doing this to honor my mother."

"If you live to be crowned, I hope that obstinacy will serve you well as queen," Elena growled.

"Han Alister is pledged to secure my safety—that was your doing, remember?" Raisa said. "And Fire Dancer has agreed to help. We've worked out a plan, and we need to follow it."

All eyes turned to Han, who stood, feet slightly apart, arms folded across his chest, his brilliant hair feathered by the downslope breeze. His hunter amulet glowed against the sober black of his tunic.

Fire Dancer had left the group to fetch the panniers he'd been carrying all day. Unstrapping the lids, he lifted out a glittering steel breastplate and gauntlets with the Gray Wolf emblem emblazoned on them.

"Armor?" Elena said. "You're wearing armor? That's the plan? You think *that* will protect you against wizard flame?"

"No, Grandmother, but it will protect me against other kinds of assassins," Raisa said. "Remember, Queen Marianna died in a fall from a tower. Captain Byrne was shot through with arrows. This way, wizards won't be able to hire others to do their dirty work for them. They'll have to come out into the open if they want to take me on."

Elena fingered the breastplate, running her worn fingers over the beading at the neck and the faint runes etched into the sides. She looked up at Raisa, eyes glittering. "This is Demonai work. Who made this, Briar Rose, and when? There's considerable power in it."

"I made it," Dancer said, setting the panniers aside. He stood and turned to face her. "It's my work."

An angry murmur arose among the Demonai warriors.

"You?" Elena stared at him. "But that's impossible. You're a—"

"I'm a flashcrafter, Elena *Cennestre*," Dancer said, lifting his chin. "Or mean to be."

"Who's teaching you?" Elena demanded. "Because whoever it is plays a dangerous game."

"Just stop it!" Raisa said. "How can we expect to win against our enemies when we keep bickering among ourselves?"

This is my life from now on, she thought. Sorting out squabbles among wizards, clan, and Valefolk.

"Wizards are not allowed to craft magical weaponry, Your

Highness," Elena said. "It concentrates too much power in their hands."

"That's not part of the Næming," Dancer said, setting his feet stubbornly. "That's not written."

"It's not written because no one ever expected that a jinx-flinger would be born into the camps," Nightwalker said. "Or would live long enough to—"

"Fire Dancer's gifts come from the Maker," someone said in a loud clear voice. "Who are we to question the Maker's will?"

Raisa swung around. It was Night Bird, the young Demonai warrior. The one who still worshipped at the altar of Reid Nightwalker.

There followed a stunned silence. Dancer and Han flat-out stared at her, but Nightwalker looked the most astonished of all.

"Perhaps Dancer's unique talents are just what we need right now," Night Bird went on. "Perhaps we should welcome any gift that helps keep this queen safe."

Reid Nightwalker's expression turned from astonishment to betrayal. "Night Bird, think again," he said. "Some gifts are better declined."

"Who decides that?" Han said. "Not the Demonai."

"*I* have decided," Raisa said in a loud voice. "I have decided to accept Fire Dancer's gift, and that ends the discussion. You all will go down and join the others at the memorial site. Han, Dancer, and I will remain here until it is time for the service to begin."

"Why don't you ride down with us now?" Nightwalker asked, eying Han, making no attempt to hide his mistrust.

"I need to be seen as queen of all the people of the Fells—Valefolk, wizards, and the Spirit clans," Raisa said. "I'm already dressed in clan garb. If I ride in with upland clan, I'll appear to belong to you." Surveying the sea of frowns around her, she added, "Don't worry, I don't mean to die today."

Reid Nightwalker insisted on staying behind with Raisa and a small party of Demonai—in case of ambush, he said. Whether by Han Alister or somebody else, he didn't say. Raisa and her party stood in the fringes of the trees, watching the rest of the Demonai descend to the tomb. Including Bird, whom Nightwalker sent on with the others.

Raisa sat down with the copy of the *Book of Temple Prayers and Liturgy* she'd brought from Marisa Pines. Han and Dancer rested under a tree, talking softly, their hands on their amulets, storing as much power as possible in the time they had left. Reid Nightwalker and his warriors kept watch on events below. Willo sorted through the bundles of cloth that had come out of her saddlebags.

Raisa read and reread the passages assigned to her, struggling to concentrate, speaking the powerful words under her breath, committing them once again to memory.

Raisa had studied the prayers in preparation for her name day, but she'd never actually attended a state funeral. Queen Lissa, her grandmother, had died before Raisa was born. Marianna, too, had ascended to the throne at a young age. Raisa couldn't help wondering if her mother would have done better had she had more time to grow into the job.

Now Raisa faced the same dilemma. Would it be too much power, too soon, for her?

A slight noise broke into her thoughts. She looked up to find Nightwalker standing in front of her. "They're bringing Queen

Marianna's body in procession up the mountain," he said. "It's time for us to go."

Raisa stood, and Nightwalker put his hands on her shoulders, leaned in and kissed her forehead. "Be safe today, Briar Rose," he said. He shifted his eyes to Han and Dancer, then back to her. "Be wary."

"All will be well, you'll see," Raisa said, looking into Nightwalker's eyes, willing him to believe her. Willing it to be true.

"I hope you are right," Nightwalker said. "This is difficult for me." He smiled faintly, bowed his head, then turned away. The remaining Demonai warriors mounted up, then clattered over the hill and out of sight, leaving Willo, Han, Dancer, and Raisa alone.

Raisa geared up for the war ahead, knowing that when it comes to politics, looking the part is often half the battle.

Willo had sorted several garments into piles. She gave Han a bundle of black-and-silver fabric. "It is not my best work, Hunts Alone, since it was done so quickly," she said. "But I think it will serve." Her dark eyes studied him as if trying to divine his purpose.

Han only nodded, clutching the garment in his arms. "Thank you." He turned and strode away, toward his horse.

Raisa had little time to be curious. Willo handed her a thick quilted jacket—armor padding of a sort. Raisa removed the shadow cloak and put the jacket on over her clan garb.

Dancer unbuckled the breastplate, then held it open as Raisa slipped her arms through. He fastened it down the front, shifting it so it sat squarely on her shoulders. She poked her arms into the gauntlets, and he fastened those as well. He did good work—they were lightweight and well finished. The magic in them buzzed against her skin.

Willo draped a crimson cloak across Raisa's shoulders. It carried an image of a snarling gray wolf in intricate stitches. "I hope you know what you are doing," she said, shifting her gaze from Raisa to Han to Dancer. "This will mark you out like a banner."

"So Lord Bayar won't need his magic glasses to see me," Raisa said. "Perfect." She ran her fingers over the stitches. "This is beautiful," she breathed. "How in the world did you . . . ?"

"I had made it ahead to honor your coronation," Willo said. She smiled sadly. "I had no idea I would be giving this gift so soon."

"Thank you," Raisa said, and embraced her, the armor a barrier between them. "What will you . . . ?"

"I will stay here and wait for you," Willo said quickly, as if she'd been anticipating the question. "I have already mourned Marianna according to the Old Ways. I've spoken to Averill. He understands, as I hope you do."

"Of course," Raisa said, confused. "But . . ."

"Your Highness?" Han's voice broke into their conversation. Raisa looked up to see that Han and Dancer were already mounted.

Dancer waved his hand and galloped over the crest of the hill and disappeared. He would ride ahead, finding a vantage point where he could keep an eye on the Bayars and other wizards present and prevent any magical attacks.

Han sat on his horse with his back very straight, his face as cold, still, and pale as sculpted marble, his vivid blue eyes the only color. He wore the coat Willo had made for him. It was black and silver, decorated with paint and stitching. Metallic serpents squirmed up the sleeves from hem to shoulder. A gray wolf and a raven faced each other on the lapels of the coat, and the back was embroidered with a wizard staff coiled with serpents, thrust through the Gray Wolf crown.

What's that about? Raisa wondered. He was of common birth, so would have no family crest. Then again, some commoners devised a signia when they rose in the world.

Han didn't seem to be the sort to care about those sorts of things.

The gray wolf must signify that he was in her service. But why would he go to so much trouble to proclaim an obligation that he no doubt found onerous? Also, he must have discussed it with Willo long before their trailside conversation. The feeling returned that she was being played by a master.

"Your Highness?" Han repeated. It still sounded peculiar when he said it. He jerked his head toward the top of the hill. "Are you ready?"

Raisa managed to haul herself into Switcher's saddle despite the added weight of the armor. The mare crow-hopped a little at the unexpected burden.

"Yes," Raisa said, steadying herself. "Let's go."

CHAPTER TWENTY-FOUR
FAREWELLS

Han looked down the freshly named Marianna Peak to the preparations under way downslope. From this distance he could make out spots of color, like splashes of paint. Bright bluejacket blue splashed around what must be Captain Edon Byrne's modest tomb.

Han wished he'd had a chance to discuss his plans with Corporal Byrne. That bluejacket was a good one to have at your back.

He wished he'd had a chance to pick Crow's brain in preparation—to ask his advice. It had been a mistake to surprise Crow by introducing him to Dancer just when he needed his help the most. He wondered if he'd ever see him again.

If wishes were horses, beggars would ride, Mam used to say.

The Demonai pavilion flew the unlidded eye banner, and the Demonai themselves were clustered upslope from the dais, like the brown and pale green of the springtime forest. Bird was down there somewhere.

She'd surprised him by defying Reid Demonai. She'd always been strong-willed and opinionated, and he guessed that was likely to cause friction with Nightwalker. It would be interesting to see what would happen from here on.

Well. Not all that interesting. What happened between Bird and Nightwalker was not his business.

The Gray Wolf banner snapped in the breeze, high atop the tent where the Princess Mellony must be housed. And the Wizard Council had its own pavilion, bearing the flame-and-sword motif of the High Wizard.

They reminded Han of armed camps facing each other, like what he'd seen in war-torn Arden. He recalled what Crow had said about leverage. Apply a little pressure where it will do the most good, and a lot can be accomplished. There was opportunity in the thousand-year-old faults that split the peoples of the Fells. Han meant to take advantage. It was the only way to win this thing. The only way to get what he wanted—once he decided what that was.

The dais was a flower garden of color—packed with the nobility dressed in their best. It was, after all, a joyous occasion for somebody. Another queen would soon rule over the Vale.

Somebody had made that happen, and Han needed to find out who, and why.

The lower slopes of Marianna were layered with the muted tones commoners favored—colors that wouldn't show dirt with repeated wearings. Five-day colors, Mam would have called them.

The very ground seemed to heave and ripple as thousands of people jockeyed for a better view. Latecomers had no hope of getting within miles of the ceremony. Cat would be down there somewhere, too, working her own kind of magic.

A long procession of mounted bluebloods snaked its way toward the pavilions at the center of the burial site. Even at a distance, Han could tell they had their rum togs on. That would be the dead queen's body making its way to the site of the memorial. The crowds on the lower slopes parted grudgingly to let her through. Han was accustomed to a festival atmosphere at executions and blueblood funerals. It was something out of the ordinary, at least, for those with monotonous lives. But the mood of this crowd seemed grim and threatening.

A thin blue line of guards divided the crowds from their betters upslope.

The queen's bier was followed by an honor guard of bluejackets. Amon Byrne rode in the lead, cradling the urn holding his father's ashes. And immediately behind him, a riderless horse, standard military issue, with boots reversed in the stirrups.

Han looked sideways at Rebecca—Raisa—the queen. She might have been an elven warrior from stories, with her magicked armor, her made-to-measure sword, and her windblown cap of hair. Her Gray Wolf cloak fluttered out behind her in the breeze.

A memory came to him—Rebecca in the alleyway at Oden's Ford, stalking toward him, her blade in her hand, leaving a would-be attacker flat on his back on the cobblestones. Rebecca promising Han the same treatment if he didn't get out of her way.

The images reverberated in his mind until he felt half sick. Were these really one and the same? The friend he knew and the heir to the throne of the Fells?

When he focused on Raisa, he saw that her nose had gone

pink, and her eyes fixed on the queen's bier glittered with unshed tears.

He looked away, beating back sympathy. The only words spoken over Mam's and Mari's bodies were his own awkward prayers—and they'd nearly died unspoken on his tongue. What use would it be to call on a Maker who would allow Mam and Mari to burn to death?

Raisa was learning the lessons he'd been taught a long time ago—what could happen when you crossed a powerful blueblood.

Those bearing the casket had reached the pavilion where the memorial was to be held. The linen-wrapped body was lifted into place on the flower-decked bier that had been prepared for it. Corporal Byrne handed down the urn, which was placed in a position of honor below the queen's casket. Then he dismounted and stood at attention with the rest of the honor guard. The bluebloods flowed into the high-priced seats close to the stage.

It was time.

Han looked up at the sky. Storm clouds piled up behind Hanalea, streaming over the lower peaks like long arms reaching out for the crowd. The sky to the west was a peculiar green, and lightning flickered over the West Wall. The wind picked up, sweeping down over Marianna, reminding any who had forgotten that spring was a fickle season in the mountain home.

Han's neck prickled. Say what you wanted about the Gray Wolf queens, they had a magical connection to the Spirit Mountains. He hoped it would make his job easier.

He glanced at Raisa, and she nodded, lifting her chin, green eyes wide and unblinking. Fearless.

"Careful you keep your seat," Han cautioned her, wishing he could issue a clearer warning. "I don't know how the ponies will react to all this."

She nodded again, gripping her reins, lips pressed tightly together.

All right, then. Han extended his free hand toward her, igniting the linkages he'd already established. They both began to glow, kindling brighter and brighter until they shone like two stars fallen to earth. Raisa extended her hands, and they trailed flame in a wide arc, like wings. Their ponies, too, flickered with brilliant flame, resembling the horses the sun god was said to drive across the sky.

The phantasm surrounding them grew, expanding so that they appeared to be twice their actual size. At the very least, Han thought, it would make them tricky targets if the magical barriers failed.

Then the wolves came—terrible and wonderful, with flaming eyes and razor-sharp teeth and great ruffs of hair about their massive shoulders. They were wolves the size of horses, with teeth the size of belt daggers.

The wolves were real—to Han's eyes, at least. They'd been appearing to him ever since he'd joined himself to Raisa in his desperate attempt to heal her. Han had only wrapped glamours about them—increasing their size, enhancing their appearance, and making them visible to everyone.

Now they resembled the monstrous beasts from Mam's scare-stories—the hellhounds that the Breaker would ride at the end of days.

Thirty-two wolves preceded them over the hill, descending

toward the crowd on the mountainside. Nearly two score Gray Wolf queens since Hanalea.

When Han and Raisa crested the hill, light spilled down the mountainside ahead of them, dispelling the cloud shadow.

We must look like a sunrise, Han thought. A new day. He smiled to himself. He'd given himself a visible role in this drama on purpose. Though it would make him a target, it was time people started seeing him differently.

He was making show, along with Raisa.

Heads turned as they walked their horses down the mountain, side by side. The Demonai warriors were farthest upslope, and they were watching for them. The clanfolk turned and faced up the mountain, shading their eyes against the glare.

The sound of their voices washed over Han. "The wolf queens come to greet their sister Marianna!" they cried, as planned. "Here come the Gray Wolf queens!"

The Demonai drew off to either side, leaving a wide path down through the middle. They dropped to their knees as the wolves passed through.

By now Han was close enough to see the reaction among the bluebloods. Atop the dais he was pleased to see Speaker Jemson in his fancy Temple Day robes. Jemson squinted up at them, his forehead crinkled, his expression faintly perplexed.

The platform was thick with wizards—Han recognized the High Wizard, Gavan Bayar, and Micah and Fiona, too, along with a half dozen others.

Lord Bayar squinted at them, his free arm slung over his eyes. It seemed he couldn't tell who they were, blinded as he was by Han's brilliant sending.

All three Bayars positioned themselves between Han's fetch and the dignitaries on the stage. They kept their hands on their amulets as if they wanted to use them but couldn't figure out what spell to cast.

A bulky sword-dangler in an elaborate Highlander uniform laden with military glitterbits leaned over to speak to Lord Bayar. Bayar shook his head, scowling, without taking his eyes off Han and Raisa.

Behind them, Averill Lightfoot Demonai, the queen's consort and Raisa's father, stood next to a pretty blond girlie with wide blue eyes. Lightfoot rested a reassuring hand on her shoulder, or maybe it was to keep her in her seat. Tall and slender, she wore diamonds at her throat and wrists and a kind of baby crown on her head.

She didn't look at all like Raisa, but Han guessed she must be the younger sister, Princess Mellony.

She was impressed by his sending, at least. She looked scared to death.

The bluejackets had formed up, swords drawn, making a fragile barrier in front of the dais. They had starch, Han thought, confronting wolves that looked like they could swallow them whole, two at a time.

The wolves did not attack, however. They lined up in front of the bluejackets, then sat on their haunches, exposing their great teeth.

All was silent for a long moment, save the snap of the banners in the wind. Even the crowd on the lower slopes had gone absolutely quiet, as if holding its breath.

"Who are you?" Lord Bayar demanded. "How dare you

disrupt our memorial for Queen Marianna with a conjure-piece?"

Raisa replied in a high, clear voice, "Do you not know me, Lord Bayar?"

Han's eyes were on the Princess Mellony as Raisa spoke. Mellony flinched and went ashen at the sound of Raisa's voice. Averill leaned down and spoke into her ear.

A tall, sturdy woman with a long gray braid pushed forward to stand behind the Princess Mellony, resting her hands on her shoulders. Tears streamed down the woman's face. "Sweet Sainted Lady!" she called in a carrying voice, almost as if she'd been coached. "It's the Princess Raisa home again! Long live the Gray Wolf line."

"While some may be fooled by a wizard's fetch, I am not," Lord Bayar said, raising his voice as if to drown out the woman. "Though it is a pretty piece of conjury, it is in poor taste. It has only frightened those who would honor our late queen. Please identify yourself, or leave us in peace. If you do not comply, I don't care who you are, I will have you before the council."

"Lord Bayar," Raisa said. "I am Raisa *ana*'Marianna, the heir to the Gray Wolf throne, here to mourn my mother. Not even a wizard with a heart of stone would deny me that."

With that, Han allowed the brilliance that surrounded them to die to a faint glow. At the same time, he directed more power into his magical shields, glad he'd overloaded his amulet in the past few days.

A murmur ran through the crowd like wind through aspens.

Han saw a flicker of movement on his right side. It was Dancer moving up along the side of the dais, eyes riveted on the High Wizard, reinforcing the barriers from the other direction, ready to act if needed. No one but Han seemed to notice him; Dancer was wrapped in a glamour, and they were all fixed on the apparition before them.

Micah stood rigid, his eyes fixed on Raisa as if he'd seen a ghost. He closed his eyes, then opened them again, as if she might disappear in the interval.

Fiona's pale eyes fastened on Han, raking over him like a steel-toothed comb.

Lord Bayar had a rum street face, Han had to admit. When his black eyes lit on Han, they tightened a bit, the only sign that the High Wizard recognized him. Otherwise his expression displayed only disdain and impatience.

"Do you really expect us to believe that this is the princess heir?" The High Wizard shook his head as if he couldn't fathom that Han would make such a low play. He turned back toward Mellony, inclining his head. "I'm sorry, Your Highness. It is a cruel trick, to arouse your hopes like this. With sorcery, it is easy to make one thing look like another. This woman is probably just a glamoured-up street doxy."

With that, the blood left Raisa's face, leaving two spots of furious color on her cheeks.

"Lord Bayar!" she said, her voice as clear and frozen as lake ice in January, as carrying as temple bells. "Perhaps you would like me to tell everyone why I had to leave the Fells against my will."

Micah twitched, his complexion turning from marble to porcelain. The crowd on the slopes below murmured and shifted.

Bayar seemed to prefer to focus on Han. The High Wizard extended his hand toward Han, who forced himself not to flinch away. "Madam, you are judged by the company you keep. This *boy* is Cuffs Alister, a common thief."

At that, another murmur rolled through the crowds downslope from the pavilions. *"Alister! That's Cuffs Alister!"*

"That's Cuffs Alister?" the sword-dangling general blurted, seeming to echo the crowd, "But . . . but look at him! He's a *wizard.*"

"A common *thief,*" Lord Bayar repeated through gritted teeth, "who has somehow learned sorcery. We believe he's entered into an unholy alliance with demons who require blood sacrifice in payment. It may be that he's also acquired illegal magical tools from his allies among the copperheads."

The High Wizard seemed to grow taller, gaining in brilliance as if competing with Han. He kept his face toward Han and Raisa, but his audience was the bluebloods behind him.

"As some of you already know, last summer Alister was implicated in a series of brutal street murders in Southbridge, done by magical means," Bayar said. "When I confronted him, he attempted to assassinate me. He fled the country when Queen Marianna put a price on his head. Now he's returned, apparently meaning to take advantage of this time of transition to destroy us." He gestured toward the line of bluejackets in front of the stage. "Corporal Fallon!" he said to a swarthy man with sharp features and a blue-black shadow of beard. "Seize him!"

Han wasn't sure what the High Wizard hoped for. Perhaps he thought Han might respond with a magical attack, and in the confusion the Bayars would have the chance to kill both him and Raisa.

Understandably, Corporal Fallon did not rush forward. He

looked from Bayar to Han, and took one reluctant step.

Raisa edged her pony in front of Han's and extended her hand, palm out. "Hold, Corporal Fallon, if you are, as you claim to be, the sworn defender of the Gray Wolf line."

Fearless, Han thought in grudging admiration.

Corporal Fallon held, his eyes shifting from Raisa to Han, his hand on the hilt of his sword. He licked his lips and swallowed hard.

"Han Alister saved my life, Lord Bayar," Raisa said. "Like it or not, he is the reason I stand before you today. I owe him a debt of gratitude, not a berth in gaol. Therefore I have issued him an unconditional pardon. Anyone who lays hands on him will answer to me."

Han looked Lord Bayar in the eyes, thinking, Here's yet another reason for the High Wizard to howl after my blood.

Bayar gazed at Han and Raisa, his hand on his amulet, eyes narrowed as if judging the strength of the barrier Han had erected.

Han sat straight in his saddle, fingering his own amulet, chin cocked up, looking down his nose in a way that unmistakably said, *Bring it on, Bayar. But you'd better kill me with your first shot.*

Something primal inside Han craved that attack, lusted for the chance to finish it now, one way or the other.

Patience, Alister, he thought. Never attack unless you are in a position to win.

Han glanced at Fiona and Micah standing just behind their father. Micah's eyes were still locked on Raisa. Fiona's, on the other hand, were fixed on Han, her brows drawn together in appraisal, biting her lower lip.

Han's attention was drawn to ground level as a score of bluejackets led by Amon Byrne pushed into the space between Han and Raisa and the guards that lined the stage. They faced the High Wizard, swords drawn. Some faces were familiar to Han from Oden's Ford—Garret Fry and Mick Bricker, Talia Abbott and Pearlie Greenholt. The Demonai warriors moved up on either side of them, longbows at the ready, protecting their flanks.

"Kneel before the princess heir," Lord Averill said in a loud deep voice. "And thank the Maker she has returned to us." Averill dropped to one knee, bowing his head, followed by the gray-haired woman who had spoken out.

Byrne's bluejackets fell to their knees. The Demonai dipped sideways in an almost comical fashion, acknowledging the princess while keeping their eyes and weapons trained on the wizards on the stage.

Jinxes are slower than arrows, Han thought.

Speaker Jemson went down, his robes billowing around him. Elena knelt beside her chair. Dancer knelt at the edge of the pavilion, keeping his head up, his hand on his amulet, and his eyes fixed on the Bayars. But no one else.

They hung there like that for a long moment, as if balanced on the honed edge of a sword. And then it began, from downslope, a rhythmic rumble of voices that grew and spread into a deafening roar.

"Rai-*sa*! Rai-*sa*! Rai-*sa*!" There were even some shouts of "Al-is-ter!"

Han looked beyond the pavilions with their brilliant banners, beyond the queen's bier and the bluebloods on the platform to see the crowds of commoners seem to ripple as they fell to their knees.

Han had expected it, but it was still good to see and hear. Cat Tyburn had done her work well.

And slowly, dramatically, like leaves falling from a tree, the others followed suit. First, the Princess Mellony, dropping to her knees beside her father. Then some other bluebloods Han didn't recognize, including the badged-up general. And after that, the bluejackets that protected the dais. Including Mason Fallon.

Still no wizards. They huddled in an unhappy group, like vultures evicted from a warm carcass.

And then Micah Bayar swept back his cloak and dropped to his knees, bowing his head, his amulet swinging forward. Fiona glared down at him like she wanted to stomp on him.

Ho, Han thought. Micah breaks with his family? That's interesting.

Three other wizards went down. Then the Mander brothers and a middle-aged russet-headed plump wizard who must have been their mother. And Master Gryphon.

Master Gryphon?

Han stared. His former teacher Gryphon stood between two older wizards, an elegantly dressed man and woman with long aristocratic noses and thin unhappy mouths. As Han watched, Gryphon swung his canes aside, and the older couple each took an arm and lowered him to the stage. They knelt as well, on either side of him, heads bowed, but Gryphon stared up at Han, a look of ferocious curiosity on his face.

Questions ricocheted through Han's mind.

Why would Gryphon be here, when the spring term had already begun?

Had all the students and faculty at Oden's Ford ditched school in favor of politics?

Han forced his eyes elsewhere. Fiona was down now too, leaving only Lord Bayar standing. The High Wizard looked about, shook his head, and smiled his crocodile smile.

"By the Maker's grace," he said softly, studying Raisa's face as if he were finally ready to be persuaded. "Is it really you, Your Highness?"

"It seems that I've managed to convince everyone in the queendom but you, Lord Bayar," Raisa said dryly, looking out over the crowd.

Reignited, it roared, "Rai-sa!" and "Briar Rose!" and "Alister!" and what sounded like "Death to Bayar!" though it was comingled and hard to sort out.

And with that, the High Wizard sank gracefully to his knees. The bloody-handed, heartless bastard actually had tears in his eyes. "Forgive the cynic in me, Your Highness. We have already lost our beloved Marianna. Given this season of tragedy, I had convinced myself that you must be dead as well." He shook his head. "I couldn't bear to even hope that it was you."

Which was likely true enough.

The crowd roared its approval, the sound breaking over them like waves on a beach.

Raisa stood in her stirrups as if to make herself as tall as possible. Because she was on horseback and slightly upslope from those on the stage, she could speak over their heads to the multitudes beyond. Her armor glittered in the sun, and her cloak fluttered and snapped in the wind.

She lifted both hands, palms up. "Rise!" she said in that

carrying voice that was becoming familiar. "Please make yourselves comfortable. It is so good to be home. I have missed these mountains and the people who dwell here—uplanders and Valefolk, the Spirit clans and charmcasters."

She paused for a long moment. "I came home because I wanted to see my mother's face and hear her voice again. Now that will never happen.

"There are many difficult questions to be asked and answered in the coming days—many decisions to be made." Raisa's gaze rested on the assemblage on the dais. "But today I have come, and the ancient queens have come"—she waved at the circle of mammoth wolves—"to honor my mother, Queen Marianna. She is the link in an unbroken line that goes back to the warrior queen, Hanalea, who healed the Breaking and saved the world. Such links are not lightly broken. The deaths of queens stir the beasts that lie beneath the dirt. They stir questions in all of us, about what has been and what is to be."

Han listened in amazement as Raisa spoke on. Does she carry those kinds of speeches around inside her all the time? he wondered. Just in case? Or do they just hatch out whenever they're needed?

However she did it, it was something he needed to learn.

The rest of that afternoon passed in a smear of images. Han dismounted and helped Raisa down from her horse under the glare of the Bayars. He and Amon Byrne mounted the steps to the dais together, just behind Raisa. They stood to either side as Raisa embraced her sister Mellony and Averill Demonai and the woman with the long gray braid. She greeted the others more formally, but had a smile and a word for each—even Lord Bayar, whom she greeted with a rum street face.

The Demonai still stood to either side of the dais, their long-bows held loosely in their hands, arrows nocked but pointed at the ground, their eyes fixed on the wizards on the stage. It was less a treaty than a standoff.

Under Jemson's direction, Raisa spoke a prayer over the dead queen, commending her to her rest in the Spirit Mountains. She greeted her ancestors, the Gray Wolf queens, naming them from memory. She asked them—and her mother—to watch over her and guide her as she led her people forward.

That makes no sense, asking for guidance from Queen Marianna, Han thought. She's made a mess of things.

The speaker touched on memories of Marianna as a young girl—her talent for dancing, her skill on the basilka and harpsichord, her love of the hunt. She had been widely hailed as the most beautiful and eligible princess in the Seven Realms, attracting a relentless parade of suitors vying for her hand. People cheered her wherever she went—she was the glittering centerpiece of a fairy tale they all could believe in.

Then the fairy tale ended. Queen Lissa died, and Marianna ascended to the throne at fifteen. Civil war broke out in Arden, and the young queen was challenged by an influx of refugees and a decline in trade revenues. The Council of Nobles recommended an isolationist policy and her generals spent vast amounts on mercenaries. Taxes were raised again and again.

Worried about being drawn into the wars to the south, Marianna passed over the glittering princes and chose to marry Averill Lightfoot—a suitor from inside the queendom who had the strength of the Spirit clans behind him. When wizards and

Valefolk complained about their fairy-tale princess marrying a copperhead, Marianna defiantly planned the most elaborate wedding ever seen. It was said to have cost one hundred thousand crowns and beggared the treasury for years to come.

Even in Ragmarket and Southbridge, people still had souvenirs from that wedding stashed away. Mam had kept a copper coin with Queen Marianna on one side and Averill on the other.

It's a sad thing, Han thought, when the best a speaker like Jemson can say about you is that you could throw a good party.

That wasn't all he said, of course, but that was how Han's bitter ears bent it.

Raisa lit the pyre, and the flames spit sparks into the storm-darkened sky. Lightning flamed over Hanalea, and the wolves lifted their muzzles and howled, a sound that raised gooseflesh on Han's neck and arms.

While the queen burned, Raisa called Amon Byrne forward. He stood poker straight beside her while Raisa delivered a eulogy for Edon Byrne, Captain of the Queen's Guard.

"I have loved and hated Edon Byrne," she said. "I have loved him for his clear eye, honest soul, and blunt speech." She paused. "I have hated him for his clear eye, honest soul, and blunt speech." She smiled at a smattering of laughter and applause. "Our most valuable servants are those loyal enough to risk telling us the truth—not always what we want to hear, but what we need to hear. Edon Byrne was such a man. In the end, he gave his life for my sake. He will be sorely missed."

She walked forward and looked down at the bluejackets surrounding the dais. "The Byrnes are people of few words, impatient with long speeches, and so I will honor him with a short one.

I commend him to the embrace of the Spirit Mountains, and know he will watch over his queen and all of the Gray Wolf line in death as well as in life."

Her voice rang out, echoing among the peaks. "Enemies of the Gray Wolf line had best take notice."

Han looked straight at the Bayars.

Raisa swung around, facing downslope again. "And so, the unbroken line of captains and queens continues. Amon Byrne, please step forward."

Amon took a step forward, standing at attention, chin up, eyes straight ahead.

"Give me the Sword of Hanalea," Raisa said, extending her hand.

Byrne drew his sword and extended it to Raisa, hilt-first. She took hold of the heavy sword with both hands and lifted it so it pointed skyward.

Strange, Han thought. Raisa didn't physically resemble the images he'd seen of Hanalea. The legendary queen had been tall and blond and willowy, with long flowing tresses. This queen was small, with a cap of cropped dark hair, her green eyes brilliant against her honey skin. Yet she looked like a warrior, all in armor with the sword in her hand, facing off against the thousands.

"Ordinarily, this would wait until my coronation," she said. "Ordinarily, the Lady sword would pass from one captain to another. But these are not ordinary times. Queen Marianna and her captain died within days of each other. It seems important to reforge the link between captain and queen as soon as possible lest my enemies think they see an opportunity in our losses.

"In the same vein, we will schedule my coronation as soon as it can be arranged," she added, her eyes sweeping over the crowd and the assembly on the dais. "There is too much business before us to delay."

She looked up at Amon Byrne. "Kneel," she commanded.

Byrne fell to his knees, still somehow at attention, his eyes fastened on Raisa.

Raisa tapped each shoulder with the flat of the blade. "Rise, Captain Amon Byrne, Commander of the Queen's Guard."

Han looked over at the Bayars in time to see a quick look exchanged between Micah and Fiona. Lord Bayar tilted his head toward the general next to him, who was filling Bayar's ear with something. Bayar was completely expressionless.

Princess Mellony seemed a bit blindsided by the cascade of events. She gripped the arms of her chair, her blue eyes wide, shifting from Raisa to Amon, and then to Micah, as if for a clue.

But Micah gazed at Raisa with a half smile of grudging admiration.

They know they've been outplayed, Han thought. The more Raisa accomplishes out in the open, in front of witnesses, the less that can be forced on her behind closed doors.

Han had no illusions that it would stop them, but it would complicate things at least. Raisa had marched into the old neighborhood with her gang, and made show to those who wanted to challenge her.

It was well done.

By now the queen's pyre had burned down to ashes, fueled by the holy oils the speakers used. Raisa smiled at her sister, taking her hands and gently lifting her to her feet. She embraced Mellony again, her younger sister towering over her. She led Mellony over to the bier, where they stood, hand in hand. As Han watched, Raisa leaned over and whispered something in Mellony's ear.

Speaker Jemson sprinkled a powder over the flames, and a plume of gray-and-white smoke spiraled up, organizing itself into a sleek, fine-boned wolf with blue eyes. She descended to the ground, landed lightly and walked forward, stiff-legged, her ruff bristling about her head, to touch noses with the assembled wolves.

Thunder growled over Hanalea, and the rain came slashing down in huge drops that exploded as they hit the dais. The wolves turned as one and loped away, vanishing into the rain-thickened air.

CHAPTER TWENTY-FIVE

HOMECOMING

It was a great day.

It was a terrible day.

Raisa had never felt braver.

She had never been more frightened.

She had never been lonelier.

She had never felt more loved.

And now she was on her way home.

The fierce courage that had fueled her during the long service at Marianna's tomb had ebbed, leaving exhaustion in its wake. She rode, embedded within her guard, Amon to her right and forward, Han to her left and behind her, surrounded by Demonai warriors, with Reid Nightwalker and her father, Averill, Lord Demonai, always within sight.

Behind them came her former nurse, Magret Gray, and the other Maidens of Hanalea, their pendants displayed outside their cloaks, honoring the line they'd sworn to serve.

The time will come, Raisa vowed, when I'll be able to ride unescorted through the streets of my own queendom.

The Princess Mellony rode alongside her, her long golden tresses plastered to her forehead and neck, her lips blue and teeth chattering from the cold. She wore a lightweight silk cloak in black and royal blue, which was soaked through.

Blinking raindrops from her eyelashes, Raisa tugged her hood up. Like most clanwork, her Gray Wolf cape was a marriage of beauty and function, and its tightly woven oiled wool fibers turned the downpour. Still, her forward motion as she descended the long slope of Marianna slapped the rain into her face. Water ran in rivulets down her neckline and between her breasts.

Mellony kept twisting in her saddle, looking back to see where Micah was, as if to make sure he was still there. He rode alongside Fiona just behind the Demonai warriors.

I need to pay more attention to Mellony, Raisa thought. I need to woo her away from those who've held her in thrall. She's all I have left—she and Averill.

They'd never had much in common. Before Raisa went to foster at Demonai Camp, their three-year age difference had seemed like a chasm that could never be bridged. Raisa prowled the streets with Amon and his older friends while Mellony played with dolls and tea sets under the shelter of their mother's warm regard.

Raisa had returned from Demonai to find that Mellony and Queen Marianna had grown even closer, leaving Raisa feeling more like an outsider than ever.

She leaned toward Mellony. "You look cold and misera-ble," she said. "Didn't you bring anything to shed the rain?" She instantly regretted it. It sounded like she was being critical rather than sympathetic.

And that's how Mellony took it. The corners of her mouth curved down. "Who knew it would start to rain?" she said. "The weather wizards did not predict it."

"If you ride into the mountains, you have to be prepared for changeable weather," Raisa said, unable to stop herself in her exhausted state.

"You should call Micah forward," Mellony said loftily. "We often go riding together. He knows how to shield against the rain."

"Just because he knows how to do it doesn't mean it's a good idea to use wizardry for such a purpose," Raisa said, thinking guiltily of how Han had dried her cloak in Oden's Ford. "You should be wary of allowing wizards to charm your person."

"You're one to talk," Mellony said, pouting. "When you show up entangled in a wizard's fetch."

That sounded too much like Lord Bayar's words.

This wasn't going well.

Before Raisa could think to ask it, Amon Byrne slowed his pace, angling his horse in closer. He draped his thick Guard cloak over Mellony's shoulders, then spurred ahead again to give them privacy.

Protector of the line.

They'd left the slopes of Marianna behind and were now crossing the relatively flat Vale, making better time as the rain had diminished to an annoying drizzle. The hardpan road presented its own hazards, however—huge puddles hid large craters in the surface.

It needs repair, Raisa thought, like everything else. Where will we get the funds?

"Where have you been all this time, anyway?" Mellony went on. "We thought you were dead." She sounded almost as if Raisa had pulled a nasty trick by being alive.

"I was in Oden's Ford most of the time," Raisa said. "Attending classes at the academy."

"You were going to *school*?" Mellony raised her fair brows. "You ran away to go to *school*?" As if this were inconceivable.

Raisa glanced about, wary of getting into the meat of the story with so many eyes and ears close by. "They have wonderful teachers there, and students come from all over the Seven Realms. I learned so much." An idea struck her. "*You* could go there, you know," she said. "You could study whatever you like. I think we should send more students to the academy than we do. Not just wizards."

Mellony's eyes went wide with alarm. "Now that you've come back, you mean to send me *away*?" Her voice cracked.

"No, no," Raisa said quickly. "Not unless you want to go. I only thought it would be a great opportunity for you. When you returned, you could serve on my council. I'll have need of counselors I can trust."

"I love my teachers and tutors," Mellony said, her voice rising. "I love being at court. Why would I want to go anywhere else?"

I would love to go back to Oden's Ford, Raisa thought. That's a mistake I make constantly—thinking Mellony wants the same things I do.

She's changed while I've been gone, Raisa thought. In the

past, she'd always relied on her sunny, uncomplicated personality. Now she seems angry and suspicious and resentful.

Thirteen is a hard age, Raisa thought. She's had a hard year and a heartbreaking week.

"Never mind." Raisa reached across and touched Mellony's shoulder. "Come, let's not fight on the day we buried our mother."

"It's your fault she's dead," Mellony said, jerking away from Raisa's hand.

That fanned the flames of the guilt Raisa was already feeling. And frayed away what remained of her patience. "How can you say that?" she demanded, forgetting to keep her voice down.

Amon glanced back at them, eyebrows raised, lips tight together. Now Han nudged his horse forward so he came abreast of them. "Your Highness, you and the princess could use some privacy. I'm nearly used up, but I think I can manage." Touching his amulet, he gestured, and a curtain of silence descended, blocking out sound all around them.

He reined in his horse so he fell behind them again, following at a respectful distance.

Mellony raised her chin as if to say, *See? You have your wizards, too.* But what she said was, "Is it true he's a thief and a murderer?"

Maybe, Raisa thought of saying. Or, *probably*. "He used to be," she said. "He was streetlord of Ragmarket."

"A wizard streetlord," Mellony said, swiping rain from the tip of her nose. "That's romantic, in a way."

"I doubt he'd describe it that way," Raisa said. "Anyway, he didn't become a wizard until after he'd left the streets."

"What do you mean, *become a wizard*?" Mellony said. "Wizards are born, not made. Unless Lord Bayar is right, and he's made some kind of deal with the Breaker." She shivered. "Do you think that's possible?"

"If he made a deal, he made a poor bargain," Raisa said. "And I know for a fact that he's a better trader than that."

"He *is* handsome," Mellony allowed, "in a wicked kind of way. I don't think I've ever seen eyes that blue on a man before. And the way he looks at a person—almost unnatural, like he can look right through your clothes. And dressed all in black like that, his hair . . ."

"Mellony," Raisa said gently. Charm or not, she wanted to stay away from the subject of Han Alister, with him riding so close by. Matters were complicated enough. "You were talking about Mother. How it's my fault she's dead."

Mellony didn't speak for a long moment, until Raisa began to wonder whether she would answer at all. "Mother was broken-hearted when you left," Mellony said finally. "She blamed herself. She thought she should have seen it coming and somehow prevented it. She barely ate or slept, and she grew thin and weepy." Mellony looked over at Raisa. "So we were all miserable and worried while you enjoyed yourself in Oden's Ford."

"*Enjoyed* myself? Do you know how hard I was working?" As Raisa said it, she knew she was being dishonest. Despite everything, she *had* enjoyed herself.

Mellony rolled her eyes. "You're a fiend for hard work, and you know it," she said. "You always had to work harder than anyone else, whether it was schoolwork or hunting or—or anything. You always had to make everyone else look bad."

Everyone else, no doubt, meant Mellony.

It was time to tell the truth. "Did Mother tell you why I left?"

Raisa said, leaning close to her sister.

Mellony nodded. "She said you had a crush on Corporal Byrne." She jerked her chin toward Amon, riding just ahead. "Mother said you ran off when she insisted you marry someone else." She lifted her chin defiantly. "And Corporal Byrne was at Oden's Ford, too. Wasn't *that* convenient?"

"That's not true," Raisa hissed, stung. "I did not run away to be with Amon Byrne."

"Really?" Mellony raised her eyebrow. "Are you calling Mother a liar?"

Raisa pressed her lips together to keep any more words from spilling out. She didn't want to speak ill of the dead. And yet she wanted to honor Mellony with the truth. She was tired of lies, tired of the awkwardness and suspicion between them.

"You never seemed interested in getting married anyway," Mellony persisted. "You always said you wanted to kiss a lot of boys before you narrowed down to one."

Well, yes. Raisa had said that.

"I'm not saying Mother was a liar," Raisa said diplomatically. "I'm saying she did not tell you all of the truth. Yes, I left when she insisted I marry someone else. Do you know who that some-one was?"

"It doesn't matter now," Mellony said, facing forward as if she somehow knew that she wouldn't want to hear what Raisa had to say. "You left, and Mother died." She slammed her heels into her pony's sides, meaning to ride forward and away, but Raisa caught hold of her horse's bridle.

"It was Micah Bayar," Raisa said. "She wanted me to marry Micah Bayar."

Mellony shook her head, slinging water all around. "No," she said. "That's not possible."

"It is possible because it's true," Raisa said.

"No," Mellony repeated. "Micah would never—"

"Micah was willing," Raisa said. "I was not."

Mellony stared at her, tears pooling in her blue eyes. "I don't believe you," she said, and wrenched her horse away, spurring him forward until she was beyond the range of easy conversation.

Well, Raisa thought, so much for clearing the air.

Someone must have sent a bird to Fellsmarch, or maybe riders with fresh horses had outpaced them to the capital, wanting to be the first to announce the news of Raisa's return. Or maybe Cat Tyburn had arranged this reception, too. However it happened, the news had preceded them, so that when they entered the capital, the Way of the Queens was lined with people on both sides, cheering and waving scarves and kerchiefs.

Although the Way was broad, the crowds surged in close, reaching out to touch their returning princess. The Guard tightened its perimeter, and Amon and Han took up positions on either side of Raisa, using their horses to keep anyone from coming too close while the Queen's Guard forced a path forward toward the castle close.

To Raisa's embarrassment, some in the mob of people cursed and jostled the Demonai, calling them copperheads, baby stealers, and worse. They weren't used to seeing clan in numbers in the city.

Sweet Lady in chains, Raisa thought. Somehow I have to bring all my peoples together—wizards, Valefolk, clans. We spend too much energy fighting with each other. It makes us vulnerable.

Speaking of vulnerable. She thrust her finger into the pouch at her waist, pulled out the wolf ring talisman, and slid it once more onto her finger. It seemed unlikely there would be any wizard attacks between here and home, but still. It made her feel safer to have it on.

Ahead, Raisa could see the glittering towers of Fellsmarch Castle poking above the buildings, a sight that tugged at her heart. So much had happened since she'd last seen them. She pounded down regret like bread dough before its second rising. Learn from it, she thought, but don't waste energy on what cannot be changed.

And it *was* good to be home. She looked about, drinking in the details she'd missed for so long—the twisting side streets, the steps built into the alleys that climbed the slopes in the outer city, the northern accents clamoring around her, and, yes, the stink of cabbage cooking and wood fires and the filth that ran in the gutters.

She took a deep breath and let it out, allowing her shoulders to slump a bit in relief, already looking forward to a hot bath and good northern food. As she did so, she caught a flicker of movement on the roof of a building ahead. A dark silhouette rose into view, its motion fluid and sinuous. It stilled itself, taking careful aim. Instinct caused her to shift sideways and down, to present a narrower target. She opened her mouth to shout a warning.

Amon swore and lunged toward her as something like a fist slammed into her right chest, nearly unseating her and bringing tears to her eyes.

Bedlam ensued. Before Raisa knew what was happening, Amon had scooped her from her saddle, cradling her close and leaning over her so that his body covered hers.

"Make way!" he roared, in a hoarse, unfamiliar voice, urging his horse into a gallop, willing to ride down any fool who didn't get out of his path.

Bricks and tiles flew as a blast of wizard flash hit the roof where the archer had been. It was Han Alister, discouraging any second attempts.

"Mellony!" Raisa gasped. "See to my sister's safety."

She saw flickers of blue to either side, breathed in the acrid scent of wizard flame, heard shouted orders and the twang of longbows. They thundered into the broader, straighter streets near the castle, through the gate that led into the castle close.

Still, Amon did not slow. Raisa could smell the moat and hear the hollow rattle of hooves over wood as they crossed the drawbridge at a dead run. They passed under the portcullis and into the interior courtyard of Fellsmarch Castle.

The portcullis slammed down behind them.

She was home.

She raised her head, twisting around so she could see. The courtyard was packed with blue-jacketed guards and rearing horses. To her relief, she saw Mellony, still astride her pony, led by Mick Bricker. She looked pale as parchment, but apparently unhurt.

Han and his friend Fire Dancer planted themselves in the arch leading to the drawbridge, gripping their amulets like they might have to fight off raging hordes of assassins.

"Call a healer!" Amon bellowed, right into Raisa's ear. "The princess heir's been shot."

Raisa ran her fingers over the plate armor just below her collarbone. It was badly dented and pierced partway through, but had held against the assassin's arrow, if that's what it was. The missile must have fallen away in the street.

Raisa attempted to squirm free of Amon's grip. "Really, Amon, I don't think I'm—"

A familiar voice broke into her protest. "Captain Byrne! Give her to me!"

It was Magret Gray, who'd already dismounted and shed her rain-drenched cloak. Magret opened her arms and Amon lowered Raisa down into them. Raisa looked up into Magret's familiar face, streaming with tears, etched with new lines of pain.

Were they new, or had she just never noticed?

Magret's hair was grayer than before, caught into its customary thick braid that extended nearly to her waist. When Raisa was a toddler she used to cling to that braid and suck her thumb when she needed consoling.

Mellony's face came into view at Raisa's elbow, tear-stained and terror-stricken. "Raisa," she whispered, "I'm so sorry. Please don't die too."

"I'm not planning on it, not any time soon," Raisa said. "Magret. Please set me down. I'm fine, just bruised is all."

But Magret's grip was as difficult to break as Amon's.

"Let's get her into the keep," Amon said. "Kiefer, I want a dozen guards on the door. Talia, get over to the Healer's Hall and bring Lord Vega on the double. Mick and Hallie, take a triple and go out and see if you can track down the archers. But be careful."

Guards took off in all directions, an explosion of blue uniforms.

"I'll help," Averill said, his eyes brilliant with anger. "I know the streets."

"No." Amon shook his head. "Depending on who's behind

this, you might be a target yourself. I'd like to keep you close for now."

Averill opened his mouth to protest, but Nightwalker said, "I'll go, Lightfoot. My warriors will be just outside the close and I know the streets as well as you do."

"The archer who shot me was on the roof of Kendall House," Raisa told him. "The arrow might be lying in the street near where I was hit. That might tell us something."

Nightwalker nodded, his face grim and determined. "We'll find them, Your Highness." He slipped past Han and Dancer, disappearing through the archway into the growing dusk.

Magret strode toward the keep, still carrying Raisa in her arms.

"Magret. Set me down," Raisa said, exasperated. "Please believe me when I say I'm just bruised. I've been shot before, and I know the difference."

At that, Han swung around to look at her, his mouth twitching with amusement and relief. It was the first genuine smile she'd seen on him in a long while, overlaying a face haggard with worry.

"Byrne, we need to do a better job of protecting the queen," he said. "Before we know it, she'll be showing off old battle scars to her ladies whenever she's in her cups. It won't help our reputations any."

Amon nodded without smiling. "I agree. We need to do a better job, and we will." He turned to Raisa. "Humor me, Your Highness," he said, stubborn as ever. He nodded to Magret. "Take her inside."

CHAPTER TWENTY-SIX

AGREEING TO DISAGREE

There was no saying no to Magret Gray. The former nurse carried Raisa into one of the salons on the first floor of the palace. There she removed Raisa's armor and padding, stripping her to her camisole, and put her down on her back on one of the couches, under a blanket. She pressed an icy cloth against the purpling bruise above Raisa's right breast.

The court healer, Harriman Vega, a wizard, arrived with four assistants. Han Alister followed them in and stood next to Raisa, arms crossed.

Lord Vega scowled at Han. "Wait outside, please, while we examine Her Highness," he said in a high, supercilious voice.

Han shook his head. "I'm staying," he said, immovable as stone. "After what's happened, Captain Byrne isn't in a trusting mood. I promised him I wouldn't leave her side."

And he trusts you? Raisa thought. That's different.

Magret stood, hands on hips, giving Han a look of undiluted hostility.

"Your Highness, please," Lord Vega said. "Surely you don't want this young man looking on while we—"

"He stays," Raisa said, with a sigh. I might as well get used to having no privacy at all, she thought.

Still, her cheeks burned as Lord Vega undid the cord at her neckline and pulled down her camisole. The wizard healer tried to keep his body between Han and Raisa, but Han moved enough to make sure he could see the healer's hands and hear what charms he spoke. His face was again as unreadable as one of the stone faces of Hanalea.

Vega and his assistants all had to take a look.

"As you can see," the wizard said to his assistants, still trying to block Han's view, "the arrow did not pierce the skin, so even if it were a poison daub, there is no danger to the queen's life. The armor apparently stopped the projectile, although the force of the blow has caused considerable bruising." He looked up at Raisa. "Was the arrow launched from close range?"

She nodded. "I would guess no more than twenty feet."

"Then you are most fortunate you were wearing this armor, Your Highness," Vega said, lifting Raisa's breastplate and weighing it in his hands, peering at the dent made by the arrow. "It's lightweight, but magicked to turn any but the strongest blows. I suppose it's of copperhead make."

"It's clanwork," Raisa said. And it's maybe wizardry too, she thought. I need to thank Fire Dancer for saving my life.

"Observe," Lord Vega said to his assistants. He laid his hands over the bruises and spoke a charm. Han leaned in close, cocking his head so he could hear, ignoring Vega's glare.

Within seconds, the ache in Raisa's chest had eased somewhat and the purple swelling diminished.

"Thank you, Lord Vega," she said, rolling her shoulders to test her range of motion. "That is amazing. I hope you won't have too many ill effects."

"It is my calling, Your Highness," Vega said modestly. "There is a personal price to be paid, of course, but I would gladly sacrifice my health on your behalf."

Raisa couldn't help glancing at Han, who'd nearly sacrificed his life on her behalf. And maybe regretted it now.

Lord Vega and his minions also examined the healing wound in her back from the ambush in Marisa Pines Pass. At this rate, she'd collect as many scars as Han Alister.

"May I ask how this was treated, Your Highness?" Lord Vega asked, running cool fingers over her upper back. This wizard was remarkably good at controlling any leakage of power, compared to Han and Micah, at least.

Or maybe Han's presence was keeping him on his best behavior.

"I was treated at Marisa Pines Camp," Raisa said, "by Willo Watersong, a clan healer."

"It's mending well," Vega said grudgingly, poking at it. "Though I don't recommend that people seek treatment in the camps except in an emergency. It's difficult to predict the effects of the herbals they use. Not only that, once the copperheads have meddled in an illness or injury, it can make it more difficult for an academy-trained wizard to diagnose and treat the problem."

"I'll bear that in mind," Raisa said, sliding her arms back into her gown and retying the cord at her neck. Magret draped a thick shawl over her shoulders, as if to provide a little additional coverage.

"Is there anything else? I think I'd like to rest now." She looked pointedly at the door.

"I'll be back to examine you again in the morning," Lord Vega said. He looked up at Magret. "You, there. If there should be any change in the queen's condition, if you have any concern at all, don't attempt to treat it yourself. Send a servant to the Healer's Hall to fetch me."

"I will, my lord," Magret said. "Thank you, my lord."

Lord Vega and his assistants swept from the room, stuffed full of their own importance.

"What a pompous ass," Magret said, when he was out of earshot. "'Course you can't throw a rock without hitting a pompous ass of a wizard."

Raisa laughed as Han blinked at Magret in surprise. "Magret, meet Han Alister," she said. "Han, this is my nurse, Magret Gray."

Magret's eyes narrowed. "Alister!" Her eyes dropped to Han's wrists, then flicked back up to his face. "The gang leader and murderer?"

"Magret!" Raisa put up her hand. "Alister is—"

"Used to be," Han broke in, shrugging his shoulders. "You one of the Pearl Alley Grays?"

Magret eyed him balefully, keeping her hands planted on her hips. "Used to be," she said. "What is *he* doing here, Your Highness?" she asked, without taking her eyes off Han, as if he might make a move on her.

"He's going to be staying here in the palace," Raisa said.

"He's . . . um . . . kind of a bodyguard."

"No," Magret said. "He can't be staying here in the palace. Not this one." Her eyes fastened on the amulet that hung around Han's neck, and she took a step back, raising her hands as if in defense. "He's handsome enough, I'll grant you that, but he's a fiend, Your Highness. Truly, he is."

Raisa looked from Magret to Han. "What are you talking about? Do you know each other?"

Han kept his eyes on Magret. "Maiden Gray," he said softly, "I'm sorry about Velvet."

"Don't call him that!" Magret shouted. "Don't you call him that. His name was Theo. Theo Gray."

"I'm sorry about Theo," Han amended.

Velvet. Raisa recalled the boy in the velvet coat who'd been with Cat Tyburn the day Han had rescued her from the Raggers. The razorleaf user who'd meant to rob her.

They're all dead, Han had said. All of the Raggers except Cat.

"I should have known you for a wizard," Magret said. "That's the only way to explain it, him taking to the streets like he done. He was a good boy before you lured him away from his family."

Unconsciously, Magret had slipped into the kind of street cant that Han used. Or had used.

"Who was Vel—Theo—to you?" Raisa asked Magret.

"He was my sister's boy," Magret said. "My nephew. My sister died of remitting fever. I raised him 'til he was four. Then he went with his father, who took him for a street mumper."

A memory came back to Raisa—playing at blocks with a boy her own age when she was three or four. A boy who somehow belonged to Magret, though she'd never married.

"Then he falls in with Cuffs and his gang," Magret went on. "Turned to slide-hand and razorleaf and shoplifting."

"He was starving," Han said. "His da disappeared and he was mumping on his own, doing a little slide-hand and second-story work along with. He started up with the River Rats. He came to me later, after Southies took over their turf."

"He could've come to *me*," Magret said. "He should have. But you charmed him. You—you—silver-tongued demon. He wouldn't leave even when I begged him to."

"He was a leaf user by then," Han said. "Not many are able to leave it. It isn't your fault you couldn't save him."

"You're right, it isn't my fault," Magret said, drawing herself up, her voice dripping with scorn. "It's *your* fault."

"Magret," Raisa said gently. "Han's been out of that for more than a year."

"My Theo was tortured and killed and burnt by wizardry," Magret said, still glaring at Han. "You're a jinxflinger. Don't try and tell me you don't know what happened to him."

"I won't try and tell you that," Han said, his blue eyes focused on Magret's face. "I do know what happened to him. He was killed by wizards looking for me. So it *was* my fault, though it was never my intention." He was making no excuses, not even attempting to defend himself.

Magret stood, fists clenched at her sides, staring at him, her mouth dammed up as if to keep her words from spilling out.

"If you want to know more, I know a girlie was his streetlord at the time," Han said. "I'll ask her to speak with you."

"I don't want your help," Magret said fiercely. "I don't want to talk to any streetrats. I want you to leave so I can see to the Princess Raisa in peace."

They all jumped and turned when Amon Byrne rapped on the door frame. "Your Highness," he said apologetically. "Sorry to disturb you, but the door was open, so . . ."

"Come in, Amon," Raisa said, relieved to have the tension in the room diluted. "I'm fine. Dancer's armor saved my life. Have you found out anything?"

Amon scanned the hallway, then carefully closed the door behind him and crossed to her side. He held up a crossbow bolt between his thumb and forefinger, the tip wrapped carefully in muslin. "Nightwalker found this. Bodkin-tipped, meant to pierce armor and kill. Common as weeds along a roadside. Except"—he waggled it in his hand—"it's got a poison daub on the head. I'd like to have Willo look at it and see if she thinks it's the same as was used before."

"Good idea," Raisa said dryly. "It would be good to know if it's the same people trying to kill me, or a whole different group."

"Seems like whoever it was took his one safe shot and ran," Amon said. "Guards are still swarming through the city, the Demonai warriors too, but I'm not optimistic."

Raisa glanced at Magret. Her nurse was cutting her eyes toward Han and shaking her head, putting her finger to her lips.

"Magret," Raisa said wearily. "Like it or not, Han is here for my protection. He's already saved my life once, maybe twice. We have to trust him. We need someone gifted, given what's been happening with Lord Bayar and the Wizard Council."

"Speaking of the Bayars, Micah is outside," Amon said. "He's been waiting out there for more than an hour, and he won't take no for an answer. He insists on seeing you and verifying that you are alive and well. Hayden Fire Dancer is keeping him company." He smiled faintly, the first smile Raisa had seen on him in a while.

"I'll tell him no, and make it stick," Magret growled, turning toward the door. "The conniving, scheming lowlife." She seemed happy to have another wizard to direct her ire against.

"No." Raisa held up her hand to stop Magret. "Let him in. Maybe we can learn something from his reaction, see what he knows."

Han straightened, and he and Amon exchanged glances. Raisa studied them, frowning. Something had changed between them, some kind of barrier had fallen. They almost seemed like co-conspirators now. She wasn't sure she liked that.

"You're not going to see him in your cami, Your Highness!" Magret said, looking scandalized.

"Oh, let's just get it over with," Raisa growled.

"All right. I'll fetch him, Your Highness." Amon left again.

"I'm not going to receive him lying down like an invalid, either," Raisa said. She slid off the bed, her bare feet thumping on the floor. Wrapping the blanket closely around her, she sat down in the chair next to the bed. Magret twitched the fleece up over Raisa's shoulders, providing maximum coverage.

Han stood behind her chair, his hands resting on the back to either side of her. Raisa's skin prickled and pebbled at his nearness.

"I should just get dressed again," Raisa grumbled, trying to ignore it. "I've got a lot to do."

"Your Highness, there's no point. Soon as we send the

jinxflingers away, I'll take you upstairs for a long, hot bath," Magret promised.

Moments later, Amon returned, with Micah and Dancer. There was a grim, angry set to Micah's mouth, a stiffness to his posture.

When his eyes lit on Han, he stopped short in the doorway, looking from Raisa in her blanket to Han as if he couldn't believe the evidence of his own eyes.

"What are *you* doing here, Alister?" he demanded. "I couldn't believe it when I saw you ride up at the memorial service, dressed like some kind of prince. How did *you* get involved with the princess heir?" He looked at Raisa. "Do you know who this is? Do you know what he's done? He's a murdering, thieving—"

"*Sul'*Bayar!" Raisa said. "I thought you were here to inquire after my health, not malign and interrogate my bodyguard."

"Your bodyguard?" Micah looked Han up and down, shaking his head slowly. *"Him?"*

"Indeed," Raisa said, losing patience. "Get used to it or get out." Sweet Lady in chains, she thought, I am so weary of wizards.

Closing his eyes, Micah took a deep breath, then released it, mastering himself in that way he had.

"As you wish, Your Highness," he said, with a smile that didn't quite reach his eyes. "I am already used to it."

He came and knelt in front of Raisa. When he lifted his head, his black eyes raked over her, drinking in every detail. Like he would tally up every cut and bruise and healing wound.

"Raisa," he said, "are you really all right?" He reached for her hands, and she snatched them back, out of reach. Han shifted his weight behind her, and Raisa knew without looking that he'd gripped his amulet. Amon moved up next to Micah, his sword ready in his hand.

"Just—just keep your distance, Micah," Raisa said, raising both hands, palms out. "I'm already jumpy. And I have absolutely no reason to trust you."

Pain flickered across Micah's face, but he rested his hands on his knees, in plain view of everyone.

"Of course," he said. "I had to see you, to see for myself that you were all right. You're not hurt? You're not wounded at all?"

Raisa shook her head. "No. I was very lucky."

"Yes. You were." Micah looked at Han and Amon almost accusingly, then back at Raisa. "I can't tell you how relieved I was when you appeared at the memorial service."

"Were you?" Raisa's voice was cool and indifferent. "Were you really relieved?"

Micah drew his brows together in a frown, tilting his head. "Well, yes, of course. The last time I saw you, we were in the middle of a battle."

"That's right," Raisa said. "And you put me there. How did you and Fiona manage to escape? And the Manders as well?"

"We were able to recover our amulets," Micah said. "After that, it was relatively easy to conceal ourselves." He shrugged. "To be honest, Prince Gerard seemed more intent on finding *you*, Your Highness. He turned west, to Tamron Court, while we traveled north. When I returned home and found that you had not arrived, I didn't know what to think."

"And immediately found somebody else to marry," Raisa said. "I had no idea you were so determined to settle down."

"I am as much a prisoner of family and politics as you are,"

Micah said. "That did not keep me from worrying that something had happened to you. I thought perhaps Montaigne had recaptured you, or that you were trapped in Tamron Court."

"Something did happen to me," Raisa said. "On my way home, I was attacked and nearly killed in Marisa Pines Pass."

"Attacked?" Micah shook his head slowly, as if to deny it. Micah was a consummate actor, but Raisa thought his surprise was genuine.

"Yes, attacked by someone who was expecting me to come that way."

Now Micah leaned forward, intent on her. "Who was it? *Who* attacked you?"

"They were out of uniform, but they appeared to be members of my own guard," Raisa said.

Micah's eyes narrowed. "Then it wasn't . . ." He stopped himself, took a deep breath, let it out. "It wasn't the copperheads, then?" But she had the impression he'd changed what he meant to say.

Well, I can hold back information as well as you, she thought. She shook her head. "Hardly," she said. "The clan healers saved my life."

"What about . . . those who attacked you?" Micah asked, his eyes fixed on her face. "Have they been questioned? Do you know why they attacked you? Were they just renegades, or . . . ?"

"They are all dead," Raisa said, shrugging, but watching Micah closely through her lashes. "I guess we'll never know."

Micah sat back a little, looking disappointed and unsettled rather than relieved.

"So," he said, "there have been two attempts on your life

within a space of weeks." He looked up at Amon Byrne and Han Alister. "And where were you two during all of this? Or do you only surface after the assassins have fled?"

Again, Raisa sensed Han stirring behind her, and she felt the heat of him through her skin. It seemed to roll off him in waves.

"I beg you, Raisa, take better care," Micah went on. "It's clear to me that your soldier and your so-called bodyguard are not enough to keep you safe. You cannot keep tempting fate. These are dangerous times."

"*You* were the one who dragged me away from Oden's Ford," Raisa said. "If you hadn't kidnapped me, I'd still be there."

"For how long?" Micah asked. "Don't you think that those who tried to kill you would have tried again?"

"You would know better than me," Raisa said. "What's the plan, going forward?" She leaned toward him, as if he might really answer.

Micah glanced at Amon and Han, and Raisa knew he hated holding this discussion in front of this particular audience. "What I did at Oden's Ford was for your protection. Even if you managed to stay alive, had you not returned, the Princess Mellony would have been named princess heir, and maybe queen by now."

"Well, that would have worked well for you, wouldn't it, since she seems to be smitten with you," Raisa said.

"I am *not* pursuing your sister," he said, rising to his feet. "I am telling you to take very good care, Raisa. Please." He bowed. "Welcome home, Your Highness. I will call upon you again." He nodded at Han and Amon. "Gentlemen. Using that term loosely, of course."

And so he left, leaving Raisa more confused than enlightened.

CHAPTER TWENTY-SEVEN

ON THE LOOSE IN THE PALACE

Fellsmarch Castle was like a small city in itself, familiar to Han in unexpected ways. The servants' corridors reminded him of Ragmarket's back alleys, where you could travel long distances unobserved by most. The audience chambers and salons were like large public squares, where the bluebloods gathered to make show and catch the attention of their rivals.

Han explored the palace and the close, mapping it in his head as he had Ragmarket and Southbridge.

True to her word, Raisa had moved Han into an apartment next to hers—Magret Gray's former quarters. She didn't have much choice of places to put him, because her room was fairly isolated in one of the gateway towers, beneath the glass gardens on the roof.

The glass gardens where Alger Waterlow once trysted with Hanalea, the warrior queen.

Seeming immune to Magret's scandalized disapproval, Raisa

relocated her nurse into quarters in the other gateway tower, some distance down the hall. The Maiden haunted the corridors at all hours like a tall stately spook with a lantern and long gray braid.

Magret made it clear that she detested Han—that she blamed him for what happened to Velvet. It was too bad because Han rather liked the iron-spined nurse. He still had hopes of winning her over—but maybe he was fooling himself.

Raisa demurred when the High Wizard and her council suggested that she move into her mother's elaborate quarters in the main palace. That could wait until after the coronation, she said. The queen's chambers held too many painful memories to move in so soon. Also, she had a sentimental attachment to her old rooms. Anyway, she preferred to mourn her mother in seclusion, not burdening the court at large. Besides, she would likely redecorate the suite once her grief had abated somewhat, and that would be easier if it were not occupied.

She had a dozen arguments, and her story often changed depending on the audience.

Han admired her politician's ability to say no and keep saying no while making it seem like no one wanted to say yes more than she did. Still, he was surprised by her decision to stay where she was. It seemed like claiming the queen's rooms would reinforce the inevitability of the coronation to those who still might hope for a different outcome.

From all appearances, resistance to Raisa as queen had evaporated after her sudden reappearance at the memorial service. Han knew that it had only been driven underground. Even if Raisa survived her coronation, an assassin could make sure her reign was short-lived.

Amon Byrne was taking no chances. He kept handpicked bluejackets on duty outside Raisa's room whenever she was in residence, and they accompanied her wherever she went, even inside the palace.

Han's suite was small by palace standards—intended for a servant—but it was almost too big for him—consisting of a room to sleep in and a room to sit in and another room for spares.

He had lived most of his life with the rest of his family in a single room. If there had been more than three Alisters, they'd still have shared a single room. Except for when they visited the privy, most families in Ragmarket did everything in one room, whether it was eating, sleeping, piecework, laundry, dying, birthing babies, or making love.

The furniture in Han's suite was heavy and ornate, like the kind in some of the fancier parts of Southbridge Temple. The bed in particular was huge and lonely, and Han rattled around in it, plagued by an excess of space and bad dreams.

It was so deadly quiet at night it was hard to fall asleep. Even with his shutters open, most nights all he could hear was the splashing of the fountain in the courtyard. It was almost a relief when lovers crept out there in the moonlight, breaking the silence with their whispers, laughter, and sighs.

Except it only made him ache for what he'd lost.

He tried to distance himself from Raisa. He told himself she was just another blueblood liar who'd use him and discard him; who would ride right over the underclass when they got in her way. Pining after a princess, as Cat called it, was the road to humiliation. He'd never be more to her than an interesting diversion.

But the reality of her kept getting in his way.

Twice now, he'd nearly lost her for keeps. Once in Marisa Pines Pass, and once in the attack just outside the palace gates. If not for Dancer's armor, she'd be dead or badly injured.

He revisited the memory of their entrance into the city again and again—the crushing pain, the vacancy where his heart used to be, the realization that he had failed once again to protect someone he loved.

It was like poking at a deep bruise, verifying that it had not yet healed, reminding himself of his vulnerability.

Of hers.

And so he'd set himself this impossible task.

He could protect himself—and if he failed, well, he'd been ready to pay the personal price for failure all his life. But how could he keep Raisa alive when so many enemies seemed bent on killing her? How could he become powerful enough to make a claim on her—to make her take him seriously as a suitor? How could he convince her to see him as a peer—someone who could partner with her in every way?

And how could he do all that without putting her in even more danger? Willo's warnings echoed in his ears.

He didn't yet know the answers, but he knew this—he wouldn't put her at risk by allowing a romance to blossom between them until he was in a position to defend it.

Raisa was brilliantly savvy about some things, but she'd never truly understood how it was between bluebloods and street-runners. She'd never had to. She didn't seem to realize that any hint of romance between them would bring both the clans and wizards down on them.

He'd have known the rules on his old turf. Here, following his instincts would get them both killed.

If you don't know where you're going, you'll never get there, Jemson used to say. At least now, Han knew where he was going, and who with. He'd just have to find his own path.

Raisa's first "tutoring session" had not gone well. The tension was so thick you could've spread it on bread and called it a meal, as Mam would say. Raisa was constantly on the move, pacing back and forth and talking and waving her hands like she could fill up the chasm between them all on her own.

Han sat in a straight chair, his hands gripping the armrests, hearing every third word. His mind's eye strayed to that rose tattoo on her collarbone, to her tiny waist, to the green eyes shadowed by thick lashes and black brows set against her tawny skin.

It was a special kind of misery to recall her fresh-air scent and forthright kisses. It had been a pleasure to kiss someone who seemed to enjoy it as much as he did.

An inside door connected Han's quarters to the queen's, meant to allow the servant that was supposed to be living there to come and go in privacy. While attending Raisa in her rooms, Magret kept it locked, and rattled the lock several times a day—a warning to the wizard on the other side.

Han mastered the lock his first day. And then it took all the self-discipline he had to stay on his side of the wall.

He fetched his own water from the pump in the courtyard and either ate in the dining hall or carried food back from the kitchens himself. While he wanted to fit in with bluebloods, he wasn't going to chance food or drink that had been sitting unattended in the hallway or carried by a servant. There were too many people who would like to see him dead, and too many slick clan-made poisons that could be added to food and water undetected.

Each of his rooms had its own fireplace. Darby Blake, Han's personal servant, had the idea he would slip in when Han was out and replenish the stack of wood and fill the water pitcher and empty the chamber pot. Han had to break him of that because he'd laid charms on all the doors and windows to keep out intruders. Servants could be threatened, charmed, or bribed. So Han carried his own wood from a bin along the corridor just outside his room and set his chamber pot outside when it needed attention.

Darby was always there, ready to receive his slop jar like it was a privilege or a gift.

For Han, living in the palace was a lot like living in Ragmarket—surrounded by enemies, with death always a footfall away. Only plusher. There were several dining halls. Like taverns, some catered to the quality and others to the working class. The food was always good and there was plenty of it, even though others in the queendom might be starving. Any time of the day or night, food could be had.

His sitting room led onto a terrace that overlooked the courtyard in the center of the palace. The stone walls of Fellsmarch Castle afforded plenty of handholds and footholds for an experienced second-story thief. The walls took him to the roof, to the glass gardens up there, and the roof took him wherever else he wanted to go.

Han was amazed at how many rooms there were in the palace, some of them used only rarely. Even after several weeks, there were parts of the palace he'd not yet explored, including the Bayar stronghold. No doubt they'd have laid traps for intruders, knowing Han was in the castle. He wanted more training on detecting and disabling magical locks and killing charms before he ventured there. And that meant he had to find a way to make up with Crow.

Han's proximity to the queen, and his apparent role as her favorite, made him the subject of endless servant gossip. At first the maids froze like deer when he passed by, and the chamberlains elbowed each other and clamped their mouths shut when they saw him coming.

Their attitude toward him was a mixture of fear, fascination, and pride of ownership. His reputation as a ruthless streetlord, thief, and knife fighter had preceded him into the palace. Added to that were the stories about Queen Marianna's memorial service, churned and expanded by the palace rumor mill.

A wizard from Ragmarket? Who'd heard of such a thing? He was one of them, and yet he wasn't. Wizards breathed the rarefied air on Gray Lady and moved in blueblood circles. Wizards hired folk to give orders to their servants so they wouldn't have to talk to them directly.

The Gray Wolf queens were known to be lusty and venturesome in matters of love, and the servant underground assumed that Han was their queen's dangersome plaything who would soon be discarded for someone more biddable.

Han figured bets had been laid on how long he would last, and whether he'd go quietly when the time came. He would have wagered himself, but he didn't know what odds to demand.

Only bluebloods seemed unaware of the ongoing speculation.

The notion that the queen of the realm would romance a thief seemed beyond comprehension to them. Which was a blessing, and he meant to make it last.

Han made a special effort to win over the servants. His mother had worked in the palace for a time, and he was well aware of how powerful a network the palace underground was, how much information it carried, and how gossip could remake a person.

He was free with Queen Raisa's coin when he asked the palace staff for favors, and he made sure to learn their names and stories. He made it clear that he would make it worthwhile for those who brought him information. He would double the payment of any who sought information about him.

He also made it clear that anyone who entered his room intending mischief would die a horrible death.

Han had never realized that queens worked so hard—at least this one did. Maybe the old queen hadn't done much of anything in the past year, or maybe it just seemed that way. Raisa toured the city's fortifications, reviewed the Highlander Army, and attended services in temples all over the Fells. She sat through meeting after meeting—with her stewards, with the Queen's Council, with the committees laying plans for the coronation. Some meetings were routine, while others had to do with projects Raisa herself was pushing. It wasn't easy. Her advisers couldn't agree that water was wet and the sky was blue. Also, there didn't seem to be any money.

As Raisa's bodyguard, Han attended nearly all of her meetings. He hoped to learn something useful—who was who and what was what. But it wore him out—it was all talk, talk, talk, and nothing much accomplished. He stood through most, vibrating like a plucked string, impatient at wasting so much time.

It struck him how alone Raisa was. There seemed to be few people at court the queen could trust. Even her father, Averill, had a clan agenda that might not fit with her own. She was always onstage, whether at meals or at a recital, or in conference with her economic advisers.

At one afternoon meeting with the Queen's Council, she managed to get into a row with just about everyone.

They were seated around the table in her privy chamber (which Han thought was an amusing name, given what was often slung around). As was his custom, Han stood propped against the wall, looking as ruthless as possible.

"General Klemath," Raisa said, lifting her chin in that way she had when she meant to do battle, "as the contracts with the mercenary forces come due for renewal, I want you to dismiss the foreign brigades and send them home."

"Send them *home*, Your Highness?" Klemath stared at her in astonishment. "These are dangerous times, my dear. I know the brigades are expensive, but surely there are other places to cut costs." He ticked off each point on his thick fingers. "There is conflict with the Waterwalkers on the western border. Arden is a threat to the south. The army might be needed to help the guard if we have a domestic rebellion." He looked up at the ceiling, making a point of ignoring Lord Averill. "There is unrest among the upland clans. They are always unpredictable. Now is not the time to be frugal with the army."

"I think you will find that tensions between clans and Valefolk will diminish once the blooded queen is on the throne and we are convinced that she is no longer in danger," Averill said. "In the meantime, we will do whatever it takes to maintain the tenets of the Næming and protect the Gray Wolf line. As long as attacks on our villages continue, we will stand ready to defend ourselves. May I remind you that in many areas of the countryside, the Demonai are all that stand between the people and the flatland brigands."

"I don't mean to cut funding to the army," Raisa said, holding up her hand to quiet the debate, "at least not to the degree that it puts us in danger. I intend to field as many soldiers as now, but I want to move to native-born soldiers. Men and women who have a loyalty to the Fells, who know the land, and will fight hard to defend it."

Klemath raised an eyebrow. "If there is a rebellion, Your Highness, it would be best to field professional soldiers who have no possible allegiance to slumdwellers and street thieves."

"Except that your foreign soldiers have no particular allegiance to me," Raisa said.

"But they do as they're told," Klemath said, like he was trying his best to be patient. "Your homegrown army might betray you."

Klemath is native born, Han thought. Strange that he's so married to the notion of southern mercenaries. Maybe he's lining his own pockets. Maybe he's on the dawb from the mercenary brokers and doesn't want to give that up.

"It is not the primary job of the army to fight our own citizens," Raisa said. "People in the Fells are close to rebellion because there are no jobs and no way to make a living. The wars in the south have idled hardworking people. Wouldn't it be better to use our funds to put our own people to work?"

"Has there been a problem, Your Highness, with the mercenaries?" Klemath asked.

"There has been a problem, General, with people starving in the Fells while we send money to sell-swords and brokers in the flatlands." The spots of color on Raisa's cheeks signaled that she was losing patience. "I've been out to the camps. Most of our soldiers seem to be from Arden and Tamron. You'd think they'd have plenty of fighting to do at home."

Klemath raised his hands helplessly and turned to the others on the council. "Gentlemen?"

"Gentlemen!" Raisa repeated. "That's another problem. Why aren't there more women on my council?"

They all looked at one another, each waiting for someone else to speak. They were all men, save one spare, red-haired woman Han didn't know.

"Well, ah . . ." Lord Hakkam flailed about for an answer. "The members—it's the office, not the gender, you know."

"I'm going to fix that," Raisa said to herself.

"Your Highness," Lord Bayar said, with an indulgent smile, "with reference to the mercenary issue, perhaps it is wise to listen to your counselors. We are here to help, after all."

"I know you are kindhearted, Your Highness," Lord Hakkam said, patting Raisa's hand. "But you are as yet unschooled in military matters. Although the mercenaries are expensive, it is dangerous to make so radical a change during this transition period. Above all, we want to keep you safe." Hakkam served as her financial minister as well as chair of the Queen's Council.

"The Guard keeps me safe, uncle," Raisa said, firmly withdrawing her hand. "And the good will of my people, which I mean to earn."

Amon Byrne cleared his throat. As Captain of the Queen's

Guard, he was an ex-officio member of the council, but he didn't speak out often. "We use only native borns in the Queen's Guard, and it has worked well for us. Until recently, our army was native born as well."

"And we lost Queen Marianna despite her native-born Guard," Lord Bayar said.

"Are you suggesting it was murder?" Byrne asked, looking the High Wizard in the eyes.

Bayar backed off. "I am only raising the possibility, nothing more," he said. "I am saying I still have questions about how she died."

"Really? I thought perhaps you had the answers," Averill said.

I did too, Han thought. Why is Lord Bayar raising questions about Queen Marianna's death when he's likely the one who did her?

"That's enough!" Raisa said. Into the silence that followed, she said, "Anyone who has solid information about my mother's death should speak to Captain Byrne. We will not sling accusations here in this council."

This is like a rival gang standoff, Han thought. With Raisa trying to be streetlord over all of them.

Raisa waited, and when nobody said anything, went on. "Regarding the reshaping of the army, I thank you for your advice, but I have made my decision. This is not an impulsive move. I have been looking at this issue for some time. I will rely on you, General Klemath, to provide proper training to our new recruits."

"Yes, Your Highness," General Klemath said, bowing his head. "As you wish. But with so many other pressing obligations,

I hope you realize that it can't be done overnight."

This change will be so gradual as to be unnoticeable, Han thought. In a year, we'll have no more than a handful of native borns in the army, and Klemath will still have his mercenaries.

"I don't expect you to do it without help, General," Raisa said sweetly. "As Captain Byrne is experienced in working with native-born soldiers, he will assist you in implementing this." She laced her fingers and rested her chin on her hands. "Also, Speaker Jemson has contacts in Ragmarket and Southbridge, where I expect many of our recruits will come from. Lord Averill is similarly connected in the camps. The clans have been under-represented in the army, and I mean to field a force that reflects all the peoples of the Fells."

She paused, looking at each man in turn. "The four of you are accountable for this. You will meet at least weekly, and I will expect monthly progress reports."

Irritation flickered across Klemath's face, then quickly extinguished. Jemson frowned, looking as if he wished to say something, but did not. Byrne's expression said that he would see it done if that's what his queen required.

She's put him in a spot, Han thought. The bluejackets and the army already hate each other. But she doesn't have much choice if she really means to make this happen.

"What other business is there?" Raisa asked, stretching her arms out in front of her and rotating her shoulders like they hurt.

"This arrived from Tamron Court via the garrison at Tamron Crossing," Klemath said sullenly, extending an envelope toward Raisa. "It is addressed to you, from Gerard Montaigne, Prince of Tamron."

Prince Gerard! Han stiffened. He and Dancer had had a run-in with Gerard in Ardenscourt. Gerard had tried to "recruit" them for his wizard army. If not for Cat Tyburn, he might have succeeded.

Strange that Klemath would give Raisa the message at this meeting, Han thought. Why wouldn't he just forward it to her with other dispatches from the border?

Unless he already knew what it said and wanted to see how queen and council reacted to the message within.

Raisa stilled herself for a long moment, took a deep breath, then took the envelope from Klemath. It was thick, creamy stationery, sealed with a wax stamp. Ripping the seal free, she slid a folded sheet from the envelope.

She unfolded it and spread it out on the table. Tucking her hair behind her ears, she bent her head to scan the message, so Han couldn't see her expression. She appeared to read over it twice, running her finger along the page as if to assure herself that she was reading every line.

When she raised her head, her complexion resembled the tawny marble they dug from the quarries in We'enhaven, set with the emeralds of her eyes. Pressing the heels of her hands into the table, she tapped on the page with her fingers, staring straight ahead.

"Well?" Lord Bayar asked impatiently. "What does Montaigne have to say?"

Raisa flinched as if startled, and looked at the High Wizard, her eyes unusually bright.

"What is it, Your Highness?" Bayar said, leaning forward and reaching for the letter. "Perhaps we could shed some perspective on—"

"Here, Lord Bayar," Raisa said, thrusting the page toward him. "Why don't you read it aloud for the council?" She sat back, arms folded, gripping her elbows to either side.

Bayar scanned the page quickly, then looked up at Raisa as if seeking clues as to how she might respond.

Clearing his throat, he bent his head over the paper and began to read.

CHAPTER TWENTY-EIGHT
LOVE LETTER FROM ARDEN

To Her Majesty Queen Raisa of the Fells,

I write in the fervent hope that this finds you well and to offer congratulations on your imminent coronation.

Please also accept my condolences on the sudden and yet remarkably timely death of your mother, Queen Marianna. It is well known that relations between the two of you have been strained of late. Her accident, while unfortunate, has cleared a major obstacle from your path. It appears that you, like me, do not hesitate to shape events to your advantage. This only reinforces my notion that we are natural allies and could be more than that.

"Blood of the demon!" Averill swore.

Clearly, this was not a message intended to be read aloud in company.

Or perhaps it was.

Han watched Raisa's face. It retained its stonelike quality, stamped with a faintly interested expression. He could tell that she was watching all the other faces in the room.

"Daughter," Averill said. "You should not entertain this kind of slander. The notion that you would have had anything to do with your mother's death is ludicrous."

"And yet many suspect me," Raisa said. "Especially outside of the Fells." She gestured to Bayar. "Go on."

It will take some time to reestablish order in Tamron and rid the kingdom of spies and traitorous elements. The abuses and excesses of the recent king have stoked the fires of rebellion among both nobles and commons. They must understand that those days are over. Indeed, the former prince and princess are at risk of assassination by their own people. You will be glad to know that I am keeping them well secured within my keep.

The current confusion does, I believe, present an opportunity for us to expand our holdings. My brother, Prince Geoff, continues to lay claim to the kingdom of Arden. He has reinforced his borders with Tamron and brought his army west to meet any threat from us. This leaves his northern borders lightly garrisoned and unprotected.

I understand that the Fells maintains a standing army of more than five thousand horse and foot soldiers.

Bayar looked up from the letter. "Remarkably accurate count, wouldn't you say?"

"Remarkable," Raisa murmured.

Bayar resumed reading.

I propose the following, the details of which are to be negotiated by our representatives:

The Fells will invade the kingdom of Arden from the north, committing at least three thousand of its troops to this campaign. The Fellsian Army will drive south as far as Temple Church and hold its position there. This will divert the Ardenine Army away from the western border and allow us to advance from that direction to take the capital.

"It would also make any future alliance with Geoff unlikely, if not impossible," Averill said.

Raisa nodded, lips tight together. "Go on," she directed Bayar. He continued reading.

Once Arden is securely under my control, I will withdraw most of my army from Tamron, leaving the Tomlins to rule as my regents there, assuming that they can be made to understand certain realities.

Finally, I propose an immediate marriage contract between us, with the marriage to be solemnized as soon as our military objectives are accomplished. It would be best, of course, for our betrothal to remain secret for now.

Following our marriage, we will jointly rule the larger kingdom of Arden, Tamron, and the Fells. You would, of course, retain your title of Queen of the Fells, a title that our daughters would inherit.

We needn't stop there. Given your line's history, we would have a natural claim to the rest of the Seven Realms. With our combined resources, we can add these jewels to our crown. You will be the beautiful and glittering symbol of a new age of peace and prosperity.

Do give this proposal careful consideration. I think you agree that this arrangement presents significant advantages to us both, if we act quickly.

I also hope you are able to set aside the unfortunate incidents along the border between Tamron and Arden and know that it was my desire to cement a match with you that drove my behavior. These times call for bold and aggressive action.

Best, Gerard Montaigne, King of Arden and Tamron

Bayar tossed the pages onto the table with a snort. "The new king of Tamron takes you for a fool, Your Highness."

Raisa laced her fingers, resting her hands on the table. "Do you think so, Lord Bayar?"

"During that *unfortunate incident,* as he calls it, Montaigne murdered young Wil Mathis in cold blood," Bayar said.

Raisa nodded. "I was there."

"Not only that," Bayar continued, "some speculate that his agents may be responsible for the murders we've seen recently, right here in the city."

"Murders?" Raisa looked from face to face, fastening on Captain Byrne's. "What murders?"

"Five of the gifted have been murdered in the past fortnight, and the bodies left in Ragmarket," Byrne said. "The murders seem indiscriminate, connected only by the fact that all of the victims were wizards. One was a member of the assembly, but the last two were students slumming in Ragmarket. They were found in a back alley with their throats cut and their amulets missing, painted over in blood."

That caught Han's attention. Cat had mentioned that there'd been several murders of the gifted in Ragmarket and Southbridge. She'd asked around, but nobody seemed to be bragging about it.

Whoever's running that crew has starch, Han had thought at the time. Or a death wish.

"Why would Montaigne kill wizards in Ragmarket?" Raisa asked.

"It's just one theory," Byrne said. "As you know, Your Highness, Montaigne has abducted wizards and forced them into his army. But it's likely he's been having difficulty getting his hands on magical weaponry. So he might be killing wizards in order to collect their amulets. Or seeking to reduce the supply of gifted in the north."

Bayar rolled his lace cuffs. "Some say Gerard Montaigne is

behind it. Others believe we should look closer to home." He turned his head very deliberately and looked at Averill Demonai. The red-haired wizard leaned forward, nodding her support.

"By all means, look closer to home," Lord Demonai said, glancing up at the ceiling. "After all, wizards have a long history of preying on each other. Perhaps some have chosen this means to address the shortage of flashcraft."

"Isn't it more likely to be gang related?" Raisa's gaze flickered to Han, then fixed back on her captain.

"That could be," Byrne said, "but the gangs usually leave wizards alone."

"All right," Raisa said wearily, as if she were adding this problem to some mental list. "Let's get back to the matter at hand." She looked around the table. "What about the rest of you? What do you think of Montaigne's proposal?"

Is she really considering it? Han wondered. He'd met Gerard Montaigne, and he wasn't buying anything the prince was selling.

"I agree with Lord Bayar," Byrne said, "whether or not Montaigne has anything to do with those murders. My guess is, since he hasn't been able to defeat his brother on his own, he's hoping the army of the Fells will distract Geoff long enough for him to gain a foothold." He paused. "Our losses could be devastating. Our army is trained for mountain fighting, where our smaller numbers aren't such a disadvantage. Out on the Arden plains, we can be flanked and overwhelmed."

"Let's not be hasty," General Klemath said, adjusting his bulk in his seat. "While there is some truth to what Captain Byrne says, his knowledge of our army and the tactics of flatland warfare is limited. Many of our mercenary soldiers have trained in Arden and Tamron for just this kind of fighting. In this instance, it may be that our employ of experienced mercenaries will lead to success rather than failure." He smiled smugly, as if he felt redeemed.

"A strong marriage to the south would cement your position," Klemath continued, "and discourage those who might seek to take advantage of a young and inexperienced queen."

Why is Raisa's general offering political advice? Han wondered. What's his dog in this fight?

Lord Hakkam nodded in agreement. "There may be opportunity here, if we proceed carefully. Whether any alliance with Arden would be acceptable to the Council of Nobles would depend on how claims for land and holdings are adjudicated and whether southerners have any claims on properties here in the north."

Tilting his head back, Hakkam looked down his nose at the others. "If we come to Gerard's aid, it would seem that grants of lands and estates in Arden should be ceded to us as victors. There's the potential that many of us could do very well on a larger stage, with more resources." He smiled, his eyes lighting with avarice. "Arden and Tamron! Think of it—miles and miles of fertile fields and riches such as we've never seen in the Fells."

He's in as long as he gets shares, Han thought. Everybody here is voting his own interest. Running this council is like herding cats and rats together and trying to keep anybody from having a meal.

"I was just in Arden," Han said, "and it's not what you think. They've been at war for almost a decade, so it's pretty torn up. A lot of the crops have been destroyed, and they've been pouring money into their armies for so long there's been little to spare for building and repair."

They all looked at him as if a dog had suddenly spoken up, offering military advice.

"Well, then," Hakkam said, folding his fingers carefully together and wrinkling his nose like he smelled something bad. "Likely many of the major landholders have been killed, so there will be properties available and in need of management. There may also be the opportunity to negotiate advantageous marriages with prominent families in Arden or Tamron."

"That may be, Lord Hakkam," Averill said, "assuming that Gerard wins. I've not been impressed with his military efforts so far. If Geoff wins against us as Gerard's allies, I suspect we won't be making any marriages to the south."

He paused. "Your Highness, you already know my opinion of Gerard Montaigne. He's a snake, and a snake doesn't change its basic nature if you dress it up and give it a fancier title. I think it wise to look both inside and outside the queendom for a match, but as a father and a counselor, I cannot advise that you go to Montaigne. You would never sleep soundly in his bed."

A ghost of a smile passed across Raisa's face, coming and going so quickly that Han wasn't sure he'd really seen it.

Maybe Montaigne wouldn't sleep soundly, either, Han thought. That cheered him. But only a little.

"We may be able to secure our objectives without committing to your marriage to the Prince of Arden, Your Highness," Lord Hakkam said. "Perhaps he would be satisfied with another match. My daughter Melissa, for example, is cousin to you, and a marriage between them would strengthen our ties outside the queendom."

"It would be a grave error to allow Gerard Montaigne to gain a foothold here," Lord Bayar said. "The next thing we know, we'll have the crows of Malthus flocking into the cities and taking over our temples."

"That will never happen," Lord Averill said, glancing at Speaker Jemson, who, as usual, listened more than spoke. The expression on Averill's face reminded Han that he had been and still was a Demonai warrior.

"Come, Gavan," General Klemath said to Bayar, ignoring Averill. "Surely we can work this to our advantage and manage this in a way to keep us all safe. I'll match our wizards against Gerard Montaigne any day. There is some risk, but there is much to gain in this."

"Arrows are faster than jinxes," Han murmured. Once again, they all stared at him.

"Alister is right," Byrne said. "Used strategically, wizards could play a pivotal role in a military campaign. But we're not used to cooperating in that way. We've not fought such a war in a thousand years."

It was a peculiar marriage of interests—Lord Averill and Captain Byrne and Lord Bayar and Han Alister agreeing on anything was as rare as gold in Ragmarket.

"I think you'll find that the Council of Nobles will concur that an alliance with Gerard Montaigne presents a rare opportunity," Lord Hakkam said. "Especially now that he holds Tamron. Perhaps we should meet with his representatives before we come to a decision."

"By all means, let us open negotiations with Montaigne's representatives," Raisa said. "That commits us to nothing, and we may learn more about his intentions. At the very least, it may keep him at bay as long as he thinks it is a possibility. While I am not keen on a match with Gerard, I certainly wish to keep all options open when it comes to the best interests of the realm. I think we have to be practical in such matters, whatever our personal inclinations. Uncle, I will leave this in your hands."

Hakkam smiled like a sharp that spies a nick-ninny mark. "I will keep you apprised of developments, Your Highness."

Ignoring the scowls on Bayar's and Demonai's faces, Raisa folded the letter, returned it to its envelope, and set it aside, closing the subject. "Is there anything else before we adjourn?"

Lord Bayar stood. "Your Highness, as you know, the queen appoints one member to the Wizard Council, who speaks for her interests. Our next meeting is scheduled a week from now, and it would be wise for you to have a representative there. We will want to choose a new High Wizard as soon as possible to provide you proper protection." His gaze swept over Han, as if he were an example of improper protection.

"Really?" Raisa said, raising an eyebrow. "It's scheduled in a week, is it?" She drummed her fingers on the table.

Bayar should have known better. Either he was blind to Raisa's moods, or he didn't care to try to read her. "As time is short, may I suggest my daughter Fiona?" he said. "You grew up together, and, as you said, it would be useful to have another young lady on the council."

A young lady who would like to nudge Raisa right off the throne, Han thought.

Raisa folded her arms, a sign of resistance. "Don't the Bayars already have a seat on the council? In addition to your role as High Wizard and chair?"

Lord Bayar nodded. "As my eldest, Micah, has turned eighteen, he will assume the Bayar seat on the council. I, of course, will continue as chair until a new High Wizard is chosen."

So Micah's the older twin, Han thought. Add Fiona, and that'd be three Bayars on the Wizard Council. That wasn't such a good idea, especially if they were getting ready to pick a new High Wizard.

"Thank you, Lord Bayar," Raisa said. "I appreciate your suggestion, but I have already chosen a representative to the council."

Lord Bayar's head came up, and he wiped a look of startlement off his face. "Really, Your Highness? So quickly? Is it someone I know?"

"Alister has agreed to serve," Raisa said, nodding toward Han, where he stood against the wall. Once again, heads turned like beads on a string.

Street face, Han said to himself, looking back at them.

Gavan Bayar didn't bother to hide *his* opinion.

"Your Highness," he protested, turning back to Raisa. "No doubt Alister would bring a refreshing new perspective to our deliberations. However, despite your generous pardoning of him for past crimes, he would be ill suited to represent your interests among members of the oldest and most illustrious families of wizards in the queendom. His rather colorful history doesn't prepare him for his duties there."

"I don't know, Lord Bayar," Raisa said, her voice like sweet poison dripping into their ears. "The wizard council has been described to me as a nest of vipers. It may be that his streetfighting experience will serve him well in that environment."

The council members shifted in their seats, looking everywhere but at the powerful High Wizard and the stubborn young queen. Han crossed his arms, affecting nonchalance, looking frankly back at anyone bold enough to meet his eyes.

"Princess Raisa, I beg you to reconsider," said the red-haired woman. "There is some question as to whether Alister is truly gifted. He's come out of nowhere, we know nothing about his family, and it seems his power has manifested only recently."

"Lady Gryphon is right," Bayar said. "There is talk that his so-called gifts are not gifts at all, but a manifestation of demonic possession, fueled by blood sacrifice."

Takes a demon to know one, Han thought.

"I'm from Ragmarket, Lord Bayar," he said, pulling away from the wall and standing, feet slightly apart. "And I came by my gifts in the usual way. As to why they didn't surface earlier, well, there are reasons."

Han's gaze flicked to Lord Averill, who wore his trader face, then back to Bayar.

"As for my family, my father was Danel; he died as a mercenary in the southern wars," Han went on. "My mother's name was Sarah, called Sali, and my sister was Mari. They died last summer. But then you already knew that. Every time you forget, I'll remind you. That's the blood sacrifice I made to be here, and that's enough."

His words sent ripples through the council like a stone dropped into a pool. Han looked from face to face, and the only friendly one was Jemson's. And Jemson looked worried.

Lady Gryphon cleared her throat. "That's exactly my point, Your Highness. My son Adam was recently named to the council.

When you compare his pedigree to that of a street thief, I think you'll find that—"

"Lady Gryphon, your son was my teacher at Mystwerk House," Han said. "If you have any questions about my credentials as a wizard, I suggest you send a note to Dean Abelard."

"As it happens, Dean Abelard is on her way back to the Fells," Lady Gryphon said. "We shall certainly ask her opinion; though, realistically, as a first-year student, you'd have had limited contact with the dean of Mystwerk House."

"Actually, I saw quite a lot of Dean Abelard," Han said, straightening his stoles. "She was . . . she was sort of a mentor to me." He hadn't intended on playing the Abelard card so soon, but just now it was a useful distraction.

Bayar's eyes narrowed. Micah and Fiona would have already put a word in his ear about Abelard and Alister.

"Whatever Abelard says, Your Highness, you must weigh the risk in having such a person close to you," Bayar began.

"This conversation is over," Raisa said, bulling right through whatever Bayar intended to say. "I have made my decision, and Alister is my choice. It was my hope that the council would accept it with grace. Failing that, they had better learn to live with it."

Lord Averill studied Han, eyes narrowed as if wondering what his sell-sword was up to.

Lord Bayar kept his eyes fixed on Raisa, and there was something in his gaze that gave Han the chills. He hadn't survived on the streets as long as he had by overlooking murder in his enemies' eyes.

The High Wizard inclined his head. "Very well, Your Highness. If Alister is your choice, we will certainly arrange to

welcome him to the Council House on Gray Lady next week."
He still did not look at Han, as if acknowledging his presence
would give him too much credit.

"I look forward to it," Han said, displaying his streetlord smile.
He tried to ignore the voice in his head—the one that said, *Kill
him now, Alister. Kill him now before he tries again.*

"If that is everything, then we stand adjourned," Raisa
said abruptly. "Alister, Captain Byrne, Lord Demonai, Speaker
Jemson, stay behind."

She's intentionally rubbing salt into the wounds she already
made, Han thought.

The rest filed out, stiff-backed and silent.

Byrne poked his head out the door and spoke to someone just
beyond, no doubt one of his bluejackets. Then he closed the door
and returned to the table.

After a moment of awkward silence, Averill said, "You've
made some enemies here today, daughter."

"Do you think they were ever my friends, Father?" Raisa said
bitterly, standing and pacing back and forth.

"They've never been your friends," Averill said, "but now
they have reason to think you will be difficult to manage."

"Good," Raisa said. "I won't be managed, and I won't be
condescended to. 'These are dangerous times, my dear,'" she
mocked. "As if I don't know that. They need to know that times
have changed."

"There have already been two attempts on your life," Speaker
Jemson said.

"Four, actually," Raisa said, toying with the hilt of the dagger
she always carried.

"Four, then," Jemson amended. "I must admit I am worried, Your Highness."

"So am I," Raisa said. "But if we force their hands, they may make a mistake and we'll have the proof we need. Otherwise, I can't think of any way we'll find out what really happened to my mother."

"Or *we'll* make a mistake, and you'll be dead," Byrne said. "They only need to get lucky once. We need to be perfect every time."

My thinking exactly, Han said to himself.

As if she'd heard him, Raisa swung around and glared at Han. "What about you?" she demanded. "You've scarcely said a word. What do you think about all this?"

Han gathered his thoughts, surprised to be asked his opinion. "I think it might have been smart to wait until after the coronation to pick fights with Lord Bayar," he said. "It's like poking at a wasp's nest—do it enough and you'll get stung, no matter how careful you are. Trust me, I know."

"You! You should talk," Raisa said, opening and closing her hands as if she wanted to wrap them around somebody's neck. "Do you think you made any friends in there?"

"Oh, they hated me already," Han said, shrugging. "Don't get me wrong: I think you're right to start with the army. Until you're in control of it, you're at risk. It's like running a gang that's blood-sworn to your second in command. You don't dare dismiss him 'cause they'll turn on you. You already know that Klemath will fight like a demon to keep control of the army. If Klemath and Bayar throw in together, all you got is the guard." He shrugged, nodding toward Byrne. "No disrespect to Captain

Byrne, but that's what Queen Marianna had, and she's dead."

"Briar Rose, you can't be serious about a marriage with Gerard Montaigne," Averill said, giving Han a "shut up" kind of look. "Please—tell me you're not serious."

"As long as I pretend to entertain the proposal from Montaigne, that keeps him in the south and drives a wedge between Klemath and Hakkam and Bayar," Raisa replied. "They've been in bed together too often recently. The Council of Nobles will side with my uncle, especially if mercenaries do the fighting, and the crown pays the bills. Lord Hakkam will spend at least as much energy trying to engineer a match with my cousin Melissa as in serious negotiations for my betrothal." She rolled her eyes. "Until I can get control of these people, I have to keep them from ganging up on me."

"Was that why you had Lord Bayar read it out in council?" Jemson asked, understanding dawning on his face.

Raisa twisted the ring on her finger, smiling grimly. "Klemath had certainly read it already. There's no telling who else. That thing has been opened and resealed so many times, it's a miracle it's still legible."

She looked pointedly at Han. "You were saying?"

Don't underestimate this girlie, Han reminded himself. Don't ever do that. Some bluebloods grow up fast—just like streetlords.

He cleared his throat. "I agree you need to push the thing with the army, chancy as it is. Soon as it's safe, you ditch Klemath and put someone in place who's beholden to you. So I think what you did was right, though maybe I would've done it at a different time."

Raisa gazed at him for a long moment, then gave a quick nod. "Yes. Well. All right, then."

"I did not realize you planned to name Hunts Alone to the Wizard Council, Your Highness," Averill said, frowning. "When did you make that decision?"

Lord Demonai obviously thought he should have been in on it. Han waited, wondering if Raisa would say anything about his demand to be named to the council.

She didn't.

"What choice did I have?" Raisa said, like she wasn't happy about it. "I wasn't going to send Fiona Bayar. This way, Alister can keep an eye on them."

"General Klemath was right about one thing," Speaker Jemson said. "These are dangerous times."

Raisa said briskly, "What's done is done. I expect you three to hold Klemath's feet to the fire on the army issue. I want to see real progress within three months. Look over those mercenary contracts and see which ones are up for renewal. I'll issue a writ that no new contracts are to be ratified without all four signatures. If you get resistance, let me know." She sighed, rubbing her eyelids with the tips of her fingers. "I'm sorry to put you in this position," she said, speaking through her hands. "I wish I had someone in the army I could trust."

"Give me a little time, Your Highness," Byrne said. "I'll make a few inquiries and give you some names. Some of the officers are native born. Another possibility is to transfer some good officers from the Guard to the Army."

"That's what we don't have, is time," Raisa said. "So much to do, so little time and money."

With that, she dismissed them. As Han passed through the cluster of bluejackets around the door, he looked back to see Raisa standing alone in her privy chamber, head down, twisting the wolf ring on her right hand.

She's more worried than she lets on, Han thought.

CHAPTER TWENTY-NINE
A GAME OF SUITORS

Gerard Montaigne wasn't the only one interested in a match with Raisa. As word spread throughout the Seven Realms that the missing princess heir had resurfaced and would be crowned Queen of the Fells, the flow of suitor gifts recommenced, from inside and outside the queendom. It was a mixed blessing. Raisa still hoped to put off marriage as long as possible, but her coffers were nearly empty and she wanted to continue to support the Briar Rose Ministry in Ragmarket and Southbridge.

To everyone else, an unmarried crown princess was seen as a loose end that should be either clipped or knitted up as soon as possible.

Dissonant messages of consolation on her mother's death and congratulations on her impending coronation arrived from the other monarchs in the realms, salted with opening bids in the marriage auction. Some offered younger sons who needed thrones to sit upon, others suggested the joining of the Fells to "kingdoms" as far away as Bruinswallow and We'enhaven.

Although Raisa *ana*'Marianna was not yet crowned, and rumor had it she was keeping a thief as a paramour, and that she likely had a hand in Queen Marianna's death, most were willing to overlook that in consideration of the queendom's mineral-rich holdings. They'd heard the northern queens were all witches anyway.

Everyone abroad seemed eager to help a young orphaned queen govern her queendom. Everyone at home seemed anxious to get her married off as soon as possible, as long as it was to their favorite.

The Klemath brothers reemerged as suitors amid a plethora of local hopefuls.

The foremost marriage candidate from the uplands was Reid Nightwalker. He spent more time in the capital than Raisa could ever remember, because of his assignment to Averill's guard. The Demonai warrior launched a quiet courtship—bringing gifts of fur throws and leatherwork and clan-made jewelry, perfumes and aromatics from the markets. Clearly, he hoped to follow in Averill's footsteps, and marry a queen.

Raisa and Nightwalker took long walks through the gardens sometimes, her Gray Wolves following a respectful distance behind. Sometimes they rode into the hills surrounding the Vale, but always with an escort. Nightwalker listened more than he spoke, and he didn't push as hard as he had in the past to go beyond kisses and caresses.

I could do worse, Raisa thought, as a political match, anyway. She ticked off the advantages: Nightwalker was unquestionably committed to Fellsian interests. He wouldn't be trying to make the Fells a minor province in a faraway realm. He would support her efforts to clean up the Dyrnnewater and keep the Wizard Council in check. A marriage to him would reinforce the ties between the clans and the Gray Wolf line.

And it would serve the Bayars right, after all of their plotting and scheming to marry Raisa off to Micah.

All in all, Nightwalker seemed like the safest choice, the same one her mother had made. On the personal side, at least he was closer to her age than Averill had been to her mother's. He was lithe and graceful and handsome. Although it was unlikely he would remain faithful to her, that wouldn't affect the line, at least.

Micah Bayar was another matter. With Raisa's return, he abruptly left off his pursuit of Mellony. As a result, Mellony moped about, tearful and sullen much of the time, trying Raisa's patience.

You're just thirteen, Raisa thought. And a princess. Get used to it.

Me, I'm done with romantic entanglements. Everybody I get involved with is either forbidden or unavailable or mad at me.

For instance: Han Alister was by turns brisk and businesslike, cold and unreadable, or slightly mocking. He deftly deflected or ignored Raisa's many attempts to restore or rekindle their friendship.

They'd had one "tutoring session," and it had been a disaster. Alone together in her privy chamber, she'd rattled on like a runaway horse, dissecting the politics at court until she was entirely bored with herself.

Han had sat there clenching the arms of his chair, stony-faced and glaze-eyed, like he wasn't hearing half of what she said. Raisa was exquisitely aware of him, constantly measuring the physical and emotional distance between them.

Their next two sessions had been canceled and rescheduled— once by him, for undisclosed reasons, and once by Raisa because of a conflicting meeting.

Why does he even bother? she thought. I am at a total loss for what to say to him that would do any good. I don't know how to go about rebuilding trust between us—or if that's even possible.

There is one thing I can do, Raisa thought. I can't give Han Alister a pedigree, but I can give him a title. And a home to replace the one that was burnt on Marianna's orders. Maybe that would make him feel more secure—more at ease at court.

She thrust away the nagging thought that neither her father nor the Bayars would be happy about it.

I'm not here to make them happy, she told herself.

Plans for her coronation proceeded amid the hard work of governing. Invitations to the coronation ball were sent out, and acceptances flooded back from throughout the Seven Realms. Some were likely curiosity-seekers who wanted to see what the headstrong princess heir would do next now that she was on her own, without maternal supervision.

Those who hoped to woo and wed her would come, for fear she might be married off in a hurry and they would miss an opportunity.

Others were no doubt looking to enjoy a week of hospitality at somebody else's expense. Or maybe they were eager to see what a real witch looked like.

Most of the thanes from Arden declined, citing the demands of the ongoing war. But, to Raisa's surprise, King Geoff Montaigne of Arden sent word that he would attend, along with his queen and two children.

He must be feeling more confident about his hold on the throne, Raisa thought; to leave Arden at this time. From what the queendom's spies reported, Geoff had mustered near unanimous support among the war-weary southern thanes.

Raisa hoped he wasn't another Gerard. At least this Montaigne was already married.

There was no response from Tamron, either from the Tomlins or Gerard Montaigne. She guessed that was a good thing—it would be awkward to have two kings of Arden in attendance. Meanwhile, Lord Hakkam's negotiations with Gerard's representatives dragged on.

Raisa submitted to multiple fittings under Magret's supervision. She needed a dress for the coronation ceremony itself, a gown for the ball, dresses for all the parties that would occur before and after. It wouldn't do for Raisa to wear the same thing to more than one party.

"Maybe I could just swap with somebody," Raisa groused. "We shouldn't be spending this kind of money on clothes I'll probably wear once."

Magret rolled her eyes. "As if anyone could fit into your clothes," she said. "And you would swim in anybody else's. A coronation happens once in your life, Your Highness. As does a wedding," she added pointedly.

Raisa made sure that Mellony was well outfitted also. She hoped that the series of social events would lift her younger sister out of her funk. And, indeed, while Raisa tolerated the fittings, they seemed to cheer Mellony considerably. Raisa's younger sister loved trying on clothes. Like Marianna, she was fond of parties.

There were long sessions in the Cathedral Temple with Speaker Jemson, rehearsing for the coronation. That's my life from here on in, Raisa thought dispiritedly. One ceremony after another. But Speaker Jemson was kind and funny. He took the coronation seriously, but it helped that he didn't take himself too seriously.

The Gray Wolves had been assigned to Raisa's personal guard, and so would play an important role in the coronation ceremony. At rehearsals, they stood stiff and solemn, brows furrowed in concentration. In a way, it made it worse that they were friends. Raisa knew they would never forgive themselves if they made some misstep that marred her big day.

Raisa missed her easy camaraderie with the Wolves. They were constantly around her, but now the barrier of rank stood between them. It was hard to relax with someone who came to attention whenever you entered the room.

Amon had carried the Waterwalker staff Dimitri had given Raisa all the way from Oden's Ford. They resumed practice with it, three times a week, in the barracks yard. It was a good workout but, more important, it was the only alone time she had with Amon these days. It allowed them private conversations, away from listeners in the palace walls.

Four days after she announced her appointment of Han to the Wizard's Council, Raisa walked back from the stables at dusk after a long ride across the Vale with Reid Demonai and an entourage of guards. She was flushed and sweaty, muscles loose, the tension dissipated by hours in the saddle. She and Nightwalker had parted with a kiss at the stable door.

He wanted more than that, of course. Expected more by now. She just wished she could conjure up a little more enthusiasm.

Talia Abbott and Trey Archer were on guard outside her room. Raisa paused in front of her door and smiled at Talia. "How is Sergeant Greenholt settling in?" she asked. Pearlie Greenholt, Talia's Ardenine girlfriend, was new to the Fells. The former weapons master at Wien House, she'd been named sergeant under the new Captain Byrne.

"She likes it well enough, Your Highness," Talia said with studied politeness. "Thank you for asking."

Raisa raised an eyebrow. "Really?"

Talia snickered. "She says it's too bloody cold up here and she's tired of walking on a slant all the time. Plus she misses the fresh fruits and greens we had year 'round at the Ford. Says all the turnips and cabbage give her the farts."

Raisa laughed, knowing Pearlie would be mortified if she knew what secrets Talia was sharing with the queen of the Fells. But Talia, at least, was short on formality.

Back in Raisa's room, her bath waited on its burner, steaming in the chilly air, but Magret was nowhere to be seen. She must be down with one of her headaches, Raisa thought. She ordered a light supper sent up, and wearily stripped off her riding breeches, jacket, and underclothes. As she sank into the hot water, her thoughts returned to the question that had been deviling her since she lost her temper with her advisers.

Had she made the right decision in putting Han Alister on the Wizard Council?

Would Han be able to help her on the council, or would he be shunned as the outsider he was? Or worse, murdered for his arrogance? Averill had made it clear he disapproved. It was what Han had wanted, but . . .

She must have fallen asleep. She woke to a hard rap on the door, and assumed it was supper arriving. Climbing from her bath, she toweled off and shrugged into her dressing gown. She walked into the sitting room, but when the sound repeated, she realized it came from the inside door to Han's suite.

She put her lips to the door. "What do you want?" she said.

"I believe we have an appointment, Your Highness," Han said through the door.

Appointment? Oh. Right. It was time for their rescheduled tutoring session.

Blood and bones. She wasn't ready to face another evening with a cold, distant Han Alister. It was just too painful.

"This isn't a good time, after all," Raisa said, looking down at bare toes peeking out from under her dressing gown. "Could we meet later in the week?"

"I need to talk to you. Now," he said brusquely. After a pause, he added, "We had a bargain, right?"

Raisa sighed. "Yes," she said. "We did." She unlocked the door and yanked it open. Han brushed past her into the room, not seeming to notice her state of dress.

She noticed his. Her tailors had been busy. He wore a blue silk coat that matched his eyes, and black trousers made to fit.

Maybe I should ask them to dress him in a burlap, she thought. *He'd be easier to resist.*

He walked to the window, rested his hands on the stone sill, and looked out over the city. Han's back was board straight, feet slightly apart, shoulders square and tense.

He's angry, Raisa thought. What now?

"I've ordered supper," she said. "Have you eaten? We can talk while we eat."

"I'm not hungry," he said, still staring out the window.

"Look," Raisa said, goaded beyond endurance. "There's no point in meeting if you're going to—"

"I hear I have a castle on the Firehole River," Han said to the window. "And a title."

"Oh. Yes," Raisa said, in a rush. "I meant to tell you, but I haven't seen you since I worked out the details. Ravengard, it's called. The castle is good sized, stone and timber, though in need of repairs. There's quite a bit of property with it, good hunting and pasturage. A few outbuildings. Not so good for farming, but—"

"Don't you think it would have been a good idea to tell me?" Han said, swinging around to face her. "It's the talk of the court. I'm the last to know about it."

"I meant to tell you," Raisa said. "It just slipped my mind. I didn't realize word was out." But of course it was. Rumors spread at court like the night itches in Ragmarket. "I thought you'd be happy. To have a home, I mean," she added lamely. She'd hoped that property and a title would help bridge the chasm between them.

"And maybe I would be, if it was done differently." He shook his head. "Don't you get it? It makes me look a fool that I didn't even know about it. Like you were gifting a favorite instead of meeting an obligation."

Raisa winced, biting her lip. "I was tired of Lord Bayar calling you 'Alister,' and 'the thief,' so I thought I'd give you a title."

"Do you think that will stop him?" Han snorted. "*Alister* and *thief* don't bother me so much. At least they're accurate. It's when they call me your doxy that I object." His voice shook, and it seemed to take a moment to master himself. He was all sharp corners and frayed edges tonight.

Raisa blinked at him, but he swung away again, scowling into the fireplace.

His anger confused her. She hadn't thought of him as someone who would be overworried about gossip.

Maybe even the rumor that they were lovers repulsed him.

She came up behind him and touched him on the elbow. He flinched but didn't turn around.

"People will talk at court," Raisa said. "There's no way to stop them."

He said nothing.

"They're talking about me as well," she said. "It's my reputation too."

"You think I'm worried about my bloody *reputation?*" Han finally turned and looked at her. "If they think you favor me, if they think I'm your pretty-boy plaything, they'll come after both of us. The only thing that stands between me and them is fear and respect. I've got to make show."

"We're not in Southbridge anymore," Raisa said. "It's not like you're muscling into another gang's territory."

"No?" Han raised an eyebrow. "That's what you think. Walking into the Wizard Council house will be a lot like walking into Southbridge after midnight wearing Ragger colors and carrying a sack full of gold."

"You're the one that demanded a room next to mine," Raisa

retorted. "You're the one that asked to be on the council. What did you think would happen?"

"The thing is, you can't be waving me like a red flag in front of the Wizard Council." He gripped her arms and looked down at her. "Listen. For both our sakes, you have to act like you hate me. Like you don't want me here at all."

"I hate you?" Raisa rolled her eyes, exquisitely aware of his hot fingers on her upper arms. "Well, that makes sense. That's why I gave you the room next to mine and named you to the Wizard Council."

"Let them think you're doing it against your will," Han said. "Maybe you're doing it under pressure from Dean Abelard. They already think I'm crewing for her. Or maybe I'm blackmailing you. If they think you don't really want me on the council, they won't guess I'm your pair of eyes."

"I don't want people to think I can be bullied," Raisa countered.

"Better that than they think we're allies," Han said. "We got to amuse them for a while until I get my game going. After that it won't matter."

What *is* your game? Raisa thought. Are we really allies? What are you really after? Revenge on the Bayars? Is it all about that?

"It's a little late to convince them we're enemies, don't you think?" Raisa said. "After the Queen's Council meeting and all."

Han laughed, but it had a bitter edge. "Nah, they'll go for it. Despite the rumors, bluebloods don't want to believe you could be allies with a streetrat. It turns their stomachs. They'd be happy to know different."

We're not all like that, Raisa wanted to say. But knew it would do no good.

"But that still puts you at risk," Raisa said. "If people think you're my enemy, it'll be open season on you. Everyone—even my friends—will be out to get you."

"Trust me, it's even riskier if they think you and I are tight," Han said. "That makes nobody happy. The Wizard Council begins to think about hushing both of us and putting Mellony on the throne. The clans'll be all over me if they think there's something between us. Your father is already jumpy because you put me on the council."

"But you'll be all alone," she said. "You can't fight everybody."

"*I'll* be alone?" He looked her up and down, his mouth quirking into a half smile. "Who's more alone, you or me? I don't have many friends, but at least I can count on those I have. Nobody's cozying up to me in order to get ahead."

Raisa took a quick breath, meaning to disagree. Then released it without speaking. He was right, of course.

Han smiled like he knew he'd scored a point. "I can take care of myself. I have some allies, and I'll find some more; you'll see." He paused, searching her face, his gaze traveling from her eyes to her lips. "I'm really very personable when you get to know me," he whispered.

Releasing his hold on one arm, he tucked a stray lock of hair behind her ear.

Raisa was acutely conscious of how close he was, the pale stubble on his cheeks, the memory of past kisses.

Coming up onto her toes, she reached up with her free hand and pulled his face down toward her. She kissed him with a kind of desperation, winding her fingers into his hair to prevent escape.

He put his hands on her shoulders as if he meant to push her away, but then slid them down onto her shoulder blades and lifted her up and into him. His lips seemed to sizzle against hers, sending a current all the way to her toes.

Once he got started, he couldn't seem to stop. He kissed her lips, the corner of her mouth, the space beneath her chin and behind her ear, leaving heat behind wherever his lips touched her skin.

He was breathing hard, and she could feel his heart hammering under the silk.

"Sweet Hanalea," she murmured, gripping his lapels, her own heart thudding painfully. "I have missed you so much."

"Look," he growled, swallowing hard. "This is not a good idea. I just . . . I'd better go before we . . ."

"Don't go." Desire sluiced through her, washing away all good intentions. She slid her hands to the back of his neck, drawing his head down again, stoppering his mouth with hers and crushing her body against his.

He scooped her up, carried her to the couch, and deposited her on it. Squeezing in next to her, he pulled her close. Raisa pulled his linen shirt free of his breeches, sliding her hands underneath. They lay together in a muddle of velvet and silk. Raisa's fingers brushed Han's muscled shoulders and back, down to the curve at the base of his spine, mapping the evidence of old hurts.

Han's lips grazed her skin, giving her the flaming shivers, his caresses wilting what remained of her resistance.

"I'm sorry," he breathed, kissing a sensitive place behind her ear. "I didn't mean to do this. It's just . . . really hard to resist when you—"

A knock came at the door, and they jerked apart. It was the door to the corridor this time. Han rolled to his feet in a heartbeat, straightening his clothing and combing his fingers through his tousled hair.

Raisa sat up reluctantly. She couldn't help thinking Han was used to quick getaways from interrupted trysts.

The tapping was repeated. "Your Highness?" a woman called. "May I bring your supper in?"

It took Raisa a moment to get her voice going. "Just leave it outside," she said, her speech thick and strange.

After a moment's hesitation, the woman said, "I can't leave your supper in the corridor, Your Highness. You know it isn't safe."

"I'm not hungry," Raisa murmured to Han, raising both hands to stay him when he turned toward the door to his quarters.

Han shook his head. "I'll go," he whispered, leaning so close that his warm breath tickled her skin. "I was right to start with. This *isn't* a good idea, and it won't happen again." He moved silently to the connecting door. "Good night, Your Highness," he mouthed. He stepped through and closed it behind him with a soft click.

Bones, Raisa thought, frustration like a stone in her middle. Nobody was acting like they were supposed to.

She stood, rearranged her gown, and waited for the blood to stop lurching through her veins. Outside the glow of the firelight, shadows shifted in the gloom, light reflecting off golden eyes and white teeth.

Of course, she said to herself miserably. A danger to the line. Everything I do or want is a danger to the line.

She stepped to the door, unlatched it, and took several paces back. "All right," she called to the servants outside, her voice nearly normal. "You can bring it in."

The door swung open, revealing a tall, broad woman in an ill-fitting blue uniform, carrying a tray covered in a napkin. Someone she didn't know, Raisa realized. The soldier's eyes swept the room quickly, then she stepped forward and to the side, revealing two men behind her, armed with swords.

They rushed toward Raisa as the woman dropped the tray onto the table with a clatter. She turned and bolted the door behind her, then scooped a brace of knives from under the napkin, one in each hand.

It all seemed to happen in slow motion, like a dream in which Raisa's feet were fastened to the floor, her cries stuck in her throat. The two swordsmen came at her from either side, smiling because they knew that with the door bolted they'd have time to finish their work even if she called for help.

They would be on her before she could wrench open the door to Han's suite, assuming it wasn't locked. Raisa fled screaming into her bedroom and slammed the door behind her. She struggled to slide the bolt across, leaping back as blades splintered the wood of the door.

Dimitri's staff stood propped in the corner of her room, and Raisa snatched it up, holding it horizontally across her body as the latch gave.

She smashed the end of her staff into the face of the first man through the door. It hit with a satisfying wet crunch, and he dropped his sword and went down like a rock, clutching at his face with both hands. Before Raisa could bring her staff back into position, the other two were inside.

The woman with the blades dropped her knives and picked up her fallen comrade's sword. Again, they came at Raisa from two sides. Even given the length of the staff and her hard-earned skill with it, she couldn't defend against both at once.

Raisa continued to shout for help, thrusting at first one assassin and then the other in order to stay out of the reach of their blades. Where was her guard? Talia and Trey should be right outside. Why weren't they responding?

Then, beyond the assassins, Han materialized in the doorway, rimed with light, one hand on his amulet, the other extended, looking like the Demon King himself. He spoke a charm in a cold deadly voice.

The sound startled her attackers, and they started to turn.

Flame boiled through the doorway, engulfing the soldier in the lead. The man screamed and jittered in a macabre dance, batting at his burning skin.

The remaining assassin half turned, distracted by what had happened to her comrade, and Raisa took this opportunity to smash her staff into her throat, a killing blow Amon had taught her. The assassin crumpled in place, her head at an odd angle.

The terrible stench of burning flesh stung Raisa's throat, penetrated her nose, and brought tears to her eyes. She shrank back against the wall, coughing violently. Her stomach threatened to evict its contents.

The flaming assassin lurched across her room to the window. Raisa didn't know if he was thinking of escape or only hoping to quench the flames in the river below.

Han charged across the room after him. The traitorous guards-man crouched on the broad stone sill for a long moment, then launched himself through the open window and fell like a flam-ing star from her sight.

Raisa flattened herself against the wall, the tip of her staff drooping to the floor and banging against it as she shook uncon-trollably. Han crossed the room to her, taking hold of her arms to keep her from toppling over. "Are you all right?" he asked, looking fiercely into her eyes. "Did they stick you? Even a minor scratch?"

She knew he was thinking of poison, and she shook her head mutely.

Han released her and stalked across the room. He bent over the two assassins on the floor of her bedchamber, pressing his fingers against their necks, looking for a pulse. He looked up, shaking his head. "Next time, try and leave somebody alive to question, all right?" he said.

"You should talk," she retorted, a bit of her usual starch returning. "Setting people on fire like that, you . . ." She stopped abruptly, thinking of his mother and sister.

"Th—thank you," she whispered. "Thank you for saving my life yet again."

"No," he said suddenly, unfolding to his full height. "It was you. It was all you, understand? I was never here."

Raisa stared at him, momentarily forgetting about throwing up. "What are you talking about?"

"It won't help our plan if your enemies think I saved your life again," Han said. "Stands to reason you'd be grateful, right?"

"Our plan?" Raisa stammered, unclear that they had one.

Han chewed his lower lip, thinking, the fingers of his right hand beating an uneven rhythm on his thigh. Then he picked up a lamp from the table, blew out the flame, and smashed it on the floor. Oil splattered everywhere.

"What are you doing?" Raisa cried, leaping back to avoid being cut by flying glass.

She heard shouts outside in the corridor, followed by bodies slamming against the locked door. "Your Highness!" someone shouted outside the door, his voice ragged with fear and desperation. *Bam!* He hit the door again. "Raisa!"

It was Amon.

Han rested his hands on her shoulders again, looking down into her eyes. "Here's what happened. You set one man aflame with the lamp and he leaped from the window. You clubbed the other two to death with your staff."

Raisa planted her feet stubbornly, shaking her head. "No. Absolutely not. I'm not going to—"

"*Please,*" he said. "Please, please do this. It's almost the truth, and, believe me, it's safer this way."

It's *almost* the truth?

The door into the hallway splintered, making them both jump.

"Better let Captain Byrne in before he injures himself," Han said. He gazed at her a moment longer. "You're a rum smasher with a staff," he said. "Good thing. But I'm not going to let this happen again."

He ghosted through the doorway to his rooms, closing and locking the door behind him.

Raisa ran into the outer chamber as the door gave way and four guards shouldered into the room, swords drawn. One of them was Amon.

They immediately surrounded Raisa, putting her to the inside of a circle bristling with steel. Other bluejacketed guards poured in behind him, fanning out through her suite of rooms.

"It's over," Raisa said wearily, swiping a splatter of blood from her face with the back of her hand. "There were three of them. One went through the window. The other two are in the bedroom. Dead."

"Blood of the demon," Amon swore, looking around the room, not relaxing his ready stance until he'd verified that there was no one available to kill.

Mick Bricker emerged from Raisa's bedroom, an awestruck look on his face. "There's two in there, just like Rebec—like Her Highness says. Both dead."

Amon cocked his head, looking at Raisa. "You killed three assassins all by yourself?"

Raisa shrugged, avoiding the question. "Do you recognize them?"

Mick shook his head. "Never saw 'em before, but I don't know everyone that's in the Guard. There's too many that are new."

Raisa slumped quite suddenly into a chair. She couldn't seem to stop shivering, and Amon took off his jacket and draped it over her shoulders. It smelled like him, which soothed her.

"What happened to Talia and Trey?" she asked. "They were just outside as I came in."

"They weren't there," Amon said. "I was going to ask if you knew what they. . ." His eyes widened, and he swung around and began barking orders, sending Mick out to look for the missing guards, two others to the guardhouse for reinforcements.

Then he sat down in a chair opposite Raisa. Leaning forward, he began, gently but relentlessly, to question her.

"How did they get in?" he asked. "Tell me everything."

"I had ordered supper in my room. Someone knocked on the door and said she'd brought it up. When I opened the door, three of them rushed me."

"Who did you talk to about supper? Who knew you were expecting someone?"

"I told Trey," Raisa said. "I don't know who he might have told. Obviously, the kitchen staff. One of them would have gone down and watched Mistress Barkleigh put the tray together. They could have waylaid him on the way back. His duty assignment's no secret. It wouldn't have been hard to figure out who the tray was for."

Amon's eyes strayed to the tray next to the door.

"There was no food," Raisa said. "Only knives."

Mick burst through the door, only to find himself faced with a prickling hedge of blades. When the Gray Wolves saw it was Mick, they dropped the tips of their swords.

Mick raised both hands to ward them off, his face haggard and grim. "Sir. We found them stuffed into a linen closet off one of the side corridors. Trey is dead, and Talia—she's bad hurt," he said. "Their throats were cut. Jarat went after the healers, and Magret—the maiden Gray—she's looking after Talia."

Raisa pushed to her feet, numb with dread. "Where is Talia?" she demanded, taking a step toward the door. "I want to see her."

"Your Highness, you'll do more harm than good out there,

while the healers are seeing to her," Amon said. "And I can't allow you to go anywhere until we're sure the corridor is clear." Gently, he pushed her back down into her chair.

Tears scalded Raisa's eyes. Trey Archer was new to the Gray Wolves, and supporting a family of five. And Talia—was it only a half hour ago Raisa had been bantering with her in the corridor?

"Send someone after Pearlie," Raisa said woodenly.

"It's already done," Mick said.

Raisa sat forward, gripping the arms of the chair, seized by a mixture of grief and smoldering anger.

"I'm going to find out who's responsible for this, and that person will pay," she swore. "This will not go unrevenged. People need to know that an attack on my guard is an attack on me."

When she looked up, her entire bluejacketed guard was kneeling in a circle around her, tears streaking down some faces.

"This day and every day, Your Highness," Mick said, very formally, "I think I speak for everyone here when I say that it is an honor to fight shoulder to shoulder with our Warrior Queen."

CHAPTER THIRTY
ALLIES

Han had been away from Ragmarket for less than a year, but it looked different to his eyes—smaller, somehow, the streets narrower, meaner, and more crooked, the houses shabbier.

It was likely the same as before. He was the one who had changed.

People in Ragmarket lived vagabond lives, so it wasn't surprising that some of the vendors at the market were different. The tenants along Cobble Street had turned over during his absence. There was a vacant lot where the stable had stood, though the blacksmith forge where he'd buried the Waterlow amulet still crouched in the yard, painted over with streetlord symbols.

It was easier to move about than before. He kept a glamour wrapped around him so people naturally stayed out of his way without really noticing him. There was less jostling from slidehanders and canting crews, fewer come-ons from the fancies and second-story aunties. He was just one more shadow in a shadowy part of the city.

Evidence of the Briar Rose Ministry was everywhere—in the banners proclaiming free meals, and temple criers promising free books and healers for the sick. The speakers drew them in with food and medicine and safe shelter. They kept them there with classes for *lytlings* and grown-ups in trades and the arts, in religion and reading and mathematics.

Despite the warming weather, the river seemed to stink less than before. During one of those interminable palace meetings, Raisa had launched a project to move the flatland refugees away from the river's edge into tent camps to the east of the city. Under the direction of the army, adults had been put to work digging pit toilets and building permanent houses, in exchange for medical care and a reliable food supply.

Some put their backs into it, tired of idleness and starvation, and recognizing the benefit of what they were doing. Others elected to return home, to take their chances in the flatlands, where the work was easier and food more plentiful, even in wartime.

Either way, they weren't dumping their scummer into the river anymore.

Han threaded his way confidently through the tangled streets, heading for his old crib. Along the way, he detoured up over roofs and through taverns crowded with evening trade. He slid into doorways, waiting and watching to see if he'd shaken the tails that had followed him from the palace. Next time, he'd have a chat with them, but now he had other priorities.

By the time he reached Pilfer Alley, he was clear of them. The entry was marked with his flash-and-staff gang sign—a warning to stay away.

Han went in through the warehouse, dropping through a trapdoor in the roof onto a catwalk. Using his first month's stipend from the queen, Han had quietly bought title to the building under an assumed name. Property in Ragmarket was cheap, and he didn't need a landlord snooping into his business.

Looking three stories down, he saw Dancer, his head bent over his long worktable, wearing the peaked pallor he took on whenever he was in the city. He'd set up a metalworking furnace on the first floor, built of clay tiles and vented all the way to the roof.

Three other people waited for Han on the ground level of the warehouse. Cat, whom he'd expected. And Sarie and Flinn, whom he'd never expected to see again.

Han froze momentarily, torn between relief, delight, and alarm that Cat had brought them here without his approval.

When she heard him overhead, Cat came to her feet, a knife in each hand. Seeing it was Han, she returned her blades to their hiding places and stood waiting, hands on hips, chin up like she was ready to do battle with him.

Han embraced the two former Raggers, tears unexpectedly stinging his eyes. "You're supposed to be dead," he said, clearing his throat. "Cat said the demons killed you."

"They should be dead," Cat said. "But they got away, and decided it was best to disappear for a while. They took ship with a pirate and crossed the Indio and back."

"Those pirates cut your tongues out?" Han said, raising an eyebrow. "Good you got Cat to speak for you."

"Pirating didn't agree with me," Flinn said, shifting from one foot to the other. "Money was good, and I got to see Carthis, but turns out I get seasick something awful."

He looked good—though still small, he was taller than before, bronzed from the sun and muscular from hauling sails around.

So much better than dead.

Sarie Dobbs had acquired an impressive tattoo of a dragon during her overseas adventure. It stretched from her wrist to her shoulder, curling around her arm. "I wanted to bring a real dragon back, but my captain wouldn't go for it," she explained, extending her arm. "She was afraid it'd set the ship on fire."

Han had heard there were dragons in Carthis, but he wasn't sure if Sarie was joking or not. Though they shouldn't have been there, he was just so glad to see them it was hard to speak his mind. A weight of guilt slid off his shoulders, a small piece of the load that he'd been carrying around.

"Cat says you're a jinxflinger," Sarie said, appraising him with narrowed eyes. "I always knew there was something flash about you and those cuffs." She touched her wrists.

"Are you back in the game, then?" Han asked Sarie and Flinn. "You two going to form your own crew, or go with somebody else?"

Sarie and Flinn both looked at Cat, then back at Han, shifting uncomfortably.

"I told them they could join with us," Cat said.

Han scowled at Cat. "That wasn't your call to make," he said.

Cat's face clouded up, promising the storm to follow. "You were the one said I should recruit some help."

"Not Sarie and Flinn. I don't want them put at risk again

on my account. Plus, you shouldn't have brought them here. Nobody can know where I'm staying. It's not safe." He turned to Sarie and Flinn. "I have a crew, but they keep their distance and work through Cat. Cat and Dancer are already in it. You're not."

Now Sarie scowled back. "You think we're not, after they done Sweets and Jonas and Jed? Sweets was just a *lytling*. I know you lost your family, but we got scores to settle too."

"It's not just scores for me," Han said. "I'm in this for other reasons. Reasons that got nothing to do with you."

Sarie and Flinn looked at each other, then back at Han.

"You always had plans," Sarie said. "Bigger than Ragmarket, bigger than Southbridge, bigger than any other streetlord. We want shares. We want to help."

"You don't want shares in this. It's a lack-witted, harebrained scheme. A fool's quest. A lost cause before I even start." It never ceased to amaze Han how people were so keen to throw away their lives by joining up with him.

Though maybe if he told them he meant to marry a queen, they'd realize how lack-witted he really was. And stay away.

"Then why you doing it, then?" Sarie asked, all suspicious.

"It's just something I got to do. I don't have a choice," Han said. "You do."

Sarie's eyes narrowed, her face pinking up the way it did when she got angry.

She doesn't believe me, Han thought. She thinks I want to keep her out of my crew.

"Look," Flinn said. "Hear me out. We was all in Cat's crib the day the demons come. Me and Sarie and Flinn and Sweets, Jonas, and Jed. Sarie and I was in the back room, and when we heard them smash their way in, we slid into the stash space under the floor."

Flinn looked up at Han, his eyes dark and haunted. "The demons tortured them. They kept asking where you was. We lay under there and heard the others screaming and screaming until they died, but they never give us up. We never even tried to help them. We ran instead. Now every time I close my eyes I see Sweets and I hear him screaming. That's why we come back. We couldn't get away from it, no matter how far away we ran."

"It's not your fault," Han said. "There's nothing you could have done against wizards."

"Maybe," Flinn said. "But blades is quicker than jinxes. *You* would've tried. We *could've* tried. And *you* can fight wizards, being one yourself. We want in. We can be the blades, and the runners, and the pairs of eyes."

Han wavered. He *did* need allies. He *could* use the help. He had a job for Cat that would take her away from Dancer. He needed somebody to gather information and keep an eye on the doings in Ragmarket.

But once again he'd be putting his friends in danger in order to advance his own schemes.

"I hear you're working for the Princess Raisa," Sarie said, changing strategies. "Cat says the Rebecca that sprung us from Southbridge Guardhouse was the Princess Raisa in disguise. I don't forget them that help me."

"Anyway, me and Sarie already decided, before we knew you was still alive," Flinn said. "We plan to get a crew together and hush the High Wizard and as many others as we can manage."

"*None* is what you can manage," Han muttered. "Don't you

get it? You're outmatched. The only ones'll be down on the bricks is you."

"Then give us a job we *can* manage," Sarie said, leaning forward so her nose was inches from Han's.

The thing was, Han understood. In Ragmarket or Southbridge, you needed a crew and a gang lord with a plan and a reputation to survive. No matter what he or she asked of you, it was better than being on your own.

After a brief charged silence, Dancer spoke.

"This might help," he said. He held up a beaten copper pendant, inscribed with Han's Demon King gang sign—a vertical line with a zigzag across. "It's a talisman, similar to the ones the Demonai wear. It will make them less noticeable to charmcasters, and less vulnerable to charms. It should protect them from anything other than a direct hit. I can make one for each of you."

"All right," Han said, giving in. "I'll tell you the same as I told Cat—you can't be having side jobs if you pledge to me. If you decide to leave, you tell me first and keep shut after. Until then, you do as I say. You can't be picking and choosing the jobs you do. My street name is the Demon King. You use that name even when you think you're free of snitches. You tell nobody where this place is; you don't come here without good reason. You'll meet up with the rest of the crew elsewhere."

"How will we get in touch with you?" Sarie asked.

"You go through Cat, or leave messages under the sign at the market. I'll do the same. You'll have a place to sleep and plenty to eat and some jingle in your pockets, but nobody's getting rich on shares. If you can't live with that, walk away now."

They didn't. Instead, they went down on their knees and

spoke the oath, using blood and spit to finish it.

"What do you want us to do?" Sarie asked, as soon as she was on her feet again.

"You know Ragmarket and everybody that lives here," Han said. "Somebody's trying to murder the princess—the Briar Rose—and he's likely to be hiring again, since he just lost three assassins."

Their eyes went big. "Blood of the demon!" Flinn said. "Who'd want to kill her? Folk in Ragmarket and Southbridge talk like the Briar Rose is a saint."

"Them that are hiring are unlikely to be from our neighborhood," Han said dryly. "But they may hire here, all the same. It'll help that people like her. Talk to them you know are in the business. See if you can find out who's looking for shoulder-tappers and bravos. They'll be looking for quality and willing to pay a rum price."

Flinn and Sarie nodded.

"But be sharp on it and keep it on the hush. We're likely up against the same as did Velvet and the others."

"That's it?" Sarie looked disappointed.

"One thing more," Han said. "See what folks are saying about some dead charmcasters got their throats cut and been left in Ragmarket. See if anybody's put the word out they're buying amulets." He nodded toward Dancer. "And mind you, watch Dancer's back. He's gifted, and there's some that might have reason to hush him."

"I've got Dancer's back," Cat said, putting her hands on his shoulders.

Sarie and Flinn stared at the two of them, as if unwilling to accept the evidence of their eyes. "You're walking out with a copperhead?" Sarie said finally.

"You got a problem with that?" Cat said, eyes narrowed.

They shook their heads.

Dancer set his work aside and rubbed his eyes. "The way I see it, the sooner we get all this settled, the sooner I can leave the city."

Cat scowled. "Just give it time. You'll like it once you get used to it."

Cat and Dancer together is like a fish taking up with a bird, Han thought. Neither can live in the other's turf.

"I have a different job for you, Cat," Han said. "And I don't know if you're going to like it."

CHAPTER THIRTY-ONE

STRANGE BEDFELLOWS

When Raisa entered the sick ward in Healer's Hall, her usual clutch of guards in tow, the apprentice on duty nearly passed out from fright. Then she dropped to her knees, her forehead nearly touching the floor.

Raisa gestured for her to rise. "Where can I find your patient Talia Abbott?" she said. "She would have come in three days ago."

Trembling, the apprentice pointed to the other end of the hall. "Last bed on the left," she squeaked. "By the window." She fled out the door.

Leaving her guard at the door, Raisa walked the length of the ward between rows of narrow pallets as the stench of ripe slop jars smacked her in the face. Those patients that were able pushed up on their elbows, staring. A low mutter of voices washed to the other end of the room, and back again.

Some of the patients stretched their arms toward Raisa as she passed by. "Queen Raisa!" they cried. "It's the Lady herself. The Briar Rose! Touch us! Heal us!"

"I'm no healer," Raisa said, gripping hands on either side. "But I wish all of you a swift recovery."

She found Talia lying on a cot at the far end, propped against the wall, her neck swathed in snowy bandages. A chalk and tablet lay atop the covers at her side.

Pearlie sat in a chair next to the bed, her head bent over a book she'd been reading aloud to Talia. She looked up when Raisa approached, then jackknifed to her feet, cheeks rosy with embarrassment.

"Your Highness!" Cradling the book in one arm, she saluted, her fist against her chest.

"Sit," Raisa said. "Please, continue reading. I just wanted to see for myself how Talia was doing."

"Oh, no, Your Highness, please, you have a seat," Pearlie said, gesturing to the chair she'd just vacated. "I'll get another." She sprinted away.

Raisa sat down next to the bed. Touching her fingers to her own throat, she said, "How is your voice? Any improvement?"

Talia shook her head and scribbled something on her tablet, holding it up so Raisa could see. *Resting it. Hoping.*

Raisa was full of questions, but she hated to ask any because then Talia would have to answer. "I brought you a book," she said, extending it toward Talia. "It's one of the Spinner romances you like. I hope you've not read it."

Talia scanned the cover, then shook her head again, smiling.

Now Pearlie was back with a second chair that she placed on Talia's other side.

Raisa took Talia's hand. "Do you mind if I ask Pearlie a few questions so you don't have to write so much?"

Talia rested the tablet on the bed and nodded her head.

"What do the healers have to say about Talia's injuries?" Raisa asked.

"The assassin crushed Talia's voice box and injured her voice cords," Pearlie said, speaking Common with her musical Ardenine accent. "Lord Vega's apprentice treated her the first day. The wound is closed, at least. The swelling's gone down, so she can breathe better and it's less painful." She looked at Talia for corroboration, and Talia nodded. "It's still hard for her to eat and drink. Sometimes it slides down the wrong way, and she coughs, and it hurts."

Something Pearlie said caught Raisa's ear. "His apprentice? Lord Vega didn't treat her himself?"

Pearlie shook her head. "No, ma'am, Lord Vega only sees to the nobility and those that come from Gray Lady. He has 'prentices from Oden's Ford over the summer, and they see to most everyone else." Turning her face away from Talia, she blotted at her eyes with her sleeve.

"Vega didn't examine her at all?"

Pearlie hesitated. "No, ma'am. Lila Hammond was the one that saw to Talia; she works hard, and she means well, but she's just a first year." She touched Talia's hand. "You're never going to get better if you don't eat more."

A flurry of footsteps in the hallway drew Raisa's attention. Harriman Vega, the wizard in charge of the healing halls, swept in, trailing apprentices behind him like a ship with a white wake.

"Your Highness! I wish you had let me know you were

coming," he said. "I would have been happy to attend you in your rooms, if you had—"

"It was my intention that this visit be informal," Raisa said, thinking, Nothing's informal anymore. "I don't need treatment, but there's someone here who does." She nodded toward Talia.

Vega's disinterested gaze swept over Talia. "I don't know what the girl has told you, but she has been treated, Your Highness," he said. "She would have been evaluated when she arrived." He gestured toward the linen wrappings around Talia's neck. "Her wound has been dressed. Obviously."

"But there is more to be done," Raisa said. "She has not recovered her voice, and she has difficulty swallowing. Wouldn't you follow up in such a situation?"

Vega waved his hand dismissively. "If the matter were brought to my attention, perhaps. But we have hundreds of patients. We must accept that sometimes these injuries result in . . . permanent disabilities."

Raisa gripped the arms of her chair, biting back the first response that came to mind. "Sometimes we must accept it, but only after every avenue has been explored. This soldier was injured when she stood between me and an assassin. She deserves better." She gestured, taking in the other residents of the ward. "How many of these patients might recover with more intensive treatment?"

Lord Vega threw up his hands. "I do not know, Your Highness, but we have limited resources, as you know, and—"

"I understand that, Lord Vega," Raisa said, rising and putting a hand on his arm. "But I mean to change that. I'm asking you to take personal responsibility for Private Abbott's treatment and recovery. Her health is a priority for me. More importantly, I'm asking that you establish a system of follow-up for those with more serious injuries." Seeing Vega's horrified expression, she added, "I do not mean that you must heal them all personally—I realize the physical impossibility of that—but you must use your extensive knowledge and experience to direct their care."

Lord Vega inclined his head. "As you wish, Your Highness," he said, puffing up like a peacock.

"If our high magic resources are limited, then perhaps we should integrate some clan healers into the service in the healing halls," Raisa said, bracing herself for the reaction she anticipated.

"Copperheads?" Lord Vega's eyes narrowed. "I hardly think we are so desperate as to resort to backwoods sorcery, Your Highness. And I will tell you right now, there's not a wizard in the Vale would dare submit to a copperhead healer or take one of their potions, for fear of being poisoned."

"That may be, at least at first," Raisa said. "But there are many in the Vale who swear by clan remedies. I know some in the nobility who have also benefitted from their herbals and poultices. I have personal experience with clan medicines, and I know they work."

From Vega's expression, Raisa might have been suggesting that they use blood sacrifice in order to steal souls. Something the clans were often accused of.

She sighed. One step at a time, she thought.

"We'll continue our discussions on that," she said. "In the meantime, let's begin by reinforcing our current system. It's one thing to offer stellar care to the nobility. But imagine a healing service where every citizen receives premier treatment. Your reputation will spread throughout the Seven Realms. Students from the academy will clamor to apprentice with you. Faculty will travel here to observe your methods."

"That's a possibility, I suppose," Vega said, straightening his wizard stoles and flicking imaginary dust from his robes. "Although, in all honesty, we have had no difficulty securing—"

"That additional support will make it easier for us to leverage your expertise," Raisa said, looking into the wizard's face. "We will also recruit more fully trained healers to assist you. This healing service is critical for the well-being of everyone in the City of Light. It has been neglected for too long."

"Yes, Your Highness," Vega said, nodding, looking mollified. "I couldn't agree more."

"Thank you, Lord Vega," Raisa said. "I am prepared to be dazzled." She smiled, and the healer preened under her approval.

"One more thing," Raisa said, as if she'd just thought of it. "Sergeant Greenholt is to have unlimited visiting privileges with Private Abbott when she is off duty."

"I will arrange it," Vega said. He looked down at Talia as if seeing her for the first time. "Hammond and I will be back to re-evaluate you when she returns from supper."

Talia and Pearlie stared at Raisa, wide-eyed, as the healer sailed away.

"I'll say one thing," Pearlie said, "you sure know how to sugar up the poison."

"That's what this job is all about most of the time," Raisa said, making a face. She rose. "Pearlie, you keep me apprised of how Talia is progressing. I'll be back to visit in a few days."

Is there anything in this queendom that is working well? Raisa thought as she left the healing halls. Is there anything that doesn't need attention? There are not enough hours in the day.

Raisa was walking back to the palace through the gardens, trailing her usual wake of guards, when someone stepped out of the shadows next to the path. Raisa took a step back, hearing swords whispering free all around her.

It was Micah Bayar.

"Micah. It's not a good idea to surprise me like that," Raisa said. She fingered her dagger, reflexively glancing down to make sure the Gray Wolf ring was in place on her finger. "What do you want?"

"I would like to speak with you, Raisa, that's all," Micah said, holding his hands out at his sides to show they were empty. He ran his eyes over her escorts, who were bristling with weapons. "In private."

"That's not going to be possible," Raisa said. "I'm sure you understand."

"Please, hear me out," he said, "and consider what I say carefully." In a louder voice he said, "I'm going to remove my amulet now, so please don't run me through." Slowly, his eyes on the Gray Wolves, he lifted his amulet over his head and set it down on a stone bench in the garden. Then he sat at the other end of the bench and placed his hand on the stone next to him. "Sit with me. Please. Your guard can remain in sight, but far enough away that we won't be overheard. If I try anything, they can lope over and lop off my head."

Raisa hesitated, biting her lip. "How do I know you don't have another amulet hidden on your person?" she said.

Micah smiled faintly. "Have mercy, Your Highness," he said.

"I could strip, but it is a chilly evening. Besides, you seem to have an immunity to any magic I can conjure." He raised an eyebrow.

Raisa debated telling him that her guard could hear whatever he wanted to tell her. And yet she found she wanted to hear what Micah had to say—something he wouldn't say in front of her guard. She had the feeling she would learn something useful.

Raisa wondered what Amon and Han would think of this idea. Then decided she didn't want to follow that thought any further.

"All right," she said. Turning to her guard, she said, "Stay here, and stay alert."

Raisa walked over and sat down on the bench next to Micah, leaving a little distance between them. "What is it?"

Micah studied her for a long moment. "I am disarmed, Your Highness. I am totally without my usual weapons."

"You are never without weapons," Raisa said.

He tilted his head toward the guards. "What I mean, is, I'm not used to meeting beautiful girls under so many pairs of eyes."

Raisa half rose. "Is that what you think this is? If so, then—"

"Please. Sit." Micah waved her back down. "I apologize. I never seem to know what to say to you anymore."

"You could start by telling me the truth." Raisa drew her jacket more closely about her shoulders. "I've grown up. I no longer respond to flattery."

"I spoke the truth," he said. "But I suspect you are looking for a different kind." He looked down at his hands. "I want to start over," he said. "I want to ask permission to court you."

Raisa just stared at him wordlessly. That was the last thing she'd expected him to say. "After everything that's happened between us, now you expect me to accept you as a suitor?" she said finally.

"I'm tired of pushing myself on you," he went on. "I'm not used to it, and it is humiliating."

"There are lots of girls at court. Why do you feel the need to push yourself on me?" Raisa asked. "Are you under pressure from your father?"

Micah gazed at her for a long moment, then shrugged. "Yes," he said. "If you want the truth. But that's not why I'm here. I'm here for myself."

There was a smudge of dirt on Raisa's breeches, on the inside of her thigh. She licked her thumb and rubbed at it, then looked up to find Micah's eyes on her. She brought her knees together and dropped her hands in her lap.

"What is it you hope to gain by courting me?" Raisa asked.

Micah raised his dark brows. "What is the usual objective of courtship, Raisa?"

"There are any number of possibilities, as you well know," Raisa said irritably. "In our case, we cannot marry, and so—"

"I would beg you to keep an open mind on that," Micah said. "You are the queen now, or soon will be. For a thousand years we have been imprisoned by the past. You have the power to make changes. The future is in your hands, if you will only seize it."

Raisa tilted her head. "So, having failed at forcing me into a marriage, you hope to take me by persuasion this time?"

"I like to think," he said, "that had I tried that first, I might have succeeded."

"I'm not the only person you have to persuade," Raisa said. "Do you think you could win over my father? Or Elena Demonai?" She rolled her eyes, picturing that interview.

"You are the first person I need to win," Micah said. "I'll

worry about them when you say yes."

"Well, I have to worry about them now," Raisa snapped.

"They are not the only people you need to worry about." Micah closed his eyes, took a deep breath. "Don't you realize the danger you're in?" he said, eyes still closed.

"Maybe not. Is there something you want to tell me?" Raisa said, putting her hand on his arm. "Who killed my mother, Micah? Who is trying to kill me?"

Micah leaned in close, speaking into her ear so his breath stirred her hair and warmed her cheek. "I don't know who killed the queen," he said. "And if I knew for sure who was trying to kill you, I would handle it myself."

Against all reason, Raisa believed him.

"Well, then." Raisa shifted away from him. "Come back when you have those answers."

Micah hissed out an irritated breath. "I can't protect you if you won't let me near you."

"Based on your history, why should I feel safer with you?" Raisa muttered.

"I'm just saying it would be safer if you were a little less outspoken. If you seemed to go along with things a little more. If it seemed like there was a chance that you might . . . accept me. If you threw the gifted a bone."

"Like what?" Raisa demanded. "Crowning you king?"

Micah raised his hands, palms out. "Take this whole business of naming a street thief to the Wizard Council. The council is enraged. They take it as a lack of respect. They think you're tweaking them on purpose."

"Is that what this is all about?" Raisa narrowed her eyes. "You

Bayars wanted me to appoint Fiona instead?"

"Fiona has her faults, but she would be a far better choice than Alister," Micah said. "Trust me, you won't rest easy with him looking out for your interests. He is in this for his own gain." He paused. "You must know that there are all kinds of sordid rumors flying around about you and that thief. The last thing I heard was that you'd named him to the peerage and handed him a holding on the Firehole River."

Raisa's cheeks burned. "What do you think, Micah? Are you listening to the rumors?"

Micah dismissed that possibility with a flick of his hand. "I know better than that. I can't imagine you would have any interest in a street thug. But none of this helps. He's a wizard. If the copperheads believe you're bedding Alister, he'll end up in some ravine with a Demonai arrow through his eye. If you're going to be linked to a wizard, at least let it be someone who'd have the support of the council. Alister has no support from anyone." He paused, eying her as if debating asking the question. "Why is he here, Raisa? What do you see in him? Why does he have access to you and I do not?"

Micah reached for Raisa's hand, then jerked his hand back as if recalling that his touch might not be welcome. He flexed his hand, rubbing his fingertips against his palm, releasing tension.

"You pardoned him for trying to kill my father," Micah went on. "Have you asked yourself who's murdering wizards in the city now? Need I remind you that the killings commenced about the time he returned to the Fells? And that the bodies have been left in his old neighborhood?"

Raisa's stomach flipped unpleasantly. "It is easy to fling

accusations," she said. "That's all I've heard for weeks. I'll tell you what I told the Demonai when they accused your family of murdering my mother. Bring me some evidence and I will act."

"We are watching him," Micah said. "Sooner or later, he is going to make a mistake."

They sat in stony silence for a long moment.

Han was right, Raisa thought. If people come to believe that there is anything serious between us, it will be his death and maybe mine.

Make them think you hate me, he'd said. She wasn't sure she could pull that off. But maybe she could introduce some doubt.

"Look," she said. "Alister won't be a problem if you let me handle this my own way. I'm juggling a lot of competing interests right now. Putting him on the council was part of a larger bargain—the least of evils. It was the price I had to pay for a bit of peace."

"I knew it!" Micah said, pounding his fist into his palm. "Who's backing him? Who's he working for? Abelard?"

Raisa shook her head. "I'm not going to discuss this any further. I've said too much already. Now, if there's nothing else . . . ?" She made as if to rise.

Micah held up his hand to stay her. "I've already admitted that I wish you had named Fiona to the council instead," he said. "But that is *not* what this is all about. That is not why we are holding this conversation. I'm just trying to give you some helpful advice. I don't want anything to happen to you. I don't want that on my conscience." His face was parchment pale, his black eyes bright and hard as obsidian.

Raisa leaned forward. "Micah, if you know of some threat to

the Gray Wolf line, it is your duty to tell me. Or prevent it. Or bring it to the Queen's Guard."

Micah shook his head, released a sigh, and stood, lips tight, his face hard and bleak. "You really don't understand, do you?" he said in a low, bitter voice. "That's exactly what I'm trying to do—keep you alive. I've risked everything for you—my family and my future. All you need to do is show a bit of . . . flexibility. But, no. You'll get yourself killed, and there is nothing I can do about it."

Raisa shivered, her jacket no longer sufficient to keep her warm. There had been—what—four or five attempts on her life since Lord Bayar's assassins came to Oden's Ford? How long before somebody succeeded?

Beyond Micah, in the shadowy garden, gray shapes milled and circled, their eyes catching the torchlight, reflecting it back like temple candles.

A turning point. A critical choice. But what is the right one?

Micah might be here on his father's orders. He might have come to persuade her to reverse her decision and name Fiona to the council. He might be trying to frighten her into doing the bidding of the Wizard Council. He might hope to fool her into receiving him as a suitor.

All of those things might be true, but Micah had saved her life more than once. For whatever reason, he seemed to have an interest in keeping her alive.

She'd been impatient, and lost her temper with the Queen's Council. It might feel good to antagonize Lord Bayar, but she could pay a high price. She needed to better cement her position before she made any more enemies.

She considered the cost of playing the game. She wouldn't swap Fiona for Han Alister on the Wizard Council. She didn't want three Bayars on the council, and she'd given her word to Han.

"Thank you for your time, Your Highness," Micah said, interrupting her mental debate. "Good evening." He turned to leave.

"Wait," Raisa said, pushing to her feet.

He half turned and stood waiting.

There was one thing she could do—a calculated decision in a situation that demanded a cold heart and a clear head. Something that might stay any action against her long enough for her to build her own defenses.

"You have persuaded me, Micah," Raisa said. "To this degree—if you are truly worried about my safety, you may tell your family that I have agreed to allow you to court me—with discretion. That I am guardedly receptive to your overtures. I will do my best not to contradict that story in public. But I'm not making any promises beyond that."

He inclined his head, his face expressionless.

"We cannot wave it like a bloody flag in front of the Spirit clans. And given your history, I'm sure you understand why I cannot risk being alone with you."

"I accept those terms," Micah said. "But I'm giving you fair warning—I will do my best to change your mind."

"I'm giving *you* fair warning—sooner or later, you're going to have to choose between me and your father. Whatever happens between us, you'll have to decide where your ultimate loyalty lies."

"I have already decided, Your Highness." Micah bowed, then

turned and walked away, losing himself in the shadows.

Raisa stood, looking after him, wondering if she'd made the right move. Would she be able to convince Lord Bayar that she'd accepted Micah as a suitor, hide that from the clans, and still keep him at a distance?

Would she be strong enough to keep him at a distance?

Back in the palace, Raisa found Han Alister waiting at the door to her room, chatting with the bluejackets stationed there. Cat Tyburn was with him, but Raisa wouldn't have recognized her if she hadn't thrown back her head and laughed her throaty laugh just as Raisa arrived.

Cat was wearing a dress—had Raisa ever seen her in a dress?—flouncy and in a deep apricot that set off her dark skin. Bangles graced both wrists, and her hair was raked back into a twist. Her lips were rouged dark as black raspberries.

Raisa and her entourage skidded to a halt in front of the door.

Han bowed, and Cat managed a curtsy. "Your Highness," Han said. "Lady Tyburn and I hope you can spare a few moments." He tilted his head toward her door. "In private?"

"L—Lady Tyburn?" Raisa squinted suspiciously at the two of them. "Well—a few moments, I suppose," she said. "I had some reading to do before supper."

They followed her into her privy chamber and waited until Mick closed the door behind them.

Magret emerged from Raisa's bedchamber. "Your Highness, I expected you back sooner. I wondered if you wanted to bathe before . . ." Her voice trailed off as she set eyes on Han and Cat. Her lips tightened into a hard line.

"I'll bathe after dinner, thank you," Raisa said, poking through the envelopes on the tray inside the door. "You can be at leisure until then."

"I don't mind staying, my lady," Magret said, raising her eyebrows extravagantly. "You might need something, or perhaps your—*guests*—might need some refreshment."

"They won't be staying that long," Raisa said. "They won't need entertaining."

Magret folded her arms. "Maybe it's not my place, but it just isn't safe to be in here alone with—"

"You are *dismissed*, Magret," Raisa said firmly. "I will see you after my late meeting."

Magret stalked out, muttering something that sounded like, "Jinxflingers and thieves. A queendom at her feet, and she consorts with jinxflingers and thieves."

At least she was too well bred to slam the door behind her.

Well, Raisa thought, Micah Bayar was right about one thing—Han Alister has no support from anyone.

"Hah!" Cat said, looking after Magret. "Most people don't hate me until they get to know me."

"That's Velvet's aunt, Maiden Magret Gray," Han said. "She blames me for what happened to him."

"That old fustiluggs is aunt to Velvet?" Cat rolled her eyes.

Raisa dropped into a chair, suddenly exhausted and feeling besieged. *"What is it you wanted to discuss?"*

"Cat wants to apply for a job," Han said, giving Cat a nudge forward. "Don't you?"

"A job? What kind of job?" Raisa looked from Cat to Han.

Cat curtsied again, her eyes downcast. "If you please, ma'am," she said, "I'd like to be taken on as your chambermaid."

"You? A chambermaid?" Raisa said, astonished. "Ah—are you—are you qualified?"

"Ma'am, I spent a year at the Temple School at Oden's Ford," Cat said. "And before that, I was at Southbridge Temple School, off an' on. Speaker Jemson, he'll give a reference. He was the one wanted me to go to Oden's Ford, so I could get on as a lady's maid. I can get references from the Ford, only that might take a while."

"Well. Um. That's impressive," Raisa said. "But I don't usually do the hiring for—"

"If you like music, I'm a rum player on the basilka," Cat rushed on. "Also the harpsichord, mandolin, the lute, and recorder. And I can sing some, too."

"Cat, it certainly sounds like you are talented—"

"Catarina," Cat said. "That's my given name. It goes better with the job."

"—but there is considerable competition for these kinds of positions," Raisa went on. "My servants usually come to me with experience as a lady's maid. Why should I hire you instead?"

"Well. I know I would need training in that part," Cat said. "I know you likely don't hire maids from Ragmarket. Not directly, anyway."

"But Lady Tyburn has other talents," Han prompted, raising his eyebrows at Cat.

"You be quiet," Raisa said to Han. She looked at Cat. "Whose idea was this?" she demanded. "Yours or his?"

"Well, Cuffs, he asked me to apply," Cat said. "And I thought, well it makes sense. Even if it's a wizard comes after you, blades are quicker than jinxes."

"What?" Raisa's head was beginning to ache.

"See, I'm the best knife-fighter in the city, now Shiv Connor's dead," Cat said. Long wicked blades materialized in each of her hands. "You can ask anyone."

"We thought Catarina could be both chambermaid and body-guard," Han said. "Two for the price of one."

"How many bodyguards does a body need?" Raisa said, rubbing her temples. "I've got bodyguards stumbling all over each other."

"We need somebody inside your room," Han said. "After what happened to Talia and Trey, I'm thinking a guard outside your door isn't enough. I can't always be right next door. And, so far, all of the attempts on your life have been with conventional means. Knives and swords and strangle-cords."

"I want to hear from Catarina," Raisa said, waving a hand to hush Han. "Why should I hire you?"

"Well." Cat poked at the twist on the back of her head, tuck-ing in a curl. "You have the bluejackets as bodyguards, I know. And Cuffs. But I think you need another blade up your sleeve. Someone who has connections all over the city. Somebody who has an ear to the ground and knows who's hiring bravos and who's to be hushed. Somebody that won't stick out in the streets." Cat cocked her head. "But that person's got to be able to come and go inside the palace, too. And talk to all kinds of people. And do things on the quiet that maybe you don't want folks to know about."

Raisa frowned. "Such as?"

Cat dug the toe of her fancy slipper into the carpet. "Spy-ing and filching where it does the most good, second-story work if need be, putting a bribe into the right pocket or a word in the right ear at the right time." She looked into Raisa's eyes. "You probably don't like the idea of doing things on the down low," she said. "But that's the turf you're walking right now. You got enemies that'll do whatever it takes to win. You got to have weapons of your own."

Raisa ran her fingers through her hair. "Unlike my enemies, I won't do whatever it takes to win. I'm not looking to hire an assassin or thug."

"I'm thinking more like spymaster," Cat said.

"Cat was the one that roused all of Ragmarket and South-bridge to come to the queen's funeral," Han said. "She had two days to do it."

"How old are you, Catarina?" Raisa asked.

Cat shook her head. "I don't know. I'm past my name day, though," she added, folding her arms and gripping her elbows to either side. "I'm sure of that."

"She knows who you're up against," Han said, seeming to understand where Raisa was going with this. "And she's older than her years."

"It would be a great favor to me if you'd take me on," Cat said, drawing her brows together as she concentrated on her speech. "It would do me good to spend more time with quality. It would help me learn about manners, politics, and such."

"Signing on for this role is a good way to get yourself killed," Raisa said, the memory of Talia and Trey fresh in her mind. "If you want to leave the streets I can put in a word that will get you a position with almost any noble family in the Fells. You're smart. Given a little more polish, you'll move up quickly."

"That's not what I want," Cat said stubbornly.

"She has her own reasons for wanting to help," Han said. "If you say no, I'll find other jobs for her to do. Likely more dangerous than this."

Raisa debated. Why was Han so keen on placing his former girlfriend in her rooms? There were so many possibilities. Was it really to prevent attacks by assassins? Or would Cat serve as a barrier to keep the two of them—Han and Raisa—apart?

Would it allow him to keep better track of Raisa's movements while permitting him more freedom to come and go as he pleased?

She looked at Han, who stood, head cocked for her answer, absently rubbing his right wrist where the cuff used to be. His face gave her no clues.

Did she really want Cat Tyburn looking over her shoulder during her rare moments of solitude? Maybe. If it helped her stay alive.

"All right," Raisa said. "We'll give it a try."

CHAPTER THIRTY-TWO

FOR THE GOOD OF THE LINE

After three weeks on the job as Raisa's chambermaid, Catarina Tyburn still rattled around Raisa's suite like a pair of chicken-bone dice in a velvet bag. She was never still—always poking her head into the closet to make sure no one was creeping out of the tunnel, staring out the windows to spot assassins hiding in the gardens, reconnoitering with the guards in the hallway to estab-lish that they were still alive and on guard. Her constant motion set Raisa's teeth on edge, but she knew how hard Cat was trying, and managed to restrain herself.

The maidservant part of the job went mostly neglected unless Raisa asked her to do something specific. Cat simply had no clue what the job entailed. Magret Gray caught things up when Cat was away, and she never missed an opportunity to point out the novice maid's shortcomings.

For instance, one morning, Cat brought out the dress Raisa meant to wear to a reception for the Guard and left it draped over a chair. When Magret arrived, she arranged it on Raisa's dress form and circled around it, hands on hips, muttering to herself.

Raisa tried to concentrate on her book, but Magret's grumbling grew louder and louder as she took a brush to the skirt.

"I'll try the steamer, but I don't know if I can get these wrinkles out by tonight. It's a disgrace, sending the queen of the realm out in something that looks like it was stuffed in a drawer or crumpled up on the floor. In my day, servants took pride in the appearance of their ladies." And so on.

Raisa put a finger in her book to mark her place. "Magret? Is there something you want to tell me?" she said.

"No, ma'am." Magret continued to brush at the velvet. "Never you mind. I'll do my best to sort this out."

"Do you have concerns about my new chambermaid?" Raisa persisted.

Magret swung around to face Raisa, her hands on her formidable hips. "Your Highness, I'm wondering why she's here, and so is everybody else. Some of us come from Ragmarket, aye, but we take the long way here, working our way up with hopes of one day serving the queen and her family. All the servants are buzzing about it, but they are afraid to say anything to her for fear she'll cut their throats."

"Really?" Raisa said in a deceptively calm voice. "Since when is it the role of my servants to dither and debate over my choice of employees?"

Magret sniffed. "It's our role to look after you, ma'am, as best we can. We want to see you well served. And it's more work for the rest of us when she doesn't do her job proper."

"She came recommended," Raisa said. "Maybe she has some rough edges, but—"

"Who recommended her?" Magret burst out. "That blue-eyed devil lives next door? Oh, he's a handsome one, and he dresses up nice, but that doesn't change who he is. I've seen the way he looks at you, Your Highness. Like he's hungry and you're dinner."

Raisa's cheeks heated as the blood rushed to her face. She came to her feet, fists clenched at her side. "I have no idea what you're talking about," she said.

"I know all about Cuffs Alister," Magret went on. "He used to take his pick of girlies in Ragmarket, breaking hearts all around. Ladies and laundresses, it didn't matter. Why, I've heard stories of how—"

"Magret, Han Alister saved my life," Raisa said stiffly, resisting the temptation to put her hands over her ears. "And nearly lost his own to do it. I owe him a debt of gratitude that I can never repay."

"Well, he'll make you pay," Magret says. "Mark my words. That one never does anything without weighing out the gold and figuring shares."

"All right, you've warned me," Raisa said. "Now that subject is closed. Let's discuss Cat . . . arina. You are absolutely right. She does need training." She paused, for a heartbeat. "I want you to do it."

"Me?" Magret looked horrified. "Oh, no, Your Highness, I couldn't—"

"I'm promoting you. I'm naming you Mistress of the Queen's Bedchamber," Raisa said. "You'll supervise my personal servants and be responsible for teaching them what they need to know to be the best they can be."

Magret pressed her lips together so whatever she was thinking wouldn't spill out. It wasn't hard to make a guess, though.

Raisa touched Magret's arm. "I am aware of Catarina's short-comings as a chambermaid. She will never be a stellar servant—that's not what I'm looking for—but she can be improved. I'm asking you to trust me on this and do the best you can. Will you do it?"

Magret gazed at Raisa for a long moment, then nodded grudgingly. She opened her mouth to say something else, when someone tapped at the door.

"Excuse me, ma'am." Magret went to the door.

It was Amon. Raisa could see his tall frame in the doorway beyond Magret's broad back.

Amon had asked for an audience with her. Several times. And Raisa had put him off. Her instincts told her that any formal audience with Amon wouldn't bring good news.

She resisted the urge to flee into her inner chamber and claim a headache, but he'd already seen her.

Magret turned toward Raisa, a question on her face. Raisa nodded wearily. "Come on in, Amon," she said.

He entered, and Raisa saw that he wore his dress blues, the Lady sword at his side.

She gestured to a chair by the windowed wall. "Please. Sit down," she said, and sat as well. "Would you like anything? Some cider? Something to eat?"

"No, thank you, Your Highness." Amon shook his head, then eased himself down, perching on the edge of the chair, his hands on his knees. "I won't stay long."

"I'm sorry I've put you off," Raisa said, fluttering her hand. "It's been relentless, and I knew I would see you at the reception tonight."

"I understand, Your Highness," Amon said, in his Formal Amon voice. "I know we see each other almost every day, but I felt I should schedule an appointment. For this." He glanced at Magret, then looked down at his hands, where the wolf ring gleamed on his right hand.

A cold lump of dread formed in Raisa's middle. She knew what this would be about.

"Magret," she said, not taking her eyes off Amon's face, "please leave us."

She thought Magret might object, but she bowed her head and backed from the room. Magret made no secret of the fact that she thoroughly approved of and trusted Amon Byrne.

"So," Raisa said, when the door had closed behind Magret, "what is it you wanted to talk to me about?"

"As you know, Annamaya Dubai has come home," Amon said. "She's staying in the dormitory at the Cathedral School temporarily, since her father is stationed on the border of Arden."

"I know," Raisa said. "I've seen her at court. How nice she came home for the summer. Though I would have thought she might stay on at school."

"She is hoping to find a position here at home," Amon said. He cleared his throat. "If she could earn a little money, it would help next year at school."

"Ah," Raisa said, nodding. "When does she go back?"

Amon's gray eyes locked on hers until Raisa looked away.

"She won't be going back. She has decided to transfer to the

Cathedral School," Amon said. "She has only one year left."

"Oh? I'm surprised she'd come back here," Raisa said. "The Cathedral School is good, but the Temple School at Oden's Ford is the best in the Seven Realms."

Amon plowed on doggedly, as if telling a well-rehearsed story. "I had to leave school suddenly, as you know, and with my—with my new responsibilities, I won't be going back. So Annamaya decided to come back home, to be closer to me."

Well, she's sort of clingy, don't you think? Raisa wanted to say. But didn't.

"I hoped you might be able to give her reference for a position here at court," Amon said. "She's had three years at Oden's Ford. She has letters of reference from her masters at the Temple School, but your recommendation would mean a lot."

"Well." Raisa fluttered her hand again like it was some kind of captive bird. "Of course. I mean, I haven't spent a lot of time with her, but from what I've seen, I—"

"I would like you to get to know each other better," Amon interrupted uncharacteristically. "I think you would like her if you got to know her."

How had Amon gotten the impression Raisa didn't like Annamaya?

I need to be a better person, Raisa told herself. I *will* be a better person, the Maker willing. An unselfish person. I just don't know if I can do it right now, along with everything else.

"I'm sure we will become great friends," she said, rattling on like an idiot. "Since she'll be here at court and . . . here in the Fells. Permanently, it seems."

Amon gripped Raisa's hands, taking her by surprise. "Rai,

Annamaya and I would like to announce our betrothal at the reception tonight," he said.

"B—betrothal?" Raisa stuttered. "To—tonight?"

Amon rushed on now that he'd stumbled into it. "Remember, back at Oden's Ford I said we meant to announce our betrothal in the summer, after I returned home?"

"So soon? I mean, you said you weren't planning to marry until after you finished at the academy, and—"

"Right. But now that won't happen, so there's no reason to wait," Amon said. His grip on her hands had tightened, and it cut off circulation to her fingers.

She should have said, *Oh, that's fabulous news! You'll make a perfect couple.* But somehow, her usual ability to dissemble deserted her when she was with Amon.

Instead, she managed, "Well, what a . . . happy . . . and surprising surprise! Thank you for letting me in on your secret ahead of time."

Amon studied her face. "Well, it hasn't been a secret. And I—as the Captain of the Queen's Guard, I'm expected to let the queen know about marriage plans."

"Really?" Raisa said. "Do I have to approve them, too?" She tried to say it lightly, but the quaver in her voice gave her away.

She'd lost Han, and she'd lost Amon, and Micah was a snake, and Nightwalker was exhausting. She felt like the belle of the ball standing on the sidelines with an empty dance card.

Amon bit his lip, his face a mask of misery. "I have to marry, Rai," he whispered, looking down at their hands. "And I'm eighteen now. I think it might be . . . easier . . . if I were married." He looked up rather hopefully. "Don't you think?"

Raisa shook her head. "Nothing will make this easy," she said. "Marriage just seems so terribly, awfully final. Even though I know we can't be together, it's still hard to give you up for good."

"You are not giving me up," Amon said. "I will always be here—you know that."

She nodded, gathered herself, and managed a wry smile. "I do know that. I am being unreasonable. Of course, you of all people know that I am not a reasonable person. Because you are my friend, I am telling you how I feel, in my selfish heart."

Raisa leaned forward, looking into his gray eyes. "But know this, Amon Byrne. I wish you every possible blessing in your marriage. No one deserves happiness more than you—I mean it."

She released her grip on his hands and stood, clutching her skirts to either side. "Thank you for the warning. It will help . . . tonight."

Amon stood also. "Good-bye, Your Highness," he said, in a strangled voice. "Thank you for meeting with me. I'll see you tonight." He saluted her, his fist pressed over his heart, then backed to the door and was gone.

That night, Raisa *ana'*Marianna hosted a reception for officers of the army and the guard. She wore an unwrinkled dress of green satin that matched her eyes. She danced with all the officers, encouraging the Princess Mellony and her ladies of the court to join in.

Midway through the evening, the Captain of the Guard, Amon Byrne, asked her blessing on his marriage to Annamaya Dubai, a student at the Temple School at Oden's Ford and the daughter of one of the officers in the army of the Fells.

The couple knelt before Raisa, and she raised a glass to toast their marriage and their future happiness, noting that they were exceedingly well matched. Taking Annamaya's hands in hers, Raisa lifted her to her feet and stood on her tiptoes to kiss Captain Byrne's tall lady on the cheek.

"Thank you for sharing Captain Byrne with me," she said, smiling. "I know we will be great friends."

There followed a series of toasts, led by Raisa, who promised to dance at their wedding, which would likely be in the fall.

All of those present agreed that the newly betrothed pair was a charming couple and congratulated Raisa on a successful party.

That night, Raisa lay awake for a long time, staring up at the high ceiling, imagining that she heard Han Alister breathing in the next room.

CHAPTER THIRTY-THREE
MORE STRANGE BEDFELLOWS

Having Cat next door as Raisa's chambermaid gave Han more freedom of movement—and less. He didn't feel like he had to stick to his room all the time, keeping his ear to the door, waiting for someone else to take a turn at trying to hush the queen-to-be. When Raisa was out and about—within the palace or outside—there were two of them now to split the responsibility of keeping her safe. Three, counting Captain Byrne.

But he felt less able to come and go from Raisa's rooms at will—which was a good thing when it came to resisting temptation.

The princess heir wasn't there much anyway. Raisa entered into an endless whirlwind of parties and receptions as the coronation loomed closer. Amon, Han, Cat, and Dancer began meeting each morning to discuss security and strategies for protecting her during the festive turmoil, what with comings and goings and strangers in the palace. The Gray Wolves stood twelve-hour shifts, seven days a week, without complaint. They took a personal interest in keeping their friend safe.

Magret Gray was the official gift wrangler, recording and storing the coronation gifts that poured in. Han inspected all of them for hidden hazards, such as magical snares, sorcery, poisons, or the like. It also gave him the chance to see who was cozying up to the queen. Lots of movables flooded in from the down-realms, including a gaudy tiara from Gerard Montaigne. Han couldn't help wondering who was walking around bareheaded in Tamron now. Or maybe the previous owner had had her head chopped off and so had no need of tiaras anymore.

The Bayars sent more lavish presents of jewelry and silver candlesticks. Han gave them an especially close going-over, calling on Dancer's expertise as well. They seemed to be unmagicked. It didn't matter much, because Magret Gray locked them away without even showing them to the queen-to-be. She wasn't taking any chances with wizards bearing gifts.

The maiden still gave Han the evil eye, refusing to speak to him directly, even though he went out of his way to be polite to her.

Han began thinking that he should give Raisa something for her coronation, too. He wanted it to be unique and yet meaningful. But it also needed to be something he could afford. He'd just bought a building, after all.

Finally, inspiration struck. He talked his idea over with Dancer, who thought he could get the piece made in time for the coronation if he got to work right away. There was a silversmith at Demonai that would help him with it.

Han and Amon and Cat and Dancer attended all the parties and dances, too, working out a schedule of handoffs that kept the queen-to-be constantly under surveillance by at least two of them.

Unfortunately, this meant that Han spent a lot of time watching Raisa circling the ballrooms and salons with Reid Nightwalker and Micah Bayar. To Han's dismay, Nightwalker seemed to have moved permanently into the city. Weren't the Demonai supposed to be up in the Spirits patrolling for jinxflingers?

And Bayar—Han assumed those dances were driven by protocol, but still. How could she stand to have him touch her?

There were other suitors, too—locals and foreigners—mostly minor bluebloods who hoped to make a marriage with a queen. Han made note of them, got to know their names, matched them up with the gifts flowing in. Cat assigned members of her crew to shadow Raisa's suitors in the city, to find out where they went and whom they met with.

The Klemath brothers were eager and persistent, like a pair of overgrown puppies, but Han wasn't too worried about them. Raisa seemed resigned to marrying for the good of the realm, but even duty had its limits.

All of this surveillance left little time for dancing himself. Which was all right. The only person Han really wanted to dance with was somebody he dared not show an interest in—publicly or privately. Private often became public in a castle with a thousand ears.

He did get in a little practice. Han didn't have a dance card (an odd blueblood scheme for lining up dance partners), but if he did, it could have been filled for every dance. There seemed to be no shortage of highborn women interested in getting to know him better.

One of the most persistent was Melissa Hakkam, Raisa's cousin and daughter of the head of the Council of Nobles. Han found it hard to believe that she and Raisa were related. Missy giggled constantly, like a dedicate deep in her cups. She hung on Han like a thorny vine, and, as usual, Han got the blame. Her father, Lord Hakkam, glared daggers at him every time she twined her arms around his neck.

It wasn't like he'd offered any encouragement.

Most of his classmates from Mystwerk were home for the summer, and the girlies he'd schooled with seemed to have forgotten what a pariah he was. Though likely some of them were crewing for the Bayars, trying to lure him someplace private for a shoulder tap.

One night, he'd just handed off queen-watching to Cat and was helping himself to some potent blueblood punch when some equally potent blueblood fingers wrapped themselves around his arm.

He swung around, nearly flinging his punch into Fiona Bayar's face. She wore her glitter-pale hair loose around her shoulders, and a black dress that was mostly bottom half. She'd filled in the plunging neckline with ropes of pricy baubles.

"Come dance with me, Alister," she hissed. "I want to talk to you."

It was the first she'd spoken to him since Oden's Ford. The first he'd seen her since the old queen's funeral. The first he'd seen her since Raisa had assigned him to the Wizard Council instead of her.

Han gulped down his punch and wiped his mouth on his sleeve on purpose. The punch glimmered his middle pleasantly. "You sure you want to be seen with me?" he said, making a show of looking around the room.

Lord and Lady Bayar shared a large table with other blueblood wizards, including the Gryphons. Han was surprised to see Adam Gryphon, his former teacher, sitting with the rest of them in his wheeled chair. Han hadn't seen him at any of the other parties, and he didn't look happy to be at this one. Gryphon was watching Han and Fiona, his brows drawn together in a puzzled frown.

Fiona tugged at Han's arm, dragging his attention back to her. "Never mind them. I'm spying on you," she said. "I'm supposed to be winning your trust."

"Supposed to be?" He raised an eyebrow. As if that would ever happen.

"Are you coming?" Fiona jerked her head toward the dance floor.

She was ordering him around again. It was a habit with her.

Well, Han thought. I do want to know what she's up to. He took her elbow and walked her into the midst of the dancers.

They circled the floor in silence for a few minutes.

"Well?" Han said.

"Where did you learn to dance?" Fiona asked. "You are better than I expected."

"I'm always better than people expect," Han said, still keeping that little bit of distance between them.

"I understand that now," Fiona whispered. "I'm beginning to realize that you have . . . great potential." She paused. "That was brilliant, getting yourself appointed to the council," she went on. "Even though it was at my expense. However did you persuade the queen to do that?"

"I can be very persuasive," Han said. "You'd be surprised." On the sidelines, he saw Missy Hakkam chatting with a crew of bluebloods but keeping her eye on him. They swept past

Raisa dancing with Nightwalker. *He* wasn't keeping any distance between the two of them. Raisa's eyes were closed, her head resting on Nightwalker's shoulder.

Han couldn't help himself. He pulled Fiona closer against him, allowing a little heat to flow through his fingers.

She smiled at him slit-eyed, purring like a cat on a warm hearth. "Have you thought any more about my proposal back at Oden's Ford?" she asked, sliding her hands up to his neck and resting her head on his shoulder.

"The one where I give you my amulet?" Han said. "And you get to be queen of the Fells?"

"I notice you haven't been wearing it lately," Fiona said, looking down at his chest, where the Lone Hunter amulet was on display.

"I wear it," Han said. "Just not where you can see it. With all you Bayars around, that'd be like waving a bag of gold in front of a slide-hand's face. And in case anybody's thinking of tossing my room, I wouldn't chance it if I were you."

She laughed. "If I send anyone, I'll make sure they're expendable." She paused, the smile fading. "I haven't forgotten that you saved my life in Aediion. I'm in debt to you."

That and a copper will get me a pork bun, Han thought.

Han scanned the Bayar table again as they swept by. Adam Gryphon slouched back in his chair, head tilted back, his blue-green eyes fixed on Han and his dance partner.

Oh. Right, Han thought. Gryphon is sweet on Fiona. Was that why he'd come home—to court her? Don't worry, Master Gryphon, he thought, I'm not really getting into your game.

"I'm surprised to see that Adam Gryphon is back from school, too," Han said.

"His parents brought him back here to assume the family seat on the council," Fiona said. "He would have been better off staying where he was. The Gryphons are fooling themselves if they think there's any chance he'll ever . . ." She clamped her mouth shut, maybe thinking better of what she was about to say. "Forget Adam. Let's talk about us. What if I came to you with a different proposal? Would you be interested?" She looked up at him, lips slightly parted.

"Different how?" Han said. "A better one, I hope?"

"Of course," Fiona said. "That was just the opening of negotiations." She pressed closer against him.

They passed Raisa and Nightwalker again, tight as ticks in Ragmarket. This time, Raisa was staring at Han and Fiona, a frown on her face.

"I don't think we should be talking about this here," Han said. "Your family and friends aren't the only ones looking on."

Fiona nodded. "You're right." She drew back a little. "But if you are willing to listen, we should talk soon." Her lips twisted in disgust. "The princess heir has agreed to allow my brother Micah to court her," she said. "In secret, of course."

Han tried to prevent surprise from splashing over his face. "She has?" he blurted. He couldn't help looking around for Raisa on the dance floor again.

"Easy," Fiona snapped, jerking her arm away from his hand. "You're leaking."

"Sorry," he said, getting his flash under control. "I'm just surprised is all, after everything that's happened. Why would she do that?"

Fiona smiled grimly. "Why do you think? Micah is handsome

and charming and quite persuasive himself. And he works fast. So if we want to prevent a betrothal or elopement, *we* need to work fast. I'm willing to snarl up Micah's plans in my own interest, but it could get very complicated if my brother marries her."

Complicated? You could say so, Han thought, his belly twisting into a knot. It could get complicated when I murder your brother.

The song ended and they coasted to a stop. And, there, so close he could have spit on them, Han saw Micah Bayar shooing off a glowering Nightwalker. Micah gripped Raisa's elbows like they belonged to him, smiling down at her, ready to claim the next dance and more. And she was smiling back at him as they glided away.

Micah works fast, Fiona had said. Han's temper flared. It was bad enough watching her with Nightwalker. How could she even stomach Micah after all he'd done? What was she thinking?

Micah and Raisa swept past again. Micah's hand was at Raisa's waist, pressing her closer, his head bent down so he could whisper lies in her ear, his lips practically touching her skin.

I should have killed him when I'd had the chance, Han thought, flexing the fingers on his blade hand. I need to put the Bayars out of the wizard business for good.

"Will you *control* yourself?" Fiona snapped, jerking away and rubbing her arm. "What's gotten into you?"

"Nothing," Han said, refocusing on Fiona's face. "It's nothing."

Fiona eyed him as if she didn't quite believe him. "We'll talk soon—I'll find a way." She took a step back from Han. "In the meantime, think about what I said."

CHAPTER THIRTY-FOUR
SECOND
THOUGHTS

Magret Gray was as good as her word. She did her best to smooth away Cat's ragged edges and teach her the basic duties of a chambermaid. With Magret's backing, Cat forged links with the upstairs staff and learned the names and ranks of nearly everyone who frequented the palace on a daily basis. Both Cat and Magret seemed to be determined to make a go of it.

Still, it wasn't easy. Raisa's Mistress of the Queen's Bedchamber wasn't used to having her authority questioned when it came to protocol and manners. Though Cat's year at the Temple School had shaped and rough-polished her, she didn't take criticism well. She always had to know the why and wherefore along with the who and the what.

Sometimes Raisa returned to her suite to find Magret and Cat icily ignoring each other. Once, they were so caught up in a shouting match that they didn't even hear her come in.

Magret? Shouting?

Raisa didn't have time to referee. Her coronation was officially scheduled for her seventeenth birthday. Guests poured into Fellsmarch as the date drew closer. At first it was mostly home-grown nobility and wizards from all parts of the Fells. Every scrap of guest space in the castle and all of the other buildings within the close were filled to capacity. Those of lower rank found them-selves stranded outside the walls, pining to be inside.

Some of the choicest apartments inside the close were still empty, reserved for royalty arriving from the down-realms, includ-ing the king of Arden. Most would arrive immediately before the coronation, and stay through the ball and the receptions that followed.

Micah Bayar and Reid Nightwalker attended nearly every party, each dancing with Raisa as often as possible and keeping a weather eye on his competition. Han was always there also. She often spotted him standing against the wall, his eyes following Raisa and her suitors around the room.

It couldn't have been easy to focus, with all the distractions. Han received considerable attention from the ladies of the court, as well as foreign visitors. A ruthless streetlord, a thief, a gifted member of the Wizard Council, and heartbreakingly handsome—what more could a lady want—in a paramour, anyway?

He danced *constantly*—with Missy Hakkam, with his class-mates from Mystwerk, and with Pearlie Greenholt, since Talia was still convalescing. He was always at the center of a fluffy crowd. Raisa couldn't help noticing whom he danced with, and how often, and how gracefully he circled the floor, his golden hair gleaming in the torchlight.

Especially since he never danced with her.

Missy Hakkam was a glittering planet in orbit around Han, when she wasn't flirting with this or that minor prince from the down-realms. Raisa's cousin seized every opportunity to touch Han, to hang on him, and she giggled furiously at everything he said.

But that wasn't the worst thing. At a party two nights before the coronation, Raisa saw Han dancing with Fiona Bayar. As Raisa circled past with Nightwalker, Fiona had her arms wound around Han's neck, her head resting on his shoulder, pressed in so tight you couldn't get a hand between them.

Find a back hallway somewhere! Raisa thought crossly.

On second thought, no, don't, she amended.

As Raisa watched, Fiona tilted her head up, smiling at something Han said. She didn't have to tilt far, she was so bloody tall.

Don't you know how risky it is, getting that close to Fiona? Raisa thought. She's just after your amulet, you know. Anyway, I thought you hated the Bayars. Don't you even know how to hold a proper grudge?

Traditionally, the princess heir spent the night before her coronation ball sequestered, praying to the Maker and her ancestors for guidance. Raisa dutifully dressed in temple trousers and a tunic and instructed the guards outside the door to admit no one.

After Magret left, Raisa knelt before the altar in her sitting room and tried to focus. It wasn't that she couldn't use a little divine intervention, given her present situation. But her mind kept straying to other things, bouncing from present to past.

Raisa couldn't help thinking of her name day, almost exactly a year ago. Waiting with Magret for her father to come, to escort her to the temple. Gavan Bayar had come instead, which had precipitated a whole chain of events that was still playing out. She would be seventeen tomorrow. She'd been just a year from name day to coronation.

Raisa felt claustrophobic, much as she had a year ago. It was as if once again a trap was closing around her, doors closing on possibilities. She was suffocating. She needed fresh air.

Pushing to her feet, Raisa hurried through her bedroom, past the elaborate temple robes laid out next to the bed, past the dress form in the corner draped in her ball gown. She plunged straight into her closet, raking aside dresses until she reached the back wall. Clawing open all of the latches and bolts Amon had insisted on installing, she pressed her hands against the hidden door. It swung silently outward.

Raisa flew down the dark tunnel, finding her way by touch, not bothering to light a torch. Finally the corridor widened, and she knew she'd reached the bottom of the staircase to the garden.

Groping blindly, she found the ladder and began to climb.

When she reached the top, she pushed with both hands, wrestling aside the stone covering the entrance. When she emerged in the garden temple on the roof of the castle, it was full dark, though the moon was on the rise.

Raisa walked out into the garden, under the glasshouse roof, breathing in the moist air of the conservatory, redolent with summer hyacinth and mountain jasmine. The great starry dome of the sky soared overhead, making Raisa feel very small. Too small for the job she'd taken on.

Moving to the edge of the terrace, she looked down on the city below. Wizard lights embroidered the streets, pooling in doorways. Carriages rattled along the Way, no doubt bound for one party or another. A wisp of music floated up to her—a basilka, it sounded like, playing Hanalea's Lament.

Raisa shivered and turned away.

Returning to the small temple, she knelt again on the stone floor and began the Meditation of the Queens in a low, fierce voice.

"Hail Marianna *ana*'Lissa *ana*'Theraise *ana*'Adra *ana*'Doria *ana*'Julianna *ana*'Lara *ana*'Lucinda *ana*'Michaela *ana*'Helena *ana*'Rissa *ana*'Rosa *ana*'Althea *ana*'Isabella . . ." She continued through all thirty-two queens since the Breaking, ending, as always, with Hanalea *ana*'Maria. "Hear me! Your daughter Raisa calls on you."

As she continued with the words of the prayer, the temple around her shimmered and faded into mist. The familiar lupine forms of the Gray Wolf queens came forward, sitting in a circle around her, curling their tails around their feet.

Here was green-eyed Althea, and gray-eyed Hanalea. And the blue-eyed wolf Raisa had seen at her mother's memorial— slender and graceful, with pale fur and small delicate paws. Her form shimmered, pale and insubstantial. For a moment, Raisa thought she saw the image of a woman.

Raisa came forward on her knees. "Mother?" she whispered, her voice trembling.

The blue-eyed wolf ducked her head, as if ashamed, then turned tail and disappeared into the mist, her tail pluming behind her.

"Yes," Althea said. "That was Marianna. She has not yet accepted her wolf form, I'm afraid."

"But . . ." Raisa extended her hands as if she could drag her mother back. "I need to talk to her. I want to find out what happened. If—if it was an accident. Or if—"

"She won't be able to speak to you," Hanalea said, her gray eyes kind and sad. "Not for months. What we do—communication across the veil—it's unnatural. It takes time to master."

The implications of this penetrated slowly, like a chilly draft under the door. "Well, I need to know—did she kill herself? Was it an accident? And, if not, who killed her?" Raisa looked from Hanalea to Althea, hoping to read something in their wolf faces.

The Gray Wolf queens looked at each other. Althea put her ears back and showed her teeth at Hanalea. Hanalea shrugged, if wolves can be said to do such things.

"We've been given the privilege of remaining in the Spirits," Althea said. "We watch over the City of Light instead of crossing to the shadowlands. With privileges come restrictions. We cannot change history by giving you information you wouldn't know otherwise."

"That's not helpful," Raisa snapped. "I was promised the gift of prophesy. I can't govern with a pocketful of platitudes and vague warnings and reassurances. You told me the Gray Wolf line is hanging by a thread. I want to know how to keep it from breaking."

Hanalea and Althea looked at each other.

"All we can do is help you recognize what is in your own heart, Raisa," Hanalea said softly. "You have access to all the knowledge and all the gifts you need to survive, if you will use them. You will have the chance to right a great wrong."

"What about my mother?" Raisa asked. "Did she have

everything *she* needed? Theoretically, anyway?"

Once again, they looked at each other as if they were straying close to the boundary of what was permitted.

"You must use all the strengths of the Gray Wolf line in order to win," Althea said.

"The time will come when you will be forced to make a choice," Hanalea said. "When that time comes, choose love."

The Gray Wolf queens rose as one, turned, and trotted into the mist.

Raisa slumped back on her heels, head bowed, seized by a fear of failure. What use was it to know that she *could* win if she only knew how to go about it? Losing would cut that much closer to the heart.

Choose love! As if that were an option for the Gray Wolf queens.

Though she'd learned a tremendous amount in the past year, it was still too short a time. She'd thought she would have years to prepare, years to work with her mother as a queen in training.

Tears burned in her eyes. There's likely never been such a weepy queen, she thought.

A thought struck her. She could run away, like she had a year ago, when her mother had tried to marry her to Micah Bayar. She could be halfway to Delphi by morning, and continue on to Oden's Ford. She could enter the Temple School and become a dedicate.

And the Gray Wolf line could unravel in her wake.

It's just as well, she thought dispiritedly. What kind of dedicate would you be? You can't even manage to meditate for a night, let alone a lifetime.

It's not fair, she thought. I should be going to parties. I should be kissing lots of boys. I'm too young to be queen. Too young to be sparring with wizards.

Relax, she told herself. There's not a wizard in sight.

And then something made her look up to see Han Alister standing in the doorway of the temple.

She didn't know how long he'd been there staring at her, but it seemed to take him by surprise when she looked up and caught him. His usual street face was gone. In its place was a wistful vulnerability, a kind of feverish and hopeless desire.

Magret had said he had a hungry look about him. Was that what she'd meant? And what exactly was he was hungry for?

And then it was gone, replaced by what he called his street face, and Raisa thought maybe she'd imagined it.

He walked toward her, tall and broad-shouldered, dressed in black, a frequent choice for him these days. But tonight his clothes were uncommonly elegant. Lace cuffs drooped over his hands, and his coat was finely tailored.

"Your Highness," he said, bowing stiffly. "Almost Your Majesty. Having second thoughts about climbing onto the Gray Wolf throne?"

Raisa rocked to her feet, swiping away her tears. "How did you get up here? How did you find me? I'm supposed to be alone."

"I came up the side," Han said, nodding toward the edge of the roof as if she should have figured that out on her own. He made a show of looking around. "I thought maybe I'd find Micah Bayar up here," he said.

"Why would Micah be here, of all people?" Raisa snapped.

"Last night, at the dance, you two were snuggled in so close I worried he might strum you on the fly," Han said.

"Just stop with the thieves' slang, all right?" Raisa said furiously. "I have no interest in taking up with Micah Bayar again."

"Again?" Han raised an eyebrow.

Raisa folded her arms, lifted her chin, and said nothing.

"Anyway, that's not what I hear," he said. He paused, and when she volunteered nothing, added, "I can't believe that you would let him put a hand on you again."

"It's complicated," she said, in no mood for confession. "I'm putting on a show, and not for you. Anyway, what about you and Fiona?"

His eyes narrowed. "Fiona? What about Fiona?"

"At the dance. I never saw two people so wrapped around each other—who were standing up, that is."

"I can handle Fiona," Han said.

"That's exactly what you were doing," Raisa said sweetly. "*Handling* her. Why is it that I should be reassured that you can manage Fiona, but you have no confidence that I can manage Micah? That's condescending, Alister."

Han shook back the lace and counted off the reasons on his fingers. "Because he has the morals of a flatland slave trader. Because he's a wizard and you're not. Because he's a Bayar. Because no girlie that catches his eye is safe from him." He paused. "Because I think you still have feelings for him, and he will use that against you."

"You are wrong," Raisa said flatly. They stood glaring at each other for a space of time, and then Raisa sighed. "Let's not fight about the Bayars tonight, all right? Did you really come up here to talk about them?"

"No," Han said. "I wanted to see you one last time before the coronation." After a moment's hesitation, he took her arm and led her over to the bench by the fishpond—the same bench Raisa and Amon had shared the night he'd returned to the Fells from Oden's Ford more than a year ago.

Raisa sat, drawing her knees up and wrapping her arms around them. Han sat next to her, staring out at the pond, seeming at a loss for something to say.

At least the cold, distant Alister was gone, temporarily, at least.

"Tomorrow night, there'll be fireworks," Raisa said, to fill the silence. "At the end of the ball. This would be a good place to watch from." She chewed on a fingernail, then dropped her hands quickly. It wouldn't do to ruin her hands for tomorrow.

Probably a lost cause anyway.

"Remember the night we met at Oden's Ford?" Han said, still looking straight ahead. "There were fireworks that night, too.

"I do remember," Raisa said. "It seems like a long time ago."

"Not so long," Han said.

A breeze swept down off Hanalea, rattling the glass, carrying the sting of high country snows. Raisa shivered, and Han slipped an arm around her shoulders, drawing her close. The heat of him soothed her, loosening the tight coil of worry wound up inside her.

"There's something about a roof, isn't there?" Han said. "It makes you feel like it doesn't matter what's going on below. All of those things that get in the way of your dreams—you're above them. Anything is possible."

"Anything is possible," Raisa repeated. Once again, her eyes welled with tears.

What was the matter with her? She *wanted* to be queen. She'd fought for it, struggled to get back to the Fells to protect her right to the throne. Was she just weepy over her mother's death, all those lost opportunities, or was it something else?

Was she closing a door that could never be reopened? Was she making a trade she would eventually regret?

Choose love, Hanalea had said. Raisa was acutely aware of Han's presence next to her. Once she was queen, that door would be closed forever.

"You know, this is where Queen Hanalea used to meet with Alger Waterlow," Han said, shocking her out of her reverie.

"What?"

"They used to come up here and make love in this rooftop garden," Han said, stretching out his long legs. "Before they ran off to Gray Lady. Now *there* was a queen who wasn't afraid to take a chance."

Right, Raisa thought. Hanalea took a chance, and see where it got her.

"Who told you that?" Raisa said. "I never heard that story." She shivered again, as if ghosts were stroking her shoulders with their cold fingers.

"Some stories don't get told these days," Han said, allowing a subtle warmth to flow between them. He stroked her hair, brushing his fingers along the back of her neck, raising gooseflesh.

You're not making this any easier, she thought.

After another long pause, he added, "You don't have to do it, you know."

"What?" Raisa turned her head to look at him.

"You don't have to go through with it. You don't have to be

queen. You can be whoever you want." For once, his face was dead serious.

"What do you mean?" Raisa said, swiping at her nose. "I don't have a choice."

"You always have a choice," Han said. "Take me, for instance. I can be anything I want if I want it badly enough. If I'm willing to do whatever it takes."

"Really." Raisa raised an eyebrow. He made it sound so simple. "What happens to the Fells if I bow out?"

"Nobody is irreplaceable," Han said.

"How long do you think I would last if I relinquished the crown?" Raisa said. "I'd be a constant thorn in the side of whoever came to power—even if it were Mellony. I would be a rallying point for rebellion—more of a target than I am now."

"You don't have to stay here. That's why they call it the Seven Realms." He reached over, covered her hand with his free hand, as if to increase the points of connection between them. "And there's always Carthis if you want to get even farther away."

"What in blazes would I do in Carthis?" Raisa growled. "And why would I want to go there?"

Han laughed softly. "I'm convinced that you would land on your feet, Your Highness. You'd likely be running the place before long."

"I don't know anybody in Carthis," Raisa said.

He took a breath, then forged ahead. "I could come with you. I would help you—however you wanted."

Raisa looked up, surprised. Han's blue eyes met hers—intense, focused, with no evidence of mockery.

The offer sat awkwardly between them. What did he mean?

What was he proposing? That she run off with him? He hadn't come out and said that, but . . . did he feel as she did—that her coronation as queen would end any chance they could be together?

"If I have to be running things, I might as well do it here." Raisa massaged her forehead. How could she explain it to him— the ties she felt to these mountains, to this small, imperfect queendom with its constantly squabbling tribes?

Raisa wanted to be here when the sun poured over the eastern escarpment in the morning and flooded the City of Light. She wanted to be here in the spring when the Dyrnnewater escaped from its banks, fed by the melting snows high in the Spirits. She wanted to see the aspens glittering on the slopes of Hanalea, to ride bareback in clan leggings and shirt through the slanting autumn sunlight. She wanted to eat high country black-berries in summer until the juice dribbled down her chin, and dance clan dances until her heart clamored and her feet stung.

Being away from the Fells had only reinforced her love of home. As did the choice he was asking her to make.

She looked up at Han, groping for something to say, but he shook his head. "Never mind, Your Highness. I never thought you'd run away from . . . from all this." He waved his hand, taking in the palace, the city below. "You're not the sort. I just thought it might help you figure out what you do want. What you're willing to fight for. What you'll give up in trade."

"You can't have everything," she said.

"I can. And I will. I will find a way," Han said, almost as if he were trying to convince himself. His usual streetlord confidence had drained away.

She put her hand on his arm, looking into his eyes. "I hope you will . . . continue to be my friend," she said. "I hope that you won't let rank and ceremony come between us."

The expression on his face said, *It already has.*

Raisa's heart seemed to seize in her chest. What if he went away? What if he turned against her? What if this was—what did he call it—a take-or-leave offer? How would she survive?

I can be anything I want, he'd said.

"I have something for you," he said, breaking into her panicky thoughts. "A present. That's actually why I came."

"A present?" She blinked at him, taken by surprise.

He thrust a small deerskin bag toward her, almost like he was embarrassed.

Unlike Micah, Han was not the present-buying sort. Though he *had* bought her flowers once, in Oden's Ford, when he'd been late for a tutoring session and knew she'd be angry.

Likely, growing up, he'd never had the money for presents.

"It's for your coronation," Han said. "Dancer made it, so in a way, it's from both of us."

"But he already made me that beautiful armor," Raisa objected. "That was more than enough."

Han cleared his throat. "All right. It's just from me, then."

She weighed the pouch on her palm. "You didn't have to get me anything."

"Why not? Everyone else did." He looked down at his hands. "The Bayars have sent you enough glitterbits to fill a stall at the market."

Raisa tugged at the drawstring, forcing her finger into the opening. She dumped the contents of the pouch into her hand.

It was a ring in white gold set with moonstones, pearls, and sapphires.

"Oh!" she breathed. "It's beautiful. Whatever made you think of it?"

"It's modeled after a ring that belonged to Hanalea," Han said. "It was—it was a favorite of hers, I guess." He hesitated, as if he would say more, but decided against it.

Raisa tried it on. It seemed to fit her ring finger best, which was good because she wore the wolf ring on her forefinger. She turned her hand this way and that, so that the stones caught the moonlight.

She knew she shouldn't accept it—it was too personal and costly a gift. And yet . . .

The shadows under the trees shifted and swam with gray bodies, brilliant eyes, razor-sharp teeth.

Raisa shuddered, as if someone had walked over her grave. "I never knew Hanalea owned a ring like this," she said. "How did you happen to hear about it?"

"I—ah—I spoke to someone who is kind of an expert on Hanalea, and he described it to me," Han said. "This is what Dancer came up with." He paused, and when Raisa said nothing, he added, "If it doesn't fit, he says he can resize it."

"No, it's fine, it seems to fit as it is," Raisa said. "Thank you."

"Just don't tell anyone who gave it to you," Han said. "If you—if you decide to wear it, I mean."

"I will wear it." She tilted her face up toward him. "I will cherish it. I just wish . . . I just wish we . . ."

As if to stop her words, Han pulled her toward him, pressing his lips down on hers so hard it took her breath away. Power channeled through her, undirected but potent, making her head swim. The wolf ring on her finger grew hot as it drew the power in.

Raisa wrapped her arms around his neck, molding her body to his, aware of the friction between them. Winding her fingers into his hair, she thought, I won't give him up, I won't. I. Will. Not.

But then Han straightened his arms, breaking off the kiss and pulling away from her. He looked down into her face, his breath coming shallow and quick, his eyes a fierce reflection of some kind of struggle within.

He threw his head back, the column of his throat jumping as he swallowed. Drawing a deep shuddering breath, he looked down at her again.

"Nearly all my life I've taken what I wanted, when I wanted it, with no thought for the future, since I wasn't likely to have one," Han said. "Do you know how hard this is for me? *Do you?*" He gave her a little shake like it was her fault.

"Listen," she whispered, sliding her palm along his cheek, cupping it under his chin. "It doesn't matter if we cannot marry. We can still be together—when we can—even if I make a political marriage to someone else."

I cannot believe I'm saying this, Raisa thought. I truly am turning into my mother.

But Han Alister was shaking his head, his face a mask of regret.

"I want to be with you!" Raisa's voice broke on the words she'd been unable to say back at Marisa Pines. "I don't want to lose you. Why can't we have something even if we can't have it all?"

"Because I won't share you with anyone else," Han said. "I won't be your down-low lover. It's all or nothing, Your Highness. I won't settle for less."

"I have to settle," Raisa muttered. "Why can't you?"

He kissed her again, this time long and slow, savoring it. Then came gracefully to his feet.

"You'd better go to bed," he said, extending a hand to help her up. "You have a big day tomorrow."

He waited until she reached the top of the staircase, then turned and disappeared into the darkness.

Giving up on meditation, Raisa went to bed, but it was a long time before she slept.

CHAPTER THIRTY-FIVE

A BAD BARGAIN

The coronation of a Gray Wolf queen was a two-day affair. On the morning after Raisa met with Han in the glass garden, she endured an entire morning of highly ceremonial meetings with her subjects and allies called the Greeting of the Witnesses.

Prior to the splintering of the Seven Realms, it had been customary for representatives from each of the realms to bring tribute to the capital of Fellsmarch to honor the soon-to-be queen.

These days it was just a tradition, though everyone in attendance still brought a small token gift for Raisa.

All morning long, she was acutely conscious of Han standing just behind and to one side of her throne, his face as unreadable as any ceremonial mask. The words that had passed between them the night before hung heavily in the air, distracting her.

Truth be told, even after everything he'd said, she'd been relieved to see he hadn't departed during the night, seeking a less complicated, less dangerous future.

Raisa wore the ring he'd given her as a coronation gift. She was sure he noticed it, though he said nothing about it.

One foreign visitor Raisa was pleased to see was Dimitri Fenwaeter, lord of the Waterwalkers, whom Raisa had met in the Shivering Fens on her way to Oden's Ford.

Then, Dimitri had been new to his position, after his father was killed by soldiers from the Fells.

Dimitri had grown taller and filled out in the year since she'd last seen him, and he had a new confidence about him. He'd brought her a linen marsh cloak, embroidered with leaves and ferns in subtle mist colors.

To put a fine point on it, Raisa was still Dimitri's liege lady, as the Shivering Fens was still ruled by the Fells.

"I hope things are well along our border," she said in Common, smiling and stroking the fine linen.

"I would let you know if they were not, Your Highness," Dimitri said solemnly. "The new commander at the West Wall is a woman, but she is surprisingly fair and easy to deal with." He was teasing her.

"Perhaps she is fair and easy to deal with *because* she is a woman," Raisa replied.

Dimitri laughed. "You may be right," he said. "Speaking of fair, I have not forgotten that you owe me *gylden*," he said. "You also promised to send me a clean river."

"I'm working on it," Raisa said with a sigh. "Let's talk again after the coronation, before you go back home."

When Raisa returned to her rooms, Magret helped her strip off her formal coronation clothing. She lay down on her bed in her cami and drawers, meaning to take a nap before dinner. She hadn't slept much the night before, thanks to Han Alister, and she needed some rest if she hoped to keep her face out of her plate that evening.

She was just drifting into sleep when a knock rattled the door. Cat came and stood guard at the foot of her bed, while Magret rushed to answer, grumbling under her breath. After a few minutes of whispered conversation, she shut the door and returned to Raisa's bedside, her face a thundercloud of disapproval.

Raisa propped up on her elbows. "What is it, Magret?"

"There's a messenger from Lord Hakkam outside. He says the king of Arden has finally arrived." Magret sniffed, to show what she thought of disrespectful, tardy kings. "He and his party are at Regent House and he'll be joining you for dinner. He's requesting a brief audience with you before dinner so he can offer his congratulations in person since he missed the ceremony this morning."

There goes nap time, Raisa thought. I don't like King Geoff already.

Reading Raisa's expression, Magret said, "Your Highness, I'll say you're resting, and the flatlander king will just have to wait until dinner."

Raisa shook her head wearily. She sat up, swinging her legs over the side of the bed. Her feet didn't even touch the floor.

"No, I want to get the measure of the man, and that will be impossible to do at dinner, or at the ball after. And I don't want to be meeting with him at midnight." She yawned. "Will the queen of Arden be at dinner?"

Magret shrugged, frowning. "I'll find out. There was no mention of her."

Raisa sent word to the dining steward to rearrange the seating protocol. Magret helped her into the gown she'd chosen for dinner and the ball after. She brushed out Raisa's hair and kept Cat on the run fetching and carrying jewelry and brushes and paint and powder. In a spare moment, Cat slid into the red satin dress she'd been saving for the dance. It was sliced high on both sides to afford freedom of movement. Raisa knew her maidservant/bodyguard would have blades hidden beneath the satin, though Raisa couldn't fathom where.

Raisa decided she'd like more eyes and ears when the king came to call. "Fetch Lord Alister from next door, if he's there," she said to Cat.

"Lord Alister?" Cat grinned and curtsied. "Yes, ma'am," she said, and flounced out.

Magret sniffed. "*Lord* Alister? You can dress him up in silks and satins, but you'll never—"

"Hush, Magret," Raisa said. She poked her head out the door, bringing Pearlie Greenholt to full attention. "Can you send word to Captain Byrne that I'm receiving the king of Arden in my sitting room and I would like him to be present?"

And then she thought, Is it even proper to receive a king in your sitting room? Likely not, but state visits had been few and far between when Marianna was queen, so Raisa didn't have much to go by. Plus, it was his own fault for showing up unexpectedly.

Cat returned in a few moments with Han in tow. Raisa suspected he had been trying to catch some sleep also, since he was a bit rumple-haired and yawning and he'd missed fastening one of the buttons on his jacket. Amon came soon after and stood against the wall, his uniform perfect as always. He'd been at attention all day, it seemed.

Raisa settled herself into a chair, spreading her full skirts around her. The chair was on a small riser, which gave her a little height over the rest of the room. They waited. Finally, a commotion in the hallway said the king of Arden and his entourage had arrived.

Raisa's uncle, Lord Hakkam, entered, bowing and wringing his hands. He seemed unaccountably nervous. "Your Highness," he said, his broad forehead gleaming with sweat, "the king of Arden asks permission to bring his guard in with him."

"Tell the king of Arden no, he cannot bring his guard in with him," Raisa said acidly. "The Fells may seem an uncivilized and dangerous place, but surely no more dangerous than Arden has been."

"Yes, Your High—Your Majesty," Hakkam said. "I just want you to know that I—I never realized that—I was as surprised as you at—at what had happened. It was never my intention to keep anything from you. When he—when the king arrived, I sent a messenger to you immediately. I hope you realize that I only have your best interests—and those of the queendom at heart."

Raisa stared at him. Is it because I'm still half asleep, or is this man not making sense at all? Or is guilt making him stumble-tongued?

If she hadn't been half asleep, perhaps she would have asked more questions.

"Let's just get it over with," Raisa said, feeling the beginnings of a headache.

Han murmured something to Cat, jerking his head toward

the door. Cat followed Hakkam into the hall.

A moment later, Cat hurtled back into the room as if chased by demons. She stationed herself in front of Raisa, a knife in either hand, all of her genteel patina swept away. "Cuffs! Look sharp! It's him, the whey-faced, gutter-swiving, prig-napping bastard! He's here!"

Han looked as mystified as Raisa. "*Who's* here?" He too stepped in front of Raisa, taking hold of his amulet. He looked from Cat to the door, unsure whether to open fire.

The door opened, and in walked her uncle, Lassiter Hakkam.

Followed by Prince Gerard Montaigne, youngest of the unhappy Montaigne brothers.

Raisa stood frozen, staring at them. Montaigne was beautifully turned out in a deep green velvet coat, cream trousers, and tall boots, his cloak bearing the Red Hawk emblem, a circlet of gold on his head. Raisa glanced quickly at his scabbard. It was empty, so her guard must have taken his sword at the door.

Good, she thought, remembering poor Wil Mathis dead at Montaigne's hand.

Raisa glanced at Cat, whose knives were again concealed, but she still stood between Raisa and Montaigne, balanced as if to spring if necessary. When and how would Cat and Han have met Montaigne? Whenever it was, they seemed to have formed a strongly negative opinion.

The prince of Arden stopped just inside the door, glancing quickly around the room. His eyes narrowed a bit when he saw Han and Cat. So he recognizes them too, Raisa thought.

Montaigne's gaze shifted to Raisa. He inclined his head slightly, as appropriate from one monarch to another.

"Your Majesty," he said with a thin smile. "Please accept my apologies for not arriving in time for your witness ceremony."

"I had expected your brother Geoff, who responded to my invitation," Raisa said, managing to maintain an even tone. "I did not realize that you were coming."

"I am here in my brother's place," Gerard said. "He cannot be here, unfortunately."

A loaded silence thickened the air.

"I see." Raisa folded her arms, her mouth going dry, and a leaden weight collecting in her stomach. There was no way Geoff would send Gerard as a representative. "Do go on," she said.

Out of the corner of her eye, she saw Lord Hakkam shifting from foot to foot by the door, as if thinking he might need a quick escape.

"I bring bad news. My brother was attacked by brigands on his way here, and he and his entire family perished," Gerard said, making no attempt to look sorry.

"Brigands?" Raisa cleared her throat. "I am most sorry to hear that." Which was absolutely true.

Gerard smiled. "Given what happened, you can imagine why I am wary of traveling anywhere without my guard. Still, I felt it was my duty to come since I am the last surviving Montaigne brother. And now the undisputed king of Arden."

CHAPTER THIRTY-SIX
A DANGEROUS DANCE

Somehow, Raisa managed to get through dinner without throwing up on the new king of Arden or anyone else. She accomplished that by eating very little.

Montaigne had been placed next to Raisa, as befitted another head of state. He had no gift of social conversation (not that Raisa was in the mood) but talked mostly of armies and politics and the challenges of governing Tamron, crushing resistance, and bringing the nobility to heel.

Raisa suspected that his choice of topics wasn't because he saw her as a peer or confidante, but because those were the only things that interested him. Or because he saw this as an opportunity to intimidate her.

He also asked numerous questions about the military and political situation and structure in the Fells, which Raisa deflected by giving vague answers and then changing the subject. She did not trust Gerard Montaigne, and although he likely had plenty of spies in place already, she was not going to be one of his sources of information.

All through dinner, Raisa struggled to rein in her acid tongue. You are a grown-up, she said to herself. And a queen. You cannot indulge your temper. You have to be strategic, and weigh every word. He is here to gather information. It's best if he underestimates you.

There's no need to let him know you despise him. Not yet.

The head table hosted foreign dignitaries mostly, including various dukes and princes from the down-realms, the kings and queens of We'enhaven and Bruinswallow, and a prince from the Southern Islands loaded down with a fortune in jewelry.

I don't even *like* most of these people, Raisa thought. And I trust them even less. She couldn't help but think back to plainer meals in the barracks at Wien Hall, the easy camaraderie over shared misery.

Finally they moved on to the ballroom and formed a receiving line to greet guests as they arrived. The Gray Wolves were off duty now. Raisa had ordered that they attend as guests instead of bodyguards.

"Talia!" Raisa embraced the grinning guard, who had arrived with Pearlie. At last, somebody she wanted to see. "It's so good to see you up and around."

"Captain Byrne, he says I won't be able to laze about much longer," Talia said, her voice low and rough but understandable. "I'm back on duty tomorrow. Thanks to you, Your Highness." Talia squeezed Raisa tight and then backed away as Pearlie looked on, tears standing in her eyes.

Cat came through the line with Dancer. He wore a clan coat

of the finest deerskin, beaded and embroidered with flash symbols and small talismans—a kind of magical armor.

Cat kept a possessive hold on Dancer's arm, eyeing the brilliantly plumaged guests uneasily. She was on duty in the ballroom. And still edgy among bluebloods.

Han passed through the line alone. He bowed low to kiss Raisa's hand. She felt the quick pressure of his hot hand as he murmured, "Your Highness."

Amon arrived with his fiancée, Annamaya, who looked resplendent, practically glowing in canary-colored silk. And all of the Bayars, a study in black and white.

Reid Nightwalker came by himself also, though Raisa guessed he was unlikely to leave unaccompanied. Though some women in the Vale wouldn't consider walking out with a copperhead, others found his deadly reputation and exotic good looks intriguing.

Nightwalker was among the first on Raisa's dance card, and he requested one of the vigorous clan dances, which left Raisa flushed and breathless and weak in the knees. It wasn't easy to carry off in a ball gown.

After, he fetched her a glass of wine. "You dance like a clan princess," he said, nodding in approval. "I had hoped you might wear clan dress tonight."

"We'll celebrate in the camps as well, after the coronation ceremony tomorrow," Raisa promised. "My father and grandmother are planning it. And I'll dress for the occasion then. This is more of a flatland party, after all."

"I'll look forward to having you to myself, Briar Rose," Nightwalker said. He leaned closer. "It is good to see one of clan blood on the throne of the Fells." He bowed, then turned and crossed the dance floor toward his waiting admirers.

After that it was one dance after another, each time with a new partner. It seemed that Raisa was expected to dance with every important male guest at least once. Many of them tromped on her toes, being unfamiliar with northern dances.

Too bad I can't dance with two at a time, Raisa thought, and get through this more quickly.

Micah surfaced midway through her list. She had to admit, it was a pleasure dancing with him after so much wrong-footedness.

"Well," he said, looking into her eyes, "there were times that I did not think you would live long enough to be queen."

"No thanks to your father," Raisa said, nodding to where Lord and Lady Bayar stood watching the dancers.

"No thanks to my father," Micah agreed.

"But thanks, in part, to you, I suppose," Raisa said generously. Micah was looking almost honorable in comparison to Gerard Montaigne.

Micah smiled faintly and drew her in closer, brushing his lips over her neck.

Raisa stiffened and drew back. "Careful, Bayar," she said. She couldn't help looking around for Han. He'd made her self-conscious, which was maybe the idea. She didn't see Han, but she did see Nightwalker watching them, his face a thundercloud.

"Accept my apologies, Your Highness," Micah said, not looking sorry at all. "It's just that you are irresistible tonight."

"Try harder," Raisa said bluntly.

"How does it feel?" Micah asked. "Being queen, I mean?"

"It's not official until tomorrow, remember," Raisa said. "But it's already a little daunting, I'm afraid. I don't like it that Gerard

Montaigne rushed up here within days of murdering his brother. Now he's got two big armies and nothing to do with them."

"I don't like it either," Micah said. "It would help us if his brother had lived a little longer. Do you think the thanes will go with Gerard? Or will those who supported Geoff rally around someone else?"

"I don't know," Raisa said honestly. "We need better intelligence from Arden."

"We need better weapons," Micah said. "Then the intelligence wouldn't matter so much. If the Wizard Council perceives that Montaigne presents an imminent threat, I cannot say what they will do."

"Oh, don't start," Raisa said. "Let's see if we can get through the rest of this dance without talking about politics."

"Mmm. What should we talk about instead?" He stroked her hair. "Remember how we used to slip away from boring parties?"

"Don't think that's going to happen tonight," Raisa said. Lifting her head, her gaze fell on Mellony, who watched, tight-lipped, from the edge of the dance floor. Though her sister had been the object of continuous male attention all night long, she still seemed fixed on Micah.

I hope this isn't going to go on forever, Raisa thought.

They danced in silence after that, until the song ended. Raisa drew away from Micah, but he kept his hands on her shoulders. "What are you doing after the dance?" he said. "I know somewhere we can go to be alone."

"That's *enough*, Micah," Raisa said sharply. "I'm going to be alone in my bed."

"Well, now. That's a shame, Your Highness," somebody said, practically in her ear.

They both swung around. Han Alister bowed. "I believe I'm next on the list," he said.

"*You?*" Micah looked him up and down, then turned to Raisa. "*Alister's* on your dance card?"

Raisa looked. "It seems he is," she said, surprised to see his name there. He'd never danced with her before, not at any of the pre-coronation parties.

"Why you?" Micah said, his brow furrowed.

"Why not?" Han said. He stood, chin cocked up, his stance and expression holding a promise of violence. A streetlord challenge.

"What *is* that on your stoles?" Micah said, giving back disdain. "A crow? I would have thought a rat would be more appropriate."

"It's a raven," Han said. "Known for being smarter than you think." Taking Raisa's hand, he led her into the dance while Micah stared after them. After the events of the night before, Raisa didn't know what to expect. But he kept her at a proper arm's length, as if this dance were something he just had to get through—maybe to make a point with Micah.

"Try to look like you don't want to be with me," Han said, his eyes flicking over the other dancers.

"How do you know I *do* want to be with you?" Raisa said tartly. Han looked startled at first, and then his mouth twitched, fighting off a smile.

Raisa didn't care. She was tired of being yanked this way and that by Han Alister: hot kisses and intoxicating embraces followed by a stiff arm.

It was the first time they'd danced together since their lessons in the upstairs room at the Turtle and Fish in Oden's Ford. She was acutely aware of the distance between them, the placement of his hands on her shoulders and hips.

"You're really not bad, Alister," Raisa said. Memories of Oden's Ford sluiced over her—of uncomplicated kisses and a friendship with fewer barriers between them.

Han was bent on business, not memories and small talk. "Besides his guard, Montaigne has a couple dozen servants with him who look a lot like soldiers or rushers," he murmured. "Cat put a tail on them. If he has other people here, we want to know about it."

"Where did Cat find a crew on such short notice?" Raisa said.

"She's been recruiting in Ragmarket and Southbridge." He leaned in. "She says to tell you she'll kill Montaigne for you if you want. No one will ever tie it to you."

"What?" Raisa grabbed Han's lapels and pulled him closer, glaring at him. "Tell her to forget it. I don't send assassins after people, especially my guests, no matter how despicable."

"I told her you'd say that," Han said, smiling and nodding to Missy Hakkam, who looked on, scowling, as they circled by. He turned back to Raisa, his smile fading. "I think you should consider it, at least."

Not that it wasn't tempting. Looking ahead, Raisa could see nothing but trouble from the new king of Arden. "How do you know Montaigne?" she asked, to keep from saying yes.

"Cat, Dancer, and I had a dustup with him in Ardenscourt. He's a great one for abducting people."

"I know," Raisa said, recalling their encounter in Tamron.

"Don't drink with him, and don't go anywhere alone with him," Han said. "Not even inside the palace. In fact, don't go anywhere without me or Cat or Captain Byrne until Montaigne leaves town." He looked down at her with narrowed eyes, searching for evidence of foolhardiness.

"I'll be careful," Raisa said. She scanned the ballroom. Montaigne was deep in conversation with Lassiter Hakkam and Bron Klemath. Annamaya Dubai was huddled up with Talia and the rest of the Gray Wolves, but she didn't see Amon. "Where is Captain Byrne, anyway?" she asked.

"He's setting up a perimeter around the castle close," Han said. "Just in case the king of Arden has planned more than a friendly visit."

Raisa felt a twinge of sympathy for Annamaya. When she married Amon Byrne, this was what she had to look forward to: a lifetime of deferring to duty.

As the song ended, Han looked over Raisa's shoulder, and his face cleared of all expression. She turned to find the new king of Arden bowing before her. "Your Majesty, I believe the next dance is mine."

Han put his hand on her bare shoulder, the heat of it stinging her skin. "Remember what I said, Your Highness." And then he was gone.

In contrast to the hot wizard hands and sweaty suitor palms Raisa had encountered all evening, Montaigne's hands were dry and cold as a lizard's skin. Had it been less than a year ago that he'd repulsed her at her name day party with talk of eliminating the elder brothers who stood between him and the throne?

And now he'd achieved that. Raisa made a mental note:

when Gerard Montaigne makes threats and promises, take them seriously.

As he had at Raisa's name day party, Montaigne overleapt any pleasantries and cut right to the point.

"I am surprised to see you dancing with mages," Montaigne said. "I understood that you were forbidden to consort with them."

"I'm forbidden to marry them," Raisa said, "but they are still good for dancing."

Montaigne didn't smile. "They are good for military uses as well. But rather dangerous to fraternize with, I believe, particularly for a young lady like yourself."

"Wizards have been part of our social and political structure for generations," Raisa said. "We believe the benefits of fraternization are worth the risk."

Montaigne changed the subject. "I sent you a proposal a month ago," he said. "And you responded somewhat favorably, I believe."

That would be his proposal that Raisa send her armies against King Geoff as a kind of betrothal gift to Gerard.

"I was willing to listen," Raisa said. "But it seems that circumstances have changed."

"Yes. They have. I am no longer in need of your army, which puts us on a different footing when it comes to marriage negotiations."

"Does it?" Raisa said. "So. Am I to understand that you are no longer interested in an alliance by marriage?"

Montaigne shook his head. "I am very much interested in pursuing a marriage contract with you." He paused. "Though

I am not so much interested in an alliance as a consolidation of holdings."

And I'm not interested in either one, Raisa thought.

"Your Majesty," she said, "I had not even dreamed that we would be discussing this tonight. I expect you must have your hands full, with your new responsibilities. As I hope you can understand, there is much to do here in the Fells before I consider . . . external affairs."

"On the contrary, I believe I have a certain momentum," Montaigne said. "You have seen what I can accomplish in a short time. I see no reason to delay the inevitable. The resources in the Fells are complementary to our own, and would help restore our depleted treasury. This would be the next logical step."

You honey-tongued romantic, you, Raisa thought, doing her best not to roll her eyes. As usual, it's all about you and what's best for you. She was suddenly eager to get Gerard Montaigne out of her queendom as quickly as possible.

She cast about for an excuse. "I will carefully consider what you've said," she said. "But you should know that here in the Fells, it is customary to remain in mourning for a year after the death of a parent. That prevents hasty decision-making while in the throes of grief. I could not consider celebrating a marriage or negotiating changes in political structure any time soon."

The song ended, and they came to a stop. "Good evening, Your Majesty," Raisa said. "Safe travels home." She curtsied a good-bye, trying to pull free, but Montaigne kept hold of her arm, dragging her toward a windowed alcove at the side of the ballroom.

"I'm not finished," he said. "Perhaps I've not made myself clear to you."

Raisa set her feet, resisting, and suddenly they were walled in—Amon Byrne, Han Alister, Cat Tyburn, and three of the Gray Wolves—with Micah close behind them.

"You take your hands off me before I have you arrested," Raisa said, her voice like ground glass.

Montaigne let go of Raisa's arm.

"I don't know what customs you keep in the south," she went on, "but I will not be manhandled in my own court. By anyone."

"I understand that you have much to think about," Montaigne said, pretending to ignore Raisa's small army. "But you of all people should understand that I am not endlessly patient. When your mother became an obstacle, you removed her. Just as I will not hesitate to remove anyone who gets in my way." He paused a moment to let that sink in. "I offer you a role and a voice in a greater kingdom of Arden—an offer that may be withdrawn at any time. I suggest that you choose carefully and render me an answer sooner rather than later."

He turned on his heel and walked away, without even a suggestion of a bow.

"Montaigne!" Raisa called after him, her voice ringing out above the music and clamor of voices.

He swung around to face her. "Yes?"

"No need to wait and wonder. I'll give you my answer now," she said.

Montaigne turned and stood waiting, his lips forming a faint smile.

He expects me to give in, Raisa realized, astonished. He expects me to say yes.

He is used to bullying women into doing what he wants, she

thought. He's never bothered to learn to read them.

Maybe it was Raisa's imagination, but it seemed the ballroom went silent around them, waiting to hear her answer.

"The answer is no," Raisa said, in a loud, carrying voice. "I would rather marry the Demon King himself than marry you. I suggest you look elsewhere for a bride. And heaven help the one you choose."

Two spots of color appeared on Montaigne's pale cheeks—whether fury or embarrassment at this public rejection, Raisa couldn't tell.

Now he inclined his head a fraction, his blue eyes as pale and cold as wind-roughened ice. "Thank you, Your Majesty, for being so direct with me. Good evening."

Raisa watched him walk away with mingled feelings of relief and dread. It was a relief to put an end to the charade that she would ever consider a marriage with Montaigne. But she knew he would find a way to make her pay for his public humiliation.

I should have let Cat kill him, she thought.

CHAPTER THIRTY-SEVEN
CORONATION

The coronation ball had been for the nobility, wizards, and military officers—bluebloods, Han would call them. Valefolk of all ranks were invited to the Coronation Day party. And there would be a feast and dancing in the Spirits for clanfolk.

Even in celebration, her people were divided.

First to temple. Magret helped Raisa into her temple robes, draping the elaborately embroidered clanwork coronation garment over her shoulders. It was studded with jewels, and so heavy Raisa nearly staggered under the weight.

It seemed symbolic of the load of responsibility settling onto her shoulders.

When she was ready, her father, Averill, her sister Mellony, her cousin Missy Hakkam, and her grandmother Elena came to escort her to the Cathedral Temple. Amon was there also, solemn and heartbreakingly handsome in his dress blues, the rest of the

Gray Wolves lined up at attention behind him. Raisa swallowed a lump in her throat.

Han Alister wore the black-and-silver coat he'd worn to Marianna's funeral, the one Willo had made for him, inscribed with subtle gray wolves and ravens, the serpent and staff on the back. He displayed what Raisa had come to think of as his court amulet—carved of translucent stone, in the shape of a hunter. She knew he would be wearing the serpent amulet against his skin.

He met Raisa's eyes, and energy and tension and secrets crackled between them. His gaze dropped to the pearl-and-moonstone ring she wore next to Hanalea's wolf. He bowed deeply, his raven stoles nearly touching the floor. When had he come to look so at home at court?

Had she herself changed that much in the past year?

Mellony and Missy lined up behind Raisa, each grabbing a fistful of fabric. They would help carry her train.

"Good thing I don't have to wear this thing but once," Raisa grumbled. "There's no way I could dance in it."

Magret fussed with the folds of Raisa's robe, arranging and rearranging. The newly made Mistress of the Queen's Bedchamber was dressed in a fine gray wool dress, her Maiden pendant glittering at her neck.

"It's all right," Raisa said, taking Magret's hands. "Thank you for everything you've done, and will do, for the line." She went up on her toes and kissed her former nurse on the cheek, wet and salty with tears.

Amon came and stood on Raisa's right-hand side, Han on the left. It felt good to have them there.

"Let's go," she said, lifting her chin.

They walked down the long corridors, the heavy brocade fabric swishing over the marble and stone floors. The formal passageways through the palace were nearly deserted—everyone who was anyone was already at the temple. Servants stood in doorways, however, and lined the broader corridors. Even the cooks and kitchen staff took a few minutes from their preparations for the feasting that evening to watch the princess heir pass by for the last time.

The next time they saw her, she would be queen.

The little procession entered the courtyard, walking along the gallery between the castle proper and the Cathedral Temple. Han slid his hand inside his coat and murmured a charm. Light arced over them, looking like a magical arbor entwined with roses, but Raisa guessed it was a clever means to deflect any assassins' arrows or magical attacks.

As they came into view, more servants cheered and waved handkerchiefs from balconies. "Happy name day!" they shouted, and "Long live Raisa ana'Marianna!"

Temple dedicates stood to either side of the great double doors of the cathedral. They pulled them ajar as Raisa and her entourage approached.

Raisa halted in the doorway, scanning the room. The cathedral was packed, every seat on either side of the aisle occupied. The hall thundered with the sound of feet hitting the floor as the congregation rose to greet the princess heir.

Raisa walked down the aisle, head held high, Han and Amon falling back a bit so that she was visible to everyone. At the front of the temple, Speaker Jemson waited in the ceremonial robes that speakers had worn for every coronation since Hanalea.

Good thing they're one size fits all, Raisa thought—just like mine.

Again, the cacophony of noise and color reminded Raisa of her name day ceremony. But this time, the Gray Wolf throne sat empty on the dais, twined with rowan and roses instead of her mother's white gardenias, a symbol that times had changed. Still, Raisa couldn't help thinking of it as her mother's throne.

Below, at floor level, and to either side, were the less elaborate chairs occupied by representatives of the Spirit clans, the Wizard Council, and the Council of Nobles. Her grandmother Elena took her place next to the clan seat, and Gavan Bayar and Lassiter Hakkam came forward and stood for the wizards and the Vale nobility.

Events seemed to slow to a crawl as Raisa's mind raced faster, collecting images, sounds, body language, expressions, and reactions.

Raisa halted just in front of the dais, turning to face the room. Her attendants fanned out to either side. Again, Han conjured a canopy of glittering magic—wolves and roses and the unlidded eye—the symbol of her father's clan.

The Gray Wolves lined up against the wall, rigidly at attention. Han and Amon stood on either side of the dais, an honor guard of sorts. Mellony, Missy, and Averill took seats in the front row, Averill slipping his arm around Mellony's shoulders.

Just behind them, Magret sat very erect, her nose pink, dabbing at her eyes.

Mellony leaned forward, looking across the aisle to where Micah and Fiona sat in the front row, clad in their usual black and white, looking straight ahead. Their faces were like fine porcelain—white and hard and yet somehow brittle.

Raisa saw a spot of red out of the corner of her eye. It was Cat Tyburn standing in the shadows of a side corridor, wearing her satin dress from the ball. She seemed to have taken a fancy to it. Cat stood, head cocked, surveying the crowd for trouble.

Farther back were guests from outside the queendom seated according to rank and protocol. The seating had been rearranged yet again, as Gerard Montaigne had sent his regrets, saying he would return home immediately. Raisa almost wished he were there, under her eye, where she could watch him. She couldn't honestly say she regretted what she'd said, but maybe her timing could have been better.

Behind the throne, crowded to either side of the altar on the dais, stood Raisa's ancestors, the Gray Wolf queens. They eddied and shifted like vapor, their brilliant eyes glittering in the light from the torches and candelabras overhead.

Raisa looked over at Han, wondering if he could see them too. If he did, he didn't acknowledge them. He stood cradling his amulet, scanning the audience for potential dangers.

This is like a wedding, Raisa thought. The bride and her attendants at the front. The wizards on one side, the clans on the other, like two families that don't get along. The Valefolk, as always, were forced to divide themselves between the two.

And me? I am marrying the Gray Wolf throne—the most jealous of lovers. She'd chosen it over Amon, over Han, likely over any chance at happiness in love.

Don't be maudlin, she scolded herself. Life is full of difficult choices. At least I get to be queen.

Jemson walked to the center of the aisle and turned to face

Raisa, his back to the crowd. He smiled down at her and winked. "Greetings, Gracious Lady," he said. "Who are you, and what brings you to temple today?" It was the first of the traditional Three Questions.

"I am Raisa *ana'*Marianna, the Princess Heir of the Fells," Raisa said, loudly enough to carry to all corners of the hall. "I have come here to claim the Gray Wolf throne."

"By what authority do you claim the Gray Wolf throne?" Jemson asked sternly.

"My mother, Queen Marianna *ana'*Lissa, has joined our ancestors in the Spirit Mountains," Raisa said. "I am Marianna's heir, entitled by blood and ability."

"What is your lineage?" Jemson asked.

Raisa recited the new line of queens, beginning with Hanalea, and ending with her mother and herself, familiar from all of the temple days of her life, familiar from her name day a year ago.

Jemson nodded. "I am satisfied that you qualify by blood, Your Highness," he said. "Now I have three questions that relate to ability."

These were new questions, ones she had not answered at her naming. It was assumed that a named princess heir would have time to become more capable before her coronation.

"To whom do you answer, Raisa *ana'*Marianna?" Jemson asked.

"I answer to the Maker, to the line, and to the people of the Fells," Raisa said.

"How do you signify, Princess Raisa?" Jemson asked. "By what do you pledge?"

"By my blood," Raisa said. Drawing the Lady dagger that had

belonged to Edon Byrne, she sliced her palm and allowed her blood to drip into the large basin on the altar.

Jemson handed her a clean white cloth to wrap around her hand. Lifting an elaborate ewer, he poured water into the basin and swirled it. Clean, clear water from the Dyrnnewater, high in the Spirits.

"Who will help you in this, Raisa *ana*'Marianna?" Jemson asked.

"The queendom rests on three foundations—wizards, the Spirit clans, and Valedwellers," Raisa said.

Jemson dipped a cup into the basin, lifted it dripping. He gestured, and Elena, Lord Bayar, and Lord Hakkam came forward. Jemson passed them the cup, and they each drank from it in turn, glaring at one another over the rim.

Amon and Han came from either side to drink. Jemson invited the front row up, and Mellony, Missy, and Averill Lightfoot came forward and drank. Mellony's pale cheeks were even paler than usual, and Raisa knew that her sister had imagined herself in Raisa's place.

Averill smiled at Raisa, his face alight with pride. Was it because she was his daughter, or because there would be a mixed-blood queen on the Gray Wolf throne?

Micah and Fiona approached from the other side. Micah's eyes met Raisa's as he shook back his hair, tipped the cup, and drank. Fiona kept her eyes focused on the cup.

One by one, the people in each row were invited forward to drink the blood of the Gray Wolf queen. About half the crowd stayed in their seats. They were dignitaries from the rest of the Seven Realms, who had no intention of declaring fealty to Raisa.

"We are thereby pledged to preserve the Gray Wolf line and the queendom," Jemson said, drinking from the cup himself and then setting it aside.

Remember that, Raisa thought, looking at the Bayars.

"Kneel, Your Highness," Jemson said.

Raisa dropped to her knees, the coronation robes puddling around her.

Jemson lifted the ornate Gray Wolf crown from its velvet cushion, raising it high. "By the authority vested in me as Speaker of the Cathedral Temple of the City of Light, I crown you, Raisa *ana*'Marianna, Queen of the Fells, thirty-third in the new line." And he settled the crown on her head.

On the dais, the Gray Wolf queens bowed their heads in acknowledgment of their new sister queen, and dissipated like vapors.

Raisa rose, stiff-necked, conscious of the weight of the crown, worried it might topple off. Jemson stepped aside. Her attendants assembled behind her, and she processed grandly down the aisle to the applause of the assembled nobility.

Likely the last time they'll unite to cheer anything I do, Raisa thought.

As she crossed the courtyard she heard a clamor from the balconies but was afraid to look up, for fear of losing her crown. Rose petals spiraled down all around her.

Once safely inside the palace, she lifted off the crown with both hands and handed it to Amon, exchanging it for the lighter tiara.

She climbed the grand staircase to the third floor and turned down the corridor, trying not to trip over her coronation robes, her attendants trailing like fancy plumage.

Thousands of people had collected in the courtyard below—men, women, and children. No doubt some had come because they'd never been invited into the castle close before and they were curious. But many of them wore roses pinned to their clothing, some of them real and others fantastical constructions of fabric and lace, bright spots of color on gray and brown.

When Raisa appeared at the railing, a thunderous shout went up from the crowd. "Rai-sa! Rai-sa! Rai-sa!" and "Briar Rose! Briar Rose!"

Raisa extended her hands, and the crowd shouted, "Who are you, and what brings you to temple today?"

"I am Raisa *ana*'Marianna, Gray Wolf Queen of the Fells," she replied, and the cheering started up again, dying away only when she raised her hands for quiet.

"Peoples of the Fells! A coronation is an ending and a beginning," she said. "The ending of a period of uncertainty, the beginning of a new era. The end of Marianna's reign, the beginning of Raisa's. The end of a princess, the first steps of a queen. The end of childhood"—she paused, wrinkling her nose—"and now I suppose everyone expects me to be a grown-up."

Laughter rolled through the crowd.

"In some ways I will never grow up. For instance, I continue to believe in miracles. But I know that miracles come to those who work very hard. I pledge that I will work very hard for you."

Another cheer went up.

"I continue to believe in the people of the Fells. Although we have had hard times, and there are threats on every side, we will overcome any adversary if we will just work together—Valedwellers, wizards, and Spirit clans. You listen to each other, and I will listen to you.

"Finally, in addition to hard work, I believe in parties." This was greeted by a roar of approval. "Tonight we celebrate. I will be dancing, and I hope you will be dancing too. Thank you!"

As she turned away, cheers hammered her back.

And so it was done. Raisa was queen of the Fells—thirty-third in the new line of Hanalea. She'd been born for this—and raised to it. She'd fought for it, and at times she'd thought she might die for it. She had a long history of tragedy and triumph behind her, and a lifetime of hard work ahead of her. It was time to get started.

EPILOGUE

The coronation party continued in Fellsmarch long after the official one was over. Guests spilled out of the castle close and into the streets, bluebloods mingling with ragpickers and black-smiths and stable boys. Food and drink had flowed freely at the new queen's party, and the streetwise residents of Ragmarket and Southbridge filled their bellies and then their pockets and carry bags. In times like these, who knew when more food would come their way?

Some in the crowd would have celebrated the crowning of the Demon King himself, so long as it involved jackets of ale or drams of stingo and blue ruin.

From the roof of Southbridge Guardhouse, Sarie Dobbs surveyed the crowd with the practiced eye of a slide-hander. A pocket diver could have had a field day with a crowd so deep in its cups. But so far there'd been little evidence of trouble. Even streetrats were disinclined to target those celebrating the crowning of the lady known as Briar Rose.

Cuffs—or the Demon King, as he called himself now, their streetlord—had asked them to keep eyes and ears on the celebration, to pass through the rougher sorts of inns and report back anything that might threaten the safety of the queen. He'd called on them since most of the prime bluejackets were partying along with her.

Who would've guessed—me and Flinn playing at bluejackets, Sarie thought, grinning at Flinn on a roof across the river. Her grin faded as she considered the high cost of sobriety on a night like this.

The fireworks were long over, the vivid colors still engraved on Sarie's eyeballs. It was getting past darkman's hour, and even the most dedicated soakers were stumbling home in the gray light of morning.

Motioning to Flinn, Sarie skinned down the drainpipe to the ground. They'd make one more sweep through the streets of Ragmarket and then head back to their crib.

Along the way, they growled at some of the *lytlings* and street kiddies, scaring them toward home. On their way down Pinbury Alley, on their old turf, Sarie spotted a pair of fine boots poking out from behind a dustbin.

Dustbins were new to Ragmarket, one of the queen's bright ideas. She seemed to think folk would put scummer and trash in them instead of leaving it in the gutters.

"Hey, now," Sarie said, "it an't safe to be sleeping over here with them boots on." She nudged one of the boots with her toe, and something about the way the leg rolled away told her the boots' owner wouldn't be needing them anymore.

"Flinn!" she hissed. "Get over here."

Two bodies lay behind the dustbin, a woman and a man, all glittered up in blueblood finery, the wizard stoles around their necks splattered with blood. Their throats had been cut right through the windpipe.

Flinn stared down at them, swearing under his breath.

Sarie knelt next to the bodies and patted them down. Whoever had done them had left their purses behind. And the boots.

"Their flashpieces is gone, though," Flinn pointed out. He was right—their amulets were missing, and jinxflingers never even went to the privy without their flashpieces.

Sarie and Flinn searched the area, but didn't find them.

Flinn squatted next to the corpses, scanning their clothing in the growing light. "Look at this," he said, sweeping his hand down the torso of the wizard with the boots.

There, faintly daubed in blood, was a vertical line with another line zigzagging across it.

Flinn sat back on his heels. "What does that look like to you?" When Sarie said nothing, he thrust the talisman Cat's copperhead had made into her face.

Sarie looked again. Now she saw it—the stylized serpent and staff. The gang sign of the Demon King, Cuffs Alister's new street name.

"That don't make sense," she said, after a long pause. "He's left the Life."

"But he's got himself a crew and a crib and he said himself he's got a game going," Flinn muttered. "Said he didn't want to let us in because it was too risky."

Sarie waved at the two on the bricks. "You think these ones

had a hand in what happened to his mam and sister?"

"Does it matter?" Flinn said.

"You think he's out hushing wizards at random?" Sarie said.

"Him or Cat Tyburn, maybe—she's rum with a blade."

She shook her head. "He's a charmcaster himself. Anyway, Cuffs is too smart for that."

Flinn licked his lips. "Remember what he said down in Filcher Alley. He wouldn't say what his game was. But, you know, he did call it a lack-witted scheme. A fool's quest. Maybe that's why he didn't want to let us in."

"He'd of taken their purses," Sarie said. "Make it look like footpad work."

"Unless he was making a point," Flinn said. "Why else would he sign his work?"

Sarie tried, but her weary mind couldn't come up with another argument.

"Maybe Cuffs an't in his right mind," Sarie said, frowning. "Remember how he was after Mam and Mari burned. I never seen anyone that draws trouble like he does."

"The bluejackets will be stumbling through here before long," Flinn said, judging the angle of the light.

Sarie thought on it. "Here's what we'll do." She wadded up the end of the wizard stole in her hand and pressed it into the neck wound, saturating it with blood. Then she mopped it over the symbol on the corpse's coat until she'd blotted it all. "Good thing these is fresh," she muttered. She handed one of the purses to Flinn and stuffed the other into her carry bag. "Let's take these too. Make it look like a slash and grab."

The next thing Sarie knew, Flinn was tugging off the boots.

"They're clan made," he said, when she glared at him. "And they look like my size."

By the time the sun broke over the eastern escarpment, Sarie and Flinn were on their way back to their crib. Sarie hoped they'd managed to cover their streetlord's tracks, but worry tugged at the corners of her mind.

He keeps this up, he's bound to be caught, she thought. And this time they'll dangle him for certain.

ACKNOWLEDGMENTS

A special thanks to my dual (not dueling) editors, Arianne Lewin and Abby Ranger. Your love and enthusiasm kept me going, even while you asked the unanswerable questions that made my books better.

Thank you to my long-suffering critique partners, Marsha McGregor and Jim Robinson; the YAckers: Jody Feldman, Debby Garfinkle, Martha Peaslee Levine, Mary Beth Miller, and Kate Tuthill; to Twinsburg YA writers Julanne Montville, Leonard Spacek, Jeff Harr, Don Gallo, Dorothy Pensky, and Dawn Fitzgerald, for being willing to read pieces and parts, but never the entire thing.

Thank you to my extraordinary agent, Christopher Schelling, for continuing to assure me that I'm not high-maintenance.